I0646020

NO WORDS AFTER I LOVE YOU

S.E. REICHERT

5 PRINCE PUBLISHING

Copyright © 2025 by S.E. Reichert, NO WORDS AFTER I LOVE YOU

All rights reserved.

This is a fictional work. The names, characters, incidents, and locations are solely the concepts and products of the author's imagination, or are used to create a fictitious story and should not be construed as real. No part of this book may be reproduced in any form or by any electronic or mechanical means, including information storage and retrieval systems, without written permission from the author, except for the use of brief quotations in a book review.

Published by 5 PRINCE PUBLISHING & BOOKS, LLC

PO Box 865, Arvada, CO 80001

www.5PrinceBooks.com

ISBN digital: 978-1-63112-397-9

ISBN print: 978-1-63112-398-6

Cover Credit: Marianne Nowicki

First Edition 042425v.1

To Bill Downs. For buying my toast when I forgot my wallet. For listening to me, over breakfast plates and giving me hope in the existence of better men. For encouraging my curiosity and making me go deeper. For putting up with my bullshit with such grace. Plato postulated that we are drawn to the same stardust soul we split apart from, eons ago. So even though you've said that in a hundred years, nothing will really matter, you will still matter to me. Because in a hundred years, or in thousands of them, my stardust soul will always look for yours.

ACKNOWLEDGMENTS

Thank you to my daughters, Madelyn Danae and Delaney Sophia, who teach me to be strong, stand up for what matters, and to believe in myself. You are the hope of the world, my darlings. I'm so blessed you chose me in your cosmic journey to travel with.

Thank you, Chris and Bill Wickstrom, for letting me read for most of my childhood. Thank you for your unfailing love, and support. Thank you for being the ones that accepted me into your own cosmic journey.

I owe a huge debt of gratitude to Bernadette Soehner and 5 Prince Publishing for having faith in my work, even if it's a little outside the box (or has a lot of curse words).

Forever, thank you to Cate Byers. My writing is subpar at best; she's the magician that edits it into a work of art. Thank your lucky stars you don't have to read it (and its 488 ellipses) without her expertise.

Thank you to my writing group, Writing Heights Writers Association, for your support and your insights. For your unfailing passion to write your heart out and to do it all for the art, the fun, and the suffering.

Thank you to my playwriting classmates at the Chicago Dramatists who were so generous and kind with such a ridiculous novelist and who helped me shape and hone my characters.

Finally, thank you, grief. For teaching me that the only way out of the storm is through, and that carrying you is not a burden but a testament to how much I am capable of loving.

NO WORDS AFTER I LOVE YOU

MEG

I have been a fuck-up for most of my adult life. So when Bradley's grand-farewell monologue begins with "I'm just not feeling fulfilled in my purpose with you," I recognize the next cog in an ever-expanding wheel of fuck-uppery. I stop typing and spin in the cheap chair to face him.

"Your what?" I laugh. Bradley rolls his eyes, takes his keys from the side table, and tries to tuck his wallet into his skinny jeans. He tries every pocket. His words drive his motion, in an ever-increasing anger.

"Honestly, Meg, you're triggering me."

"What in the hell are you talking about? Your parents are from Vermont. What could you possibly be triggered by? Someone getting your Starbucks order wrong?"

"This is what I'm talking about!" he yells and shoves his wallet in his eco-friendly bag instead.

"Oh, honesty triggers you?"

"You used to support and uplift me."

"I recall that you used to be humble. You also used to help pay the bills." I raise my eyebrows, not in surprise but in the superiority of being older, and not an actor.

"You can't turn this on me, don't gaslight me."

My eyes roll to the back of my head. "Please stop using words from your trendy dictionary. That's not even what gaslighting means."

"It's modern language, Meg!"

"You're just not taking personal responsibility for your own reactions. I've been paying your rent for months," I say.

"Oh, so you're the victim in this scenario?"

"I didn't say that, I said—"

"You know what? I don't have to listen to this. I've already made up my mind. We're done. You're officially uninvited from my opening night."

"You entitled little shit." My hackles have raised at the sheer audacity that I even wanted to see him prance around in a Mr. Mistoffelees suit.

"You sound just like Charlie. I swear the older you get the more like him you become. I didn't sign on to sleep with a fifty-nine-year-old man." He huffs in an overly dramatic way, even for an off-Broadway actor, and storms from our one-bedroom—not even an apartment—a studio with a closet for a bathroom. A sad little space that I have no idea how I'll pay for on my own. The echoing from the door slam fades into the walls. The sanctity of quiet seems to push away the spite of his words.

Not feeling fulfilled. Triggering.

Charlie.

I turn back to my page, to the defunct paragraph I was battling with when Bradley's declaration of independence came barreling through my work. The paragraph is shit, even without the interruption. I delete it and think of calling someone who might understand. But it's too late to call Charlie. He goes to bed early. No sense in disturbing his or Gina's sleep with my latest fuck up. I get up from my laptop and kick the door, my last word to Bradley on the matter. A small and empty win for a situation that's been falling apart for months. I had let it. Because I don't know how to save things.

I wander around the space, newly empty of anyone but me. Even though it's a cycle, I have to readjust every time. I head straight to the three-cabinet kitchen, for the good stuff on the top shelf. I pour a small amount into a jelly jar and fish in the tiny freezer for an ice cube. I raise my glass to the quiet door, to the footsteps of the latest leaving love interest, now long gone.

"Here's to getting another artist on his feet," I whisper and take a sip. "Maybe next time someone will return the favor."

Next time. The bourbon scorches going down and reminds me of all the burning in my life that began when I was too little to know the danger of fire. My eyes start watering from the constant inhalation of poison and loss. When they start watering, the emotions edge towards the newly opened door, and I start crying. When I start crying, I can't stop. I ache for something.

I ache to *do* something different. To *be* something else. Something more than a sad little side plot, left again by the main character on his way up. But I don't have the answers any more than I have next month's rent or next week's article. I have silence. And the ability to fuck up. Royally.

CHARLIE

I've been a fuck-up most of my life. But I've been a lucky fuck-up. And I know how to work hard. So, even someone who fucks up a lot, can get somewhere if they're willing to learn from every fuck-uppery and make something out of the ashes. I'm an unfortunate romantic and I rarely made a living when I was young, but I was happy poor.

And so when I finally made it, I was happy too, but not because I didn't have to live on three-day-old deli bread or handouts from the Mount of Pious Judgment that is my father. No, I was happy because I had Gina. And I had teaching. And I had writing. My plays were lauded and laughed at and that was all I could want for.

Life went on this way for so many years. Fucking up, learning, changing, fucking up less. We never had a family though it was not for lack of trying. My god, we were rabbits in our younger days. Living on sex, and love, and art and acting, like gardens of stolen produce. Gina is brilliant and blonde with a voice like sweet honey and a figure that fills hands. She is loved by all. But every night when she steps down from the stage, she comes home to me. In the past it was a hovel, where the lights were seldom on, the heat was rarely hot, and the keys were always clicking.

We'd beat poverty. We'd beat the idea that families and happiness needed children in the equation. We beat a million odds. We beat cancer. Once.

Now, sitting across from the doctor, Gina's hand in mine, hot and clutching, I feel like I've fucked up again. I must have, somewhere along the line. Why else would God have made it come back? Why would he have spread it, like a veil, inside of her? Gina shrugs at me, as if it's nothing to worry over. She flashes that damn smile on her ruby lips.

"The show must go on, my darling."

Fuck the show, I think to myself, but I know she's looking to me to be braver than that. The one who she can cling to when all other options are quicksand around her.

I'M TAKING MEG TO BREAKFAST TO TELL HER. GINA INSISTED. SHE has appointments to get to and she doesn't want me 'skulking' in the waiting room. Meg Kent is one of our dearest friends. Gina calls her our orphan, but she's past forty now. We met her in Kansas, where she was a novice journalist, covering one of my plays. We've been in love with her ever since. She's our closest friend. Which is why, I argue with my argumentative wife, that *she* should tell Meg.

"But, Charlie, she loves you." Gina says, a hand over mine as if there is no room between our skin for arguments. We certainly don't have the time. I sigh. Meg loves us both. It's going to kill her. If she weren't so distracted by the latest serial monogamy saga in her life.

. . .

NOW MEG AND I ARE AT OUR FAVORITE DINER, RAYMOND'S. I scowl as I listen to old what's-his-name's recognizable story, and the familiar disappointment, but not surprise, in her voice. Despite the plot I already know, I love listening to her. She has that earthy, midwestern undertone, even after all of these years in the city. Her hair is messy, in a bun, too much of a hassle to spend time on and she doesn't wear makeup. She never looks put together. Like there's too much chaos in her creative mind to waste time worrying about her appearance. If Gina were here, she'd tsk her tongue and bring it to the front of the conversation.

But Gina isn't here, and I don't give a shit that Meg's got ketchup stains down her sweatshirt. She's beautiful, if for no other reason, than because of the very nature of her chaos. She's not 'Gina' beautiful. No one is that beautiful. Gina, shining star of the stage, with a Southern drawl that would turn the heads of any man living or dead and a smile that sends me.

But Meg has dimples, and self-deprecation. She's got snark, on Jewish old man level, and green eyes that are hard and soft at once, and her ass … I stop the train of thought and listen to the last line of old what's-his-name-leaving.

"And that's how I ended up with all the rent and none of the sex."

"Well, thank God. The guy was a grade-A moron." I grouch and try not to think of Hipster Bradley naked.

"He got into *Cats*," she says, like the man walked into the pearly gates.

I narrow my eyebrows and keep my anger behind my gaze when I stare at her.

"He couldn't get into a bag of chips with scissors. The man was a talentless hack and you shouldn't have paid his rent as long as you did."

"You're just saying that to be sweet." She sips her coffee and looks out the window. The morning is gray and pissed off, just like us. There's a pause. A moment. I have to tell her. But all that comes out is;

"When have you ever known me to be sweet? Go to hell." I say and fluff out the paper, before refolding it. The squares blur as I silently mouth the words; *Gina's got cancer. She's got it again. We went to the doctor. It's back.* So many ways to ruin Meg's day, even more.

When I look up, she's staring at me from across the table. There's a softness there, like she's reading the lines of my face. I realize I haven't brushed my hair. Not since the doctor's appointment two days ago. I must look so unkempt, yet she looks at me like she doesn't even care.

"Thanks," she whispers and sniffs back tears. I hate that. I hate when those eyes fill up, and inevitably pull me in. Make me want to stay stupid things. Or worse, do stupid things. I keep my eyes on the puzzle. I can't be pulled in, so I just put my hand over hers and squeeze it.

"How is Gina?" she asks, a crowbar to a stuck door.

Fuck. I have to say something now.

"It's back," is all I say. It's all I can manage to say. It takes a beat for the information to travel from my lips, to her ear, to her brain, to her connective tissue, and her hand turns up to grasp mine.

"Charlie, no."

"Yes." It gnaws at me when the deepening wells of her eyes spill over. "It's bad, Meg."

She takes my one hand in both of hers. How her hands are always so cold, I'll never know. Where is all her blood?

"What can I do?"

"Be here," is what comes out of my mouth. And I'm not sure if I'm saying it for my sake or Gina's. Meg sniffs, dries her eyes, as if she's pulling back her own grief for our sakes alone.

"Ok. How is she?"

"Tired," I shake my head, abandoning the paper and sitting

back. I take off my glasses and rub my eyes. The hard part is over. Now Meg will come in with her fortitude and her sass, and some battle plan to draw me out of my despair, with just enough cynicism to make it believable.

"I'll bring her matzo."

My heart aches in my chest and I feel weak.

Stupid heart. Stupid Meg.

"Conniving little gentile. I don't know why Saul even gives you soup."

"On account of me giving up the gentile god years ago, and because I'm so charming."

"Little shit."

This makes her laugh. The grouchier I get, the pricklier I am, the more she laughs and knows my game. There is sunshine for a moment until the weight of life, outside our table, sinks in.

"I'm sorry. Maybe it will work better, for longer this time."

I sigh, and lean back over the table to focus on the puzzle. I need to finish something after all. It's been weeks since I wrote anything substantial. Days since I wrote at all. The grief is blocking my creative tap. I hit my pen against the table harder and harder.

"What'll I do, Meg?"

She stops, bites her lip, looks at me and down to the tap-dancing pen. It's not a fair question. Gina's my wife. Meg's just a friend. It's not her battle, it's not her problem. But then that stupid Midwest resolve clears its throat, picks up the pieces of worry, and proceeds.

"Keep fighting, Charlie. We keep fighting, and we keep loving her until she can't stand either of us."

How could anyone not stand Meg? Me though? I'm sure the world et al, is completely done with my bullshit. "She already can't stand you." I deflect.

"Liar! She loves me."

"She does. You're coming over, right? Sunday?"

8

"With matzo and a nice knish."

"Take the language of my people out of your filthy Lutheran mouth," I smile, even as the heavy hurt settles into my heart and I sniff back tears. She leans in and squeezes my hand. And I can't help but believe, for that one moment, that we could fight this. If Meg Kent was fighting beside us.

MEG

Charlie asks me to meet for coffee the morning after Bradley's departure. I, of course, comply. Coffee with Charlie always breaks me out of my mood. If there's anyone crabbier at the world than me, it's him. Plus, I love to hear him talk. About anything and nothing. I love the way he sits back and listens, discerning brows pulled together, as though he's contemplating my words. As if I matter. I'm curious as to why he asked me and didn't mention Gina coming along. Her birthday is coming up soon, and I'm sure Charlie, in his old-school romantic way, has devised a plan he needs help with.

What a man to find, I think as I put on my worn red boots to navigate the slush-deep sidewalks. It's ten blocks but I don't have enough for fare today. When I arrive, Charlie is there, already seated, readers on and mouthing answers to the crossword. I watch his lips count through the window. The spaces, the letters, making it all fit. He looks up, a graying curl on his forehead. He waves me in.

He looks pale. Paler than I've seen him in a long while and his bright blue eyes pop against his skin. His mouth is downturned, like he doesn't want to talk first. He rarely does.

"Hey!" I puff out and the breath feels hot on my cheeks.

"Did you walk all the way?" he scowls.

"It's a lovely fall day."

"It's twenty degrees out, Meg."

I shrug and take off my coat, I settle in, nod for coffee and don't allow even a moment before I dive into the dramatic end scene of Bradley. Charlie remains a statue as I recount the far-too familiar episode.

"And that's how I ended up with all the rent and none of the sex."

Charlie's scowl deepens. "Well, thank God. The guy was a grade-A moron."

"He got into *Cats*." I say over the menu.

Charlie rolls his bright eyes over his readers and levels them on me.

"He couldn't get into a bag of chips with scissors. The man was a talentless hack and you shouldn't have paid his rent as long as you did."

"You're just saying that to be sweet." I sip my coffee and looked out over the busy city street outside. The cloudy morning spits gray flakes against people's faces as they walk by. I set aside the menu. I can't afford toast, let alone breakfast.

"When have you ever known me to be sweet? Go to hell." Charlie studies his puzzle again. I watch him from across the table. I love looking at Charlie. His wild and curly hair, unkempt and disrespectful. His face a map of a million laughs, handsome but in total, unrefined.

"Thanks," I whisper. For the moment of stability, for reaffirming my faith in men. He reaches out, without looking up from his puzzle, and places his warm hand over mine with a squeeze.

"How is Gina?"

Charlie pauses, and with him, my heart. He never pauses when talking about Gina, he's over the moon in love with her.

There is always some news, some show, some smash hit that she's working on mastering, filling up their brownstone with repeated notes and lines, and the sparkle that is Gina. There is no pause to a life so full. Charlie clears his throat.

"It's back."

The words are like a double hit to my chest. I don't have to ask what 'it' is. It's only be five years since it took root in her the first time. Now it takes root in me, with the kind of despair that steals words.

"Charlie, no."

"Yes … It's bad, Meg."

I ache with anger. I want to throw my fist into something, but I'm stupid and weepy instead, so I take his warm hand in mine.

"What can I do?"

"Be here," he says.

I sniff and look up to staunch the deluge. My crying doesn't help any of us, and he certainly doesn't need to feel worse for my tears.

"Ok. How is she?"

"Tired," he shakes his head, tucking the paper beneath his plate. I watch him take off the readers and rub his eyes. "This time is already worse."

I'm at a loss. What the hell do you say to that? I'm a fuck up, not a doctor. I have nothing to give him, even after they've given me so much. My heart aches and I'm desperate to do something.

"I'll bring her matzo." I say. *Soup* … I remember, a strange flashing memory of my childhood … *soup* somehow was a small taste of comfort in the midst of a cold and torrential storm. Soup is always a comfort.

"Conniving little gentile. I don't know why Saul even gives you soup." Charlie says, eyes swimming, grasping at his anger to keep him above the rising tide of sadness.

"On account of me giving up the gentile god years ago, and because I'm so charming."

"Little shit."

I smirk. I see his mouth mirror mine. The first smile I've seen on him since we sat down. It fades. So does mine.

"I'm sorry. Maybe it will work better, for longer this time."

Charlie sighs, he shakes his head and leans back over the crossword puzzle. He taps his pen a few times, harder each strike. Something is different. He's shaking his head. I stare at a face I've known for too long. She's not doing the treatments.

"What'll I do, Meg?"

All my bullshit relationship troubles seem like petty squabbles. Watching the love of your life, undoubtably the strongest, smartest woman either of us know, falter with a reoccurring malignancy makes Bradley, the man in a cat suit, seem like a cigarette butt on the dirty sidewalk.

"Keep fighting, Charlie. We keep fighting and we keep loving her until she can't stand either of us."

"She's already can't stand you," he says.

"Liar! She loves me."

"She does. You're coming over, right? Sunday?"

"With matzo and a nice knish."

"Take the language of my people out of your filthy Lutheran mouth," he says but I see the tears in his eyes before he tries to cover them with his smile. I lean in and squeeze his hand this time.

I WALK HOME ALONE. CHARLIE OFFERED TO SPLIT A CAB, BUT I NEED to be alone. I spend the time staring up at the buildings, and away from the faces of the people on their way to brighter futures. I think of Charlie. Of Gina. Of the cruel and relentless march of time, that feels like nothing more than a breeze in its quick passing.

I attended the University of Kansas coming off the strange

decade of flannel and recession, grunge and the death of hair bands, to the confused and angry strains of Nirvana. The world had just lost Matthew Shepard and the dawn of a new era of hateful divisiveness was simmering below the surface of the country. When Donald Trump was just a reality show host, and the common cold was the worst thing we gave to one another. When there was still hope. When there was more 'let live' to our lives.

Charlie taught there, so brief a window of time that I like to believe it was the universe conspiring to bring us together. I wasn't even a theater major. I was going into business. Clearly, a much wiser career choice. But it turned out that my research papers were deemed 'too creative' and my well-meaning Econ teacher, gently steered me into the English department. Journalism, creative writing and the arts. So, there I was, taking Charlie's class for the Humanities credit but loving his class for the truth. For the Charlie. For the everything that felt like the inner philosopher I wanted to become. It was a class of 120, I never expected him to remember me when I stopped him for an interview after his debut play was put on by Theater Lawrence. But he did.

"Kent, right? You're a journalist, now? You should be a novelist." And so began a strange and charmed connection that needled into my gray matter and planted seeds of dreams I didn't know I wanted. He was gracious. His wife was loving and warm, her smile brightening all my darkest corners. Gina and I hit it off from the start. She was a living heart, walking in the world. A big and beautiful temperament, destined for greater things than Lawrence had to offer. They relocated back to New York soon after the interview. When I graduated, I decided to take my chances, with a slingshot of resumes, out into the hardened streets of their city.

I couldn't stay in Kansas. I had nothing left but a drunk mom and a lifetime of loss and I arrived with just that, plus a couple of suitcases and no right to be here.

I haven't moved much since. But I had always remembered Charlie's class and his comment. *You should be a novelist.* He has always been a voice in my veins that asked for more. Asked for what I was worth. When I moved to New York, he and Gina helped me feel more adjusted. As adjusted as a hayseed imposter could feel in a city of fast-paced go-getters.

We would wobble. One month seeing each other nearly every week. The next month I would be empty armed, while they traveled the country for work, or I was embroiled in another failed romance. Gina would shake her head at me.

"You deserve better, sugar."

"I know."

"So, find better."

"Where exactly?" I said and poured her a glass of wine from the bottle between us. Charlie shook his head, and filled my glass with water. Jesus, one small conversation at a coffee shop in our third year of us knowing each other and he watched what went in my glass. So that my mother's downfall didn't become mine, too.

"She doesn't need a man. She needs to write her novel," he argued, before Gina could make her point.

"A novel won't keep her warm at night."

"But at least it's a better use of her time and she'll finally stop living for someone else's dream," Charlie argued, hands crossed over his chest and leaning back.

"I dunno, writing a novel is a million steps away from the society pages," I'd said.

"You weren't born to write for gossip rags, Meg Kent. You need to stop taking side-character roles." There was a fierceness in Charlie's eyes when he said that. I still remember. It was five years and three boyfriends ago. And a month before Gina's first diagnosis.

She'd beaten it that time.

But dark things lurk in small spaces and by the time she was feeling too 'run down' to make it to the cast party on another hit play, it had taken up city blocks inside her body.

CHARLIE

Gina, my bright and beautiful firefly. My reason for living, my end game, my only. Twenty-nine years my partner in crime. Twenty-nine years and she—my towering tree—ever reaching for the stars. Twenty-nine years and I—her grounding roots. She's too anxious to settle, always has been, since I've known her. Too anxious to sit still. Too afraid of missing out on the next big adventure.

And I'm scared now, because the essence of who she is, has become the driving force for her decisions this time around. And she doesn't want to ruin the short time left with throwing up, and losing her hair, and feeling weak, and tired. She wants to keep working, keep acting, one more show, one more night.

And I indulge her. Because I understand. If you can't be who you are, in the middle of a deadly storm, then were you ever that person at all? Could you imagine a world where Gina spent her few months in bed, aching for the stage and the lights, just to eke out a few more moments of misery?

She can't imagine it either. I begrudgingly go along. She finishes the last run of her show. She is ever brilliant, and ever bright, wowing audiences until the final curtain call. Standing ovations all round, though no one on their feet, or sharing the stage with her knows. She won't allow it. Only our families know. Only Meg.

That night, when the make-up comes off, and the warm bath is taken, and she's settled into her favorite robe, curled into bed next to me where I am pounding out useless words that I will later violently delete, she looks over at me.

"I'm tired, Charlie," is all she says, and lays her head against on my shoulder. I brush her soft blonde hair, felt the bird weight of her settling on my arm like a leaf settles on a pond. Barely a ripple. She passes out. I call the hospital and carry her sparrow body down our hall, out the front steps and to the waiting box of light and fury.

Now we're here. Not in a hospital for treatment, because it's far too late for that, but in hospice. And she's made it the best dressing room yet, had me bring in her fabrics and favorite bedclothes and she adorns it with lights and her favorite pictures and a conglomeration of all the things she wants to see, and re-feel, and rejoice in. Pictures of her favorite castmates and shows.

"*Annie Get Your Gun*, was my favorite," she says softly and puts a kiss on the glass frame, right over the top of Don DeVoe's face, an actor that must have done a hundred shows with her. A fine guy, nice enough, always a little too longing in the looks if you ask me. But I'm resigned to not argue with her at all. Until she says;

"I need you to do something for me."

"Anything, love," I say, and put down the laptop to come sit next to her.

"It's about Meg."

"What about her?"

"She's coming this afternoon to visit."

I hadn't seen Meg since I told her. My life, her life, were both in the season of growing apart, and I had bigger burdens to carry than the latest man-child taking up her light.

"Okay?"

"I need you, Charlie, before she gets here, to go get some coffee."

"That's it? Why can't I just call her now and she can bring it?"

"I need to talk to her alone."

"Why?"

"Girl stuff." My eyebrows, lie detectors in and of themselves, draw down.

"Bullshit."

"Charlie," Gina sighs and takes my hand; she stares at the way her thumb caresses over the back of it, running the rivulets of blue and the strings of bones beneath my skin. "You love that girl."

"Of course, we both do. She's our Meg."

"Charlie," her eyes level on mine. It's the I'm-dying-so-shut-up-and-listen-to-me look. "If you don't love that girl for the rest of your life, I will never forgive you."

"I don't understand what the hell that means." It's a small thing, but I watch her eyes dart back to the pictures beside her bed, before they come back to mine.

"It means that hearts as big as ours aren't meant to only love once."

I'm confused and I balk at her accordingly. "I don't love Meg like that."

"You just don't know it yet."

"There's nothing to know," I yell. A nurse passing by, leans her head into the room like a specter floating without a body, and asks if we're alright.

Gina smiles her best actress smile, twinkling eyes and all. "My oaf of a husband is being stubborn again. But he knows I'm right." The nurse nods and leaves as if this is a common occurrence. It probably is.

"Who would give up the chance for another great love in their lifetime?" Gina says.

"What the hell are you even talking about? I don't love Meg and I'm not going to! I love you, that's it. The *end*. You're my last and *only* great love." Gina looks sadly up at me, as though she's disappointed in my stupidity. Meg will be here any minute. I look over my shoulder. I'm sweating. My stomach flips nervously, while my brain tries to put walls up against the asinine idea.

"But you have to let her come to you."

"Gina, please stop being ridiculous."

"And she will."

"Goddamn it, don't say shit like that. It's idiotic."

"You'll need each other, when I'm gone." It's all she says before she smiles over my shoulder at the next round of medication coming her way. "Go get the coffee."

I lean down, kiss her forehead with angry lips, and leave. Even if she didn't tell me to, even if it wasn't already prearranged, I would have left for coffee because I can't breathe in that room. I'm halfway through ordering, when the horrid realization hits me that the "girl talk" she must be having with Meg is probably along the same lines. I pay quickly, grab the coffee, and rush out of the hospital cafeteria. I have to interrupt her fever-dream madness before she asks Meg to love me. What in the hell would Meg think of such a stupid request? I bolt down the long hallway and repeatedly hit the elevator button like I'm trying to get it off.

"Come on, come on." When I finally make it back to her room, all I hear is Meg's quiet voice say,

"Of course, I will."

Goddamn it. This isn't happening. I round the corner with the two cups of coffee in hands, shoulders slumped in anger of their conspiracy. I look Meg dead in her eyes and into Gina's next as though I've caught them in the act of trying to somehow salvage my heart.

"You will what?" I hand Meg a cup of the coffee, just like she likes it, too creamy and too much sugar. Bastardized. A tool to ply the truth from her. But Gina interrupts Meg's awkward, open-mouthed fumble of words.

"Kick your ass in scrabble. It's my dying wish," Gina says with a smile and a wink. But I don't smile.

I fear it's too late, especially from the strange way Meg avoids looking at me. Then again, maybe it is just the grief. The girl is trying not to cry. The girl. The forty-four-year-old girl. The one who lost her teen sister in a car wreck, the one who lost her mom to drinking. The one who never had a dad. Now she's losing Gina. She looks at my wife like she doesn't know how she's going to survive another goodbye. Like she doesn't know if she has enough heart left to lose another piece.

It suddenly isn't about Gina's stupid end-of-life-ask. It's about making sure I, somehow, guide Meg through this valley of shadows.

Despite what my wife has asked of me, I know I can't let Meg drift off. She's lost too many people and I won't be one, just because of my wife's hopeless romanticism. We all know that Meg and I don't belong together. It won't ever come to that.

"She's a terrible scrabble player. There's no way," I respond.

"Well, then, I guess she'll have her work cut out for her, won't she?" Gina turns to Meg and nods. Meg picks at the paper holder on her cup, sadness etched into the new lines around her brow.

"Give me a sip, won't you, love?" Gina says to me, and I let the whole debacle fall at my feet.

It doesn't matter what she's said. It doesn't matter what she wants me to do. I'll tell her anything. Anything she wants to hear, just to see her smile. I sit on her bed, opposite of Meg, who shifts ever-so-slightly away, and I share my coffee with my wife. My first and only great love, despite her big plans.

MEG

I walk into the hospice room, like I was her mother. With a copy of her latest reviews in the paper, a vase of fresh flowers and her favorite chocolates from a small shop off of 54th. Charlie said she hadn't been eating. I'd hoped these would be a game changer. I smuggle them under my coat and place them in her lap while I arrange the flowers. I have to keep my eyes from her, my hands busy; because I knew the moment I sat down, I'd probably cry.

"Where's Charlie?" I'm proud at how even I keep my voice.

"Oh, I dunno, stepping out with some hot, young, non-malignant thing." Gina smiles.

"Stop." I don't laugh. "That man doesn't step out anywhere without you."

Gina's eyes turn sad. More sad than normal. An odd sad on a woman who has carried sunshine, even when darkness was pressing further against her insides. "I sent him away to get coffee."

"I could have gone."

"I needed him to do it, because I need to talk to you."

"Gina—"

"Alone."

My busy hands still, my snarky comments and false hope fade like so many lulling machines around us, ticking out precious heartbeats that we both know have an end.

"Don't look at me like that," she says and shakes her head.

"Like what?"

"Like you don't know how to say goodbye to me."

"I don't," I croak and feel tears stinging my eyes.

"Well, darlin', you say it with a smile. You say you were glad to know me and that you'll never forget me."

My hand shakes when she reaches for it. "I am," my stupid voice catches and I can't breathe. "I won't."

She tsks her tongue. "Where's the smile?"

"I can't smile, Gina. I can't be happy about this." I pause and swallow down a lump of grief that's dried, and had probably been sitting in my throat since breakfast with Charlie. "Please don't go. I don't want you to go."

"Honey, now. We don't get to choose, and we can cry all day about how it ain't fair, but it won't change the way of things." She pauses to gasp and puts the tubes back into her nose for a moment. I don't so much sit as fall into the hospital bed next to her. She holds my hand. I listen to the gentle and rhythmic tick of the machine feeding her breaths. I don't know how long it takes a man to get a cup of coffee, but she shifts and I look up.

"You gotta do something for me, Meg."

"Anything," I say and sit up, ready to adjust a pillow or grab her water.

"You need to love him."

"What?"

"Charlie, you have to love him, and check on him. Every day. Until he's just sick of it. Then you need do it again the next day. And the next, and the next after that."

"Gina, please let's not talk about—"

"We've got to. We got to talk about it now." She's angry, as if there isn't time to waste on my self-pity. "How long do you think he'll be gone for coffee?"

I realize then that she's sent him away, for this very purpose. To give his care over to me. She isn't wrong, he'd hate it if he knew.

"Gina, Charlie is a grown man."

"Who's had me shoving food at him when he forgets to eat, and making him laugh when he gets too heavy in the world," she pauses to breathe before continuing with fervor. "He's had my love with him for half of his life and he will fall into the dark, if we're not careful."

If we're not careful. Team Charlie. Would he really stop living, if he didn't have someone to live for? I can't imagine a world without Charlie.

"He doesn't need me, Gina. I'm a fuck-up."

"You'll make him better."

"What's better than Charlie?"

"Charlie with you." The thought is weird and disjointed and I shake my head at it.

"Please don't go," I whisper again. "He loves you so much. I love you so much. Please, just don't."

"Charlie loves too much, and that's why he writes so well. Why he flies to the moon when he's high and sinks to the bottom when he's low. He needs someone to keep him from staying on the bottom."

"I can barely keep a houseplant alive," I say. She takes my hand and squeezes it so tightly that I wonder if she's really on death's door. She seems too strong to die.

"I need you to take care of him."

"I don't know how, I can't."

"I'm tired and I'm hurt, and I can't leave in peace, unless I know you'll do this for me."

Shit. What does it matter to agree to this ridiculous idea, if it brings her peace? Charlie doesn't need to know.

"Of course I will," I say and her hand relaxes into mine.

Charlie comes in, two cups of coffee in his hands and head down. The angry man stalking.

"You will what?" he says and shoves the coffee at me. I don't know what to say. Gina's knee nudges my thigh from beneath the sheet.

"Kick your ass in scrabble. It's my dying wish," Gina says. Charlie doesn't smile. He's silent for a minute, looking at me. As if he knows. I keep my eyes on my cup. When he speaks it isn't the outing of our conspiracy but a very Charlie-like thing.

"She's a terrible scrabble player. There's no way."

My first reaction is to argue. But when I look to both of their faces, I understand that this is one of the last times I will get to see them together. I fight the tears back even as the canyon of hurt in my chest threatens to crack open. I close my eyes and try to make a memory. Her thigh against my knee, the smell of Charlie and coffee, and the soft whoosh of air from my lungs when I sigh. I freeze it all in time, inside of me.

"Well, then, I guess she'll have her work cut out for her, won't she?" Gina turns her face to mine and nods. I can only nod back. "Give me a sip, won't you, love?" she asks Charlie who shares his coffee with her, quietness in his eyes.

I stay until my coffee has gone cold in my hands. I can't stand to drink it.

I don't want this to be our last cup.

CHARLIE

The inevitability of death is not lost on me. It won't be long and I'm trying to fight the ache in my heart with all the armaments of making every fucking moment we have left, count.

I'm reading aloud from *Man's Search for Meaning*. I'm flipping the page, wiggling the readers up my nose to get a better view, adjusting myself closer to her on the bed and she sighs.

"When we are no longer able to change a situation, we are challenged to change ourselves," I read and she takes my hand suddenly, turns her nose into my shoulder, and emits a strange little cry.

"I'm sorry, Charlie. I loved too much. While you were writing, I loved too much. I love you, too much too." The words are puffs of breath and disjointed.

"I love you, and I could never be loved enough," I say. I take off the readers and look down, but her hand has fallen and her head is heavy against my shoulder. And my heart knows, my soul knows, before the machines can even alert the rest of the world.

"Gina?" I whisper, and turn to hold her close, her head sits in the crook of my neck where now, only one heartbeat carries the world.

"No … no, my love, don't go. Please, not yet." A useless request, and the staff filters in to watch my whole being fight against her signed DNR, and instead of beating against her heart to beg it to start again, I am holding her into my skin, raging against an unchangeable fate, and begging death to take me too.

~

I can't move, don't want to leave her side. But the world thinks it strange, to lie beside something that's no longer there. Counselors talk to me, psychiatrists, doctors. Hours pass and I do not leave the room. They are giving me grace, but they're also getting tired of my bullshit. I hear two nurses whisper as they help undecorate her tomb that they don't expect me to make it a year. They scurry away like mice when I look up from her still chest, where I am laying.

Where silence becomes stifling and a heartbeat no longer with me, is the worst empty page I've ever had to face. They convince me to move, they ask if I need to call anyone. Would I like them to call anyone, on my behalf? I watch as she is carefully taken off stage, and down the hall. I am numb and worthless, and shake my head. I want to go home. To the tomb of the once was.

I pack up the box of her photos. Casts and crew, her family down south, who I call, briefly and nod to their gasping cries on the other end. I continue to de-Gina the room. There's a picture of me and dad, who's still putzing around at eighty-seven. I haven't called him yet. We have a troubled past. The cast of *Annie Get Your Gun*, and Don DeVoe's face with her lipstick printed in layers on the glass. One of Meg and us at the opening of my best-selling play to date. Arms around each other, smiles wide as the night and twice as bright. So young. On top of the world.

A world that kicked us all to the ground.

Some of us, it kicked beneath it. I sob, deep in my chest and put the photo over the breaking of my heart. I don't want to call

Meg. But she needs to know too. And I'd rather call her than my dad. I pick up my phone, I don't even know the time, I'm lost in the gray of 'after' that seems to exist outside of clocks or calendars. Hers is the only other number on the top of my phone besides Gina and my father. Her smiling eyes, waiting for me to break her heart.

When I dial, I don't expect her to answer. She never does. She hates talking on the phone. But I hear her breathy hello, as though it's a question. Like she forgot how to start a conversation. It breaks my heart, because I'm about to permanently end all conversations between her and Gina.

"She's gone," is all I get out before I collapse on the bed where she left me.

Charlie, no.

The disbelief is the only shared condolence either of us have. I hear her throw up and the line goes quiet after the retching. She's always held her grief in her stomach. I hang up and shake my head. Suddenly, all I want is to see Meg. Be in the presence of someone who isn't a hospital employee, who understands the severity of the universe closing down around the grief stricken. Meg knows grief. Maybe she'll know how I can survive it, or if I should even try. Gina's words and her last request of me jumble around with Meg's history of loss. I need to get out of this place.

My phone starts ringing and I nearly drop it, but it feels like a lifeline now and I hold on.

"What in God's name happened?"

"I dropped my phone," Meg's voice is wet and shaky.

"What the—"

"I'm fine, I'm here. I'm coming." I hear the subway rush around her, I'll lose her soon. "What do you need me to do?"

"Just be here." I hang up.

What in the hell was I thinking? I can't have Meg here. I want to hold her even worse now. Grief is a strange mess of not knowing what you want, but wanting it now.

When she stumbles in, weepy and looking like she's been sucked into soul-killing articles for most of the day, I shove a box in her hands quickly. So that I don't shove myself in her hands.

"When does your family get in?" she asks and her words remind me, up from the artistic pit of my despair, that there are real things to be handled.

"They've been called, they're coming in on Monday." Words tumble out of me but I don't feel like I'm speaking.

"Your dad?"

My grief is a raging sea, and I'm a tiny lifeboat. I cannot hold space for my father right now. I stare at her, a frozen screen.

"Right," she says, as if she understands. "Let me know when he gets in and I'll pick him up." She does not press or ask if I've even called him. It is these little graces she gives, that keep me from throwing myself down the stairs on our way out.

I ride home with her and let her stack the boxes.

She says I'd better call her when I refuse to let her stay. I can't be with anyone right now. I don't even want to be with myself. I nod. She says to sleep. My insides balk and twist. Sure kid.

When she says to try some sleeping pills and then nearly bursts into tears, it shakes me into the present.

I have been angry for her mothering of me. But she is scared. I see it in her eyes. The little girl, left behind at every turn in her life. I promise that I'll call her. And I will. How can I not, now?

She doesn't let me even have a day before she's texting me on repeat and I have to all-caps her that I'm FINE. I give her a list. Not even half of what needs to be done, but something to keep her busy and off my personal case of loss. Something to remind her she is needed. So she won't drift into her own depression and away.

I don't want to admit it's partly me, wanting to keep her close.

MEG

I'm at my desk on an overtime shift to help afford my next month's rent since I don't have a lax boyfriend throwing in his bartending tip money. Gina hasn't been far below the surface of my thoughts, but I do that on purpose. I didn't go and see her in hospice after the strange conversation about Charlie. I took extra shifts instead, as if that would balance out the scales of fear and denial. I haven't visited Charlie because I know that his time and effort should be on her, not at how badly my life is starting to disintegrate, or how I have to sneak food out of the breakroom because I can't afford groceries every second week.

No one needs to worry about me, because no one ever really did. I worry about me. I'm finishing up the crappy graphics on another crappy clickbait story, no original thought to be found, when my phone sings. Charlie's face sits beside the number and I answer without thought. He's the only person I would pick up for. His voice is a breath, as though he's leaning into my ear.

She's gone. The breath ends in a sob. My whole body shudders with disbelief.

I was going to see her one more time. I was going to be there.

I want my mouth to say words, my condolences to speak

themselves back, but I can't. I can't think and I can't breathe. I think I whisper his name, maybe I say *no*, as if he's gotten the wrong punchline, and needs to tell the joke over. It can't be right.

I was going to see her one more time. I was going to be there.

My heart pulls in on itself, a black hole, right in the center of my chest, sucking everything in tight. The painful wave hits and I lean over and vomit into my trash can. I drop my phone; I don't even say I'm sorry. I don't even hang up.

Charlie does. He hangs up.

"Ew, go home!" Stan's eyes pop over the side of our adjoining cubicles.

I stand up, woozy, grab my things, and stumble to the elevators clutching my phone and dry sobbing in disbelief before the doors even close. I call Charlie back, on my way to the subway.

"What in God's name happened?"

"I dropped my phone," I croak.

"What the—" his voice is distant a whisper.

"I'm fine. I'm here. I'm coming." Gina's words are echoing in my head, singing a chorus line of grief and disappointment in myself. But it hurts too much to listen so I focus on Charlie's instead. "What do you need me to do?"

"Just be here."

I never wanted to be a character on Star Trek so bad in my life. To just, poof, transport myself directly to the spot. I hang on the rail, looking at the call gone dead.

"I'm coming," I whisper softly as if she's on the train with me, helping me find my way back.

I don't understand the room. It's been cleared and there are only a few boxes left. It's not where I've been before. Cold and clinical, bare sheets in the bed where I last saw her. When she was alive. When I should have held her hand longer. When I should have brought her one more cup.

I want to crumple to the floor and sob. I start to. My knees do that weird buckling thing, and I can't see for the tears building up in my eyes. Charlie shoves a box in my hands and I'm obliged to hold on to it. I look up at him. He gathers his coat.

"When does your family get in?" comes out of my mouth, because he needs someone. An adult. He needs someone more capable than me. I want to be more capable than I feel, for Charlie. But I need a moment. He pauses, wavers, then like someone has shoved a steel rod up his spine he continues.

"They've been called, they're coming in on Monday."

"Your dad?"

Charlie just looks at me like he can't believe I'd even ask.

"Right. Let me know when he gets in and I'll pick him up."

Charlie's dad never travels alone in the city and Charlie will have more on his mind than trying to live up to his father. Besides, I like the man. I know he was an asshole to his son. I also know that, secretly, his dad loves him. He's told me so, in a couple of quiet corners at birthday celebrations where the theater crowd dictated the spotlight and he and I preferred to be off stage. Simon is so proud of him. Even with all the ways he niggles and pushes him; there is love. I wish someday, he would show his son that. Charlie doesn't say anything, and I follow him out with the boxes.

When we arrive, not a word spoken on the subway to their apartment, I help him get the boxes stacked beside door and he holds it open. The cold wind blowing in, as if to not allow the comfort of me staying.

"Thank you," is all he says.

"I can stay."

"I'm tired. Please. I'll call you later."

I want to hug him, but he looks raw and unholy, and I close my eyes. The day after my sister died, I felt like cactus spikes were stuck in every inch of my skin and they'd dig into anyone including myself, if the slightest pressure was applied. I remember the sting of my eyes, blinding and raw, and I just wanted to sleep, and sleep, and sleep. Forever.

"Ok. I get it. But I'm here, and you'd better fucking call me."

Charlie pauses, as if I've roused him from a script and he's had to look up to the improvisation of the actors.

"I will," he says angrily and his brow narrows. Somehow, I know he will. He's angry because he knows he has to. Because I told him to, and he's too polite to decline.

"Try to get some sleep. I know it's hard. Try some tea or Advil PM. But not too much!" I emphasize. God, did I just give him an idea? I turn back, desperate, I start crying.

"I'll call you," he reassures. His hand reaches out and touches my shoulder.

"Ok. I'm going to go save you the waterworks," I say. Charlie nods and watches me go. I turn back, at the bottom of the stoop, but he's already closed the door and turned off the light in the entry way. My heart aches in my chest like a puppy that's trying to get back inside. Whiny, stupid mess.

He'd better call me.

CHARLIE

You're never ready. That's what people say. You can think you're prepared, but you're never really ready.

You're not ready when your wife dies. You're not ready for the details and the realities that death hands you on legal paper. Not ready for the end-of-life costs, or the insurance policy she'd taken out without your knowledge. You're not ready for your wife to take care of you, even after death.

You're not ready to go through the mail and find a letter addressed to you, not in the shape of a typical condolence card, but a letter from Don DeVoe, that outlines, in disturbing detail the ten-year affair he had with your wife. And how his aching heart, filled with grief—that four-letter word in five-letter clothing—demanded he come clean.

I'm not prepared to go on in a world where everything I've ever known was a lie.

I drop Don's letter. The shaking of my hands is like the clawing of raw nerves, tremoring agents of disbelief and anger. I tear into her room, bursting through the closed door to the answering smell of her perfume, locked away since she'd been in hospice. I upend every fucking thing to prove him wrong. I dump out every drawer, tear down all her clothes, tip over every box in her closet. To prove him wrong.

But the last box, in the back corner, tips over in a cascade of letters.

Letters that are not in the shape of condolence cards.

Hundreds of them ... proof that *I* am wrong.

You're never ready for the feeling that the only thing left to do is jump off a damn bridge and end the fucking charade of life. I'm not sure if I'm ready, but I'm sure that that's what I'll do.

Because what's the point when you realize that the love you've held for twenty-nine years, was for someone whose heart was divided? And you are now alone. Not a soul to care, to grieve with. To love. I grab my coat and Gina's favorite blue scarf. I arrange an Uber to the bridge. I slam her bedroom door closed. Let it be a tomb, like our life.

My heart aches in my chest like an animal in a cage too tight. Angry, inconsolable mess. I growl, in the empty, echoing apartment and grab the front doorknob for the last time. When I rip it open, I'm confused and pissed off.

Because who's on my fucking stoop? Megan Fucking Kent.

"Hey there, stranger," she says, nonchalant to the fire of impending death in my gaze.

"Get out of my way."

"Where you goin'?" she asks, quirking that head, looking like a kid, all full of honesty and hiding angel wings beneath her plain brown coat.

"Out."

"I'll go with you." She shrugs and it's decided, even with the box in her arms. I'm not in the mood for her bullshit.

"I'm suicidal," I rage. Hoping she'll cry, or cower, or anything to save herself from the storm of inevitability in my veins. I'm dying tonight. It's not a question.

MEG

Charlie hasn't called. I've left messages, out into the ether, with no response. By the evening of the third day, I'm genuinely worried. I was young in my moments of loss, I had a world and years ahead of me. Gina's words filter in, a cool Georgian drawl.

He'll fall into the darkness. He loves hard, he falls hard. I check my phone. I text again into his darkness with no reply. I leave work early, my heart and brain racing and worried. How could I have already failed her?

I stop at Saul's. I'm starving and I just got paid, so, that's dangerous. The rent was a little late, but I've got thirty dollars to spend on the best soup in town and I'm going to take it to Charlie's. I miss his face. I need to just be near him. I need to make sure he's okay; shut out the world for a moment and fill our bellies. Mine growls at the counter. Saul just smiles.

"What can I get you? Lentil?"

That was Gina's favorite. I sigh, shake my head, and my eyes go soft. Saul's do too. The whole neighborhood feels the pit of loss.

"Do you—" I pause, swallow down the burn of tears, and clear my throat, "do you have chicken and wild rice?"

"I got some in the back. Fresh pot." He nods and I give him the biggest smile I can muster. I wipe my eyes while he's gone but I think he knows I'm on the verge. I'm not one of those beautiful starlet criers. I'm an ugly crier complete with all the puffiness. A mess waiting to break open. He hands me the soup and a bag of bread. I calculate the cost in my head.

"Uh, I don't need the bread tonight." Saul sees me fingering the bills in my wallet.

"You're headed to Charlie's?"

"How'd you know?"

"Chicken wild rice is his favorite. He only orders it when Gina's out of town."

I sob and catch myself, wiping my nose on my coat sleeve. Saul shakes his head, stares into my treacherous, weeping eyes.

"You don't pay. Not tonight. Take him the soup."

I shake my head. "I can pay."

"Next time," he says, with his own eyes shimmering, and the deal is final.

We are all a little broken, beneath this loss and the unfair truth that we still have to go on. Without her.

"Thanks, Saul."

He only nods with a wink and is on to the next customer. I hop on the subway in a daze. Charlie still hasn't written me back. What if ... my heart hammers up a notch in my chest. What if something's happened? What if he went into the dark and I wasn't there?

I wish the train would go faster. Why do we keep stopping for people? I get off, shove my way through the current going down, swimming upwards like a desperate salmon. I keep the soup intact. I climb his stairs two at a time and the ache in my chest is equal parts worry and being terribly out of shape.

"Please answer. Please answer," I whisper as I raise my hand to the antiquated brass button but Charlie rips the door open before I can even ring it. He looks wild. Unmoored. His eyes are fighting and strange, like he's made decisions. I don't know what to say. So, Kansas takes over.

"Hey there, stranger."

"Get out of my way."

"Where you goin'?" I ask and tilt my head to the side like an innocent farm girl, unaccustomed to dark thoughts.

"Out," he grouches.

"I'll go with you." I shrug at this, and the soup and bread shrug too. He glares at me; I can feel his mouth forming the sharp blades of words.

"I'm suicidal." The admission itself is a lifeline that he throws out. He could have said he had a meeting, or lawyers to talk to, or a walk to think. But he tells me this truth, because I'm the last barricade. His failsafe. I force myself to smirk and roll my eyes. I bully him backwards, my will and the box of warm food herding him.

"You're hungry."

"No," he says, a split second before his stomach rises to greet me with a groan. His back is pressed to the not-yet-closed door. "Just go, Meg. I'll see you at the funeral."

"Whose? Yours?" I pause, Charlie's eyes go soft through his anger. "Get in the apartment, Charlie. Before it gets cold." I force him back, all the way in, and slam the door closed, putting myself between him and it. I set down the box and take off my coat and hang it up next to where he's standing. He sighs, takes in a deep breath, and closes his eyes.

"Meg," he whispers.

"Let's eat," I say and take off his scarf for him. I hang it with reverence next to my shabby trench. He gives in and throws his coat over the bright blue. As though he can't look at it tonight. I take the box into the kitchen and start to unpack the hot soup and warm bread. I have to get the step stool to reach the bowls in the cabinet and Charlie just stands there watching me, shirt with its cuffs rolled up, untucked and pining for the bridge or busy street that would have ended his pain.

But the pain can fade. I know. It can become livable. I've lived with it for some time. I set down the bowls and crack open the top of the container. Charlie leans in, trying to feign disinterest.

"Is that—"

"Chicken and wild rice, from Saul's private stash," I gloat.

Charlie fake glares and his stomach growls again. "You little shit."

I don't respond but I pass him a full bowl and a chunk of fresh bread. He holds them both in his hands, warm, soft. Little things to cling to in a world that was so desperate and cold five minutes ago. He doesn't speak, but he sits at the island and I scoot up next to him.

I talk about work. I talk about an article I'm writing about AI, I talk about the next impending writer's strike. I keep my topics to things easily forgotten or let go of. I talk about anything, and leave spaces of silence for him to contribute. He doesn't, but he presses his long thigh against mine under the counter, and finishes the rest of the soup.

I offer to stay. He says it's unnecessary. The funeral is tomorrow. Which is why I should stay, I argue. We have things to take care of. He shakes his head. He's changed from the man marching to death, to someone resigned to accept it. But I'm wary, and I don't want to go back to my cold apartment. Not with his knee touching mine.

"I can take the couch."

"No."

"I'm taking the couch."

"I'm fine," he says, and I believe him, but I look at him like I'm not sure. "I'm gonna be fine," he says, and nods. "I'll see you tomorrow."

"You will," I agree with a nod. "On your couch."

"You're insufferable."

"You're tired," I whisper, and my hand reaches out, drawn there by the woman who wished I'd find a better man, and brushes away his hair. "I'll leave in the morning and go get your dad."

Charlie is suddenly accepting. He sighs before pulling away from it. "You sure you don't mind picking that asshole up?"

"I'd love to, that old fart is a hoot."

"He's a monster."

"Well, to a girl who never had a dad, he's better than an empty chair at every play and parent/teacher conference I ever had."

"I wouldn't be so sure about that," Charlie whispers. I clean out my bowl and try not to think about the years without a dad as the last softness of bread absorbs the broth and makes a communion of better men in my mouth. Men like Saul. Men like Charlie.

"Thanks, for the soup. And the company," Charlie says. I stand up and take our bowls, rinse them, and put them in the full dishwasher. I shake my head and pour the soap in to start it. When I look back, Charlie is watching me. There's a softness to the light that's shining from behind him, and I am flooded with something strange and achy. I sigh, start the dishes and come around the chair. Don't be stupid, I tell myself. Give him space. Don't be too much.

But that's what I do. Stupid things. I'm a fuck-up and I'm always too much.

So, before I park my ass on his couch, defiant that he should ever leave without me, my heart spins me around and I put my arms around him from behind. He puts a hand over mine and leans back so my nose is in his neck.

"Thanks for not dying today."

"Don't Jewish mother me," he grouches.

"Someone should." I kiss his temple and give him a squeeze before letting him go. I am banking on faith that knowing someone is waiting for him tomorrow will keep him alive. "Go to bed. We've got shit to do, bright and early."

He waves me off and I head to the living room. I lock the front door, take off my stupid boots and park myself on his couch. The house is quieter than it's ever been, and I hate it. It's the painful after, in the dark night before there's even a before to think about. I lay here, a long while, awake and afraid, that he'll slip away from me. My stomach is full, but my heart is worried. When I see his light go out, when I hear the quiet of a street gone to bed, I cover myself with a blanket from the back of the couch and close my eyes. Tomorrow will come, bright and early, and it's gonna be a rough one.

CHARLIE

To their credit, Gina's family has been helpful with some of the details for the service. For having known my wife that long, I didn't know how religious her family was. I should have guessed, being from the heated, deep south, they'd have words to say about Gina's last rites. But I don't care, because there is no God, so they could hold the pomp and pony show in a shack off of Pier 45 and it wouldn't change the darkness in the world. My dad, the quiet stoic, ever quick with a harsh judgement, is going to take the train down from his assisted living apartment in Connecticut. Meg is picking him up. Meg is doing a lot actually. I gave her a list of the little piddly shit I didn't want to do, this morning. After I woke up and the little jerk was making coffee in my kitchen, still in last night's clothes.

And she's handling it, on her phone, while going down my stupid and shaky handwritten list. The flowers, the seating arrangements, the food for after, the hotels and transportation for Gina's Southern family who would never survive the New York streets alone. It's like the little Kansas yokel has finally earned her Big Apple stripes. I sit in the middle of Gina's torn up room in the early hours of the day, forgetting how to breathe.

Hating, in the pit of my stomach, that I have to stand in front of her friends, my friends, the family we've shared for twenty-nine years, and lie.

∼

Funerals are like weddings.

The day is full of the flurries of necessities, and the gathering crowds, and social pressure to shake so many hands, and nod, and accept watered-down condolences. As if it could put your heart back in your chest knowing that the theater producer on three of her shows will miss her terribly.

Funerals are like weddings in that there are a lot of tears, and you rarely eat, and before you know it, you're in the middle of a giant monstrosity of brick and colored glass because, well, Southern Baptists made the final decision and I was in no state to care, and the man in cloth looks solemn and just a pinch annoyed as his eyes dart to your Jewish attire before he clears his throat and calls you up to speak. For an allotted twenty minutes, tops. Only I'm not the best man. I may not have even been the better man.

Today I'll be playing the part of "grieving husband".

Funerals are like weddings. There's always a crowd, but you look for the faces that anchor you and your tumbling belly, like a shore to a storm-beaten ship. I'm supposed to stand up here, and tell the world how wonderful she was, how much she'll be missed. But they all know this already. Every single one of them knows it. If they knew her, they loved her. They already know how wonderful and bright she was.

But they don't know how dark and angry I have become. How this storm rages in my veins, battering the hull of my broken ship. I look for a face to anchor me. To still my writhing guts.

My eyes lock into Meg's. She's standing at the side of the room like a goddamn usher. While I've been surrounded by the

43

picketing lines of mourners protesting a brilliant light gone out, she's been scrambling to find chairs for everyone and passing out Kleenex. She should have been next to me. With the family. But Meg knows she has no family. One less now.

I look at her there, biting her lip, trying not to cry. I shake my head at her.

Don't do it, kid. You know as well as I do, this is all just pomp and circumstance.

Meg knows that I'm dark, and angry, she knows my hull has been compromised, but she doesn't know the whole truth of it. Or to what depth the sea of rage is tumbling through me. I turn back to the crowd, a hungry gathering of birds, waiting for the breadcrumbs of my words. Surely, the playwright will wow them.

My eyes dart around them all, settling on one face. Tears trickle down the man's reddened cheeks and he locks his gaze with me. Sympathetic turns to pathetic when I recognize Don DeVoe and my heart roars, like a lion maimed but not brought down. My voice stalks through the tall grasses of anger, through the parting lines of my lips, silent and still.

Let him lean in to hear these words.

"I've never believed in God, but I believe even less now. If there ever was one, then it was her. My planets revolved around the center of her and the world did not deserve the warmth of her star. *None* of us deserved her." Don knows I mean him; the great idiot has to know. I hang my head, chance a glance at the crowd, blurred through eyes that are cruelly tearing up, despite my resolution to be angry over sad. "God doesn't deserve her either."

That's all. That's all I can get out and not point my finger at Don and his treacherous heart. How dare he ruin the last testament to my wife? How dare he show up and mourn a woman who was mine? He's the black hole of my world. I sit down next to my father who clears his throat and in it, speaks a volume of reprimands.

Denouncing God in front of the entire church on such a sacred day such as this, Charles?

"Add it to my tab, Dad," I whisper beneath my breath.

The flurry doesn't stop, and I think I sign some paperwork, and I collect the ashes, which were to be separated and scattered, between New York and Georgia. Both urns come home to the apartment, where a good, old-fashioned wake has been dictated by my late bride. A wake.

Wakes are for Catholics, I'd said. She shrugged in her robe and took my chin in her hand.

They always seem like fun, is what she had said. Of her own funeral, she wanted it to seem fun. She wanted wine and music and dancing and laughing. I have the wine. I think Meg did that. Meg ordered the food too. It's all here, and so is the endless stream of well-wishers, face after face. Graceless, awkward patting of my shoulder from nearly all. Gina was the hugger. They are not sure what to do with me.

The only thing that's not here is Meg and I look at every face that enters the apartment, every milling sheep as though she's snuck in. Where in the hell is that girl? Maybe it's my brain, trying to distract from my grief, but it's got me worried. I haven't talked to her since that morning when she asked me where to put the flowers after the service. I said I didn't care. She said she thought she could donate them.

I said God could shove them up his ass. She said she was short, but she'd see what she could do.

I unexpectedly smile in the middle of someone else's story.

Where is she? Did she get left at the church? Left by the people she loved, once more? Orphaned again?

Two hours into the introvert's nightmare, and the endless parade of people is starting to quiet. Meg walks in. I watch from the kitchen as she sneaks through the front door, as if she's trying to slip in without opening another wound. Her nose is pink, and her eyes are watery from the cold. Or maybe it's the grief.

She hangs up her scarf and that old threadbare coat. She pauses to say hello to my father, as if he deserves her softness. She's walking through, not a soul recognizing the plainness of her, the very un-Broadway nature of Meg, in her simple black dress, probably the only one she owns, and probably only because Gina helped her find it. She gives people that awkward, tight-lipped smile that one offers in these situations, perhaps a handshake or a fluttering pat on the shoulder. But no words are exchanged. My God, but she's given me something to focus on. Poetry in her plainness, an anchor in this stormy sea. I can tell she doesn't want to be here. I can tell she knows she doesn't belong. I feel like she might try to sneak out. Give me some awful excuse tomorrow, like she was there but missed me in the hustle bustle of it all. But I can't let that happen. Because she needs to know she's not abandoned. Someone notices. Gina begged me to notice her.

As she passes the kitchen I reach out and take her wrist in my hand. It's small and just the act of wrapping fingers around her bones halts her world.

I always think Meg is so much bigger, but she pulls easily into my arms and I'm just as startled as she is. The kitchen is quiet and I'm not sure why I react like such a desperate man, thinking she might leave. I'm not sure what to do now, with her so close. I cannot account for the grief in me. I am desperate. For any normalcy. For someone not in the business. Someone who knows me.

"Where have you been?" I say.

"The park."

My heart shoots up into my throat. The smallness of her cold wrist and how easily I was able to kidnap her into the kitchen makes me overpour in worry.

"By yourself?"

"I couldn't," she pauses and looks into my face. "I didn't think you'd notice."

"Didn't think I'd notice? That you weren't here? What the hell?" Words come out of my mouth. I've been regulating all day. I can't regulate with Meg.

"This is a lot of people and more socializing than I know you want to do. I didn't want to be one more obligation for you."

Martin, one of my favorite horn players from the pit of many a show-stopper, steps into the kitchen for another sandwich. He gives Meg an awkward, tight-lipped smile, and pats my shoulder lightly, before he leaves. My brain refocuses into the tired vulnerability, unguarded in her.

"Don't leave me alone."

"You're not alone. Everyone is here," she points out.

"They're here for her." I look towards the sounds of laughter and stories in the next room over. In this sea, I am alone. Meg's cold fingers are suddenly on either side of my face, making me look at her.

"I'm here for *you*," she says. I look into her eyes, a quiet shore. I feel my face pinch up like I'm going to cry and that stupid girl throws her arms around my waist and holds me. Buries her face in my chest, and holds me. She's a castle wall, behind which I can cry and not be watched. She holds me so tight.

Like someone who loves you holds you. Without reserve, without any awkward pause, without worry for societal rules or false conclusions. I'm stunned into accepting. When was I last hugged? Hugged like a Midwestern girl hugs? Warm and close and like two hearts are trying to reach each other through the cages of ribs between. Never.

She smells like cold air and the traces of someone smoking on a park bench, and shampoo that's soft and flowery. I could push her away and berate her for being too sentimental. But my body sinks into the warmth. Fuck, I need a hug. A real one. Does she know how badly I need it?

I put my arms around the smallness of her. I don't know how tightly she needs this and I know I shouldn't care, so I just hug her like I want to hug, and she shivers and I shiver back and I feel the tears welling up between us, a great lava flow started from an earthquake. I run my hands through her hair, and hold her tragic little brain next to my heart.

"My girl," I whisper and catch myself.

Which girl?

It demands an answer and I have to decide. "She was my girl."

The grief flies its middle finger to my stoicism and Meg is so warm and close and just so there, that I start to cry. And I don't know what to do, so I just let it go. She's whispering her anguish, *I'm sorry, I'm sorry, I'm so sorry* over and over like Meg was responsible for the treacherous cells or the decade long affair, or the loss of everything I thought was true. As if she was putting that on her plainly dressed shoulders.

Comfort in her warmth starts to feel like betrayal. I think she feels it too. I sniff and pull away. I'm too confused to have her so close. I'm too far into the middle of my grief and I'm bound to make poor choices. I can't look at her in case any part of this ache is still in my eyes. She tries to look at me but I pat her shoulder like Martin patted mine. Awkwardly. Boundaries thrown back up in defiance. I need to get out of this kitchen. Into a crowd where I can be unseen again. I pause and hand her a box of Kleenex before I go. I hear her sniff and pull out a couple before blowing her nose in a very moose-like manner.

The honking of it brings the first tickle of a laugh I've felt in days.

MEG

I've been nauseous, and empty all morning. A world without Gina is dark and hungry already.

In the morning, I help pick up flowers and take Charlie's dad from the train station to the apartment. I did everything that I thought Gina would do for me. But I've never been much of a nurturer. Most of what I learned, I learned from her. I pick up food, I usher in guests. I'm doing all the things.

But I'm also keeping my grief in, like an infected wound I don't want seen. I've been keeping it in, and doing the things, and checking the boxes, and showing up for her in ways I never did for my own life. Except there's that one thing she asked me to do. that I don't know how to.

Take care of him.

How? How do you do that? What can you possibly say to someone, do for someone, when the light of their world goes out and all they can feel is darkness? I remember reaching out to touch his hand, and he gave me a list instead.

I understand. When I lost my sister in a car wreck my junior year, I didn't speak, or eat, or let anyone touch me for weeks. Grief is a cocoon, and a fire all at once. It's a pair of cement shoes while you've got a noose around your neck. One minute not letting you feel anything, the next barraging you with it all. There's no right way to transition to a new normal. Because it never feels normal. Not when you've loved someone that much.

Gina and Charlie never had kids, but they had a family. Charlie's eighty-seven-year-old father. Gina's sister Kimberly, a few cousins up from Georgia, and the entire Upper West Side stage conclave who loved them since the beginning. The church is full. Gina wouldn't have wanted a church. Neither does Charlie. But he'd pretended to appease her family, to ease the tension for Gina throughout their lives. He's wearing his yarmulke. I suspect that's more to avoid a confrontation with his father in the middle of the mess.

Now, standing there, off to the side of the pews, in the eye of a devastating hurricane, there was nothing else to do to hide the wound. To stave off the grief. And it's all around me and its infectious and I can't hear the words. I'm wiping my nose on my hand, like the proper lady I am, and Charlie catches my eyes with his. His mouth is clenched down, he shakes his head.

Don't cry.

Keep it together, kid.

I sniff and nod. My eyes dry. Charlie stands at the podium, hands on either side and straightens his back to speak. But this is not like any of his lectures I ever sat through. He's so still. Unanimated. Dead. He's staring at a point in the crowd. It's an odd stare, and I'm confused, I look into the faceless mass. Maybe he can't focus with so many of us. Maybe he needed just one face to shrink the world down. I'm sad it's not mine.

He starts.

"I've never believed in God, but I believe even less now. If there ever was one, then it was her. My planets revolved around the center of her, and the world did not deserve the warmth of her star. *None* of us deserved her. God doesn't deserve her either."

Shit Charlie, I think and watch his father cringe, tightening his tallit around his shoulders. Charlie looks at me briefly, there is no smile, no warmth. No light. He walks back to his seat and doesn't look my way again. The service is short. Or at least I think it's too short for a life so full.

I leave before anyone else and wander in the park for the next two hours. Hoping that Gina will show up in some sign. Some dragonfly or flower, or in the kind smile of a random stranger. But it's cold and nothing flies. Nothing blooms. There are no kind strangers here and the wind has turned bitter. I don't want to go back to their apartment for the wake.

But I promised her.

I SNEAK IN AS SOME PEOPLE ARE LEAVING, PLAIN ENOUGH TO BLEND in with the furniture. His father is telling stories of his son and the terror he was. I think Charlie is still a terror, just an older one. I weave my way through groups, only stopping long enough for that awkward smile one offers in these situations. No words of great importance are exchanged with me. I was not important enough in this bigger, brighter world of theirs.

I'll just pay my respects, check on Charlie, and see what time his dad needs to leave in the morning. Then I'll leave the family to their grief. I'm reassuring myself of the plan when suddenly there's a warm hand around my wrist and I'm yanked back and into the kitchen.

"Where have you been?" Charlie hisses.

"The park," I stumble.

"By yourself?"

"I couldn't," I swallow and look up at him. His fingers are warm. "I didn't think you'd notice."

"Didn't think I'd notice? That you weren't here? What the hell?"

"This is a lot of people and more socializing than I know you want to do. I didn't want to be one more obligation for you." I spew out while someone steps into the kitchen for another sandwich. The man gives us both that same wake-appropriate smile and pats Charlie's shoulder before he exits.

"Don't leave me alone," Charlie says, voice edged with the desperation an introvert feels in a sea of people.

"You're not alone. Everyone is here."

"They're here for her." His face falls and I feel it. The black hole opening up between us. The sinking of Charlie into the bottom. I hear Gina's words come back to me, a hush through neurons.

You can't let him sink to the bottom.

I grab his face in my hands. I've never touched Charlie's face. My thumb gently traces the edge of his brow.

"I'm here for *you*," I say, looking right in his eyes, and before I can rethink it, I throw my arms around his middle and hold on to him. I will not go gently into an arm pat. He smells like Irish Spring and coffee, and I'm not sure if it's for his sake or mine, but he doesn't push me away. I hold on. His arms land light, like moth wings around my shoulders, then he sinks in. And the touch is tangible and it feels like the only reality I've had in the last two days. I hold on, I hold on. A shudder runs through our bodies as if an earthquake is trembling beneath us. His hands, long fingers, find my hair, thread in and he holds my cheek close to his broken heart.

"My girl," he whispers softly. "She was my girl."

Then he cries. And I don't know what to do, so I just keep holding on and cry back to him the useless words, *I'm sorry, I'm sorry I'm so sorry* over and over like the bad refrain of a song stuck in my throat. The weakest earworm ever.

The comfort of his warmth starts to feel different. I think he feels it too. Charlie sniffs and pulls away. He doesn't look at me even though I'm trying to catch his eyes. He pats my shoulder lightly, hands me a tissue, and walks back into the grieving fray.

CHARLIE IS SURROUNDED BY FAMILY THE REST OF THE NIGHT, telling stories of laughter and better times and is swept up in the ritual of helping others in their own form of letting go. I know he won't be able to let go. I won't either. Not ever.

I stick around. I make sure people are fed. I make a list of the flowers and the food, so they can be thanked later. I fill drinks, I call people rides if they celebrated her life too much. I don't drink. Not here in this place. There are too many shadows of Carl Jensen's Funeral Home in Pickering, Kansas and the vodka-laced coffee my mother started the day with at the potluck reception after Cecily's service.

Grief cries out to be drowned, to be forgotten, pushed away and numbed out. I'm not going to be numb as long as Charlie is riding the swell of it. The crowd dwindles to just their immediate family. I'm exhausted and out of place.

Charlie is on the couch, next to his father and listening to stories from her sister, and I feel like the odd ball. The fuck-up who nobody knows; the ghost of a different era skulking around the apartment. So, I go into the kitchen and I put away the leftovers. I make him a plate. I'm sure he hasn't eaten. I cover it carefully and put his name on it. I clean the countertops and leave out an unopened bottle of wine next to a glass. Charlie doesn't drink much. But he might need it after the dust has settled. I kiss the top of his head on my way out.

"See you around, professor."

His eyes are tender and he nods. "Be safe, kid."

He calls me kid like I'm not pushing forty-five.

"Eat something, you ornery old fart."

He waves me off with a smile. It's like a small and fighting ray of sun, barely peeking through impenetrable clouds. That I can call him names and he can smile.

I never worried about walking home until I left Charlie that night. My safety wasn't much of a concern. I was too old and angry these days to be bothered by it. But now. Now I had someone to take care of. She made me promise.

I check both sides of the street and walk with a confidence of a woman who'd defend something she loved. Even if that something wasn't myself. I don't teeter in my heels so bad these days; Gina taught me how to stay balanced on the tightrope of life. As my thoughts meander down the sidewalk with me, I realize that Gina was the first person to take me shopping for real clothes.

My mom gave up a lot of hope and flattering measures after Cecily died. For herself and for me. She gave up a lot of everything. Just not drinking. Which is why I only keep one bottle, the good stuff, on the highest shelf. This one has lasted me ten years so far.

Clothes were never a big deal. Just cover your parts, and don't get too full of yourself. It had to be washable, practical, and keep your ass hidden. Even when I was in college, fresh out on the streets of Lawrence, Kansas, and with a small paycheck of my own, I dressed to the standards of my mother. Don't be too proud, and cover your ass.

After moving from rural Kansas to the big city, I got my first journalist gig at Page Six. It was heartless and demeaning but I could pay my rent and at least I had Charlie and Gina.

She took one look at my Goodwill, thrown-together outfit and shook her head.

"Sugar," in her Georgian drawl, "we're going shopping for you, and there will be no arguments."

I looked down at my tan slacks that would have been dynamite if I worked at State Farm and the floods were a-comin'. My plain blazer. The white button up shirt with toothpaste stains down the front.

"Uh, well, I don't have a lot of money right now. I just started."

"All the more reason you need better attire. You cannot move up, dressin' down."

"Listen to the lady, Kent," Charlie started, but paused and the most beautiful laughter sprung from his throat.

"What on earth's gotten into you?" Gina had said, laughing herself at the contagious sound.

"Megan 'Clark' Kent, mild mannered reporter from Kansas!" He barely got out through chuckles and tears. Gina pinched his leg and gave me a smile that would have raised a thousand children with more than enough love to spare.

"All the more reason you need my help. You'll be superwoman someday and you gotta look good doing it."

The memories echo through me as I walk the twelve blocks to my shoddy apartment. All I know, about being a lady, I learned from Gina. All I know about dressing myself well, even on a budget, she'd given me. The confidence when I did not feel it. The love when I had so little to grow from, was her gift to me. My life was empty of Bradley's scripts and toothbrush, and condescending eye. But it was full of something more, that I didn't really see until there was empty space to think. What were *my* dreams? Filed in among all the other catalog cards of pleasing other people.

I was going to be a novelist someday.

I heard the dream whisper, soft and nostalgic. Something too long gone to start thinking about. But some thoughts are like freight trains. They start from the station slowly. And with every rotation of wheel they gain more traction, more speed, more power …

I hear Charlie's voice, a conductor to the smoke-billowing beast.

You need to give up the boyfriends and write that novel. You're not owning your main character. He'd scoffed in my head, as the train chunked and thrummed and deafened past me. The horn from a passing Uber knocked me back onto the curb in time. I stand on the street corner, and look back towards their home. That space would never again be filled with her sweet Southern fire. That life was done with dreams and freight trains.

You'll be superwoman someday.

"I dunno. When is someday, Gina?" I whispered back to the empty space in the big city.

The only time is now. She smiles in my brain, as though she's never really gone.

I climb my stairs, two at a time, until I am huffing and my feet hurt in the heels and I'm sweating through the one good black dress I own. I slam the door, lock it, and throw my coat on the sway-back couch. I grab the good stuff and a glass. I sit at my desk, fingers itching over my legal pad of paper. All this pain has to be good for something. All of this missing her. Of feeling bereft, already, in my obligations to Charlie. I text him.

> I'm still here. All you have to do is text. The subway runs all night.

Then I sit at my desk, I pour a drink for Gina. And one more for me.

I don't stop writing until the sun shines its orange-slice haze through my blinds, and over my desk.

CHARLIE

I'm surrounded in platitudes and stories and others letting go of her all night. It's exhausting and if I'm being honest, I'm actually mostly just smiling and nodding and watching the crowd to make sure no one goes in Gina's room and to see where Meg is. But I don't look directly at her. God no, then I'd just want people to leave and for her to warm up some casserole and we could sit on the couch quietly and just *not* think about death.

The evening rolls on and on until the last people say their goodbyes and a sudden fear strikes my heart that I will be all alone. With her memory and the echoes of a hundred voices missing her. I watched Meg, escorting the drunks down to their rides, and talking to all the others I can't get to and I don't know if I hate her for being so thoughtful, or love her for taking some of the weight. She must feel so out of place.

I finally sit down, on the couch, next to my father and listen to stories from Kimberly of Gina's first play wherein she dressed all of the neighborhood dogs up and produced a stirring rendition of Hamlet. I feel the daylight of nine-year-old Gina shining in the room and I miss her. I miss her terribly. I let my grief take the wheel while my anger sleeps in the back seat. I feel

Gina kissing the top of my head and I look up into Meg's tired face. My heart is confused and somehow still at peace. Like when you see a butterfly for the first time, or the very first perfect snowflake in winter.

"See you around, professor," Meg says.

I nod. "Be safe, kid."

"Eat something, you ornery old fart," she says and Gina's family narrows their eyes. But Meg is Meg and she knows I haven't eaten, and I am ornery. The word, *fart* is such a midwestern tell. I wave her off with a smile. I should offer to walk her home. But there are still so many people here, and before I even think to get up, she's danced through them to her coat and the door is closing behind her.

I hope she stays safe. The thought is curtailed by the hugs and well wishes and more people going home. Kimberly is taking my dad to his hotel. He won't stay here. He never stays with us.

Us.

Me, I mean. Now only me.

The silence. The silence is deafening when I'm finally alone.

I'm truly alone for the first time in years. I look at Gina's door and worry I might just die there. My phone pings from my back pocket and a strange sensation of worry hits me, like it might be Gina. Telling me not to grieve too long. That I had plays to write and stories to tell. That I still had to love Meg. My gut feels twisted and I'm not sure if it's the hunger, or the loss, or the strange cocktail of considering Gina's asinine request, I stumble into the kitchen as I open the message.

> I'm still here. All you have to do is text. The
> subway runs all night.

Fucking Meg Kent.

My heart unclenches. At least she's home safe. More than I can say for myself. I look up from her words to find the clean kitchen. Days it had been a sty. In the space between mourning, someone has cleaned it up. Probably her.

There's a plate, with my name on the tinfoil covering, and a bottle of wine with a sticky note that says "it's kosher". I scowl at it and twist open the cap. Fucking Meg Kent. I reheat the food and pour a glass.

Then I sit at my counter, like some vagabond who wandered into a diner and was given sympathy. I don't deserve anything, but the food is good and even though I don't want to taste anything or feel good about anything, the wine splashes down my throat with it all.

I fall asleep on the couch, marinara and wine down my white dress shirt and aching for dreams to be kind.

I AM UP EARLY THE NEXT MORNING. I PICTURE ALL OF THE WAYS men are meant to grieve and all the ways we're meant to move on. I don't know which is the right path for my heart but when my eyes open to the still dark, I'm not even sure what city I'm in. My father left a message on the home phone. He took the train this morning. Fine. I didn't want to say goodbye to him anyway. Gina's family flies out, they had texted about meeting for breakfast but I'm in no damn mood to entertain or listen to any platitudes. Because I woke up with Don on my mind and seeing his stupid face at the funeral.

I read the words of his stupid letter over and over again in my head. Even though now, it's merely part of the debris in Gina's room that I wish I could just burn down. I lay there, in yesterday's clothes and last year's hopes. Wrinkled and disheveled and feeling like nothing I do, no movement, no writing, no action, will ever erase or placate the sense of loss inside of my chest.

Fuck God. For doing this to me. For doing this to her. For the ruinous road he sets out before us, as we march to death. Is there anything left? My life won't shine again. I scan through my texts. Platitudes and sorrys. Some of them in short hand. Some with a fucking crying emoji attached.

Eye roll.

But then, there's Meg's.

I'm still here.

"Me too, kid. What a fucking tragedy, yeah?" I say and the echo of my agreement comes back to me. I want to implode. I want to rave and rant. But everyone who loved her is holding a dear memory this morning and there's no one to talk to.

I'm still here.

I put on a clean shirt, rinse out my mouth and pull on my coat as I leave the house. If anyone knows how to wallow properly, it's probably Meg. That girl is a grade-A, born in tragedy wallower.

I text her. No read notification. No response. I call her before I hit the subway. Nothing. The train is slower when your heart begins to worry.

I arrive in her shoddy building and the super recognizes me on my way up the stairs.

"Charlie! Good to see you. I'm so sorry to hear about, Gina. My wife and I are praying for you." Pascal says and I nod in recognition that to some people, prayers might actually mean something.

"She home?"

"Does that girl leave?" He laughs and lets me in. Meg lives on the third floor, in the middle of a near-defunct complex with the chaos of poverty on all sides. It's a studio and the perfect jumping board for people on their way to something better. But all she does is sit at the end of it and stare at the water. I sigh, raise my hand. Knock.

Nothing. Not a stirring or the sound of music from the other side. I knock again. Still nothing. Now fear ticks in. What if something happened? What if she's not alone? Thoughts of Don hit my gut and I rage at the quiet beyond the thin wood.

MEG

"Meg Kent, answer your damn door!"

Charlie's voice is a drum in my head and I pull myself up from the couch, where I've been drooling on my hand and my hair is stuck to my face. My brain is an idiot for conjuring him of all people and waking me up.

"Meg!" this time with a very real pounding on the door. I stumble over, undo the five locks and open it. Charlie is there, irate, crotchety, hand raised, shaking his fist at the world. Or me.

"What in the hell, Charlie?" I whisper and try to right my hair. There is no righting it. My dress, has been pulled sideways and my bra is showing. I quickly pull it closed.

"You didn't answer your phone."

"Huh?"

"You could have been lying in a gutter somewhere!"

"Aw, look at that, now I got a Jewish momma." I smile, lean against the door jam, and his eyes fall oddly to my mouth.

"Yeah? Well, maybe I ought to put you over my knee."

My face feels hot. I wasn't expecting that or the image that comes to my mind. I clear my throat.

"I thought Jewish moms just guilted you into compliance, not actually beat your ass. Isn't that for the Baptists?" He pushes through me. "What are you doing here? Besides making sure I'm not dead?"

"Breakfast. Or I guess brunch now. When did you start sleeping in?" he grumbles and walks through my terrible apartment like he's inspecting it to be condemned. To be clear, it doesn't take him long, he makes one circle and hits all of the areas, kitchen, desk, living room, Murphy bed.

"Since I started—" I swallow the fear and my eyes dart to the desk, filled with papers and notebooks and my laptop still open. And the bottle. I guess I'd been toasting a bit more to the lost loves of my life than I would normally.

"Drinking?" he says and scowls at me.

"Not usually, but last night was, I mean, after the—I just—" I stumble over the excuses, hearing my mother in every one of them. His mouth turns down at both corners. He grabs the bottle, still sloshing with liquid, marches it to the sink and pours it down the drain. I feel it. Deep in my blood. It hurts.

"Hey," I slam my door and come across the room. "You can't do that."

"I'm not going to watch you throw away your brilliant mind in a bottle."

"I'm not!" I gesture again at the desk. "I stayed awake over that." Charlie drops the empty bottle in the trashcan and goes to the desk. He stands, still for a moment, a frozen grouchy statue, shoulders hiked up to his ears. I watch his hand twitch.

Then his fist unclenches. Then both do. He reaches out, touches the handwritten outline before picking it up to look closer. And the pages of messy scrawl that follow it. I feel like a school kid getting their report card read for the first time.

"It's just a—" I tug at my hair and clear my dry throat, "it's just a start."

Charlie drops the notebook back on the desk, nods but not impressed, and turns back to me. "Get dressed. You need food."

"I need food? You need food, you grouchy old asshole." I try to argue to protect the tender and exposed underbelly of my new novel. He turns his back and stalks out, slamming my door, to wait outside while I dress.

CHARLIE WANTS TO GO TO BREAKFAST. WHICH ISN'T ODD IN ITSELF. Charlie loves a good breakfast, after a few hours of writing and taking his daily walk. But this time feels different. And it takes me a while to count back the days, but he's been different. Not just since Gina died, but a little after that. It's like a fire of hatred has been smoldering. It started with his angry insistence on suicide and went on to him denouncing God in church. I mean, he'd always been skeptical of religion, but never hateful.

Still, when he says, "I want bacon, from Raymond's," I balk at the idea. Raymond's is famous for a whole lot of delicious pork products. Bacon and eggs, pork chops and eggs, chorizo, sausage, any number of prohibited meats partnered with eggs. A Jewish nightmare.

"Bacon?"

"Grab your coat. It's freezing." Is all he says and I'm curious and hungry enough to not ask too many questions.

"Is your dad still—"

"He left on the 5:20." Clipped and short, like he's got other things to think about.

"That's early, are you okay alone?"

"Fine."

Charlie is decidedly not fine. Because he's quiet. Not just contemplatively quiet. Like we asked some big questions and now his brain is running through scenarios and making connections between. No, he's angry quiet. I puzzle over it, drawing connections of my own.

Is this grief? It feels like something else, something more.

Is it about the bottle? He knows I wouldn't go there, right? That I still remember too clearly the days after my sister's funeral, trying to get myself to school and to my job afterwards because I didn't know if it was my paycheck that would keep us from freezing to death that winter.

Charlie doesn't speak for the rest of the subway ride. He doesn't speak on the walk across the street and not as we enter, even when he holds the door, and I say thanks he doesn't respond. I nod to the waitress for a table for two.

When he sits down, I'm expecting him to mull over the menu, and settle on something *not* against his softly held principles. But he doesn't look over the menu. The waitress comes up, he looks at her sternly and orders two large sides of bacon.

I think my mouth is hanging open because when the waitress looks at me it feels like she can see my dry tongue. I can't order. My head swings back to Charlie.

"You were serious? Bacon?"

"Yes, Meg, bacon."

"But Charlie—"

"She'll have two eggs, over easy, sourdough toast, extra butter and a side of bacon." It's hard to ignore how well he knows me when I feel like a stranger is sitting across the table.

"Charlie."

"What? You're not sharing my bacon." The waitress leaves, taking the menus with her. We sit in silence. Silence is odd for Charlie. It's almost like I'm the ghost that trails along beside him that he can't exorcise. The witness to his life post-Gina. Maybe he needs someone to be here, for his fall into damnation by bacon. The waitress comes with the coffee and the piled plates of bacon. He leans over them and takes in a big whiff, closing his eyes like he's just been waiting for an excuse via crisis. I wonder if there's an asteroid coming. Certainly the end of the world would bring about more piety.

"What the hell? You know you aren't going to eat that stuff."

"I can damn well do what I want."

"Look, I get that your faith is shaken right now."

"Shaken, Meg?" He takes the first slice in his fingers.

"Stop. Let's talk about this."

"Why? Why do you care?"

"Because you invited me here. Even being too pissed off to explain why. Why am I here? To what? To watch you damn your soul with a big old plate of salty sin? Even outside of some makeshift deity, your system isn't used to that stuff and you're going to get sick! I want to understand why."

"Because!" he yells and his voice sounds panicked and strange. "Because, fuck God! And fuck his rules, and fuck not eating unclean foods, when he put that unclean shit into the beautiful universe of her body. Fuck God, when he gave her a lover. A lover who sent me the most sappy and awful letter about the woman we 'both' loved and then had the fucking audacity to show up at the funeral. Fuck Don DeVoe for loving her all those years, Meg! And fuck me for not seeing it, because my damn head and heart were so over the moon for our life and my work. Maybe I got lost." He stops to breathe, to think. "Maybe it was me. Maybe I got lost, in my stupid little plays while my wife had to look elsewhere for love. But, fuck a god that wouldn't give me a sign, a nudge to look up once and a while. To be a better man for her. Fuck. God."

"Charlie," I say as his words become strange companions to my memories, "that doesn't make any sense. What do you mean she had a lover?" The waitress comes and drops off my food. I don't even look at it. I can't reconcile the idea that Gina could love anyone but Charlie.

"That's enough. I don't want to talk any more about it. Hand me some toast." He stares hard at me over his pork-greased fingers and I sniff, paused in the suspension of disbelief. "The toast?" he asks again.

My hand shakes and the plates clank together when the toast

lands in front of him. My mind rewinds, to the way he stared out into the crowded funeral hall. He wasn't staring at the nameless faces, unable to focus. He was staring at the man who'd loved his wife. Who'd showed up at her funeral. Who'd spent years loving Gina in secret. I feel like the door of my airplane has ripped off midflight and I can't hear for the noise and shock shooting through my system.

"Jesus, Charlie. Why didn't you say something sooner?"

"I said I didn't want to talk about it." And he doesn't, he just wanted me to know the facts. He just wants to eat pork products and fly a metaphorical bird to the big man in the sky. Which means he can't care much for what's left of life, and it's in that moment that I'm worried. And mad, and hopeless. I feel his anger like it's my own.

Tears ask for an outlet but I shut them down. The idea that the woman I loved so wholeheartedly could do this to the man I care for so deeply makes my heart spin around, caught in a sharp-toothed blender of the impossible. The waitress comes out, with two Bloody Marys on a tray for the next table. She stops cautiously beside us. I order a vodka tonic and she skitters away, a mouse in the midst of two hungry and scraggly alley cats. Charlie scowls at me.

"Fuck God," I say back to him and raise my eyebrows. He pauses mid bite and points his finger at me.

"That's not the same thing."

"What? We can't fight our past? We made mistakes and so did the people we love, so let's fucking give up."

"You don't get to give up."

"Neither do you!"

"I'm much older and I don't have a reason to live."

"You have worlds to live for. You have your work and people who love you. You have me!"

"You don't get to drink!"

"Well at least I'm not doing it behind your back," I sob

before turning my head to stare at the street outside. For a moment it looks like Charlie will put the bacon down. I watch his fingers shake from the corner of my eye. When I look back in his face, he glares and takes a voracious bite of three pieces at once.

"Fuck me," I whisper again and let the waitress set the clear poison between us.

My world is shattered. Perfect love doesn't exist after all. I don't touch my breakfast but I drink the vodka down, all of it, until the straw slurps empty bottom, while Charlie eats.

I'm so mad and disillusioned that when he pays for the meal of sadness, I don't even bat an eyelash or pretend I want to pay. I can't anyway. We stand outside the diner's door for a long moment. He looks down at the ground, takes a deep breath and levels his eyes on mine.

"I'll give you that one, Meg. But no more. You've got bigger things to do. Go home. Write."

"Charlie, I'm sorry." I say and my world wobbles beneath our feet. "I'm sorry about Gina. I'm sorry about Don. It's shitty and—"

"Don't. Don't apologize for other people, Meg." He crams his hands into his pockets, blows out a bacon-soaked breath and shakes his head. "It's too late anyway."

I hate this darkness in him, but as I'm already brewing my own pot, I don't feel like I have the right to tell him to stop marinating. "What are you doing now?"

"What do you care?" He rubs his stomach and I can't imagine the turmoil his system is having with all of the fat and salt. Probably the same mine is having with the rot-gut poison I drank out of spite.

"Stop being an asshat," I growl back, shades of my mother's vodka tone in my mouth.

"Going home, alone. To a bunch of goddamn ghosts. And answer all the damn emails that keep coming up, and finalize all the affairs, and pay the hospital bills and all the other shit that avalanches when someone dies. Not to mention figure out what to do with the five half-shit plays I began before she died."

"Let me come help." Broken heart through my throat.

"No."

"Why?"

"I don't need you helping me through my sadness, Meg. I've got this."

"Yeah, obviously. Seems like you're coping really well." His head drops and I hate myself for the bitterness. "Are you forgetting? I've been here, Charlie. I've lost. When I shouldn't have lost. I know how much this fucking hurts. My heart knows."

He scowls. The response dies on his lips. He sighs. He looks around. His big brain is thinking. "I want ten pages by next week."

"What?"

"I want ten pages, of your new novel by next week. I'll see you Sunday at eleven, the park." That's all he says and then he leaves. No goodbye, no asking if I'm even free that day.

The desire to tell anyone who's trying to dictate my life to fuck off is really strong, and it's less censored with a gut full of booze. But my rational brain, waves a desperate hand in the sea of vodka now trying to numb my neurons and stops me. Charlie's edict feels like the professor I used to know. The man who had purpose and direction. He wants to see my pages. He wants me to write. I've asked him what I can do to help. This is what he's asking of me.

"Fine," I say weakly, but he's already gone, taking the train the opposite way to home. I would rather walk.

So I do. My brain seeped in the idea that Gina could have even kissed any other man than Charlie. But she was an actress, so I guess, why not? Was their whole marriage an act? Is that what Charlie's thinking too? My stomach hurts. Poor Charlie. Poor Gina. I have no words in me, but when I get back to my apartment, and hour later after walking off the effects of my stupidity, I make my ass plant in the chair and start and stop for a pathetic two pages.

My eyes hurt and my brain won't stop rolling over the strange and macabre rollercoaster that's become everything I once knew to be true. Hadn't I escaped Kansas to get away from the tragedy? To live in a fast and bright world, with fast and bright people? I look back at my desk as I pour myself a bowl of cereal and wonder if I should scrap those two pages and write about her.

Not Gina. Not my mom. But Cecily. My sister. The milk turns sour on its way to my stomach and I quickly release that idea. That's not the story in me. And it sure as hell isn't a story for anyone else.

After my ragingly healthy meal, I fall into bed and my brain conjures up the sight of Charlie's face, biting down on bacon as if he hoped it would kill him on the spot by divine lightning strike. My eyes open, as my heart seizes and I feel for the first time ever, what love truly must be. To throw your god under the tires of a bus. To shake your middle finger at a lifetime of belief, a legacy of generations because a *real* god, a *good* god would have saved her. Would have spared their love. Wouldn't have let her lover into that church on that day. Wouldn't have taken my sister at sixteen. A metal pole through her throat, blood draining out slowly while she stared at her best friend's limp body, half out of the windshield. A decent god wouldn't have taken my mom out of her mind and into a bottle when I needed her most.

No one ever cursed God for me, and I'm not sure I'd throw God into the trash for anyone.

My mind goes back to the hug Charlie gave me in his kitchen, hands in my hair. The way he didn't cry with anyone the whole day. But me. To the way his face lit up at the bus stop when I was floundering into the city like a fish on a line all of those years ago. To the way he angrily pointed at me to put down the drink.

Except maybe Charlie.

I curse God now for Charlie. I curse him for myself too. The opposite of nightly prayers puts me well into sleep.

CHARLIE

I mull over the entire morning. Like I'm still trying to chew through the strings of salted meat. Starting from the moment Meg opened her door, revealing the same dress she had on last night, pulled across her body like she just stumbled out of bed. A curve of flesh reminding me of a desire I used to know. Her leaning against the doorway as she called me a Jewish mother and the horrible way my eyes found her mouth, smart and seductive. The weirdest, most unhinged thing that comes out of me in response to her immature laissez-faire attitude.

About taking her over my knee … We both blushed. Fuck me.

I'd poured out her liquor. I'd judged her humble apartment, like I hadn't ever stayed in something just as bad. How I wouldn't let go of the anger inside my chest. I need my anger, it's my grief language. I sit down in my empty kitchen, a glass of Alka Seltzer fizzing next to me, head in my hands. I close my eyes and think back to her desk.

There was a list, a short outline, surrounded by balls of mistaken starts. *Novels I want to write. Stories I need to tell. What is grief? What is anger in grief? What do we do about loss? What did I gain from all my loss?* Questions, scrawled in her chaotic writing.

Is she in my head? My hand twitched towards the papers. Meg is in the delicate stages of beginning to write something worthwhile. My anger simmers low, a stovetop keeping things warm, as I sip the Alka Seltzer.

Bacon?

I hear her confusion all over again. It was stupid and childish of me. The whole morning. I suppose I could have just done it myself. But I'm hurt and I needed someone to see it. I needed someone to know. Before I set myself and my soul on fire. One small hit to my faith. One giant leap for my demise. She watched me, with increasing concern, and when I let the whole awful truth of it go, across our two plates I'd never seen Meg look more broken and at a loss. I close my eyes, I hear her voice when the drink lands between us.

Fuck God. Fuck me.

I've never been so mad in my life! Not just at her and the button she knows how to push, but at myself. Especially when she tells me that people love me. That I have her. She pointed to her own heart and Gina's words hit me in the back of the head.

Love her or I'll never forgive you.

"Maybe I won't forgive you either, Gina." I sigh, try to stay calm and take another sip to ease the ache of too much hate in my system.

Gina's infidelity was a cruel burden to lay on Meg. But it was cruel of Gina to put the weight of each other's survival on Meg and I. Nothing about this world is fair, and I'm ready to quit the whole stupid game. She sucked down that drink like she didn't give a shit anymore either.

She didn't eat. And as I watch her, in the memory, across the table, trying to keep tears in and shaking her head and the calm dullness settling into her eyes as the alcohol starts to numb out the fuckery of the world, my anger abates. Ebbs, back into the sea of all my churning emotions. What have I done to Meg? When all she's been, since the day she found out about Gina, was a calm port in the storm of loss? My stomach stumbles and shifts, grotesque and confused.

I paid. We left. No words will ever suffice. When we got outside, to the cold and gray of late December, I look at the ground. The weight of the truth is shared, but not lessened. I don't care if I ever repair myself, but I couldn't let her leave on this uneven ground. But then when she apologizes, *I'm sorry about Gina*, I feel the heavyweight punch in my gut.

I want to pull her into my arms. I'm sorry Meg; I'm sorry I was childish and stupid and angry. I'm sorry I gave you my hurt, like it was your fault that I had to carry it. I'm unfair and ridiculous. I sigh deeply and shake my head.

She called me an asshat. She was absolutely right. Days of people babying me and letting me 'feel my emotions' and be a dick had given me an excuse. But those words from Meg shock me back into remembering I don't have leave to treat her that way.

Let me come help.

I told her I didn't need it. But that was a lie. It was a damn lie and I've never needed anyone more. Because she knows. How it fucking hurts to lose something you love that much. I think of her notebook. Her scrawled writing:

What is grief? What is anger in grief? What do we do about loss? What did I gain from all my loss?

Meg knows. I feel my face soften; I try to calm my stomach with another sip. She wants to help. And I need something to … believe in.

I didn't say sorry and I couldn't hug her. All I gave her is the selfish deadline for my own benefit. So I have an excuse to not die between now and Sunday. Because Meg will be waiting, with pages for me to read. I don't look back on the gluttony, the blasphemy, or the pain still present in her. I can't.

MEG

I met Jonah at a coffee shop, where I was writing because they'd shut off my heat. The novel was a fucking mess, and I'm wobbling between some weird strata study of my failed romances and touching on romantic musings. In short, it's a piece of shit. And maybe that's because that's the only way I know how to write, dramatically and without depth. My life has been, up until this point, a series of articles that scratch surface-level itches and the murky depths below are too scary to dive into. And that stands to reason, because that's how I live. Surface level.

I'm still hurt about breakfast with Charlie, but I know I have to have something. He's waiting for something. So I start to dabble, to write down what it felt like when I was ten and my dad left, but it makes me nauseous, and that makes me think of greasy bacon, and that makes me think of Charlie's face, angry across the breakfast table as I chugged a glass of vodka. And how fucked up we both are, after Gina's death.

It turns me inside out and I am too antsy to stay in my apartment, now cold because I can't afford the heat. I'm lonely. I'm miserable. I have to write, but I'm stuck. So there I am ... best shape of my life, at a coffee shop around the corner from my apartment, wide open for the advances of anyone willing to pay any attention. I must have had three or four refills from my one cup, when the younger, mountain of a man, with his blond, haphazard bun and a well-kept beard walked by. He stopped solely for the purpose of watching my hand shake.

"You okay?"

"Strange question for a New Yorker," I said between stuttering sentences, barely thinking there was a human on the other end of the voice.

"Well, I'm from Colorado, and it looks like maybe you've reached your caffeine limit for the day." I looked up and found him. Fell into his warm, rugged smile. His distinct lack of scowling. Kindheartedness on a cold afternoon and comfort in distracting me away from the murky dark. He bought me an herbal tea and talked to me over the blank and endless screen, which grew gray and dark until it gave up on me.

I close my laptop and lose focus for the next three days. He's only here for a couple of weeks, with a show. But he's not an actor, I tell myself, reassured. He's a roadie. A working man. A man not afraid to use his hands. And I let him.

It numbs out so much of the hurt from the past months. It quiets the voices and gives me a viable excuse to distract myself away from the mess of a book that feels as empty as a widower's apartment. Jonah is my saving grace away from the scant six pages I have managed. Six pages that Charlie will hate. But I don't buy another bottle since the one Charlie dumped down the drain. Because when the world gets too hard, and the sadness starts to overwhelm me, I can find Jonah's hands and he knows how to keep the show running.

"WHERE'S YOUR WORK?" CHARLIE ASKS AS I WALK UP TO HIS USUAL bench, where he's bundled down in his threadbare coat and Gina's rich blue scarf around his neck. It makes his bright eyes brighter. Whatever the scars, whatever the pain, he still carries pieces of her everywhere he goes. I'm just distracted enough by him that I lose my place in the conversation.

"Huh?" I say and hand him a cup of coffee.

"The pages, Meg?" Then Charlie stands, studies me and scowls. "What the hell," he sighs as he brushes back my hair beneath my hat to see the bites on my neck.

"What? Jesus! I got lonely."

"So what's wrong with being lonely? We're all lonely. Lonely is how you get work done."

"I needed a distraction for a bit, okay? It's not going well." Charlie huffs and starts walking, not even looking to see if I'm catching up. I trip after him. My cheeks burn hot even in the acrid cold air. I didn't bring pages, because they're terrible. And I didn't want him to be even more disappointed in me.

"You do not need distraction. You are a girl who doesn't know what it is to be alone. I think when you get too close to your own voice, your own potential greatness, you pull away. I think that you're scared."

"I am not," I grumble. "I just—" I pause and sigh. "I don't know if I have greatness in me, Charlie. I've never been great, at anything."

"That's not true."

"Oh? Name one thing I've done right in my life."

There's a pause, he stops walking. He looks down at me. His brow pulls in.

"See? You can't. I'm a nobody. Why would anyone want to read what I write?"

"You are not a nobody. You survived a life most people wouldn't, you went on to be a journalist."

I scoff, "Journalist, psh."

"You are a writer, and you are interesting. Five out of six starving actors say so."

"Ugh, what the hell, Charlie?"

He puts a warm hand on the crook of my elbow before I can leave. "You are still kind even when the world was far too cruel to you, and you know about grief." He swallows, looks down. "You know so much about it, that you're afraid to be alone with it."

My mouth hangs open but no words make an appearance. My eyes sting. The arrow was a dead-center shot to my heart.

"When was the last time you were alone, Meg, really?"

I feel insulted by the question. As though he saying I'm incomplete and can't seem to get my shit together. That I'm a scared little child who can't face her past. I don't like how close to right he is. I don't like the way his eyes went dark when he saw my neck or the lingering warmth where his finger brushed away my hair from my neck. The pressure of his hand on my arm. I don't like that he's angry.

"When were you?" I immediately regret it. He falters. He doesn't look at me. "I'm sorry, I didn't mean that."

He looks up at the tree-lined path of Central Park where the bones of the woods are cold and dead.

"Charlie—"

"Stop. Stop using that tone like I'm an orphaned child."

"You're not a—"

"I haven't been alone since I met Gina."

"I know," I say, softer. "Me neither." But where I have had a string of mishaps and disastrous relationships, he's always and only had Gina. We're stopped, in the park, awash in the gray cold of our mutual lives.

"And what have we got to show for it?" Charlie says and looks up the empty path. Not a soul to meet. Not another beating heart to walk towards.

"Cynicism and unhealthy coping mechanisms?" I say. Charlie closes his eyes, sighs, shakes his head and keeps walking.

"You need to keep your head on straight."

"I'm trying to. I'm know I'm really close to something. I just needed to get—"

"Don't say *laid*," he waves his hand as if trying to dispel the idea.

"Why, Charlie Horowitz, are you a prude?"

"You know I'm not. It's just that sex is—" he stops. He looks at me and quickly away.

"Sex is what?" I watch his mouth quirk into a little smile and I'm surprised at the way my stomach produces butterflies at the sight.

"It's fun," he sighs and shakes his head, "but it's the same as booze, or cocaine, or anything else. It takes you out of your mind."

"Sometimes I want to get out of my mind," I whisper. "Desperately."

Charlie is silent and I don't look at him. "Me too," he answers.

What must it be like to have your one partner, half of your life, the woman you ate with, lived with, had sex with, suddenly gone? The lonely pit opens up in my stomach and I toss the rest of my coffee in the trash bin as we pass it. Lonely as I am, I will never be as lonely as Charlie is.

I don't believe it is better to have loved and lost, and I'm pretty sure, Charlie doesn't either.

"So, I should stop having sex?" I ask quietly.

Charlie looks down at me, ridiculous eyebrow quirked, and that same strange smile. "Nah, kid. Don't stop. Don't ever stop. But don't let it eat into your writing time."

"Really? 'Eat into'? That's what you're going to choose when trying to convince me not to have sex?" I lift my eyebrows at him and smile and Charlie sputters before laughing uproariously.

"Jesus, I can't take you out in public." He nudges me farther from him and the sun breaks out of the suffocating clouds. "I want to see those pages, Meg. No matter how ugly they are."

"Fine," I say and nod, but then I stop and he looks back at me. "What?"

"Fine, I will write my stupid life story. But only if you start again. I want to see a play out of you. Any play. And don't tell me you're working on one. I can tell you haven't been."

"How the hell do you know?"

"Because you're churlish."

"What?"

"I know you."

He shakes his head repeatedly as if trying to clear a foul thought from it. "No. I think I'm done with that."

"Done? What? The hell you are."

"I don't have it in me anymore."

"That's the biggest line of bullshit I've ever heard. You're brilliant."

"I can't write." he whispers. Then he clutches his free hand to his heart. "There's nothing left in here." The act of it, the expression, the truth in the gravel of his voice cuts me so deeply. That Charlie should be without a heart? The man who wrote from it, lived from it, loved from it? If he didn't have a heart, how could any of us deserve to live? How could any one of us love?

I walk back to him and stand in front of him, looking up. I've never felt so small, so angry. So desperate to make someone understand. I shake my head. A guy runs past us, steely eyes ahead in the middle of our tender moment. Sneering at the humanness blocking his path.

"That's not true," I say and want to throw myself into his arms, wrap him up and jar him back to life. But I only look up at him and he looks down at me. And the wind blows a curl of hair across his brow. "It's only been a few weeks."

"Feels like an eternity without her."

"Then find something better to pass the time." I say.

"What? Like sex with actors I meet at coffee shops?"

"Low blow, Horowitz. He's not an actor, he's a roadie, from Colorado."

"He has a man-bun, doesn't he?"

"Ugh," I roll my eyes and try not to laugh.

"So, what does Man-Bun do for you that writing doesn't? Besides the obvious?"

I pause at this question. Man-Bun, Jonah, distracts. Just like cocaine or booze. He lets me get away with not thinking about anything. He lets me not have to relive the memories that are locked away. He lets me keep going on as I always have. I clear my throat, to make a path for the dodge.

"He does have a name."

Charlie scoffs at this. We both know it's not as important as I'm trying to make it seem.

"What is it? Tree? Yukon? Brawny McSteel-Chest?" There's a strange undertone. He's always been tired of my bullshit with men. But, this time there's something malicious in the way he degrades a stranger.

"Dost I detect jealousy?" I raise an eyebrow.

"Maybe I am." The words puff out in a cloud of steam that falls against my cheek and stops my heart. We are silent. He tosses his coffee in the trash. "Maybe I am jealous." This time, it's a funny thought that's just occurred to him. Like he's admitting to himself some secret that not even he'd considered.

I've never had this feeling, like my heart is going to hammer itself right out of my chest. I lean back, even as the wind and his words conspire to push us together.

"Charlie," I say and my voice cracks.

"I'm jealous because you promised me pages and instead of writing, you're wasting your energy between the sheets of some guy who's probably not even committed enough to invest in a toothbrush for your sink."

I step away. "I'll get you pages. If you get me scenes."

"I told you, I can't."

"The world is ripe with ideas. You have tragedy and love at your fingertips, every goddamn day," I argue.

"You can't use my own lines against me!"

"Why not? They're brilliant lines. And they came from that giant head of yours with its giant eyebrows."

"Giant eye— What the hell do you know about anything?"

"I know they influence the tides."

"You're an asshole," he laughs and I want to reach up at touch his cheek. I shake my head and we stand, noses pointing at one another accusingly. He touches his eyebrows self-consciously. I love them. They're just bushy enough to be interesting, without being overwhelming or acting like a blindfold. He moves on to massage his temples. I narrow my gaze, I soften my voice. His armor is down and this is where the truth can land.

"I know that you aren't done," I whisper.

"The house is too quiet to write."

"So what? Mine is too cold. Both lame excuses."

"Why is your apartment cold?"

"Unimportant and uninteresting question. It's not the environment outside. Your brain can do the magic inside."

"Why is your apartment cold, Meg?" He asks again, this time in a worried voice that means he's at the end of his rope with my avoidant banter.

"They shut off the heat."

"It's ten below!" Charlie yells at me.

"I know. That's why I was at the coffee shop. That's how I got distracted."

"Shit." Charlie stalks away.

"I don't know why you're surprised; you know what I make at BuzzFeed and apartments are expensive. When Pascal raised the rent last month, I had to make some decisions. I'll be fine. I just have to sign up for more articles or find a freelance gig."

"No!" he turns and paces, pissed. "You don't sign up for more work because then you're not going to write your novel."

"Well, I can't pay rent with a novel that's not written. And I can't write a novel without a place to live."

"So live with me." The words feel hot and angry as though he hates me for them. We stall on the path and my cold fingers crunch into fists.

"What?"

Charlie looks to one side of the path and the other as if he's been caught. "I have some space."

He has more than that. It's a two bedroom, and they used to sleep in separate rooms, supposedly because Gina had snored so badly. I often wondered if it wasn't because she was already pulling away from him. The thought makes a dark hole open up in my heart and I touch it self-consciously. Gina's smile shines in the back of my head. Even if it would guarantee that I could watch out for him, I can't live with Charlie.

"I can't." I shake my head and feel a drop of snot threaten to escape. "I can't stay in her room." I wipe my nose on my sleeve.

Charlie glowers at me. "Of course you won't, I'm not offering you her room."

"What, am I sleeping in yours then? Won't that be awkward when Man-Bun comes over?"

"Ah ha! You said he had a name."

"Something like, Jonah, I think?" I shrug with a smile. Charlie shakes his head.

"You can have the loft. It's still got my old desk in it but I can clear that out."

"Where would you write?" I need to find a reason not to. I can't have this lining up. The truth is then I would have to write. There'd be no excuse. He would see to it.

"I can move my office downstairs. So I can see the park."

"That would be a good place for *you* to get some writing done."

"It would be a good place for us *both* to write, Meg." It's so strange a line, and he says it with a soft air of hope that I can't, under any circumstances now, refuse. Gina is on the park bench behind him, swinging her feet like a little kid, glee in her smile and clapping her hands.

"How do I know you won't hate living with me?" I say it more to her than him.

"Oh, I know I'll hate it," he says.

"Then why are we even talking about it?"

"Because, you shouldn't be freezing and I shouldn't be alone," he yells back and spreads his hands, still in his coat pockets and I look down his torso, to the weight no longer there. I see for the first time his gray skin, his dull eyes. In the weeks since she left us, I've been remiss. I haven't been doing my job.

And he shouldn't be alone.

"Only under two conditions," I say and step closer. If only to warm him with some body heat, because it looks like he's lost most of his. He looks down at me, closes his arms protectively over his chest.

"What? And don't say Jonah the Man-Bun can stay over."

"That you'll finish a play and that you'll kick me out the moment I get to be too much."

"Should be a good two-day run," he nods and turns, continuing the walk as if we hadn't just agreed to move in together.

CHARLIE

I know she doesn't have it, when I watch her walk up. There's nothing but coffee in her hands and that sly smile that tells me that Meg Kent got laid. I don't have evidence except for twenty-three years of knowing that particular smile. When I ask her where her work is, she acts as though she's forgotten and hands me a cup of coffee.

If that is the case, punishment must be swift and fierce. I didn't keep myself alive for the last ten days to not get something from this. I look over her smile. There's a flush in her cheeks. I push back her hair, to find the red marks on her neck.

Love bites! Like some amateur high schooler got ahold of her in the back seat of their dad's Ford Fiesta. "What the hell?"

"What? Jesus! I got lonely." She's not mad, she's smiling, wider. As if sex is something that should be forgiven. It should be. She should be having sex. But not at the expense of her writing. I can't risk her getting involved with some loser who's going to steal her time and her talent. Because then I won't have pages, and I won't have purpose. And then, who knows?

"So what's wrong with being lonely? We're all lonely. Lonely is how you get work done."

She mumbles through excuses, but I turn to start walking. I'm angry. Not just at her lack of pages. I miss kissing a woman's neck. I miss, kissing a woman's … anything. I think of Gina's soft skin.

I wonder if my lips overlapped where Don's had been, I walk faster. I hear her huff as she catches up to me. Meg is not Gina. Meg can have lovers. But Meg is no good at not losing herself to them. I sigh and keep my voice calm.

"You do not need distraction. You are a girl who doesn't know what it is to be alone. I think when you get too close to your own voice, to your own potential greatness, you pull away. I think that you're scared."

"I am not," she says. "I just— I don't know if I have greatness in me, Charlie. I've never been great, at anything."

"That's not true." Anger makes my chest hot. That she should not see herself.

"Oh? Name one thing I've done right in my life."

I stop walking. I look down at her, the thoughts are rampant and uncontained. You survived your dad leaving, you survived the death of your sister. You survived your mom's alcoholism and all of her worst days. You moved out on your own, you made a life, and you kept promises to your friends. You gave me joy. You made my wife happy and inspired me to write. Your laugh is stupid and beautiful, your freckles are stars at night. Promises of your words kept me alive for over a week longer than I wanted to be …

"See? You can't. I'm a nobody. Why would anyone want to read what I write?"

"You are not a nobody. You survived a life most people wouldn't, you went on to be a journalist."

"Journalist, psh."

"You are a writer, and you are interesting." I can't let the ideas that have settled into my belly like a gang of silly butterflies come out of my mouth. "Five out of six starving actors say so."

"Ugh, what the hell, Charlie?" she turns to leave. I grab her arm. The first time I've really touched her since the hug in my kitchen. I let a butterfly pass through my lips regretfully.

"You are still kind even when the world was far too cruel to you, and you know about grief," I try to swallow them down but another escapes. "You know so much about it, that you're afraid to be alone with it."

She stops talking. Her eyes are hurt. I've said too much, and all of it wrong. So, like any stupid man, I just keep going.

"When was the last time you were alone, Meg, really?"

"When were you?" The words are a slap to the face and a knife in the gut all at once, and maybe I deserve it. She withdraws quickly, at pain in her haste to defend her own destructive tendencies. I let go. I know she didn't mean that as cruelly as it sounded. Still, I can't look at her.

"I'm sorry. I didn't mean that."

I shake my head, clear that wreckage, breathe the cold air into my dead lungs.

"Charlie," her voice begs forgiveness.

"Stop. Stop using that tone like I'm an orphaned child."

"You're not a—"

"I haven't been alone since I met Gina."

"I know. Me neither," she says, quiet to the space around us, stopped in the park. We are drowning in this gray sea, this shared realization of how little company we have left us. I sigh, my next words are escapees from my new widowed existence

"And what have we got to show for it?" I look up the empty path. It's strange to not see a person for a short span of time. Like we're manifesting our loneliness together.

"Cynicism and unhealthy coping mechanisms?" she says with a shrug. Fuck, I want to laugh at that. *Don't laugh.* I tell myself, *don't encourage her.*

I close my eyes, turn away, and keep walking.

"You need to keep your head on straight."

"I'm trying to. I'm know I'm really close to something. I just needed ... I needed to get—"

"Don't say *laid*." I stop her, even though the thought has already crossed my mind.

"Why, Charlie Horowitz, are you a prude?"

Am I? I look down at her. The brief and unfathomable thought of her pale skin at the mercy of some young man's irreverent mouth and greedy hands, hits me like a shovel to the side of the head and I have to immediately look anywhere but at her.

"You know I'm not. It's just that sex is ..."

"Sex is what?"

What is sex? I smile and think of the laughing, sweaty joy, the softness of tender praises in quiet rooms and wandering hands in the back of a cab. I think of Gina and me backstage, young and in love and the suppleness of her thighs and the way her lipstick smeared on my chest, marking me as hers. The creation and expansion of cosmos, and the shuddering stillness of our singular atoms. Sex is life. And death. And all the drunken wonder in between. I won't ever have that again. I'm no longer qualified and my partner is gone.

"It's fun," I sigh, trying to talk to a younger version of myself. "But it's the same as booze, or cocaine, or anything else. It takes you out of your mind."

"Sometimes I want to get out of my mind," she says. "Desperately."

"Me too," I say. Suddenly I'm grieving the loss, not just of my wife. But of intimacy. Of touch. Of kissing. God, I love kissing. Maybe even more than sex. Something about the formidable interplay, the exploration, the pressures and tastes and sharing of heat. The roving hands and foreheads pressed together when you catch your breath. I'll never kiss anyone again.

I feel like I've had a limb amputated. As though I'll be stuck with the ghosted nerve endings but never be able to use the part again. I want to cry; I feel the burn behind my eyes.

"So, I should stop having sex?" Meg shocks me back into the park and away from the coffin of my lips. How unfair would it be that Meg should never be kissed or held, or loved into oblivion? I could never take that from her. Even if I have taken it from myself.

"Nah, kid. Don't stop. Don't ever stop. But don't let it eat into your writing time." I regret the words as soon as I say them.

"Really? 'Eat into'? That's what you're going to choose when trying to convince me not to have sex?" she lifts her eyebrows at me and smiles. Naughty, horrible, wonderful girl. I feel like plaster is cracking off of my face for the width of my smile and something bursts out of me. It feels like a flight of swallows, like the loud exuberance of song birds. It's … a laugh. Deep and real.

"Jesus, I can't take you out in public." I gently push her away, like a terrible kid sister in the back seat, too close to me. She laughs. What is this lightness I feel? It cannot be coming from my own chest. I clear my throat. "I want to see those pages, Meg. No matter how ugly they are."

"Fine," she says. But then she stops. I look back at her.

"What?"

"Fine, I will write my stupid life story. But only if you start again. I want to see a play out of you. Any play. And don't tell me you're working on one. I can tell you haven't been."

"How the hell do you know?"

"Because you're churlish."

"What?"

"I know you."

I shake my head. I could write a hundred plays with all the things Meg Kent *doesn't* know. "No. I'm done with that."

"Done? What? The hell you are."

"I don't have it in me anymore."

89

"That's the biggest line of bullshit I've ever heard. You're brilliant."

"I can't write." The confession floats between us and I reach up to touch my heart that uttered it against my will. But this is Meg, and I can talk to her. Because she knows better than anyone, the struggle. So I let the weakly beating muscle cough out the rest. "There's nothing left in here."

She walks up to me, stands in front of me, looks up as if she's about to slap my face. A jogger passes by us, Meg glares after him trying to find something to hit. She looks like she wants to pounce on me.

"That's not true," she says. I step back and look down at her, surprised that she should argue my emptiness. The wind picks up. "It's only been a few weeks."

"Feels like an eternity without her."

"Then find something better to pass the time."

"What? Like sex with actors you meet at coffee shops?" That was low, even for me in simmering in my excused-by-grief pot.

"Low blow, Horowitz. He's not an actor, he's a roadie, from Colorado."

"He has a man-bun, doesn't he?"

"Ugh," she rolls her green eyes and laughs.

"So what does Man-Bun do for you that writing doesn't? Besides the obvious?"

"He does have a name."

"What is it? Tree? Yukon? Brawny McSteel-Chest?"

"Dost I detect jealousy?" she chuckles.

"Maybe I am." I close my mouth.

What in the hell was that?

We are silent. I throw away my coffee cup. I sigh, turn back around, hands in pockets and level my eyes on hers. "Maybe I am jealous." I say again. She leans closer to me. I can feel warmth from her body reaching out across the cold ocean of my self-imposed suffering. She leans closer, says my name.

I close my eyes. A lonely heart is a confused heart and I'm not jealous because I want her to be mine. I'm jealous because … because why? Think of something, Horowitz, quick.

"I'm jealous because you promised me pages and instead of writing, you're wasting your energy between the sheets of some guy who's probably not even committed enough to invest in a toothbrush for your sink." My writer brain cranks to life and saves my ass. Maybe I'm not done after all.

"I'll get you pages. If you get me scenes."

"I told you, I can't." Panic sets into my chest. A deadline? A project? What is she trying to keep me occupied away from the stench of my grief?

"The world is ripe with ideas. You have tragedy and love at your fingertips, every goddamn day!" I stop short. That little shit. Pulling a quote right from my lectures.

"You can't use my own lines against me!"

"Why not? They're brilliant lines. And they came from that giant head of yours with its giant eyebrows." I stop again. The air is silent between us.

"Giant eye— What the hell do you know about anything?" She knows how to keep the train rolling, faster and faster, away from my self-pity and towards the age-old joke of my big, old-man eyebrows.

"I know they influence the tides."

"You're an asshole," I laugh again, twice in one day, and the pigeons on the concrete coo in response. I want to reach down and squeeze her when she raises her laughing eyes at me. I touch my eyebrows, pet them down to calm my mind. She's watching me, smiling. I close my eyes to the sight and massage my temples. My resistance is waning. She knows this.

"I know that you aren't done." She's close to me now. Her nose nearly to mine as I look down.

"The house is too quiet to write." I throw that out. Dumb.

"So What? Mine is too cold. Both lame excuses," she returns. I open my eyes and drop my hands.

"Why is your apartment cold?"

"Unimportant and uninteresting question. It's not the environment outside. Your brain can do the magic inside." Talk about a fucking dodge. I move closer. She sways back.

"Why is your apartment cold, Meg?" I ask again.

"They shut off the heat."

"It's ten below!" I yell at her.

"I know. That's why I was at the coffee shop. That's how I got distracted." She shrugs.

"Shit." I start to walk away from the immediate and ridiculous thought that pops into my head. I absolutely cannot, under any circumstances, entertain that idea. She's a grown woman. I'm a grown man. It simply would not work. She's following me.

"I don't know why you're surprised; you know what I make at BuzzFeed and apartments are expensive. When Pascal raised the rent last month, I had to make some decisions. I'll be fine. I just have to sign up for more articles or find a freelance gig." It's her making excuses now, and I feel like we're on a merry-go-round spinning around the fear of change.

"No!" I yell to the idea that over the last twenty seconds has planted itself into my gray matter and will not leave. I put my hand to my mouth, rub it across my lips. Sigh. "You don't sign up for more articles because then you're not going to write your novel."

"Well, I can't pay rent with a novel that's not written. And I can't write a novel without a place to live!"

Fuck it.

"So live with me." Stupid brain. Stupid, horrible brain. The idea sits like a black cloud between us. It feels like a moment I'll never be able to take back. We're friends. We're alone. Neither of us is thriving and that's not a secret.

"What?"

I look to one side of the path and the other as if someone else said that, some weirdo in the bushes probably. "I have some space."

"I can't." She shakes her head and sniffs. And I think it's because she's trying to save me, until she says, "I can't stay in her room."

I glare, that hadn't even been on my mind as an option. "Of course you won't, I'm not offering you her room."

"What, am I sleeping in yours then? Won't that be awkward when Man-Bun comes over?"

"Ah ha! You said he had a name!"

"Something like, Jonah, I think?" she says, cavalier. The thought of Meg and a "Jonah" in my bed gets quickly shoved off the boat and into the proverbial whale's mouth, never to be thought of again.

The thought of just Meg in my bed ...

I clear my throat and push that thought closer to the railing.

"You can have the loft. It's still got my old desk in it but I can clear that out."

"Where would you write?" she shakes her head, and fills her smile. I feel a songbird in my chest, a lifting of some great weight. I shrug to try and bring it back down on me.

"I can move my office downstairs. So I can see the park." I feel like somewhere above us in the cloudy gloom, an angelic Gina is applauding this horrible idea.

"That would be a good place for *you* to get some writing done."

"It would be a good place for us *both* to write, Meg." How can I sound so certain, when I feel so off balance, and strangely hopeful.

"How do I know you won't hate living with me?" she says.

"Oh, I know I'll hate it."

"So then why are we even talking about it?"

"Because, you shouldn't be freezing and I shouldn't be alone,"

I yell back and spread my hands. She looks down at the way my shirt clings to my body. A thousand different thoughts could enter my mind, at the way she studies me, but the self-conscious idiocy of worrying that I don't look anything like Jonah is what sticks.

"Only under two conditions," she says and comes up to me. I close my arms quickly. I'm not a body she would notice, and certainly not one she'd want to touch. All the same, I discourage it.

"What? And don't say Jonah the Man-Bun can stay over."

"That you'll finish a play and that you'll kick me out the moment I get to be too much."

"Should be a good two-day run," I nod and turn, trying to walk away from the awful deal I just struck.

MEG

It only takes me an afternoon to move into Charlie's place. Every time I walk through the door with another box, I feel like a stranger sneaking in. But he's here, at his kitchen island, watching me struggle up the stairs and through the old brownstone's doorway with my dilapidated boxes from the Indian place down the street of my old apartment. Some of them are just light enough I can take all the way to the loft. Some require a pause for moral support between.

"Those stairs are going to kill me," I huff, a gentle plea for a little help. He scowls at me.

"I thought midwestern women did things for themselves."

"I thought men *your* age were chivalrous." I bite back and wipe my brow on the hem of my T-shirt. Charlie's eyes fall to my midriff and linger. He blushes and I feel a singular butterfly tumble around in my stomach. Curious.

"I grew up in the era of women's lib, if I helped you, how could you prove how strong you are?" I scowl back as he straightens out his paper to block his view of my sweaty, haphazard struggle.

"Cool, old man. We'll see who's strong when you help me with my mattress, because you're helping me with my mattress." I leave and he huffs behind me. I get the frame up myself, and build it. When I come down, he's nowhere to be found. That cheeky bastard, I scowl, determined to get the mattress up myself. I'll midwestern woman my way into this place. When I get out to the rented truck, there's Charlie, the mattress half down.

"What took you so damn long?" he says. I can't speak, he's nearly carried it up the first flight himself. Charlie is strong. Stronger than I really knew. Or stupider. The truck driver leaves even before Charlie gets to the doorway.

"Jesus, let me help you." I hurry and take some of the weight as we trudge it up the stairs and flop it into the frame. Exhausted we both collapse together onto the bed, breathing hard and staring at the ceiling.

"Stairs suck," I say as I listen to Charlie's breathing, feel the shudder of it in the springs beneath me. Somewhere in the back of my mind, a subtle fire begins to flicker. A familiarity. A want.

"I guess you'll have to get in shape," he says, cutting me off from the trail into what about having Charlie breathing hard next to me seems to be piquing my curiosity. I turn my head. Charlie gets up quickly.

"Find your laptop and meet me downstairs."

"Huh?" I huff and feel the sweat drip down behind my ear.

"Your laptop, Kent."

"We're starting now? But I haven't even unpacked my underwear yet."

"You don't need your underwear to write." I look up at him from the bed with a smile.

"Might want to think about that before I sit on your furniture."

"I do *not* want to think about that. Ever again. Just your laptop." And then he's gone, down the stairs.

I roll my eyes and look around. It's a small space. I think

intended for storage or guests. That's all I really am. One or the other. There's only room for the bed, one dresser, and Charlie's desk. I told him not to move it. I would use it. It's old, but as I stand up and run my hand along the smooth-worn wood, I think of all the ideas, the words, the scenes that have passed over it. From his hands, from his brain. A shiver of creative inspiration and recognition tingles through my fingers and shocks into my body.

"Meg, now!" he says.

"Je-sus! Okay!" I yell back and shuffle around in the bags and boxes until I find my laptop. I guess we're doing this thing. When I come down, he's already set up on the dining room table. I have the suspicion he doesn't eat there. I sit down across from him with a huff.

"I do have a desk now, you know. So do you."

"I want to establish boundaries. I want you to remember why you're here." He looks over his screen at me. His eyebrows are angry.

"I'm here to write," I say smally. I don't say that I'm here to make sure he eats. I don't say that I'm here to make sure he doesn't jump off bridges. I don't say that I'm sacrificing myself to the cutting block of vulnerability, to save him from his own grief. Charlie nods. "And?" I lead him.

"And what? Eat my food? Get toothpaste in my sink?"

I scowl. "And why are *you* here?"

"I live here, don't be a moron."

"Charlie, you know what I'm asking." He's silent, his eyebrows raise in surrender.

"I'm here to write," he whispers. I nod, open a new document and sit there. The cursor doing its accusatory dance on the page, a small needle always poking.

"So where do I start?"

"At the beginning."

I scowl and start typing, dictating out loud. "In the beginning there was only Charlie, and Charlie created rules. Charlie saw that these rules were good—"

"Knock it off," he grouches, but then settles in to his own running dialogue as he types. "Meg thought she was being cute, but she was really just stalling."

I type back without looking at him. "Charlie thought Meg was cute."

"Jesus," he grumbles and rubs his forehead. I'm making his life harder.

"I'm sorry."

"Just—"

"I don't work like you do. I'm not used to this direct approach. I know you want me gone as quickly as possible, so I know I need to start writing, but that comes with pressure and I—"

"That's not it," he says plainly. "I don't want you gone. But I don't want you to fall into old habits, Meg. This is a new start. This is your time. To write. To do it. To finally write your book. I'm here to make sure that's what you do."

"I just don't know how to start."

"The faucet, Meg."

"The what?"

"You remember? The faucet, you were there. I've talked about it before."

"Louis L'Amour? Writing is like turning on the faucet. Even if there's rusty gunk in it, you have to keep writing, keep the ideas flowing. You have to let it run to get to the good stuff."

He nods, a small quirk of pride on his lips. For a moment, he's not sad widowed Charlie. For that brief instant he's teaching, he's watching the 'aha' spread over my face, and he's swayed away from the months of grief burying him.

"That's the only way the magical lapse happens," he says.

"The magical lapse?" my voice sounds husky and I quickly try to clear it away, but it doesn't matter because I can't stop looking at that smile.

"When you're so engrossed in your story, in the writing, that you lose track of time and space. You know what that is, right?"

I'm choking on the strange wonder that's playing in the shadow of the old Charlie I thought I'd lost. I look down quickly at the cursor. Has it sped up, or is that just my heart?

"Come on, Meg. You've done it before." His voice is soft and I look up over my screen. Suddenly a story is flooding my mind. But it's not about Cecily and it's not about grief. His blue eyes are boring into mine. His words, *come on Meg, you've done it before*, feel like a gentle coercion and I feel my heart skip. The sweat of moving feels cold against my skin and every inch of me shivers.

"Okay," I choke out and my fingers start typing. The strange rush of heated words coming out of my fingers doesn't seem to have any reins and I'm just blindly being carried by them.

"Okay," he whispers to his screen and Charlie starts to write too.

I'm nervous, like trying to guide a galloping horse, but it is quiet and safe here and there's no noise but for the clicking of keys and the salacious and decadent space to paint pictures with these words that don't stop.

What I do know, as the short and fiery scene plays out in front of me, is that there's no way I will let Charlie read this one.

CHARLIE

The day she's supposed to move in, I wake up at two am. Not atypical for me but the nervous feeling in my gut is different. What in the hell have I done? Why did I ever ask her? I stop and stand at Gina's door for a full ten minutes before I turn the handle and go inside. It's still a wreck. It feels like a tornado ripped through. If Meg should see it … I close my eyes. She won't. She won't go into Gina's room. She's got too much midwestern reverence for the dead, and I suppose for me too. I close the door tight and pace. I try to write. I try to clean up. I've been living a strange and solitary dance since Gina was in hospice. Alone for weeks and I don't know how to accommodate another heartbeat.

This is a terrible idea. The best I can do is play it way cooler than I feel. Nonchalant. Move in, or don't. I don't care. I open the door when she arrives. Still asking me if I'm sure, even though there's a small rented truck double parked.

"Get your ass in here before the poor guy gets ticketed."

So she starts. She's efficient with the few boxes and doesn't ask for help. I'm a louse for not offering, but there's part of my heart that feels like if I help, I'm somehow moving on. Or condoning a younger woman living with me? Accepting another female under my roof. Tempting the cruel and sensual hands of fate?

I look at Gina's door, apologizing a thousand times in my heart for every beat. But when I close my eyes, all I can see is Gina smiling with approval. Like I'm finally on the right track. I grimace and pull out the paper, determined to not, under any circumstances, help Meg, or Gina's delusions, move into my apartment.

"Those stairs are going to kill me." She's breathing heavy. I scowl.

"I thought midwestern women did things for themselves."

"I thought men *your* age were chivalrous." I look up and she's wiping her face with her T-shirt, her stomach and hip bone exposed. My body responds like a goddamn lunatic. She's dirty and sweaty. She's Meg. I look away with forced disgust.

"I grew up in the era of women's lib, if I helped you, how could you prove how strong you are?" I put the paper and a thousand reprimands between us.

"Cool, old man. We'll see who's strong when you help me with my mattress, because you're helping me with my mattress." She goes upstairs, after the awful goad, to build the frame.

Old man? I'm furious. Maybe I'm not, but I'm using the small dig to make it even harder for me to see Meg as anything but a nuisance. I go outside and get the mattress, the last thing from the truck and tell the guy to head out. I'm halfway up the brownstone's steps when she comes out.

"What took you so damn long?"

"Jesus, let me help you." She scurries to take some of the weight. When we flop it into the frame upstairs my body gives me a sturdy 'fuck you' and I collapse on the springs of it.

"Stairs suck," she gasps. My mind flutters over a memory of collapsing, out of breath, next to Gina after we'd made love the last time.

"I guess you'll have to get in shape," I grumble.

I try not to think of how many men have stared up from this mattress, a naked Meg beside them. Not knowing her brilliance for the distraction of her skin. I smell, the sweet salt of her ... I get up quickly. I'm not coming up here again.

"Find your laptop and meet me downstairs." I bark at her on my way out of the space.

"Huh?"

"Your laptop, Kent." I turn back around.

"We're starting now? But I haven't even unpacked my underwear yet."

"You don't need your underwear to write." Fuck. Why'd I say that? She's going to respond. She smiles, she knows I left that wide open.

"Might want to think about that before I sit on your furniture."

"I do *not* want to think about that. Ever again. Just your laptop." I leave. I go downstairs. I look at Gina's door across the room. "This was a terrible idea," I tell the ghost behind the door. I get out my computer.

What's taking her so long? We need to start. So she can finish. So she can leave.

"Meg, now!"

"Je-sus! Okay!" she yells back and trudges down the stairs, like a put-out teen. "I do have a desk now, you know. So do you."

"I want to establish boundaries. I want you to remember why you're here," I say.

"I'm here to write," she says, voice quiet. But her eyes are deeper than the words and I squint into them. "And?" she asks.

"And what? Eat my food? Get toothpaste in my sink?"

Now she scowls. But her eyebrows can't hold a candle to mine. "And why are *you* here?"

"I live here, don't be a moron."

"Charlie, you know what I'm asking." She wants a bargain. She wants to know she's not alone.

"I'm here to write," I say. She nods, so pleased with herself, and studies her screen. I open a new file in Final Draft. The cursor blinks, black on white. Asking me for a title. A cast. A setting. Impossible asks in my state of mind.

"So where do I start?" Meg reads my mind.

"At the beginning," I answer. Jesus, that was dumb.

She starts to type. "In the beginning there was only Charlie, and Charlie created rules. Charlie saw that these rules were good—"

"Knock it off," I yell. Comparing me to God will get her ass beat. I scowl over the screen and settle into my own page. I type, ACTION. "Meg thought she was being cute, but she was really just stalling."

She types back, "Charlie thought Meg was cute—"

"Jesus," I drop my head in my hands. This was a terrible idea. Maybe *I* should move out. She stops typing.

"I'm sorry," she says.

"Just—"

"I don't work like you do. I'm not used to this direct approach. I know you want me gone as quickly as possible so I know I need to start writing, but that comes with pressure and I—"

"That's not it." I say, embarrassed that she sees through me so easily. Do I really want her gone? She is my best friend. "I don't want you gone. But I don't want you to fall into old habits, Meg. This is a new start. This is your time. To write. To do it. To finally write your book. I'm here to make sure that's what you do."

"I just don't know how to start."

"The faucet, Meg," I yell back, but I'm not mad. I'm excited. Because she's asking me. For help. About something I know how to do.

"The what?"

"You remember? The faucet, you were there. I've talked about it before." I watch her face. Like she's filing back through a card catalogue of memories, and her eyes suddenly light up. She rattles off the theory of writing I taught her, all those years ago. A spark fires in my heart, an excitement in her excitement. Nearly word for word, she talks about keeping the water running until it comes out clear. You have to keep the words flowing until they come out clear.

She does remember. She can be taught. An elation fills my chest. This feels like purpose. I want to stand up and lecture and draw diagrams and get excited. I want to instill excitement in her. I want to see her get just as caught up as I do, like I know she's capable of. Her eyes light up. She's enthusiastic and I'm disconnected, for a moment, from the months of suffering.

"That's the only way the magical lapse happens," I say.

"The magical lapse?" Her question drives me and I smile. The writer's greatest folly and gift. The magical time lapse. The flow state. The transcendence in and of the work.

"When you're so engrossed in your story, in the writing, that you lose track of time and space. You know what that is, right?" Her cheeks turn pink but I barely register that because I know she's had that before, that's what drives writers to want to write more, bigger, longer books. She looks down.

"Come on, Meg. You've done it before." She looks up at me. She's biting her lip. A strange sultry heat settles on the table between us. Something that's trying to feed us both. Her voice is low, like she really wants something.

"Okay," she whispers and just … starts. Like I've never seen her write before. Like she's locked in and inspired and I'm the best goddamn writing coach anyone has ever known! I settle in, so proud of myself that I whip up a title without really thinking of it. "The Georgian Storm"

"Okay," I whisper to the words.

Maybe this is what we're doing now.

MEG

I feel like a goddamn monk. Only allowed to work, and sleep and write. But it could be worse. Because Charlie is a quiet guy, unless he's pacing in his office or talking to himself in the kitchen when he's making coffee.

But not in a crazy way. Not in a deranged, lost-all-his-marbles way. In a writer way. And I understand those conversations. There are even moments I'd like to answer for him, but I don't want to dull the magical knife that is, in these very moments, cutting through the scar tissue of doubt and grief that's been keeping him bottled up for too long.

I hear snippets.

"But why doesn't he just get the dog himself?"

"Where was the mother-in-law this whole time? An awful woman like that would want to be close."

Charlie's plays are clever. They're socially smart and philosophically cutting. They're funny, and full of heart and hubris. Charlie is his plays and he's been too long away from himself.

If my writing suffers in these moments, it's because instead of being distracted by sex or cuddling, or fights like with other cohabiters I've had, I'm basking in the brilliance of his creative process. And that a man this brilliant believes in my work almost makes the monk's life seem like a new era I'd like to usher in. But it also makes me deathly afraid that he's going to realize I'm a fraud any day. That he'll come to the understanding that I'm not talented. That I don't have a lick of smarts in my head and that my book is nothing but a steaming pile of shit.

I know he'll kick me out. So, I try to at least make good use of the time. I try to follow through on my promises. To him and to Gina.

I remind him to eat.

And drink more than coffee.

And I make him go for a walk in the afternoon when I get home from my day job, under the guise that my brain is stuck in useless drama mode and I need to shake it lose. Which is not always a guise. I've had a lot of roommates, but never one that I haven't been sleeping with. There's always been playful romance, and sex on demand, and cuddling for movies after work. Then there's the going out and the working too much, and me assuaging their flagging egos and them finding better circumstances because I'm too busy paying the bills, and the fight and the monologue about me not fulfilling them enough, and me taking the bottle from the high shelf and toasting their new found success while I wallow in the same pit I've been stuck in for years. There's usually no writing of my own involved.

You can't be creative when you're supporting someone else's dream and being distracted by lesser things.

But living with Charlie is different. We're not here to boost each other's egos. We're here to hold each other accountable. Bradley texts once. I block his number. I have too much to do, to worry about what bullshit is on his mind. Jonah only checks in from faraway places. I let that happen. I write back that I'm writing and busy. He always has nothing but support to give.

What a strange occurrence; to have two men in my life, who actually give a damn about the happiness I'm working towards. I don't know that I'll ever get used to it.

CHARLIE

I haven't had a roommate since college. And he was some young jock from New Jersey who didn't last the first semester. Meg smells better, doesn't drink, and is the least invasive species I've ever known. She seems unfazed by my attitude and the truth is, she's barely here, with her job's odd schedule. I rarely see her. When I do, we share a meal or two. She makes me go for walks in the afternoon. *Makes me ...*

I used to walk a lot before Gina got sick. Every afternoon, at least, to take a break from the screen. To take a break from the work. Gina rarely came with. I wonder now, in those short hours of time, if she entertained anyone else? The thought is an iron anvil in my bowels and I shake it off when I grab my coat and follow Meg outside. She brings groceries every few days, stopping after work, and it makes me realize how little I've shopped since Gina died. It makes me feel idiotic that even Meg, who's not one to take care of much in life, is still managing to take care of me better than I deserve.

She throws out all of the dead houseplants. She brings in a new one for my desk.

"I'm not watering that," I say, over my readers when she sets it next to my computer.

"I'll water it, you grouchy old fart," she grumbles. I look at the bright green leaves against the backdrop of a steel city, salted with the driving snow outside. There's something hopeful about it. I look over my shoulder as she's getting a cup of coffee. She's still in her pjs because today is not a work day.

I love not-work days. I like Meg in the slouchy state of relaxed. I like that her brain is doing the big important work and the ridiculous standards of beauty can sod off. Plus, on not-work days, she fills the space. With typing and mid-morning showers, and snacks ... god, she's always snacking. She reminds me we have a deadline coming up. We're supposed to be exchanging pages at the end of this month. I watch her spoon sugar into her coffee and lick the spoon.

I turn back to my screen. Defiler of perfectly good coffee. But lucky spoon. I shake my head. Stay focused. When I write, she doesn't disturb me. The Georgian Storm comes out as one-acts, and not in character of my wife, but some faceless figure. It's lacking and drab, as if I've compartmentalized my life by the years. Maybe I'm afraid to look at it in total, I'm not sure. I just know that Meg and I had a deal and as long as I hear her typing upstairs when she's home, then I'll do my part.

There's something strange about another body in your space after so many lonely weeks. And not an intrusive body. She's not Gina, singing loudly or rehearsing lines, draping an arm over me to gain attention when I'm in the middle of a writing lapse ...

But the quiet kind. I hear footsteps, I hear the creak of her chair, and the sigh of her stretch. Sometimes she stops by my desk, but if I'm in the middle of my thought, she quietly leaves a fresh cup of coffee, undefiled, or a bowl of soup. She doesn't ask for thanks; she doesn't stop to see how it's going. When you see another writer in the middle of it, you know how it's going. And you know distraction will derail the train and kill all the passengers.

It's refreshing.

Sometimes at night, when I've been writing or obsessing, or reading much of the day, walks with Meg do me nothing but good. I listen to her frustrations of work. The daily news, the latest plays out. She never talks about her family, but after twenty years, I know why. I don't talk about Gina. Sometimes loss is too heavy a bag to carry on our walks. We carry it all day on our own. Together, we're lighter.

When we're both home, she's so quiet at times that I forget she's only a set of stairs away. I talk to my characters, I yell occasionally. I pace incessantly. Sometimes I hear her fingers stop. The pause of the gentle ticking. But she never calls out that I'm bothering her. And Meg wouldn't hesitate to tell me that I'm bothering her.

She only reminds me to eat, cleans up after herself in the kitchen, and doesn't leave a mess in the bathroom. But I sometimes stare at her toothbrush when I'm brushing my teeth at night. I think about her mouth. I think ... about kissing. The soft taste of mint against warm and giving lips. Sometimes I want to sleep in Gina's room. But I don't know how that might make Meg feel.

So, I try to keep my crazy, normal.

MEG

I still have bills. It's the unintended consequence of a Master's degree I didn't finish and taking care of too many burgeoning actors for too long. So sometimes I have to work a double shift. Which means less writing. But I'm okay with that, because to be honest, it's not going well. I think I'm a writer, but every time I sit down, the story I try to tell feels a million miles away. The Cecily in my pages is a protected memory. A statue behind glass. And my mother a gray one-dimensional cloud that never gives itself form. I suppose that's my job, right? To bring them to life, to carve them into something real? But I can't seem to break into those old memories in any way that feels true. I haven't given any pages to Charlie yet, but he hasn't shown me any of his. I smile on the subway at the stupid thought. Charlie showing me his if I show him mine.

The trouble is, some of 'mine' have taken on a romantic frenzy to them. I'm embarrassed and I feel like an asshole.

I'm an asshole. I can't deny though that the months alone have done something to my libido. I'm starting to write in things that only a romance novelist might. I tuck those pages away. Those can't be the ones I show Charlie. He'd kick me out. Maybe I should see if Jonah is in town. Maybe this time I really do just need a distraction. To get the tension out of my system, and off of the page. I reach for my phone to see where his gypsy life has taken him and if it's within a reasonable train ride, when the blip of a new message catches me up short.

How are you?

My mother, Eileen Kent, has chosen this moment to write.

As if she had any right to wonder how I am?

I don't respond. She's fishing. Maybe for money, maybe for love. Neither of which I have any to spare. But of one thing my journalist mind knows, it's that she doesn't really care, she probably just found a photo album and remembered that somewhere in her unsoaked past she had a daughter who lived. I itch to tell her I'm fine. That I have a steady job and a place to stay, to not worry. Did she ever worry about me? I go back to work and keep my head and heart on task. I try to push thoughts of men and moms to the farthest corners of my mind and let the whirlwind of celebrity life be its normal, fantastic distraction.

It's late when I finally come home. The idea of 'coming home' to Charlie fills me with a strange warmth. Like it's been my whole life that I've never had a home, and his is the first that really *feels* that way. Work was a fucking bear and I'm hungry as one. I hadn't gotten anything but coffee on my way out and Charlie was too busy writing so I didn't want to bug him about going to the store. I worked through lunch, rode the double shift hours, and now I feel like my soul was drained from my body in slow, fifty-word click baits all day.

So when I get home, it's heaven. Because I'm not alone, but I'm not bombarded with having to give more of myself. I drop my shit at the door, kick off my shoes and roll my shoulders back and forth. I know he hasn't shopped, because he's been working too, so I dig in the fridge and find Chinese from some night last week? It doesn't smell like it's spoiled yet and I'm too hungry to be picky. Just as I'm turning to take it to the couch, a bellow breaks open the room.

"How dare you not tell me?" The door to Gina's room hits the wall as he staggers out. I grip the box and feel the noodles drain their fluid into my palm. I've never seen the dull haze of his eyes, even as he's spitting fire.

"Jesus, Charlie, what the fuck?" He stops immediately and studies me, turns his head around the room. It's like he comes awake enough to be properly confused.

CHARLIE

It's all going along, surprisingly well. Which makes me start to wonder when it will all fall apart. I send out a couple of collections of one-acts. Not what Meg and I agreed on but I can't work every minute of my day on the stop-and-start monstrosity of what might be Gina's life. I think Meg would understand. She hasn't mentioned her pages either. We're exchanging tomorrow. I start to work on what I have, my gut in my throat as I settle down to create the words that Meg's discerning eye will see.

But then Don DeVoe calls. Meg is at work. At first, I hope it's her, asking for an extension so I can have one too, but instead his staged-grief tone comes over the line. I want to hang up. But I let him have ten whole seconds.

"I'm really sorry, and I'd love to just talk to you, Charlie. I think we have a lot in common if you just let me—"

I throw the phone across the room and it shatters against the wall.

The only thing we have in common is dead. I feel the room getting dark and suffocating. I feel dizzy. Grief is a microburst that hits out of nowhere and I'm glad Meg isn't home. I reach into the bottom drawer of my desk and pull out a twenty-year bottle of Scotch. Fuck Don.

I was doing so well.

I'm still dizzy as I pour a healthy sized portion for a horse, and take it with me into Gina's room. I slam the door closed and sit with the heavy weight of grief in my heart. I'm not sure if its decades or hours that pass, but I know the glass is empty and I'm not sure when Gina is coming home but when she does, I'll give her a piece of my mind.

Everything is fuzzy and uncertain. Why is her room such a fucking mess? What are all of these letters? I'm confused and I don't know the day or time. I bend to pick one up and the front door opens. It takes me a minute to listen. I stagger into a wall first, stand still ... who turned the world around?

When I hear her in the kitchen, it feels like I've been lost in some kind of maniacal fever dream and Gina is coming home late. Only I know now where she's been and what a 'cast party' really meant, and all I can see is Don's stupid and Botoxed face smiling up at me through the funeral crowd. So pious for a man who'd been screwing my wife. I'm going to give her a piece of my mind.

"How dare you not tell me?" I slur as I rip open the door and it bangs against the wall, knocking over the pictures I still have standing. Gina's not in the kitchen, but Meg startles and nearly jumps a foot off the ground.

"Jesus, Charlie what the fuck?" she yells and she's clutching her heart and the last remnants of Chinese food. She's pale in the ghost light of the fridge and my mind is dragging the shackles of the past behind me, unwilling to let go. I look around. For Gina. For Don, for the anger that has been tip-toeing slowly around the edges of my life every day since those machines rang the one long note of her death.

"What the fuck you?" I answer back, confused, wobbly, drunk

off my damn ass. Above all, embarrassed. Meg's brow closes down and her eyes narrow.

"Since when do you drink?"

"Since whenever I want to. I'm a grown man." I try to salvage my pride. I think I'm standing taller; I'm pretty sure I'm leaning.

"Yeah, real grow'd," she says and puts down the crumpled carton where her fingers had dug in with shock. She washes her hands and gets me a glass of water. She digs in the cabinet for the Advil and Tums. "Here," she sets them down on the table between us.

"I don't need you taking care of me."

"Right, because you're a grown man, I know," she says with the edge of tired in her voice that says she's taken care of a drunk numerous times before. "Drink the water."

"I don't—" I stumble. "I'm fine. I don't need it."

She sighs, walks to the living room and tucks herself into the couch, legs pretzeled beneath her, and nods to me to join her.

"What?"

"Sit down."

"Why?"

"So you can tell me what the fuck happened to get you to here, and I can tell you what the Kardashians are doing now."

Ugh, my drunken stomach turns. "Do I have to?"

"No, you *get* to," she says and looks up at me.

"Get to?"

"Yeah, Charlie. Don't you know? You get to be mad with me. You get to rant and rave and get all Shakespearian Hamlet murderous. And I'll always take your side."

"Why in the hell would you? Maybe I'm wrong."

"I wouldn't tell you if you were. Not tonight." her voice gets softer. She scoots over and pats the cushions. "What happened?"

"I didn't write today." That was a stupid thing to say.

"And?" she leads me, knowing that's not what drove me to drink.

"I'm a miserable excuse for a man and a widower."

"No, on both counts, go on."

"Don DeVoe called me," I rage. Meg doesn't placate me. She stands up and sets the noodles down angrily.

"That fucking prick. Why the hell would he do that?"

"Right? That's what I thought!"

"What did you tell him?"

"Nothing, I threw my phone—aga—against the wall." I realize now what a stupid and expensive mistake that was. I look over my shoulder at the broken body of it on the floor, the carnage of its insides spread like a murder scene.

"Wow, I didn't know you could do that to a Nokia. What are you, the Hulk?"

"I do not have a Nokia, you little shit." I start laughing which is stupid and strange and the tension of the day seems to fall off my shoulders with the hysterical deluge. Suddenly, I'm tired. Meg takes me by the hand and leads me to the couch. She picks up the carton and takes a bite.

"I miss the days of being able to slam down a receiver when you were mad. That was probably the next best thing."

"That was the stupidest thing." I grumble. The couch is soft compared to the hard floor of my wife's tomb.

Meg shrugs, takes another bite, offers me some but my stomach warns against it.

"We'll get you a new one tomorrow." She settles next to me. I feel the warmth from her thigh, my eyes find the bare toes wriggling into the cushion. Toes are strange. I've never had cause or interest to study them, but Meg's are … cute.

I should march right back to my room. No way I'm sitting next to her. In her calm little nest, eating leftovers and looking sleepy, with her damn little toes, wiggling beneath my thigh for warmth. I should not stay here, not at the end of the hardest day since Gina left, when I need human comfort so much. Too much.

"Man, today can go suck a bag of dicks, am I right?" she says and shakes her head.

I humph in agreement. It could. It wouldn't change anything though. But this, sitting on the couch with her, this feels changed. Like it's shifting the day into comfort. I'm sleepy. Maybe, it can't hurt to have this moment. Right?

I'll just sit for a little while to be polite; she'll get bored and go upstairs and we'll end the night. The memory and the hurt drains down as soon as I settle in beside her. She flips on the TV. Something we rarely do, but it's been a long fucking day and I don't care how badly my brain melts. I'd actually welcome it. She picks Mystery. Fine, better than some Hollywood rehashed action fest. Or worse, romance.

She hands me the water. I know she's right and I don't argue. When I put it down, my whole body feels heavy and she's engrossed in the show. I lean into the couch, but our shoulders touch. She burps. Fucking Meg Kent, even the little escaping of air makes her charming. More so that she doesn't say 'excuse me', she says, "Jesus, how old was that chicken?"

I smile. A stupid, drunk smile. My brain eases into the unexpected relief of her warmth next to me. The story isn't great. I don't even bother keeping my eyes open. I just sit there listening. But soon, I'm not listening to the dialogue. I'm listening to her. Her breathing. I listen, I feel the metronome of her lungs, and it starts to sync with mine. Or do I sync to her? It makes my bones feel like lead sinking below water when they collide along the same path. My world goes dark and I feel her beneath me and I'm dreaming, and nuzzling into her, and I'm thinking of being Hamlet mad, but it's too tragic, so I try to remember my favorite Shakespeare play. My favorite line from The Twelfth Night and it's something …

About love.

Something about how seeking love is good but …

But what? I hear her heart beat beneath my ear, and I need it closer, so put my arms around her in the dream, and she sinks her fingers into my hair. Seeking love is good but …

God, she's warm and smells so good, and her touch feels like if heaven had hands. Love sought is good, but …

"Love given unsought is better," I remember. "Meg, I'm sorry I drank." I tell the dream and she kisses my head; a baptism of forgiveness. It's been so long since I was in the arms of love that I let myself cry out to it and lean in. I wish every night could be this way. I'm sure I won't wish that in the morning, when I wake up hungover and alone.

Charlie, you idiot.

MEG

He's standing there, drunk and wavering, coming out of Gina's room of all places. I try not to look behind him to the darkness that seems to be littered with papers and clothes.

"Since whenever I want. I'm a grown man," he staggers. Ugh, apparently, Charlie is an angry drunk. Which is kind of a damn shame because I think I'd always secretly hoped he'd be the romantic kind. Offering poetry and slow kisses, quoting Shakespeare and gentle caresses. A piece of noodle sticks in my throat and I cough.

"Yeah, real grow'd." I get him a glass of water. I'm not going to lecture. He's had a shitty year, and I'm too fucking tired to do a decent job at it anyway. I hold the glass out to him. "Here."

"I don't," he falters to the side, "need you taking care of me." He waves it off.

I'm exhausted, I'm tired of fighting and tired of wondering what my mom wanted and tired of thinking I should write her back. I wish he was sober. I want to talk to him and ask him what it all means, and what should I do, because Charlie would know. Sober Charlie would know. But he's suffering and for once I understand, that it's not all about me. Tonight is about him.

He is in the struggle of a grief neglected and this is why I'm here. This is the real reason I agreed to move in with Charlie. To be here, when he stumbled in the dark. To keep him from staying at the cold bottom. And even if I harbor a mutual need to feel seen, and to know this won't turn into my mom's downward spiral, tonight it's my turn to give Charlie a warm place to stay. I tell him to sit. He refuses. I coerce him with an open mind and the irreverent humor he connects to. Every word is like a secret code between friends. That we're going to be alright. That life is stupid and it sucks, but we're in it together.

He tells me about Don's call, his broken phone. All the ways he's tried to bury the truth that's now resurfaced and how it drove him to try to forget.

I feel an opening in my chest, a relief I do not expect. I knew the root of my mom's addiction at the shallow level any teenager might. But she never talked about it. How it tore at her, how the stumbling numbness was better. The wasted mornings, the lost jobs, the disconnect of her life was somehow better than feeling so much pain. Back then I could only guess about the depths of her grief, so wrapped up in my own. Sitting with Charlie, baring the wounds, feels like recompense and an opportunity to understand the pain that pours the glass.

When I tease him about his phone, he laughs. Beautiful and uncontained, silly tittering waves, and I'm swept up in the half-mad, half-relieved deluge. He quiets, tears in his eyes. I take his warm hand in mind and pull him to the couch. He doesn't fight this time and settles in softly, rubs his face, shakes his head. I pick up the carton and take a bite.

I tell him I wish we could still slam phones down to hang up. That there's something to physically ending a connection, that will never be satisfied in our touchscreen existence. I feel his weight settle into the cushions and my body threatens to lean closer to his, from the gravitational pull. Maybe it's the same need, in our touchscreen existence, for actual touch.

I grab the remote, and look at Charlie. He's staring at my feet. Curious. He looks like his reserve is waning, and I'm suddenly not so mad he drank. Even if he did think I was Gina. He settles in beside me and I turn on the television flipping to a BBC mystery theater. Something to make us think about anything other than being on the couch together and the obviously rough day we've both had.

"Man, today can suck a bag of dicks, am I right?" I say and try to drop the articles and pressures and texts from my mom off my shoulders. Charlie grunts in agreement, not even berating me for such a horrible image in his head now.

Charlie and his breathing soften. I hand him the water. He drinks most of it, and takes the Advil, before setting it down, sans a coaster, in our bachelor lifestyle. Soon he's leaning closer to me. I put the empty carton down, and burp. I'm sure I'll probably deal with after-effects from that, but for now my stomach feels better and my brain is gently letting go of the day.

This is something I never shared with my mom. The sullen acceptance that we're neither our best selves today, but we'll drink our water, and take some Advil, and try again tomorrow. My mom was never sullen. She raged, she blamed, she shouted and sometimes threw things. Charlie's drunken grieving is quieter, at least now. I am not the target of his anger. Or his grief. I'm a witness and the reasonable voice in the room. Something I've never really been. It catches me in my heart. That I could take care of someone, and be their solid landing space. Me, the fuck-up.

I'm mindlessly staring at the screen, at a loss to solve the mystery of Charlie, or the show in front of us. And before I can even try to pay attention, my brain is short circuited. Charlie's weight shifts and he cascades into me. It's a slow, easy fall, like a giant tree in the forest, and I'm pushed into the cushioned arm of the couch.

I lean back and he follows me down, warm and heavy, and he murmurs against my neck. He presses his ear to my chest and he holds me so closely that my body takes him in like rain to dry ground. I don't know why I don't say anything. I don't yelp or grunt or anything. I don't wake him up. I don't push him away.

Because I don't want to. Because I'm selfish and horrible. Because it's been so long since I was touched and Charlie would never do this sober. I feel like my body gives way, a sigh of relief, a seldom-used hammock taking him into the heat of summer napping. He's snoring when I look down to where he's wrapped his arms around my waist and his head is pressed into my heart beat.

"Love given unsought is better," he whispers. "Meg, I'm sorry I drank." Then he's asleep and one of his long legs is pressed between my thighs and I let it stay. I put my arms around him and kiss the top of his magnificent brain. He half cries, half laughs and is out again. I feel like someone gave me the goddamn keys to Random House.

"Charlie, you idiot." I whisper and fall asleep, letting my hand run through his wild and soft curls.

When I wake up, he's pressed against the length of my back. On our sides, facing the screen that's asking us if we're still watching. His chin is in the crook of my neck. His legs parallel train tracks to mine, warm and long. His arm is draped over my shoulders and I smell the liquor on his breath, a strange chemical breakdown of Charlie and the sweet intoxication I want to taste. I hold on to the arm across me and close my eyes.

When was I held last? When did I last feel the warmth of another human being? When it wasn't destined to end in sex? He mumbles and nuzzles into my neck and my whole body seems to betray me with a cat-like curl into his body. Charlie grumbles in an archaic way that makes me realize he's probably even more lonely than I am. I want to cry. Charlie isn't interested in *me*. He's just lonely. He's suffering. She told me to take care of him, not seduce him in his drunken state and fall …

In love with him.

The thought is a hush through my veins and I ache for this to be a dream that we can both wake from in the next few hours and not feel guilty, or weird. I sigh, I hold on tighter with my hand and squeeze my eyes closed tight.

I used to play a game, when I was little. A game whenever something good happened—which wasn't often—or something beautiful, or something significant, I'd freeze the moment. In my brain. I'd pause, close my eyes really tight and concentrate. What I smelled, what I felt, what I tasted, what I saw, what the light was like, what the words were, what the season was. I'd press all of these observations close, into every cell of my body, just like I was pressing my eyelids closed.

I'd make a memory, right down to my genes. I did it with Gina, on the hospital bed. I did it when Charlie hugged me in his kitchen.

I feel him, long and warm against my back. The way he is always soft but tough. The way he has a strength that bends, a willow in the wind. I inhale the smell of warm cotton, his soap, the sting and oak of bourbon; I feel his curls against my neck and I trace the lines of his long fingers beneath mine.

I close my eyes really tight. I freeze the moment. I stop time, to think about all the beautiful things Charlie is. The willowy strength, the stinging ache, the passion contained, the warmth at my back. The man who has always stayed. I hold him tighter to me until I feel my muscles shake and tears burn at the corners of my eyes, I make this memory permanent. Because promise to Gina or not, my heart's strange wandering aside, and all the stumbling beautiful ways I want to be with Charlie not considered, I know I can't have him. I know this. I press my lips to his hand, squeeze it, and he becomes part of my very soul. I quietly untangle my physical body while my heart stays intertwined with him. I creep out of the living room, and upstairs to the cold empty tower that feels like I'll never hold sleep there again.

CHARLIE

The fucking dreams. There's Gina in the hospital bed and I'm holding on to her, but she slips away, sand through fingers, and the world is cold and dark. I toss and turn and fling my arm out to the empty space. My head is pounding and it rouses me, like the drummer that used to live below our old flat in Queens. I sit up, I look for someone in the darkness. Meg was here. Now there's no one.

"Shit," I whisper. Did I fall asleep on her? What the fuck is wrong with me? I stand quickly and pace in my own self-hatred. But my head throbs and I have to sit down again. I drink what's left of the water with more Advil. In the dark I hear the shower start. What time is it? I stumble to my bedroom, closing the door behind me and collapsing into the unmade sheets. Through my shared wall with the bathroom, I hear Meg humming. I cover my face and groan. I'm such a damn idiot. I close my eyes tight; I try to remember. Did I do anything? I clench and unclench my hands trying to rouse a memory. Did they touch her? Do they hold memory of that?

I remember her heartbeat beneath my ear. I remember her smell and her hands in my hair. My own hands trace over the memory of it as they run through my haphazard hair. Did I … quote Shakespeare? Out loud?

"Oh, for fuck's sake," I groan and roll over into a fetal position. I will have to move out now. I'll move to Siberia. I hear the humming stop. Frank Sinatra's *The Way You Look Tonight*, on pause and I hold my breath. Did she hear me? Did she think last night meant something? Surely, not. Meg's not an idiot. I have two choices. I can hide in my room, like a giant stupid baby. Or I can go about my day as if nothing happened. I see Gina shaking her head in my memory at my foolishness.

"I could also, face this situation like a man who made a mistake and apologize," I tell her. She smiles. *Yeah, do that*.

I sigh. I get up, I go into the kitchen, I start the coffee and get another glass of water. I'm drinking it when she comes out, wet in a towel. Not dressed as normal. She shrieks mid chorus at the sight of me and jumps, nearly losing the towel. I startle and drop the glass which shatters against the counter.

"Shit, Charlie!"

"Damn it, Meg!"

"You scared me." She comes quickly to the kitchen to help me clean up the glass.

"Get out of here," I yell. She looks up at me, just as angry, and circles under her eyes. How long did she stay on the couch with me? The regret of hurt tumbles me against the rocks of guilt and I soften. "I don't want you to cut your feet."

She stands, and I try to look away from the knot of the towel, resting on her sternum, her slight shoulders. Ivory and cream. A constellation of freckles across the pale of her. My breath catches.

"I've got it," I say softer and look away quickly. I scramble for the dustpan and she nearly leaps up the stairs for the safety of her room. I do not 'got it'. I've in fact, lost it.

What a stupid, ridiculous difference one night makes.

MEG

I'm going into work. I need to get out of the house and I need to get away from Charlie. I need to put space between my heart and all the stupid little things he does in a day that drive me just the right shade of crazy. But more than that, I need to get away from the way I can't seem to *not* feel him, pressed against my back, and wish it was the state of my life in permanence. I sneak downstairs, for a quick shower. I'll be out and dressed before he's even up. When I pass the living room, he's snoring loudly, arm flung out against the coffee table. His back is going to kill him today. I remind myself that that's not my problem. I don't even realize I've paused to look at him, until he snorts and startles me into scurrying for the bathroom.

All while under the spray I promise myself I won't think of him. Of the way he felt against me, of all the grief and pain he's holding in and not dealing with, until it barrels through his life in a raging drunk. Charlie should go to therapy. Charlie isn't 'of' that generation. And who am I to judge? Did I go to therapy? After all the shit hit me? No, because that was just the hand life dealt me and I dealt with it. Didn't I? I'm humming. I don't even realize it, but I keep it up, a soft back beat to the terror that's building in my neurons.

I'm thinking back and forward on the timeline of my life and how I learned to cope and the ways in which I've not accepted love or connection in any way that might hurt me too much when it leaves. The biggest loss of my life since Cecily was Gina. There have been no real heartbreaks between. Because I kept my heart safe. But Charlie and Gina pried open that box and built a nest inside. I wipe the mirror and tug at the bottoms of my puffy eyes.

Age is a bitch. She's like a wraith that sits on my shoulder every time I look in a mirror. *Time is running out.* She cackles at the lines and I scoff. Running out for what? To be, objectified? To be of use? Maybe I want the clock on my 'beauty' to run out. Then maybe I won't have any choice but to resign myself to the words I keep avoiding. All of these thoughts are tumbled inside of my brain, like a book case that got shaken in an earthquake. I leave the bathroom in just my towel, wet and stupid in rumination, still humming when I catch movement out of the side of my vision and shriek in surprise. I nearly drop my towel right in front of Charlie who, drops his glass of water. It shatters against the counter.

"Shit, Charlie!"

"Damn it, Meg!" he responds at the same time. The echo of one fear between us.

"You scared me." I rush to help, sorry that I was upended. Sorry for the thoughts in my head. Just … sorry

He yells at me, to get out. His eyes travel over my chest, my neck, in wary glances before he sighs.

"I don't want you to cut your feet." I back away slowly. The writer in me, plays this out, a scene. He's broken something, it's dangerous to be around. He's trying to save me. He's trying to save me from the pain. From his pain.

"I've got it," he says.

I don't think he does. Not any of it. The glass, the breaking, the dissolution of a boundary we inadvertently crossed last night. But I can't speak so I nod and go back up to my room, as quickly as I can. What a stupid and horrible difference a night can make.

I DO EVERYTHING I CAN TO NOT THINK ABOUT CHARLIE AT WORK. The never-ending slog of deadlines and posts, and bare-minimum fact-checking does some of the work. The rest is all me, telling myself in quiet moments that this doesn't have to be a big deal. That I don't have to make anything of this. Charlie and I are friends. We've hugged, we've kissed on the cheek, we've comforted each other in times of hurt, and sassed one another back into a healthy state of moving on. We are above one night of laying in each other's arms. My phone pings. I pause the rampant brain-fuck of which celebrity haircut would suit you best, to glance down.

Where are you? Are you okay?

Mom. Again. If I don't write back, she'll call. If she calls, Stan's stupid face will pop up over the cubicle to berate and then tell on me, like he saw me eating out of his paste jar in kindergarten. I sigh, check around me like I'm about to pull out the biggest contraband—emotion—and respond.

I'm at work right now, mom.

Can we talk?

I sigh and shake my head. Stan coughs through the wall. I type another sentence on the article. Jennifer Aniston is totally your face type.

> Now's not a good time.

Nothing but silence returns on the screen and I exhale all the agony. Never is a good time. It's never going to be okay. The disheartened sixteen-year-old in me crosses her arms to pout, self-satisfied.

> Soon?

Why? Why does she need to talk so badly now? I sigh and continue on with the article. She asks again. And again. And again and Stan stands up to peer down at me through his glasses.

"Hot sexting going on or something?"

"I hope so. Your mom said she liked women my age," I growl at him. Stan lowers down like a deflating balloon. I text my mom quickly.

> Later Mom, I'm going to get in trouble.

> Sorry. I just miss you.

I sigh and silence my phone. I put it in my bag and continue on. If it's one thing that could take my mind off of Charlie, I guess that was it. What would he say, if he knew? Probably be mad that I responded at all. Not mad at me. Protective for me. I close my eyes, stopping mid Anne-Hathaway bob, and pull out the memory of Charlie's long thigh pressing into mine, soft curls on my neck, his arm over my shoulders. Permanent now, in my memory. His words press against the memory, and trickle out in soft whispers.

I don't want you to get hurt.

Nothing could have touched me in that moment.

I can't stay with Charlie. If my mom is about to reenter my life, I know my old patterns too well. I'll want comfort and I will find it in any willing bed. And Charlie wouldn't survive me bringing home a guy. And he definitely wouldn't survive it if my attention inadvertently turned on him. Which it could very well do, after last night. I am a horrible excuse for a friend who's about to open up decades of wounds and bleed out on his floor. Charlie must be protected, from my grief and from me.

I don't know where I'll go, but I have to move out.

CHARLIE

"I think it's time I move out." Laura, in my script, says and my fingers follow her words. Only, they aren't Laura's words. They're Meg's and I realize that I've been stuck in my script for the last few hours of the day. The magical lapse has hit hard. I didn't even hear her come in from work. I shake my head, delete the misspoken line, and look up at her. She looks tired. We never really talked and I didn't apologize after last night. She'd left for work and I let her. And now she wants to … what?

"What do you mean you should move out?" I say. I hope my voice sounds harsh enough that she doesn't question me. I hope that it sounds aloof, like I don't remember falling asleep on her, or how she looks, wet in a towel. How every time I hear her hum, I smile stupidly before being racked with guilt. I keep wondering if I really kissed her neck or just dreamt it.

She shakes me from my thoughts. "I don't want to cramp your style."

"My style?" I raise my eyebrow to the bullshit.

"Look! I've disrupted your work just bringing it up." She points to my laptop, so I close it.

"You can't move out." She can't. She can't. I mean, she could. She probably should.

But my heart.

"But, Charlie—"

"I need you here," is all I can admit before I open my screen back up and start again.

"For what? To leave my shoes on the floor, and scatter my insecurities about, and leave coffee-stained notes all over?"

The life of the apartment. The soul of living.

"Yes," I croak. "All of it."

She throws a fit. She hates one word finality. She gathers her stuff and puts on her stupid hat, and her ridiculous red rain boots, straps on her money-empty purse.

"Where are you going?"

"Out," she says and leaves.

I sit and stare after her, Gina's scarf swinging from the vibration of how hard the door closed. Period. Finality. I should have said more. Should I go after her? Certainly she'll be fine in a big, dangerous city, upset and tired …

Gina's hands are on my shoulders and she's leaning into my ear.

If you love that girl— her voice is soft. *Don't let her get away, Charlie.*

But following her would be desperate and I'm not desperate.

You are. Gina shakes her head in between the veil of my memory and the house that once had her tea stains and high heels. Her lack of insecurity about anything. The house, is empty of both of them now.

I'm not desperate.

You are.

I am. I'm desperate to not live with this ghost alone. To know where Meg's at and that she's safe. To hear her whisper to her pages, or scratch her nose, and ask me if I've eaten, and make excuses that she then plows through to write. To have Meg, even at an arms distance, in my life.

"Fuck," I whisper and save the work before I get up. Goddamn it, I stretch my stiff body that seemed much younger even yesterday. We had missed our walks the last two days because I'd been working.

Because I'd been working.

Meg thinks she's disturbing my work. Because all I ever do is work. Because work is easier, writing is easier, creating a world is easier than grief. It's easier than all of the strange and tumultuous feelings I'm denying about Meg. Then admitting that we are all on a one-way ticket to the ground and there's no getting off the ride. And I'm scared to spend the rest of that ride alone, when someone so beautiful is living one staircase away from me.

"Fuck," I say it again and put on my shoes. I'm just going for a walk. I'm not going to find Meg. Shit, how will I ever even find her? What if she's going to a liquor store? What if she goes to the park by herself? What in the hell was she wearing?

Her knitted raspberry hat, her old gray coat, the red boots … my creative mind conjures up seeing those feet laying prone in a dirty alleyway and my heart rate climbs and I'm tearing down the hallway and out the front door. It's cold on the street and muddled with the sounds of humans. Settling in and tearing out. Yells and laughter, car horns and the gentle shush of a train below me. I watch my breath puff out in front of me in frantic little clouds. The corners of my eyes start to freeze, but I'm not crying, surely.

No, and don't call me Shirley.

I see her. My body doesn't even let me look both ways, it follows blindly, a puppy into the street, aching to catch up to her.

"Jesus Christ, slow down," I gasp through lungs that weren't expecting a high-speed chase. I land, next to her, just as she's about to cross. I see a small smile tug on her mouth and feel the weight of a million men, through eons of time, at the end of a line where a woman sat waiting. Then it grows. That smile, that happiness, relief. Shit, I'd follow her out into traffic any day just to see it. But it's the way she scowls at me afterwards, like she's *not* happy to see me, that makes my breath catch. "What are you doing?"

"I guess I'm walking after you," I say. I force the curmudgeon back into my throat.

"Why?"

"Because I needed to get out."

"Nice."

The heartbeat in my chest pulls and tugs, puckering in on the stitches I've worked so hard putting in to keep it closed. I could just keep lying to her. But we both know I'm just lying to myself. Fuck it. The one-way ticket's already punched.

"Because I don't want you to move out. Because I—" I stop. She stops. We're in the middle of the street. Neither of us moving but staring. Two gunfighters at high noon, waiting for the other to draw first.

"You? You what?"

Car horns blast around us in a cacophony of anger. I thank God for New York impatience.

"Get across you idiot," I say and take her elbow to hurry her to the other side. Her arm seems so small in my hand. I think Meg is a force, a big strong woman. But, I look down at my hand, she's bird bones and feather wisps. Teetering on the edge of breaking, but never breaking down. She pulls away and we both run for the entrance to the subway.

"Where are you headed anyway?" I want to regain control, to stop the tugging on my heart. To make this easy between us again. I need to make it easy.

"Kansas."

"Funny." My heart tells me I'm a fucking idiot.

"I don't know. Out."

"Why do you want to move out? Is it the no man-bun rule?"

"No, I don't want to bring a man-bun home." She stops for a moment and shakes her head. "I told you."

"You don't distract me."

"I'm a burden."

"You're not." How could she possibly think that? "Why in the hell would you even think that?"

"Because, I—" she stops the truth from her mouth and I'm pissed. Both of us are chewing through the restraints of a lifetime of disappointment and neither will ask the other to simply loosen the knots. Her steps down into the subway quicken, as though she's still running away.

"I don't pay rent." Is the asinine thing that comes out. I scowl at her back.

"That's bullshit. I don't need your rent. You need your rent."

"For what?"

"For when you start opting editors and marketing and all those expenses no one tells you about as a writer."

"I gotta find an editor? But I don't even have a book." She turns back, interrupted from leaving, stalled on the platform.

"You do. And it's gonna be beautiful." I stop at the word. So much of her, not just her book. I look down at her, as she turns that freckled midwestern nose up at me. She wavers closer.

"It's incomplete." *She's incomplete.*

"You'll finish." *You'll get there.*

"How do you know?" She defies my faith on the regular. But never when it's about myself. Only when it concerns her. Meg is a woman with little faith in herself.

"Because Meg Kent is no quitter." I double down and lean in closer, expecting that she'll pull away. Expecting that in the broad light of the subway truth, fluorescent and cruel, she won't like the age of my skin and the way my eyes are filling with tears. I think I want to kiss her, even in the dirty concrete underbelly, even when I have no right to. And the universe knows it's a terrible idea, because it stops the train right next to us. Where will we go?

"Come on. Let's go see a show." My brain decides and I shrug beneath it. What else do you do when the world is upturned and nothing makes sense?

"A show?" I pull her in behind me by her tattered sleeve.

"Well? You got me out of the house, and I don't think either of us should be writing when there's a new play and the Vine and Goat."

"Wait, there is?" and just like that she's distractable again and I don't have to think about death, or losing her, or kissing her, because I can talk about a world I know and love. One that is safe. It's safe to do this. With Meg. She's safe. She's safe with me.

MEG

The play was good. It distracted my mind. It put me in a new world and listening to Charlie talk about it as we walked back to our subway stop reminded me of that other life, when we were both younger, and he was filled with passion for an art that had been lost to the rest of the world. The animation, the aggravation. I remember him always being this way. He would say you could tell if a play was good, if you were still talking about it three blocks away from the theater. It didn't have to be liked, you could have hated the hell out of it, but if you were still talking about it, then it touched a nerve and it must have at least been interesting. He talked for five blocks. I didn't think about my mom on a single one of them. But when we board the subway car, he turns silent. When I look over at him, leaning against the pole as the car took its slow progression to speed, he's looking at my feet.

But not at my feet. He's looking at a memory. Somewhere far from me. Far from the subway. Or maybe a subway in a different time, after a different play. With a different girl. His hands are in his coat pockets, and the way his stormy eyes turn sad, I know.

It's been a while now since he told a story about her, heard a song and said it reminded him of her, said something on the menu was her favorite. Though I know she must be on his mind constantly. On repeat. Maybe after the funeral, and the debacle of Don, Charlie's been denying the memories. But I feel this one, creeping up from the gray metal platform, through his soul, hiding behind his eyes.

"She would have liked that one," I said softly, a dare to the monster lurking. To come out, show itself, let the wound open and the pus come out. To help him heal. Charlie's eyes snap to mine and he shakes his head.

"She would have hated it."

"What? She loved Downs!"

"Not his best work."

"Still, she would have liked it. The humor was very tongue in cheek. I can—" I stop, the tracks bump beneath us, shaking him as he stares at me. Waiting for what might come out of my mouth next, but the words are stopped short somewhere.

"I can still hear her laughing," he finishes for me. I hug the metal pole, knowing it's a playground of hepatitis. Seems safer than trying to hug Charlie right now.

"Me too." We both stare out the window at the cold, gray metal intestines surrounding and speeding by our car. "Why don't you talk about her more, Charlie? You know you can, always. You can always talk about her with me."

"There's nothing else to say," he whispers.

"I miss her. I feel like there's worlds still to say. I think a play about her would be beautiful," I argue. Why I'm poking the bear in his gray tweed coat, shaggy and teetering, I can't say. Maybe I'm still mad from the feelings in my heart. Maybe I'm mad that she left us to fend for ourselves. To get confused. She couldn't have known.

I ask how his play is going.

Charlie glares at me, like really glares. Like he's looking at a rat dragging a dead body of another rat away. He's not writing it. I can tell by the way he dodges the questions and the rising anger at the idea overtakes him. He says I'm an idiot, that he'll never forget her. That the world wouldn't understand the light she was, so what was the point?

I tell him so that he can give people hope. So that he can give me hope, that he still has something to live for, something to strive towards. So that there will be a distant future with Charlie Horowitz in it. I can't ever remember someone loving me that much. But it's the way I feel about Cecily. Eternal spring in the middle of perpetual winter. But his memories of Gina are like the cancer that took her, growing and festering, slowly taking over inches and miles of his heart. Closing him off to anything else around him. Closing him off to me. I swallow back the selfish thought.

I feel my stomach ache and the train stumbles to a halt and throws me back a bit. All of these years and I still ride like a hayseed yokel most days. Unused to the constant motion of a city. Charlie is out as soon as the doors screech open.

I follow him. We walk in silence, while the city blares, and blinks, and howls around us. He unlocks the gate, lets me in first. I unlock the door. But he still lets me in first. We hang up our coats, noses red with cold and he barely looks at me.

"Goodnight, Meg."

"Thanks for the show, Charlie." I whisper and he goes directly to Gina's room, shuts the door and I watch the light click off. It's strange and hurtful. Because I know that's where he was when he came out drunk the night we fell asleep together. What is in the room? What kind of loss is he marinating in?

"Oh, Gina," I whisper. *If you only knew what we've become without you*. I make a cup of tea and walk up the loft steps. My heart aches to knock on her door. I want to be with him. I want to be with him and his memory.

But I can't.

He's with her tonight.

CHARLIE

The play was good. Good in that there was a familiarity about being in those seats, and in the lights, and the particular energy of a crowd. It was a small and independent theater, and was hosting one of my favorite playwrights. Gina had always been undecided on the man, but I found he understood the preposterous nature of humans, and wrote well about it.

It was the perfect distraction and better than that, it seemed to keep Meg's mind away from her thoughts of running away. The warmth of her shoulder next to mine unclenches something in my heart; a guard around the fortress that gets to have the night off. Afterward, when the curtains close, I can't help but give it my typical run down. Some men break down every quarter or period of a game, but my Sunday pastime is dissecting the play-by-play of plays.

Meg listens, rapt. There are small wrinkles around her eyes, and I like them.

I like Meg with age. I try to look away from the laughing lines dancing around her mouth and continue on with the most heartening and beautiful parts, of someone else's world. As we descend the stairs of the subway I catch my reflection, not really my face, but the flash of blue around my neck. Bold jewel blue, and I look over my shoulder, sure that Gina has caught up to us. I feel her taking my arm, but it's just the turnstile brushing my coat. Words that were running like a river out of me trickle to nothing. I step onto the car slowly, behind Meg, and look over my shoulder. Just in case.

Just in case she's there, trying to catch up. Just in case, so she doesn't think I've left her behind. Just in case the last months have only been a horrible dream. Some unnamed author in the sky was writing a scene and its one they decided to cut. She'll catch up, Gina will catch up any day. And she'll put her hand in mine and smile up at me and shake her head and tell me it was all an awful plot twist. *Whoosh*, the doors close and I'm still hearing her voice.

I didn't really. It was all part of the second act crisis. Don was just a part of the play …

I feel my body become heavy and full of hurt. I sense that Meg is looking at me, and I'm trying to stand but I feel like the car's metal post is holding me up. I stare at her feet. Just hers. Because no one else is on the car with us. My eyes feel hot. I want to be alone. I want to curl up in Gina's room and beg her for forgiveness on account of the bird wings fluttering in my heart over another woman. Those tiny beats of moving on that I'd felt in my chest over the last few days. The whispers of life after Gina, that shouldn't be there.

There shouldn't be life after her.

I see her, then, just beyond Meg's feet, dancing through the streets of Rome, and blowing kisses to the audience. I see her wrapped in silk scarves and singing in our kitchen. I see her, naked and porcelain, a doll in my bed, breakable and unbelievable in softness. I see her blue eyes twinkle and bright red lips beckon, and I hear the voice, southern swagger in perfect round tones. She's in every sense I have and I feel dizzy and sick. Does Don feel this way too?

"She would have liked that one," Meg says suddenly, like a hand pulling me up from dark water. I come awake to the subway and take a sharp inhale, as though I'd forgotten to breathe under the deluge of memories. My eyes fire into Meg's and I shake my head. What is she doing here? When I should be grieving my wife, alone in my misery?

She's here because I asked her to stay.

Because Gina probably asked her to stay with me.

Because Gina asked me to love her.

I fail to breathe again and my next words come out angry.

"She would have hated it."

"What? She loved Downs!" Meg's talking about the play. Not me and the fledgling hope in my heart in her presence. I take a deep breath. We're talking about the play.

"Not his best work."

"Still, she would have liked it. The humor was very tongue in cheek. I can—" Meg stops, a voice broken by the rattle of the machine beneath us. I stare at her, muted like she hit the wall of my grief. Her eyes, damn those eyes, wet and sad. Waiting for me to say something to reassure her, that I'm okay. That it's all going to be okay.

"I can still hear her laughing," I finish the thought.

"Me too," Meg says. I look out the windows and watch the rushing gray pass us by, still feeling weak from the wave of memories that are echoing in my brain. She asks me why I don't talk about her. Reassures me that she doesn't mind. That I always can talk about Gina. But the problem is that I can't. I can't always talk about her. Her words bubble up to the surface of my cloud. She says it like she understands but it hurts her and I'm confused. Infused. A hopeless wreck of a man, undeserving of either of them.

"There's nothing else to say," I put a period on the conversation. End scene. But Meg's got reporter pluck and there's no finality until there are answers.

"I miss her. I feel like there's worlds still to say. I think a play about her would be beautiful," she leads. Maybe she's trying to shake me from my stupor. Maybe she's just as disillusioned. Maybe Gina shouldn't have left us like this, steeped in some weird confusion of obligation. I'm mad that she left us this way.

Because Gina knew everything. I feel like she knew things beyond my comprehension. All these thoughts pile up behind the faulty damn of me not telling Meg yet that I haven't really been writing that play.

"You are working on a play, right?" The rhetorical question flies out of Meg's mouth and hits me across the face like a fist. It stings. It hurts, and how dare she? Scrape at the infected goop of my heart wounds. Give me a taste of my own medicine? What is she? Grown up?

"Where are your pages? Wasn't it convenient that you missed the deadline?"

"I missed the deadline? You missed it too!"

"So? Apparently neither one of us is writing. So what?"

"So it matters. It matters that you write about her, Charlie!"

"Why?" I ache for her to stop questioning me. To stop pushing me past the level of my comfort. I don't want to grow out of this, I don't want to leave any of it on the page, and risk it falling behind me.

"So you—I dunno, can remember her. So you can immortalize her."

"You're an idiot. I'll never forget her. I don't need words on a paper to remember her."

"Then maybe you write about her to introduce her to people who never got to know her."

Volumes. It would take volumes for people to know my wife.

Decades of famine and feast. Hell, I had those things, and I still didn't know her. Did I? She is my conundrum. My lifetime of unknown. My mystery and purpose and she left me undefined. I sigh and look at Meg. Only honesty. I can only give her honesty.

"Why would you tell someone, living in perpetual winter, that there was something like spring, when you knew they could never feel it?"

The train juggles to a stop and Meg stumbles with it. I shake my head. I don't know why I'm listening to advice from a woman who hasn't found her own balance in life.

"You tell them about spring, so they have hope," she whispers but I rush past her and pretend not to hear. It's not my goddamn job to give people hope. Falsely at that.

I need to get home. I need to get away from Meg, and her questions, and the memories that rode the train with me like ghostly cobwebs, stuck to my shoes and still trailing behind me. I can't look at her, or back at them. The city is its noisy, wet symphony and it feels ten times louder and I can't talk because I know I'll shout, and Meg will get mad. So I keep my mouth shut until we reach the house. I hang up my coat, my hands pause on the scarf, feel the soft skin of it between my fingers and I ache. When I glance over at her, Meg's eyes are dropped and she looks like I hit her with a newspaper for bringing in something off the sidewalk. Her nose is pink, but I can't tell if it's from the cold or tears. I can't stand here and wonder; my heart is in no condition.

"Goodnight, Meg."

"Thanks for the show, Charlie," she says to my back. I go to Gina's room, shut the door and strip down. I hit the light and lay, naked and willing the bed to burn beneath me, so that nothing but ash will remain of the life we had. Of me. Of Gina, of the lies we told ourselves. I hear the kettle sing, low and mournful. The tinkling of spoon to cup. The soft socked footsteps of Meg going up to her own bed.

Can't a man even self-combust in peace? Without worrying

about his reluctant and heart-forward roommate upstairs? I roll over and groan into the pillows. Gina's smell is faded, like the strange tint of perfume, left on a shelf too long.

I weep against the unfairness of her fading, until I fall, graceless as I am, into a fitful sleep.

MEG

I wake up, and the first thought on my mind is Charlie, spending the night with his grief in Gina's room. I close my eyes tight again and will myself to think of anything else. Cecily's face filters into view.

My grief.

She's there, on a road trip to Kansas City, long blonde hair tattering like streamers in the wind, while she flies her hand out the window of the backseat. My mom is driving the old station wagon that has no AC, and they're singing along with Neil Diamond on the radio.

Baby loves me. Yes, yes she does.

I hate Neil Diamond. I want to listen to something newer, poppy, like Roxette or Boyz II Men, but they're singing, and we're averagely happy so I let it fly. Like the wind through my sister's hair. I'd forgotten that we were ever happy. I'd forgotten the sound of our voices raised in song, the off-pitch tilt that was more joy than talent. I forgot the way Cecily used to roll her eyes at me when mom would insist that the driver always picked the station.

What station had Cecily picked the night she died? What song was the last she heard? What notes, carried her soul out into the darkness? Away from me? My eyes shock open. I'd rather think about anything else.

When I tune my ears to downstairs, nothing stirs. He was in a mood last night. I know he's in grief, but I don't know where he's at on the spectrum now. When he asked me to not move out, it felt like a downhill glide. Easy with hope. When he rode the subway home with Gina's ghost in his pocket, we were Sisyphus again, trudging through the muck of loss. But isn't that the way? Even after so many years.

Tell your momma girl, I can't stay long sings in the back of my head, whispering the memory that's aching for me to peel back the hurt and look at it.

I can't. I have to go to work. I get up, I shower. But the song hums through my lips and I have to consciously close my mouth and think about what I need to get done today. When I get out, I don't take time to worry about my clothes. Who's there to tell me I look like a vagrant college kid anyway? I make the coffee. The door of Gina's bedroom stays closed and I'm trying to be reverent but every appliance and dish seems to be clanging out wildly and I cringe every time I make a move. I'm a three-ring circus setting up tents in a graveyard. It's nearly time to leave, and still not sign or sound from Charlie. What if he … did something last night?

No, we won't tell a soul where we gone to … my heart is a syncopated ache of clapping and strumming. I knock on the door. *Bum Bum …*

Can't stand still while the music is playing …

There's no response. The music feels loud in my head and I beg the memory to leave me be. I beg Charlie to answer, to make what's real, real again. I yell at the door.

"Coffee is in the pot, and there's waffles. Please eat something."

Nothing stirs.

"Charlie?"

I have the idea to break down the door.

She's got the way to move me, Cherry ... I take a chair from the kitchen island and hold it like an axe over my shoulder.

"Charlie?" I yell again. I hear him clear his throat. I drop the chair to my waist and set it back down.

"Okay," I hear him mutter. Far away, on a different stage of loss. Three states of despair over.

"I gotta go to work, but I'll see you tonight, okay?" I feel my voice tremble, my pitch is all off and I can't sing. "Charlie?"

Baby loves me, yes yes she does ... fades to a soft backdrop and disappears all together when I hear him grouch ...

"Okay, Meg." All of my tense muscles drop against my skeleton in relief. If he's angry he's awake and annoyed, and annoyed means he's going to come out and putter away the tension as soon as I'm gone.

"Asshole," I whisper. For worrying me. For being the only thing that's stopped the memories that threatened to put me in bed for the rest of the day. Only one of us gets go grieve at a time, and I've had years to get over it. I'm so over it,

Girl, we do whatever we want to ...

I grab my bag, my coat and hat, and head off to a job I hate in a city that helps me forget even further.

CHARLIE

I'm a poor excuse for a man. Waking up in the shipwreck of Gina's room is the worst feeling in the world. Like I've traveled back in time and straight into the aftermath of the crime. Only it's me that's torn it all down. Me that ravaged her memory. I was the storm that desecrated her grave. It was me that tore apart the room looking for something of value. What was it all worth?

I hear Meg stirring and I'm so damn embarrassed for the way I behaved, that I wait while she trudges through her daily routine, not the light footsteps of someone caught in the dawn of a new day, but someone still processing the dark of last night. I don't move. I close my eyes, until I hear her at the door.

"Coffee is in the pot, and there's waffles. Please eat something."

I am a corpse. Dead men don't move.

"Charlie?"

I don't answer of course. But then I wonder, if she thinks I'm really dead, will she barge in and see me? A naked squatter in the splendor that was my wife's room, now torn to shredded jealousy?

"Charlie?" again.

I clear my throat. "Okay," I say back, and my voice is an echo behind concrete and barbed wire.

"I gotta go to work, but I'll see you tonight, okay?" A scared Meg is on the other side of the prison wall. She'll see me tonight. I sigh and cover my face with both hands. Meg can't find me. I can't die and have her find me. Not like this. "Charlie?"

"Okay, Meg," I grouch. I hear her mutter *asshole* as she turns to leave and I feel the strange, ugly nausea of guilt filling my chest. Just last night she told me she was leaving, to not disturb me. Just last night I stopped her. Told her I wanted her here. To what? Witness my epic downfall?

I'm a poor excuse for a man.

THE REST OF THE WEEK GOES BY IN THIS WAY. EVERY NIGHT I FIND myself drawn to Gina's room, to her bed, naked and alone and trying to pull every memory off the shelf and from my neurons and play them over and over on the bare wall like a movie until the early hours of the morning, and I hear Meg knock and tell me the daily menu. And leave.

And come home, tired and sighing and kicking off shoes. I can hear the slump in her shoulders. I swear I hear her sit beside the door, her nail tracing the molding and wondering where I've gotten off to. When she's not home, sometimes I go out and eat. Sometimes I stay in and write, drivel and dumb shit, and sift through Don's old letters and throw up out of the saccharine homage he's paying to a woman he knew so little of. And so much of.

Sometimes, I come out. When Meg is upstairs, a Diet Coke for dinner which is shitty and I should tell her so. But I feel like my voice is stuck in a dry basement of my chest and even if I tried to speak, it wouldn't carry far enough to reach her. But I sit at the base of those stairs and listen to her. We've barely spoken more than a few words. We have not set a new deadline.

Dead. Line.

The clickety clip of her hands across the keys sometimes floats down to me. The woman has long fingers and they're fast, like knives piercing page with certainly hard truths. I hear her gasp and cry and I fall against the stairs and wait, willing my stupid body to go up and be with her, willing my heart to come out of the damn room where nothing but hurt has been laid down and be with the living again. Meg is weeping. She sniffling and gasping even as her fingers fly and I …

I am a poor excuse for a man.

MEG

A week goes by in the same way. I don't see much of Charlie. When I come home, he might be writing, or out with friends of the theater. Or he might be behind the door. I fear it is the always the latter. I don't offer to write with him. I'm scared of encroaching into his sanctity, his space. I don't want to be the pressure of an outside world telling him to move on. I just want to sit next to him and wait it out. Like we're in a tornado warning, huddled beneath our desks. The Kansas in me finds the safety from natural disaster in his quiet countenance. Except that he spends most of his time in Gina's room. I hear him in there, rustling, sometimes talking to himself.

I know I should be concerned, but who the fuck am I to judge? When my sister died, I shut down to a degree that left me one step shy of a runaway. I built up awesome little detachment issues that kept me from ever falling in love, and from ever getting close, and from ever caring about anything enough to be broken by it. Not when they shared my apartment or left me soon after. Not when they used me up and took off running.

Charlie didn't have that lesson early on. It must be tough to learn it now.

It makes me sad that he's learning it at all. Charlie should never have to learn how *not* to love. I try to talk to him. I knock on the door. I let him know that there's someone on the other side of his grief. That she's waiting, when he's ready. That she made him coffee and watered his plant. That there's food in the fridge and toast getting cold, and please eat.

He says, *okay.* He says, *alright.* Sometimes I hear a feeble, *thanks* … and I leave. I can't make him talk to me. I can only be here. Right? Am I doing too little?

Three days in, I take off my coat and I slump down against Gina's closed door, my back to the wall, my head against the frame. My finger paints tiny circles around the wood, where on the other side, I wonder if Charlie is doing the same. Waiting to feel like he can come alive again.

Please come alive again, Charlie. The world is too dark here without you.

Some nights I just have a soda and write, and that's shitty. I know it. But eating by yourself sometimes just makes you feel emptier then if you hadn't eaten at all. Plus, maybe there's a sick part of me that wonders if he sees me treating myself badly, he'll snap out of it. Maybe I should call Jonah. But that might drive Charlie further into despair. There are no walls in my loft and I'm an exuberant lover. I would not do that to him.

That thought sits with me, of not being an exuberant lover when I'm with Charlie. How he once told me on a cold sidewalk in the middle of a Chernobyl day that I shouldn't stop having sex. That no one should stop, but that he was finished. My brain sifts through strange little thoughts and my filter doesn't stop them. I sit at my computer. I sip my Diet Coke. I close my eyes and let the thoughts build into something disastrous and beautiful. I type but don't look at the words, I don't read them or check them for punctuation because everything about the thoughts in my head right now are punctuating. Sharp, driving … I gasp, I feel myself crying.

From the absence of touch or the absence of love, I'm not sure. But I write it all out, all about what it must be like to be loved by the hands that touch you. I'm not sure I've ever really been touched by hands that loved me. Wanted and desired, yes. An object to crave and claim, to be sure. But to be loved first?

Who in the world had that? Maybe Charlie did, I sob a little too loudly and cover my mouth. Maybe Gina did more than once in her life. I sniffle and dry my eyes and close the laptop before pouring myself into bed and shutting off my light. I close my eyes tight, my hands pressed to my body, wondering if Charlie would hear. I look back at the stairs, the drop off a cliff to the broken rocks below. Has anything survived down there?

That's when I hear him shuffle back into his room, as if he heard me listening for him. Did he hear me cry? What an idiot I must seem to Charlie. I'm sure he wouldn't blame himself for a grown woman's tears. If anything, he probably chanced an outing into the world and scurried back to his safe zone when he found me blubbering like an idiot because I'm lonely and I want meaningful sex. Meaningful sex?

Ugh, what's wrong with me?

I dry my eyes, take a deep breath and take my bra off before recommitting to ending this day. Tomorrow is going to be different.

Regardless of what Gina asked from me, I want to make sure that Charlie is up and out of that room. I will find a way to rouse him. My eyes close and I groan. I need to get laid before I say or do something stupid to the only man who's ever really meant anything to me.

He's too brilliant to be left to rot in the dark recess of a love lost. And I'm too stubborn to let him.

I WAKE UP BEFORE MY ALARM, DREAMLESS. IT TAKES ME A MOMENT to realize what's woken me. The shower is running, downstairs. I close my eyes and listen. Is there anything more comforting than to hear another person in the shower? To know that they're there, going about their little human things, doing their little routine. Naked and trusting and feeding into a sense of normalcy that I've probably been looking for my whole life?

Then there's the smell. Fuck, it drives me insane.

Let me explain.

Only three smells in the history of the world could stop me short and spin me around, completely changing the chemistry of my body and elevating the dopamine in my system.

One, dirt roads after a rain. It's home and it's comfort. It's the life-giving, opening up of a dry spell. It's promise that crops will spring back to life, green, and that death is not imminent, no matter how long the world has thirsted. It's hope and a sense that everything will be alright. It's a childhood before death and the simplicity we should all have, at some point in our lives.

Two, freshly baked bread. The smell is a twin to the sound, and a triplet to the pressure of your fingers on the hard shell when it cracks open and the steam of its birth pours out. It's in the hours of someone's time, the patience in the waiting. The work of kneading. The smoothness of dough and the subtle smell of yeast; living and breathing something into creation. It's nourishing and comfort, and the sense that you're going to survive the bane of winter. Shelter against the coldness of life.

The third … I take a deep breath, hear the pitter patter of the shower as he's lifting arms and rinsing hair, and gathering pools of water in the crook of his elbow and body before it deluges to the floor of the shower … The third is the smell of a clean man. It's not just the soap or the water. It isn't the scent of the hair product. It's something feral and instinctual.

It's the way his skin opens up and takes a breath and the reaction of his pheromones to put back in place what was lost. It's the warmth that radiates and the permeating delicious taste in the air. It's the sense that there's a purpose for your nose, and that's to be buried in someone's chest, and feel safe and warm and at ease. And turned on. I take a deep breath and moan. I turn over into a ball, eyes open and waiting for him to come out. The bathroom door opens. I can feel the warm cloud of steam reaching its tendrils of seduction up the stairs. I want to die.

It's more than just a man showering. It's Charlie, doing something life-sustaining. And it's made me feel like everything might be alright, that we're going to survive this cold winter. That maybe, we are coming around to ease. He goes into his own room and shuts the door. His door squeaks differently than Gina's. I wait to the count of twenty to make sure he's not forgotten anything and will bounce back out, half naked. I gather my things, take the stairs quickly and close the bathroom door. I start the shower and step onto the still wet tile. Even though I have my own soap, I take a moment and hold his up to my nose.

Yep. That's Charlie. Fucking Irish Spring, almost an assault of clean. He's not even Irish. I smile and put it back in its place. Today feels different. The fact that he's out of the room, the fact that he showered, all of the facts that are keeping me lifted on a cloud of hope, when last night I was sobbing into useless words. I nearly start singing in the shower, but I don't want to scare away the man who's still healing in the room next door.

I get out, still in a towel, go upstairs and get ready for work. I realize then as I shuffle through my drawers and see the time on my phone from across the room, that I've spent twice as long in the shower as I normally do. What did I do? Well, I did scrub my face, and think about the day, and smile over Charlie's soap like a goddamn idiot. I shaved. A strange thing to do for someone who's legs aren't getting touched. I haven't worried about doing any of that in weeks, but what the hell?

Charlie is out of his room and this is the kind of day you can shave your legs for.

Still, it's left me with little time for breakfast. I'll have to grab it on my way out. When I bound down the stairs, tripping on the last one, he's there. In the kitchen. Clean. Hair curling and still wet. He looks pale, thin, but awake and alert. He shakes his head at me like a puppy that's overexuberant. I try to rein it in, find some reason to be crabby and old like him. The serious mature one.

"Morning," I start but he doesn't have time for puppies and their pleasantries.

"I'm going to be gone."

"What?" I say breathless, and take my bag in my hand as it swings wildly.

"I'm going to Chicago tonight."

"Chicago?" My brain trips. *Don't ask him how long, like you're going to pee on the floor and have separation anxiety if it's longer than a day. Don't be a moron.*

"One of my older plays is opening at the Belle Theater and they asked me to come answer questions afterwards."

"Oh, for just a show?"

"For all the shows, all week." He's terse, but there's something decided in him. He's stepping out. He's putting a foot in front of the other. He's cranking his rusty joints and neural pathways back to life again. I'm not mad, and I'm not disappointed. I put a scarf and a smile on.

"Ok, cool." I don't want to say too much. I don't want to ask why he's been holed up in Gina's room, and he doesn't offer an explanation. I don't want to unbalance us. Not now, not when Charlie is out of the room and doing something that he used to do. Maybe he's embarrassed. Maybe he's running away. Maybe it's not my place to question or judge. He's my friend, and how we cope in these deserts of grief is more a matter of survival than method. He takes a deep breath, shakes his head as if he's trying to read my thoughts just as hard as I'm trying to read his.

"I just don't want to fall into a spiral and I'm looking to keep myself busy, with something I—" he stutters and I pick up where he leaves his thought.

"You love." The words fall out. I'm too at a loss to hold them back. *Just keep writing this script, Meg, don't pause too long with an ending on love. Don't make it weird, weirdo.* "It's ok. It's good. I'm glad," I nod and readjust my bag, leaning towards my exit as if I want to go and it's no big deal.

"Meg, before I go, I just want you to know that drinking the other night was a mistake. I know how unfair that was to you." He looks so damn awkward and hurt. I can't let him. Because I don't blame him for anything he's done in his grief. I am a soft dirt road, and he is the rain.

"Nope, no apology necessary. Shit hits hard sometimes and I know you're not the kind of guy to lose yourself. In the bottle or otherwise." I look at him pointedly before nodding. "Have a gross hot dog in Chicago for me."

"I absolutely will not," he says and there's a smile on his face, which bakes a smile onto mine and his smile cracks open wider, satisfying, and nourishing to me.

"Well then, at least have a good time. Enjoy it, Charlie. You deserve to have this." I say. We both do. We both deserve to breathe. We both deserve space in the things that make us who we are. I'm still wondering what that is for me.

"You're going to keep writing, right?" He points a finger to remind me what makes me who I am. I roll my eyes. "We'll trade pages when I get home."

"Sure." I turn to get out the door.

"Meg?" He yells after me and I'm so elated that his voice not a quiet and gravely cry from behind a bedroom door that I turn and return his tone.

"Yeah, Charlie. I know. I'll write."

"I'll see you when I get back, okay? Please—" suddenly both hearts in the room stop. He's not going away forever, he's saying. Whatever he's about to ask, I'm in.

"Don't bring Man-Bun over?" I finish for him.

"No! Eat, I was going to say eat. No more Diet Coke dinners, okay?" He's scowling. A fine one to talk about sustaining yourself, but I just nod. I'll sustain myself with food and not useless and easy sex or Diet Coke.

"Okay, Charlie." For a moment my hand freezes on the door knob, dislodges from it. For a moment I want to come back to him. I want to throw my arms around him because I haven't seen him in days and I thought he'd died and I thought I'd died, but we're both still here and shouldn't we hug on something like that? Shouldn't he put his head to my chest and fall into the couch. Shouldn't we … I swallow down my stupidity, my loneliness. He's watching me when I look up.

"Okay," he says and storms back into his room. The door slams behind me and I find myself on the cold street, gray above and the sound of a buzzing city working its best to make me think of anything but how lost I feel.

CHARLIE

I'm leaving. It's an opportune time actually. I'm still embarrassed by the night I passed out in Meg's arms and even more so for abandoning her after the play. Seeing her close down, stop eating, be affected by my mourning, was a tipping point for me. If I'm not going to die in my wife's room, then I need to stop pining naked in there. I can't hold my drink either and I'm a fucking jerk to do that around her, given the mess she was raised in. Still ...

I remember Meg's steady heart beneath my ear, the warmth of her. The smell of her soap, the way her fingers held my head close. How loved I felt, how the storm had been quiet and I felt somehow like I would make it through this. And I hate myself for it. Because I shouldn't make it through this, should I? I remember in dark notes how I made her stay, then abandoned her for days.

So I'm leaving. To give us pause. Space. To figure my shit out. One of my plays is opening in Chicago and I'm going to go. Because I'm tired of the old perfume smell, and the peculiar way that I'm drawn to Meg, and the usurping of my solid ground, and the itch to write and create even when my muse is in a grave not yet grown over with grass.

When I get home maybe I'll clean out Gina's room. Maybe I'll just go back in there. But the change will do me good.

I tell Meg, on her way out the door for that stupid fucking job that I wish she'd just quit, that I'll be gone for a few days, to an opening. I've done it in the perfect amount of time. She's already running late so she can't ask too many questions or worry, but it's enough time that she knows I won't be there when she gets home. Why that thought makes me sad, I don't know. Meg alone makes me sad.

"Chicago?" She pauses but her bag keeps going and hits the door frame as she's walking out. Like the rest of her life is just continuing on without her. But she pauses.

Two lines appear between her brow. Concern and worry.

My voice is harsh when I answer, because I can't let those lines sway me. She quirks her lips, in a sad way.

"Ok. Cool." The monosyllable equivalent of a thousand thoughts not ready to line up and become a sentence. I feel the sudden stone of guilt drop in my gut. I never talked to her after the night of the play. Just monosyllable noises to affirm that I hadn't died yet.

"I just don't want to fall into a spiral and I'm looking to keep myself busy, with something I—"

"You love," she finishes. "It's ok. It's good. I'm glad," she nods. But I see the young Meg, hearing excuses from her mom, empty ones. That she had no doubt nodded along with. She shifts her bag, and I know I've only got moments to make her understand.

"Meg, before I go, I just want you to know that drinking the other night was a mistake. I know how unfair that was to you."

"Nope, no apology necessary. Shit gets hard sometimes and I know you're not the kind of guy to lose yourself. Have a gross hot dog for me." She says it fast, like she can't allow me the space for my guilt. Because there are things to live for. Gross hot dogs to eat.

"I absolutely will not," I say and the world has lifted from my shoulders for a moment.

"Well then, at least have a good time. Enjoy it, Charlie. You deserve to have this." She says but it feels like she's talking to herself. Convincing her own brain that this is a good thing.

"You're going to keep writing, right? We'll exchange pages when I get home."

She rolls her eyes and turns to leave. "Sure."

I'm not sure she means it. There's a teenage petulance there and I don't blame her for holding it. I'm suddenly scared to leave her. Scared she might stumble, or scared that I will without her. I don't know the difference between codependence and comfort in this moment, which makes it even more important that I go. I know we both could use the space.

I tell her to eat. She sighs and says she will. On her way out, her hand twitches on the doorknob like she wants to come back to me, like she is thinking of … shit, she wouldn't want to kiss me or hug me, would she? Her smell comes back into my nose, the soft pads of her fingers in my hair like I'm still cratered into her softness. All of it hits me.

"Okay," I say gruffly and storm to my own room to pack, ripping the decision to make this moment more than it is, from either of our hands. I hear the door slam behind her.

MEG

I'm just coming out of the subway again, when I check my phone to see if Charlie left any flight details.

No.

But there are three calls from my mom and seven texts from her too. I never answered her. I was too busy pining or whatever the fuck you call it when your brain loses the reasoning battle with your heart. But what's on my phone now is more contact than she's tried to make in twenty years. I'm nearly to work. I text her back just that.

There's no reply.

She's effectively stolen my brain space from Charlie and I'm actually thankful for that.

It's been three days of living on my own and I'm sad to report that I'm not really enjoying it as much as I thought I would. There's an emptiness in all the space. There's too much quiet and I'm scared of Gina's door. There's too much space and I'm scared of leaving the apartment, by myself for some reason. So I stay in. Work and home, work and home. One night to the market, but then, always back home. To something familiar. To a novel that I'm floundering in, but that I promised I'd be working on.

I'M BARELY EXPECTING THE CALL. I MEAN, I ALWAYS WONDER WHEN the day will come that she finally calls and I'm too distracted to screen it out. Roused from her drunken stupor, to apologize, to ask me for forgiveness. It was a fantasy that rode with me out of Pickering, Kansas in a beat-up Ford Escort, to college. It was the dream when I walked at my college graduation and looked down from the stage to find her asleep in the reserved seat, passed out from 'celebrating'. I used to dream that when I moved to the city, thousands of miles away, that she'd meet me at the train station, to help me move into my new place in Queens, my beater car long since sold. But the platform was empty.

Well, not empty. Charlie had called me before I'd left, on my very first cell phone. A Nokia if I recall. I still remember the sound of his voice on the other end.

"Hey, Clark Kent, everything on time?"

"So far. Please tell me Gina will be the one picking me up and not you."

"Brat," he smiled. They had made a family of friends when the world had taken mine away. Maybe they were my first loves. The memory of Charlie's voice filters in again, as I remember it all.

"That's it, now I'm picking you up, just to ruin your first memory of being a New Yorker."

"You're already ruining it, you old fossil."

Charlie was forty at the time. Younger than I am now. My god how the world has shifted and changed. The politics, the technology, the everything. But two things never did. Charlie and Gina were always there. And my mother never was.

Until I pick up the phone on autopilot and hear her on the other end.

"Megan?" Clear. Not slurred. A pulse-pounding sigh of regret for answering forms in my lungs. I breathe out sounds.

"Hey—Mom," the word feels weird in my mouth. Too dry and disconnected to be anything tasteful. I close my eyes and try to remember one fond memory. One good thing. She'd leaned on me at Cecily's funeral. Her head of soft brown hair on my shoulder. That wasn't the worst memory. I know there must be more but I can't dive that deep before I hear;

"Did you get the mail?" It seems like a strange question. Stranger because the over-piled mess of it is on the sideboard. I quickly run through it. Most of it is for Charlie, some for Gina, but only from vultures that didn't know her well enough to know that she won't be answering anyone's mail now. There's a bill for me, junk for me, and a plain white envelope from Pickering, Kansas.

"Mom, what is this?"

"I wanted to talk to you before you got it. Because you're my power of attorney and the executor of the estate, they sent it to you."

"Mom, what are you talking about?" Those formal titles are reserved for people who are supposed to take care of you and your life, in the event you can't. She interrupts me.

"I wanted to be the one to tell you, honey. Please. Before you open the letter."

The words that follow, rumble through my intestines like a subway car. Jutting out in the night like rocks below your fall. The envelope flutters down beside my feet as I collapse onto the stairs and listen to my long-lost mother, the only family I have left, tell me that my world will once again shift into the darkness of loss. I can't begin to know how to hold everything that seems to crash at once inside me. A faulty dam giving way to a peaceful town's unknowing. I think I thank her for letting me know. I hang up. My fingers itch, but my heart says it can't. Can't write out these words because then they'll be real. Then the loss will be real, the abandonment complete. I keep it inside and head upstairs. I don't eat, and I don't sleep.

~

I WORK A DOUBLE SHIFT THE NEXT DAY. IT SEEMS HOLLYWOOD'S nastiest bad boy got caught with a newly minted eighteen-year-old Disney star at a drug-filled rave and the world was about to go nuts over it. Seems tragedies happened in multiples.

I don't like these stories. Not only are they mindless distraction from the real problems of the world but they encourage people to get in the middle of other people's business. Still the moral downfall couldn't have come at a better time, because Charlie is still in Chicago and I don't have anyone to talk to. I could have called. I texted once to ask how it was and only received a 'fine'. He doesn't want to talk, if he did, he would. And if I can't talk to Charlie, I don't want to risk going home and talking all night to a bottle.

I haven't recruited a new starving artist to save.

And since sitting alone with thoughts of the conversation with my mom swirling like a Kansas sized tornado in my head was about as destructive a thing as the real event, I throw myself into work to avoid it. I'm healthy like that. One coping mechanism for another.

Even though most of the writers in my pod don't bother, I did some snooping, research, anything I could to put out as many articles in an sixteen-hour period as possible. Stan tells me to go home. That the boss told him, they're not paying for another hour from me. But that's fine. Since Charlie won't let me contribute anything for my room at the top of his stairs ("It's barely a closet, Harry Potter, just write your damn book") I don't really need the money. I can actually breathe in that department. It's the other areas of my life that have me suffocating.

I gather my things and take the subway home. It's not busy at this hour, except for a couple of tweakers I have to keep my eye on, and my hand on the pepper spray in my pocket. It's such an old canister, I'm pretty sure the most effective use would be to throw it. I sigh when I get to the gates of his apartment. It feels like home, a little fortress I can lock away all of my problems, and live in fairytale-like, comfortable denial.

I try to write, but it comes out like a bad high school journal entry. I eat some leftover pizza in the fridge and take a shower. I sit down and try again. It comes out as memoir and the stumbling, blocked version of events I've buried too deep to unearth. But I owe him pages so I trudge through them. The long days have lulled me into a sense of deserved sleep. I stare at my incomplete and dishonest words, the cursor blinking behind them.

Liar ... liar ... liar ...

"I don't wanna do this tonight," I whisper to the cursor, to Charlie, to all the world's best and brightest writers who would push on through.

I'm not the world's best anything in the moment. I'm tired. And in the middle of crushing hurt with no one to distract me. I go downstairs for a glass of water. Charlie's door is ajar. He's in Chicago. Probably schmoozing with the actors and directors of his play. I think now, that he just wanted to get out of town. I'm not the only one looking to be distracted.

I just want to get into comfort. On this night, on every night since Cecily died, since my mother shut down, since Bradley and the string of half-assed loves left me, since Gina passed away, I have been uncomfortable and unloved. It's a coldness that's deeper than the caverns in my bones and I don't want to feel it tonight. I step into his quiet sanctuary. It is blue in the dim light and simple. Unmade bed, spare glasses on his side table, books stacked high and one of his shirts thrown over a chair. Pieces of him that make a meal of my loneliness.

I crawl into Charlie's bed, and immediately fall asleep.

CHARLIE

The trip is fine but I'm unsettled in my solitude. I sit in the back of the theater, as I always do, cringing at the play and after three nights I'm tired of listening to my own voice. So, I trade in my ticket and when I come home, it's a day earlier than I'd planned. I want to be back. Even with the rooms filled with sadness and the awkward reunion with a woman I'm definitely not falling in love with, waiting for me. Maybe I'm secretly hoping that she's brought Jonah the Man-Bun over and I can rest easy in the fact that she's moved on, as Meg does. If she's moving on, then maybe I can too.

When I open the door, past midnight, the place smells clean. Like while I was gone, she went through it all and wiped up the crumbs, and the spills, and the fridge full of leftovers. I stop and stare into the dark and I can tell even in that low light that the counters of the kitchen are shining and all my old coffee mugs have been washed. I don't trip on any shoes or packages or cartons. And there are hooks open for my coat. I should be happy, but I'm not.

It means she wasn't writing. I look up to the loft, the lights are out. I don't want to wake her so I drop off my suitcase and hang up my coat, I start shedding my clothes and open the door to my room. I realize, as I'm walking through the threshold that I haven't really thought of Gina the whole trip. Just pieces.

Just frames of film, scratchy and gray. *Oh yes, she loved that line. Oh, she'd hate that trope.* Detachment is easier when you're away from the perfume-laced room with love letters not meant for you are strewn about. I'm out of my pants and exhausted as hell when I realize what's wrong with the picture of my comfortable bed. Even in the dark, I see the shadows of a very Meg-sized lump on the side I normally sleep on. Curled up, blankets tucked like a caterpillar around her.

"What in God's name are you doing?" My brain speaks before my mouth filters.

A pause.

"Sleeping," she grunts.

"Here? In my bed?" I want to yell but I'm so tired and confused. Why is she in my bed?

"Charlie, come on." She mumbles and falls back to sleep as if I'm the one being unreasonable. She sighs happily. When did she start sleeping in my damn bed?

"Get up! You can't sleep here."

"No." She's resolute. I'm so goddamn tired.

"Well, where in the hell am I going to sleep?" I pause. I can't go back to Gina's room. I was just feeling some lifting of the weight. A small taste of what I am without her. I can't. I can't.

"Sleep here," drifts up from the covers.

"Meg, don't be ridiculous." Is my only protest but she sits up and scowls at me and her hair is a mess and her cheeks are flushed and she's not even opening her eyes all the way.

"Don't be a prude," she says. God, she looks tired. Her lips are a full moon, in pout. To fall into bed with a woman, the woman, whose heartbeat still echoes in my ears when the rest of the world feels too big and too loud. What would her lips feel like on my cheek, my neck … my lips?

"Meg, please." I ache for her to get up and leave.

"Charlie." She grabs my wrist and pulls me into bed. And I'm too tired and worn thin and the sight of her in my bed is more than my heart can fight. Before I know it, I'm down. There, next to her, smelling her hair as she sighs and sinks in, back to sleep.

Fuck it.

I'm too tired and she's asleep and it's not like we haven't been here before. I look up at her profile, hair falling into her face and eyelashes heavy on cheeks.

"Not this battle," she says as if she can feel me ramping up to fight. "Not tonight. You can," she yawns and my body lets loose the struggle in the presence of her comfort. "You can yell at me tomorrow. Then I'll argue that you weren't supposed to be home yet." I sigh.

Fuck, Meg, I think, and squeeze her shoulder before turning away. Back-to-back is safer.

I'm a liar if I say I don't enjoy the closeness of another human being. At least it's just her.

I'm drifting, content. Back in my bed. Feeling like myself, and oh so goddamn tired. Meg's quiet warmth is beside me, and it's a familiar weight in the mattress. Her breathing hitches.

She shuffles. What is wrong with her? Then it hits me.

Something *is* wrong.

She'd never just curl up in my bed. That would be sappy. And Meg's too hard-nosed for sappy. Does she want to talk about it? Ugh, I should ask her. But it's past midnight and …

I hear her sniff. I feel the small shake of the mattress below us. There's more warmth as if her body is trying to contain the fire of hurt that's pressing out of her eyes right now. I'm too tired for a conversation and I wouldn't know what to say anyway.

"You idiot," she whispers and shuffles again. She must be talking about me.

God, what if she leaves? I'm desperate that she doesn't. *Please don't leave me, Meg.* My heart and head cry out at once. *I'm not an idiot. I'm not,* I think incoherently and turn to the sound of her sniffling again. I reach out. It's a gamble; a lotto ticket, shaking in the wind, pressed between my fingers, ready to pull loose or grant me millions in a heartbeat.

"Don't be a baby," I mumble and pull her in close, to my chest. Her back, her shoulders are swallowed in my torso. How is Meg so small? I smell her hair as I fold her into my arms, safe. *Don't leave.* I think. *Don't leave. Let's just let the dark be the world for tonight. I'm here. You're here. We're still alive. We still feel. Just breathe, Meg.* She relaxes in my arms.

We sleep.

MEG

The weight of Charlie sinking into the bed is the weight of a giant and a moth. It is light but absorbs heavy and I feel him tense as if he knows he should fight. I yawn and feel the comfort of his nearness reminding me that there are good men in the world still.

Charlie squeezes my shoulder and draws his hand away. He sighs. I feel him turn his back to mine and through the hazy veil of night, I hear his breathing become soft and even. The weight of his world settles heavy on the mattress beside me.

I want to wake up. I want to roll over and spoon him. I want to be close to him and let the truth of Charlie weather away all of the new hurt in my heart. I want to press my breasts against his back and my nose to his neck. I want to feel his long fingers draw mine across his chest. Maybe even lower. My breathing hitches.

I'm awake now.

I look over my shoulder and the muted blue light of the room that only shows his shadow, the outline of his form, a mountainous landscape against the sad backdrop of both of our lives.

Is it him that I want? Or just someone?

God knows since my mom called, after years of not speaking, resolute that we should reconcile, and me without a healthy physical outlet to avoid that decision on, it could be what my heart was looking for. A distraction.

But I don't think so. I roll back over, eyes drifting closed. I don't want to use Charlie; I don't want to put him like a balm over the tear in my heart. I don't just want somebody.

I start to cry. I want him. I think I've always wanted him. Why else would I run to his bed when I need comfort? My eyes fill, my nose burns and I sniffle.

"You idiot," I whisper and wipe my nose on my sleeve. I turn back over and roll into a tight ball, clench my teeth and my eyes hard against the tender revelation of my heart. I feel him shift.

I need to get my shit together and go sleep in my own bed.

"Don't be a baby," he mumbles and pulls me in close, my back against his chest. I think it will only make things worse. His breath is against my temple, warm and soft. I think this will only make me sob harder. But it doesn't. Charlie permeates my fear, with calm tendrils of comfort. I sigh. I relax.

I sleep.

DREAMS ARE FUNNY. WHEN I'M STRESSED, I'M ALWAYS RUNNING late to a destination I can never make it to. When I'm sad, it's watching my dad leave down a long hallway that never ends, and me crying endlessly after him. It's my sister, being lowered into the ground and I'm lying in the grave, next to her. I get to watch as my pale body is slowly buried under handfuls of dirt. One for each person who knew me.

But didn't know me.

This dream is different. I'm on the hill, and there's the grave. Just one. But it's empty. Not me, not my sister, just a big uneven oval in the ground. And the soil is rich and dark and it smells like wet potential and something clean. I stare at it, upturned earth, alone at the top of this grassy hill, high waving wheat in the distance. The roots of Kansas, have a hard time leaving my blood.

What do I do? What is this?

Suddenly, Charlie's hand is in mine and he looks down too, like our eyes are connected and whatever I look at, he sees.

"Time for planting," is all he says, then he kneels down and scatters a handful of scrabble tiles into the dirt.

"What? That's silly, you'll never grow anything there, that's my grave."

"Then you grow it," he says and puts more tiles into my hands, closing my fingers around the corners of them until it hurts. The words hurt. The tighter I try to hang on to them, the more they dig into my palm, drawing blood to the surface of my tissue-paper skin.

"Ouch."

"Let go. Stop holding on to your words," he says. "Let go."

"You let go," I cry and sit up. Knocking my clenched fist into the side table. Charlie rolls over to hold me down. He's strong, and so much bigger than me. Warm in the cold night.

"Shh," he mutters into my neck. "It's okay. I'm still here, Gina. I'm still here."

The words hurt worse than the dream. They hurt worse than anything. The truth my brain is holding onto, the truth of every loss, of Charlie's broken heart, it's all so painful to hold. I untangle myself and stand beside the bed. He mutters and I tuck the covers closer around him. He smiles into the pillow I borrowed. I'm sure he's asleep.

Then I go to the couch, eyes wide and throat closed from all the overwhelming want that won't ever see release, the hunger that won't ever be satiated, and the past loss that has set up urban deserts in my heart. The memories I've built over, the words I've buried, that are trying to burst through the concrete. I move to the desk. His desk. I push away his scattered papers. And I write.

I write and I write until my fingers cramp up and they're blackened with ink and my eyes feel like they've been washed with sandpaper and I sob dryly before falling asleep on the page.

All of the rubble of a city I'm trying to jackhammer through, all the wreckage of years of pain I've buried and denied myself. A nightmare of wakings.

I am dreamless, spread across his desk, cheek to my marks, making cursive tattoos on my face, until the sunlight breaches in jagged oily landscape. And the only hunger I have is to continue. I rise, I stretch, I turn the page and I write, fill the page.

Flip it, fill it, flip it, fill it …

CHARLIE

Dreams are funny, for months they've been about Gina, and her dark room. Sometimes they're about Don's smiling face, talking up to me from the photo with her lipstick still pressed against the glass layered above him. But this time, I am writing.

I am at a desk, on a stage, writing. And the audience is waiting for the next words to leap from my typewriter. They spew out, curve around my head and hang in the air. If the audience gasps or laughs then I know I'm doing something. If they cry, I've reached into the metal and ink taped entrails of the machine and pulled out human frailty. It is then that I am king.

But this dream is different. I'm at my laptop, at my desk, facing the west over the Hudson. The city buildings sparkle, a thousand tiny golden eyes, and the sun is frozen in a sunset casting orange over the loose paper and chewed pencils. I squint into its never-ending demise, before looking away.

"You can't keep looking back, darling," Gina says and I reach to my shoulder where she always lays her hand. But it's empty. "Look at her, she's brilliant." The sun sparkles and dances between the hard lines of the city. Something earnest and midwestern about it. Something that is unquenchable, and timeless. Something that lasts, through the winter and the dark, and always manages to rise again.

"It hurts," I squint even further as I raise my head to look at the orb, warm and light. It filters into the dark cavity of my chest and burns me there. It burns all over. I look away, cowering behind my screen.

"You have to look," she whispers. "I'm not here anymore and you need to find the light." It's no nonsense and exactly what Gina would say.

"I like the dark. You're not here and I like the dark."

"You don't. You love the light."

"Gina—"

"Don't shut out her warmth. Stop sleeping in my cold bed. She's right here, Charlie."

"I don't want it. I don't want the light. It burns," I start to sob, eyes closed to the sun, even as it warms my face.

"Love burns."

"I don't know how to—"

"You let go." The words are real and come from Meg's mouth and the sound vibrates in my ears and the sound of someone hitting the side table rouses me away from the sun, even as Gina whispers through my blood.

Don't leave her.

I take Meg in my arms and fall back into the bed. The sun is gone, the quiet night is cool and Meg is hot and breathing hard. I snuggle in and will her body to settle. Like the sun.

"Shh, it's okay. I'm still here, Gina. I'm still here." I reassure them both and fall back to sleep. Harder than I have in days. Maybe even weeks.

When I wake up, it's sometime early, in an empty bed and I hear shuffling in the living room. I lay still for a moment, hands to my head and feel the throb of too early a day and too late a night in my temples. I'm disappointed and relieved that she's not here. But I hear the scratching, the irreplicable sound. Pen to paper. I reach over. The empty space is the hollow in a tree trunk. The center of a whirlpool, spiraling. The emptiness is Meg. I stop, I listen. She's writing. I'm suddenly wide eyed at 4:13 in the morning. I stumble out into the hall. She's at my damn desk.

Christ, I don't know how long she's been at it. But it must have been from a few hours ago, given the piles of papers and the way she's worked through one notebook and on to the next. I should be mad when I see my own writings scattering the floor, tossed aside in anger or anguish. But I'm not. Not at all. I'm fascinated.

I've never seen it from this side before.

Sure, Gina had her mad moments. Being caught in the role, forgetting to answer her phone. Being with someone else, perhaps. But this. This is something that is uncomfortable in its familiarity. As if I'm watching myself from the outside in. The control of gaze and mind, the complete loss of the world around her. Meg writes like madness has lit a fire inside of her veins and the only way she can get it out is on the page.

I stay soft in my movements and start the coffee pot. I think of all the things I wish were done for me when I was in the middle of the alpha state storm. The Magical Lapse. She'll need coffee and food. She'll need space and quiet. I collect my own papers around her like the sneakiest butler alive, and set up a desk at the kitchen island. I watch. I write. But mostly I watch. Because it's captivating, her complete loss of the world. I set down coffee and a bagel next to her.

She writes.

I shower, unpack, start laundry. She writes. I write, she writes. I make sandwiches to the disgruntled request of my stomach. I make her one too. I set it down. She hasn't eaten breakfast; she's just writing. But I'm too frightened and respectful to look over her shoulder to try and read the streams and streams of messy handwriting and typed up notes that are coming from her.

It's not a deluge. It's a monsoon. I couldn't stop it even if I wanted to. Meg has been holding on to the thick of it in her chest for too long and I'm not some goddamn Dutch boy. I won't be sticking anything in the cracks to stop it up.

"Good. Just let it go, kid. All of it." I whisper and shake my head, before starting in on my own writing and notes.

Now, it's nearly five. She hasn't eaten. She should at least have water. I pour her a nice, cold glass and set it down. The words seem to be slowing, I feel her shoulders sinking. The body is weak even when the mind is willing.

"Drink something," I beg, and the fear from the glassiness of her eyes and the sad curve of her spine makes me hold her shoulder and kiss the top of her head. I lift the water to her lips, to remind her of the real world outside. The one she has to partake in, or she'll die.

She drinks, blinks, drinks some more, takes the glass in her own hands and I step away. She sets it down and continues.

I think about going to Gina's room. Leaving Meg to the demons singing through her fingers. But I don't. The thought is a passing cloud that holds no bearing. I don't want to stay with Gina tonight. Meg is alive and on fire and I watch the yellow-orange ochre of the sun paint lines across her face and shoulders as it passes through the sky on its descent. The dream, from last night comes back to me in harsh relief. In the midst of the scribbling and ticking of her thoughts out into the world, she is the sun and it hurts to look.

Don't look away.

Don't leave her.

MEG

Charlie sets coffee next to me and I write. The sun makes an arched brow, lazy over the horizon, and I write. Charlie sighs and sets down a sandwich next to the cold coffee, but I can only write. I can only eat words, drink the memories, and survive on the things I wish were future plans, real and imagined, all of it a garish mix of the madness in me and Charlie kisses the top of my head and brings me water.

"Drink something," he whispers and there's wetness to my lips and I write and I'm consumed more in the page than I ever was in my own skin, for days or hours, I don't really know. And Charlie says,

"Come to bed, Meg."

My hand, fingertip blistered and painful, knuckles cracking and tender, drops the pen.

"Come to bed."

I am a shell, brittle and aching, and all of my blood is spilled as ink on the page and I can't know if my legs will work. I sit back, slump and feel the world shift dangerously to the left and arms are around me. And his heart is pressed to my cheek and I sob, but I have no words and I have no tears. My soul is a dry crackle of bitter leaves into his neck and he speaks such soft words.

Rain on a dry dirt road, pattering salvation in syllables.

"It's okay, Meg. I've got you now." *Meg, Megan, Meg* over and over and the whispers are kisses on my skin, forehead and temple and …

Lips?

Soft and my parched soul reaches out to catch the sweetness. *Meg*, the rain whispers down my throat and every cell sighs back in relief.

"Charlie," I croak, "Don't stand at my grave and throw words," the corpse of me begs, sure that I am dying.

"Go to sleep, Meg," the warmth whispers and his body, smelling like soap and dryer sheets wraps me up, warmer than the cold dirt that used to cover me.

When I was dying.

CHARLIE

When it's eight o'clock, I'm tired of the worry. Her words have slowed. The faucet that was flooding is now only trickling. I watch her lungs, beneath ribs, beneath shoulder blades struggle and heave. The pen tilts in her hand. Brain weary and soul spent, I know this moment. I rise, stretch. I don't know if she'll eat, she seems unfazed by hunger, but the slump of her body tells me she's tired. I'm tired too.

"Come to bed, Meg." I whisper.

She drops her pen. Stares into the chaotic splatter of words and memories in no semblance of order to me. I sigh, kneel beside her and nod as if I've made this mess of my creativity before, and it will all be okay. Even though you feel like you've lost a lot of blood and you'll never come back from it. Even though you don't know what reality means when you've driven yourself this far mad, creating an entire world on the page.

"Come to bed," I say again. She sits back. I'm not sure if she even hears me, but she huffs and her whole body shifts and slides out of the chair into my arms. She feels like a feather blanket and I scoop her up close to my chest. God, I haven't carried anyone in a long while, but there she is and I feel like I could hold her for the rest of my life, if that's what she needed. I take her, across the paper-strewn floor, past the kitchen with its uneaten sandwich and cold coffee pot, sitting like artifacts in a museum, relaying the sad and virulent events of the past day. She presses her cheek into my chest and starts to cry.

I'm upended and stupid with love for her.

"It's okay, Meg. I've got you now," I whisper. Meg, her name on my lips, in my breath, the air in my lungs, the blood in my veins, *Meg, Megan, Meg*. Each time it's uttered is a kiss to her warm skin. Her cheeks, I lay her down. Her forehead. My lips follow the tracks of tears to her parted lips.

Meg. I kiss her softly. God, her lips are warm and giving like she's parched for kisses and I want to drown her.

"Charlie," she returns the prayer, the question, the answer when the pressure of my lips has released. Like kissing her has woken her voice and my heart stops for a moment and I wait for her to berate me, wipe away the kiss and the traces of me she surely doesn't want.

"Don't stand at my grave and throw words," she cries.

"Go to sleep," I say and cover her with the blankets. I put a glass of water on the nightstand, and some toast. Shades of my mother come back to me, a wave of nurturing. And all of those moments Gina left me to fester, enraged and starving wash over me too. I leave them at the foot of the bed, take off my shoes, and strip down to my boxers and T-shirt.

I should take the couch. Her breath is even and deep.

I should take the couch, but maybe I'll stay for a little bit.

*I should take the co*uch, but maybe I'll stay for a little bit and the first word of dissent from her and I'll go. I curl up on my side, facing her. My eyes won't close. I just need to watch her. Just for a moment.

I spend most of the night wondering if she's going to die.

Afraid.

Afraid that I will lose her, now, just when she's found herself.

Just when I've found her. Talking of death, looking like the pale corpse of the woman who's been annoying me for months. Meg will be fine. It can't be any other way. Because I can't stomach another loss, and Gina would hate me forever. I fall asleep in brief stints, waking to listen to Meg breathe and stare into the fixture above the bed. Sometimes she rolls over, presses her cheek to my arm and throws a leg across my hips and my body remembers the curve of a woman.

And the softness, and the taste, and ... desire rears its ugly, selfish head and wants Meg wrapped around me, and gasping into my chest. I shuffle, I ache, I tuck myself away from her and the painful pull of everything below the waist that I thought was dead. He's not dead. He's a bonafide jerk and he's desperate for her.

I think of chickens. And insurance offices, and poor reviews. I think of moldy salmon and bad martinis and all the things that turn me off about life. Until it's too disturbing and I move to leave.

But if she wakes up alone?

You'd better stay, I hear Gina smile. I adjust my shorts. Take a deep breath, grab my laptop from the side of my bed and start working on something, anything to spend the passion in a more fitting place. Aren't I past the stage of wanting sex? Aren't I too old for the bullshit of it all? I shake my head at my own foolishness and focus on the screen. One word, one quote, one page at a time. One scene.

The dawn comes up over the horizon like a mother checking in on her kids, asking how we slept.

Not good.

Why? Too conflicted and hard?

I roll out of bed to start the coffee and when I bring back a cup, Meg's still asleep. I watch her over the edge for a moment. I don't want to leave. Not just this room, but this life.

Gina didn't. She didn't leave the room, or parties, or dress rehearsals, or opening shows in faraway cities. She stayed with someone too. She stayed until she left this life. Until she left me. I'm a defiant and stupid child, sleep deprived, and lost in my own world. I sneak back into bed, set down the coffee and start to write again, renewed even in the exhaustion.

Meg moans beside me and scoots her nose into the pillow away from the loud, insulting light. Her ass is up in the air, like a kid on a Saturday morning, still thinking they have school and protesting. I stare at it.

She's not a kid. She is round lusciousness and more womanly than I ever remember her being before. But despite thinking I'm far too old, and am strongly against the objectification of any woman, especially my friend, I can't look away from it. The strange urge to lean over and gently bite her, shivers up my spine.

Jesus Christ. I should wake her up. I clear my throat.

"It lives," I say and she looks up with one eye at me where I sit, supposedly working and playing it *so* nonchalant that I'm sure she's not *at all* suspicious.

"*Lives* is generous," she says into the pillow. Goddamn it I want to pull her close. I want to, I want to … I need to make this no big deal. For her sake even more than for my own. She rolls closer to me. I'm far too busy to notice the warmth of her skin, her legs, her back closing in on me. She is spring sun to a snow-covered path.

Focus on the work, I type and sip my black coffee. Meg likes coffee, sweet with cream. I write her name into the line. *Meg is sweet with cream*. My work is working against me while Meg is pressing against me. Shit.

"What the hell happened yesterday?" she says, and I have to think carefully.

MEG

I wake up starving, and my mouth is dry and it tastes like tumbleweeds feel. Breakable and bitter. I moan into the pillow, even as my stomach growls up from the mattress.

"It lives," Charlie's voice is soft beside me, and from my unburied eye, I look up blurry vision to where he's sitting in bed, readers on, focusing on his page while a cup of coffee steams on the side of the table behind him. I mutter, feeling the memory of yesterday's catharsis, rolling over me like a slow, heavy wave.

"*Lives* is generous," I whisper into the pillow. I want to move but I'm weak, I want to get up but I think my will has been lost somewhere in all of the words. I roll closer to him. "What the hell happened yesterday?" I say, soft, not sure if I'm asking him or myself. Charlie doesn't look at me, so I'm pretty sure the question was in my own head.

"Something that was too long coming. Something I hope happens again."

"No," I argue and turn away from him. "God, please not again."

"You think the lapse is always supposed to be pretty? You think it's supposed to be all rainbows and butterflies?"

"Huh?" I stutter and look up from the pillow.

"You've been afraid of writing for too long and when you stop letting it happen, it will make you take the time." He smiles, all-knowing, and types a few more lines.

"I don't even know if what I wrote was worth anything."

Charlie closes his laptop and takes off the readers. He sighs. "It doesn't matter. It exists now. In the world."

I open my eyes again, to watch him watching me.

"Should it?"

"Yes," he whispers back. The truest, deepest yes I've ever heard. Then he shakes his head at me.

"How did I end up here?" the memory is fuzzy. The smell and warmth of his shoulder. Sweet words whispered. Kisses? Surely, he didn't kiss me. Surely, he didn't carry me.

"I carried you."

I groan like I've been hit and bury myself under the pillow. "Well, there's one nightmare come true."

"What?" he grouches suddenly and I scowl, one-eyed from the pillow, back at him. I'm horrified but I still don't want to leave the comfort of bed with him.

"A man, hefting my ass across the house? There's no lying on the driver's license now. Mystery is gone."

Charlie looks down at me, coffee cup in midair to his lips. "You're an idiot."

"Yeah, a whole lot of idiot. Tons."

"You know how sweet the weight of a woman is in your arms? Trusting, unguarded and asking to be close? I would have carried you for miles." He takes a sip and my whole heart in one sentence. I want to cry and crawl into his lap, trusting and unguarded, and make the world angry with the perfection of it. But my brain is stupid and foggy and I'm hungry. I make a strange desperate noise as the fatigue hits me. I reach my hand out and it finds his hip. Charlie is strong, and tense. I feel his muscles twitch beneath the pads of my fingers and the long loneliness in me perks up her head to feel his warmth.

I hold on as if I can't believe such a man exists, such an island, in such a storm. My eyes drift closed again.

"You need to eat. I put up with your bullshit yesterday because I know what that mental space is, but today you need to eat."

He knows what that mental space is? When the world around me collapsed and there are only words and a story to breathe and I can't hear or see anything beyond the page? When everyone I've ever known would have berated me, called me crazy obsessive, mocked me for daydreaming myself out of reality? He's just accepting that it's who I am?

My stomach growls again, forming a strong alliance with Charlie. He puts his readers back on, types a few more lines. When the caterwauling of my hunger begins to break his stride, he nudges me with a cold, bare toe to the thigh.

"Get up. Coffee is in the kitchen. And there's bagels. I saved the pages that fell on the floor, but I didn't pile them with the rest. Only you can sort that out. I also saved the doc on your computer and plugged it in to charge, you're good to go. But first, eat."

I grumble and shift, pulling my twisted shirt out from underneath me. I just want five more minutes.

"Eat, Meg."

"Ok! Jesus!" I growl and tumble out of bed, when I look back at him to give him a proper scowl, he looks over his glasses at me and his hands pause. The sunlight is hitting me in the face and I know I must look a damn mess. But he doesn't look at me like I'm a damn mess. He looks at me like a beautiful woman, tumbling out of his bed and into a sunbeam. He smiles.

"I suppose you want me to shower too?" I grouch it, if nothing else then to break the perfection of romanticism I don't deserve. His eyebrows raise with his shoulders, the perfect Jewish man shrug that says. *It wouldn't hurt the either of us if you smelled better.* But he doesn't say anything. His eyes drop to my legs and back to his computer, fingers flying.

The light, the madness, is in his hands now.

CHARLIE

"You're an idiot."

"Yeah, a whole lot of idiot. Tons." I put the coffee down. This is ridiculous. If I had an ounce less control I might pull her into my arms and put all thoughts of her inadequacies out of her mind. My stupid mouth decides to talk instead. And that's when I know I've fucked up. When it all starts to come and there's just no stopping.

I tell her I would have carried her for miles. What romantic idiot has taken up residence in my brain? I quickly grab my coffee and try to scald my wretched tongue. My stupid lips. She's going to freak out. But she doesn't.

She makes a sweet, needful noise and her hand reaches out and grabs my thigh. I nearly shake apart. Her strong fingers sink into my muscle and it connects us in a moment that leaves the rest of the world behind. Her eyes drift closed again. She has to be starving. And if her hand stays on me much longer, I'm likely to do something stupid about the very different kind of hunger in me. I bark at her to eat.

She stays still, like she's thinking through the endless pages. Thinking so deeply, that she might not even realize that her hand is gently kneading into my muscle, strong fingers possessive on my thigh. Her stomach growls again, offering me the excuse I need to get her out of my bed. I put my glasses back on, type a few incoherent lines before her stomach becomes so loud in its protest, I'm genuinely worried for her. I nudge her thigh with my toe. She rouses.

"Get up. Coffee is in the kitchen. And there's bagels." I take a deep breath, she needs to go, or I swear to God, I'll drop my work and make us both sorry for my loneliness. My tongue rushes ahead to stave off the incoming need. I try to remind her of the work now left in the aftermath. That she has something to do, other than be in my bed. Anything but be in my bed.

She grumbles, and removes her hand from my thigh. I breathe a sigh of relief. She shuffles and moves and tugs at her shirt. I think back to the morning I took her to Raymond's after the funeral. When her dress had been pulled too far across and the black lace bra and pale skin had greeted me at her door. My body pulls tight.

She needs to leave. Now.

"Eat, Meg."

"Ok, Jesus!" She bolts up and tumbles out of bed. Then stops, to glare back at me for disturbing her emotional hangover. And I stare at her, there, bathed in the morning streaming in from the window, an isosceles of light, running from her hip to her knee. She's got no damn pants on. I pause. When did she take them off? Why did I never notice how pale her skin was, or the freckle on the front of her right thigh? Because I've never seen so much of Meg's legs and it's my utter undoing. I smile like a damn idiot. Privy to what other men have surely overlooked before, in the minute detail of a freckle.

"I suppose you want me to shower too?" There's my grumbling Meg. I shrug but keep my mouth shut so I don't offer to save water and join her. My stomach clenches and my eyes find the freckle. Wondering where the rest of them are hiding on

Meg. I quickly put my eyes back on my work. I write it all out. I write every spiking painful ache. I write the stupidity of a man when faced with something that should just be a simple and uncomplicated 'no thanks'.

I begin an essay on the ridiculous nature of innocent encounters having the power to spark something in my soul. The madness is mine now. I pretend to ignore her until she leaves the room.

My hands are shaking like a teenage boy who discovered their first dirty magazine. Only there was nothing overtly seductive about last night. Nothing she did was meant to tempt me. She's just Meg and I'm an asshole.

"Stupid brute," I surprise myself with the loudness of words in a room without her. I need to kill this feeling in my chest and its effects southward. It's only going to cause us both pain and embarrassment. She wouldn't ever be interested in me. I'm too old and she's used to a sturdier brand of man. She likes pretty guys. Like Jonah Man-Bun. I bet he's a pretty one. I'm not pretty.

"Desperate men make stupid mistakes," the line comes out and I type it down quickly. I'm desperate. She's just confused.

Still, I think and touch my lips when I hear her curse in the kitchen, we kissed last night. Softly, warm and pressing as if I was breathing oxygen into her lungs below water. Like she needed the touch to survive. She kissed me back. Her lips found mine.

She wasn't in her right mind; I tell my ridiculous body and stupid romanticism.

"You're an idiot," I reprimand myself. When she curses again, I get up to see what's going on. She's just standing in the kitchen, still pantless, staring at a bagel, holding a bloody towel. Goddamn it, the kid has it bad. Writer's hangover. Her brain is trying to find one pathway to stick with. I'm not coddling her today. I have to pull the drawbridge back up.

"What? You just gonna hold the bagel all day? Trying to build an intimate understanding with bread? Eat!" I startle her and she spills her coffee. I stare at her as she bends down to wipe it up. For Fuck's sake, Meg, don't move until you have pants on. She stands up and glances at me with wide and deep eyes. I tell my brain to not misconstrue, to not project my feelings of want into those eyes.

"I know that look," I whisper and put my hands in my pockets to keep from coming closer, I focus on her face. The way she's staring at me, her lips pink. She shuffles her legs closer together. I need to stop entertaining possibility.

"You—you do?" she stutters. God, why can't I just keep my hands still? Why am I blushing? Can she tell? How much I want her, how my body's reacting to this stupid chemical urge? This emotional connection?

"You want to—" I start.

"Charlie, you know I wouldn't—"

"Write." I interrupt. I feel the heavy iron gate fall between us. Silence follows. She breathes out.

"Write. Right."

"Eat first."

"I'll eat during," she whispers, takes her bagel and her coffee and runs up the stairs to her space. I look away to keep my treacherous eyes from watching the soft bounce of flesh. I'm a horrible friend.

MEG

Who's had me shoving food at him when he forgets to eat, and making him laugh when he gets too much in the work ...

Gina's words are in my head as I pour coffee. What would she think, if she saw us now? Him being the one that pulled me up from the dark last night? Falling asleep together. That he might have kissed me. I touch my lips, absent from the present, and a heavy weight fills my heart. She had a lover. All those years. All of those moments I thought they were perfect in love, the epitome of what it meant to find your true soul mate, and she was with someone else.

And the rational, human female side of my brain knows that this is not a big deal. Because I've been there. I've been waylaid by distractions and failed to end one thing before starting another. Humans are fallible and partial to instant gratification. If she were lonely, I spill the coffee on the counter and wipe it up with a dish cloth, because he was writing all day and night, and off to open plays, and not being present with her ... I lean against the counter, blow across the top of the creamy, brown lake in my cup, rippling up tidal waves of unsettled thought. Who would blame her?

My heart is confused and tossed around and I grab a bagel and the knife. I saw through its tough skin, and my finger with a hissed curse. I hear typing from the bedroom behind me. I hear the soft noises of our cohabitation and the underlying wave of guilt hits me. My heart and my body are now on board with the ridiculous notion. Something twisted and warm in my guts begs me to bounce back into his room and tackle him.

But we all know what happens when I fall for a guy. I fuck it up.

It never turns out well. Not for any of us. Charlie's random lines from the other room, spin my thoughts into tighter spirals;

Stupid brute

Desperate men make stupid mistakes

You're an idiot.

I don't think he wants me the same way. He was forever Gina's even if she hadn't been solely his. What must that be like? To be someone's, even beyond death? I'll probably never know. The bagel shoots up from the toaster and scares me into spilling my coffee again. My brain swirls.

I need to catch this runaway train. I need to concentrate on my work. Maybe if I can put the effort on all of the raw material I mined yesterday, I can get this novel out. Then I can get out of this house. Maybe by then Charlie will be better and not need me. Maybe we can go back to being friends. Just friends.

My stomach turns, the hunger from before has turned into an angry, hurt-filled beast that's eating me from the inside out.

You can't go from love, back to friends, the cigarette smoking, street-wise angel says from my shoulder.

Not this kind of love. Not with Charlie.

What am I even thinking? Charlie's too high class for me. He'll never love me back, so it doesn't matter. Even if I told him, it wouldn't matter.

You just better not open your big stupid mouth and tell him,

Smokey says, blowing out a ring and an arrow that hits the bullseye.

"What? you just gonna hold the bagel all day? Trying to build an intimate understanding with bread? Eat!" Charlie startles me and I spill my coffee for the third time. He's staring at me, readers and bathrobe scowling with him. My wonky moral compass disappears back into my subconscious and I put both the coffee and bagel down to grab a towel to clean up my mess. I am suddenly aware, as I'm bent over, that I have left my pants on his floor. I shoot up quickly and hold the towel over my underwear.

"I know that look," he whispers, puts his hands in his bathrobe pockets and makes me blush by just being stupidly cute. My heart hammers, my thighs shake as I grip the coffee-stained towel.

"You—you do?" God, why can't I just keep my face still? Why am I blushing? Why is my stupid lonely body betraying me and our friendship? I shift as I feel heat spread across my skin, and lower. Does he know? Can he tell? God, this is horrible.

"You want to—"

"Charlie, you know I wouldn't—"

"Write," he says it, silence descends, my fingers loosen. I breathe out.

"Write. Right."

"Eat first."

"I'll eat during," I whisper, gather the cold bagel and the half gone-to-the-floor coffee and scurry up the stairs.

CHARLIE

If there's one good thing about writing, it's that when you're caught up in the lapse of it, the real world fails to exist. And that means you can effectively avoid the romantic and sexual thoughts that spring up after your best friend tumbled into your bed. You also, inadvertently hide all of the little things about them within the characters and lines. Things you never noticed before, like how she tucks her unstyled hair behind her ear or bites her lip when she does the crossword next to you. You can ignore her presence in the balm of being busy, typing away at a play you don't want to write, which sometimes turns into two characters that sneak away to rooftops to find a place for their hungry kisses. I delete that one, and at least three more like it.

I'm trying to stay focused, but the errant poem will spring up in the middle of my chaos, about the freckle on Meg's thigh or the way she shakes her ass in the kitchen to something asinine like Lynyrd Skynyrd.

Sweet Home Alabama suddenly becomes my favorite song.

Until I hear her singing *Always on My Mind* in the shower, because I parked myself outside of the bathroom to listen to the way her simple voice echoes against the tile and the warmth of the steam seeps through the crack in the door. She's always been on my mind, and more so now, and I'm torn between the truth of it, and the way it feels sacrilegious. The way a woman nests herself in my home is a feeling I thought I would not miss.

I have missed it.

I try to recenter, I put out a few more one-act plays. Memories from my childhood, when my mother was a saint and my father was a tyrant. But it feels old and done. I catch Meg over my shoulder one Saturday morning, reading and I spin around in the chair.

"What?"

"One-acts? What about the big one?"

"Where are your chapters?" I counter. Our deal fell away when we'd tumbled into bed together.

"I'm working on … other things." She blushes, and holds on to her tea like it might pull her out of the next question.

"What other things?"

"Just, stuff." She leaves the memory of her cheeks blushing over her cup to unsettle me the rest of the day.

It's absolutely ridiculous to think that she's having the same thoughts. I sigh and start back up. These plays are fine. I can write these all day. These can be sold in pieces. For high schools and speech meets, they're fine. I'm fine. I don't need to dig deeper.

"You can dig deeper you know!" she calls from upstairs.

"Says the pot to the kettle," I yell back. Meg mumbles something. I hear the creak of her mattress springs. I want to go upstairs. I want to catch her, in bed, in our mutual vulnerability, and flop down next to her, and tell her what a horrible time I'm having at it, and can she understand what an idiot the heart is?

I sigh, I hear Meg turn and grunt. Trying to get comfortable with our shared discomfort. I take a deep breath and close my eyes. Meg's voice whispers, patters through my head.

You tell the world about spring so they can have hope.

As if I could shut her out and focus on this crap fest of a play that I never really wanted to write in the first place. It is the start of a journey that I know will tear out my heart. Or maybe just the infected bits. I think of how brave she was on the night she spilled out the story of Cecily and her mom. Of how much it hurt her to bleed it out. Of the strange difference of calm that has defined her since then. Was it the writing? Or was it the bed?

What a narcissistic idiot I am. I sigh and open a new document in Final Draft. No more disjointed half-truths. Maybe it's safer to write through the hurt than to let my thoughts travel up the loft stairs and straight into the naked and heated bed I can't get mentally out of. It would be safer to get lost in Gina's life, than to admit I'm getting lost in a much worse place in my own.

I begin it as a catalog. Just the bare bones. An outline. I can't bear to make it word for word, the harrowing detailed steps Gina walked. And so, it is a slow and painful surgery, a less lethal cut, running parallel to a life I couldn't possibly put into words. It's about her, but it isn't.

It's about the incessant ache for fame and love, and all the ways we bend our souls to not be forgotten in our lifetimes. It's Gina's story. But it's also mine. It's a love letter to New York and its victims. Those starving kids in the freezing apartments, taking any job, role, or waitressing gig, just to feel the wooden planks of a stage beneath their feet. It's about a small-town Georgian who sang like a goddamn bird and fluttered into the hearts of Broadway.

It's about the men who loved her. All of them. Why wouldn't we? Who didn't fall hopelessly in love with Gina? I need the audience to understand. I will make them love her too.

Those words will be the hardest to write. Those scenes, those conversations. I'm not sure if I can take myself out of the grief to be an observer. Those are the days that I find my eyes pulled to the kitchen whenever Meg is down to get a snack; does she ever eat a full meal? Or when she's coming home from her shift at Satan's Little News Shop.

I can almost feel the lack of her care to write from the dragging shoulders and the way she throws her head back to groan when she shuffles in. I never hesitate to yell at her that it's not going to write itself. No breaks. Not for her and not for me.

If we don't stay busy … I look up and she's glaring at me over my laptop screen as she grabs a soda and her ass sways up the stairs. We have to stay busy.

MEG

If there's one good thing about writing, it's that if you're doing it right, you can close yourself off from the real world. And that means you can effectively avoid your awkward circumstance. The one you created yourself when you fell asleep in your best friend's bed and started entertaining sensual and romantic thoughts of everything from his long fingers, to the way he wears his bathrobe. Things you had taken for granted before, like the way his hair curls across his forehead and the soft tone of his words when he talks on the phone. How he giggles to himself and rubs his face when he's written a particularly good line. I can shut it all out and just focus on this crap fest of notes that I created in what I like to call, 'the frenzy'.

Some of them are completely indecipherable. Part poetry, part ranting insanity. I try to put those aside and aim for shifting things into chronological piles. How can this ever become a novel? Haven't I been fighting my whole adult life to keep this kind of chaos from the world? Even if I did finish it, who would want to read that? My Life of Grief is not literature. It's horror. At best, a series of dime store trash novels.

But Charlie said that I should embrace what I wrote during

'the frenzy'. That when words came out that way, they were meant to be in the world. I can't show this to the world, I think as I run the pads of my fingers over the tattered paper edges, stained with coffee and tears. The world is already nine parts tragedy and one part despair. I sift through them. I pause to read.

It's not all about her death, the loss, and the neglect. I find a page in the scattered throng with a story about Cecily and I riding bikes all day, like wild halflings in the abandoned streets of Pickering, Kansas. About the freedom of no watches or phones. The endless summer days that called us home with the streetlights came on, and the cookie sheet pizza mom would make from scratch. These are glimmers on the pages, threaded through the mess of my loss.

Were these the stories that made a life? Cecily's? My own? Could they make a book?

Charlie shuffles downstairs. It's been days since we really talked.

"I'm going for a walk," he grumbles. I pounce on it. I need air, I need something. I feel my fingers tremble as I come down from the loft.

I need him.

He's there, getting on his coat and he looks up at me. For the first time in weeks, he meets my eyes, unawkward, so I take the hint that we're doing this thing now. That we're okay and seeing me in my underwear was no big deal and he probably didn't really kiss me. We're okay.

"I'm going too." I don't ask and he nods at me.

"Fine."

"Is this a talking walk? Or a brooding walk?" I ask as I put on my coat and slip into my ridiculous red boots. Charlie puts a hat on, and shoves one of his own down over my messy bun to cover my ears.

"What's your poison today?"

"I dunno," I say. "I'm feeling torn and unsure." His eyes soften on me for a moment. A kindred in mind.

"Ah, finally a real writer, are you?" He raises his beautiful brows at me and I can't not smile.

"Psh, no. I'm just a two-bit hack, out for the quick-fix journalism award."

"Get outta this house, Kent," he grumbles and gently pushes me towards the door.

"How's your play? Your *real* play," I ask not ten feet from the front door and Charlie shoves his hands in his pockets. He scowls down at the dark rings of dried gum and cigarette butts on the sidewalk as we pass by them, like a concrete river of things used and left behind. Aren't we in the right spot?

When there is only silence, it occurs to me that maybe I shouldn't have started out so strong. I could have eased him into it. A little dialogue foreplay. Foreplay with Charlie. My face feels warm. What's he into? What makes him drop that aloof old man shell? We both know he's not as old as he acts. I think he likes kissing. I think he liked kissing me.

"Terrible," he interrupts and for a moment I feel like he read my thoughts as clearly as if they were running on a tickertape across my forehead. I cringe. "I mean, it's not terrible. But it's harder than I thought it would be." He shakes his head and looks out at the street, as if he's trying to find a shortcut through the hardest parts of this process.

"Yeah, I get that," I stutter. "It's hard to know where to begin, what to tell, and what's sacred. What to let—let go of. It's harder to play God to a story that already happened."

Charlie shakes his head. "I'm no god."

I have to hold back the words on my tongue. To me he is. A long-legged god with wild curls and absurdly unexpected brain waves that seem to hit his audiences in deeper layers. We cross the street, one block from the park. Charlie sighs and holds me back from walking into a cyclist. His hand lingers on my shoulder before he takes it away again to shove in his pocket. I wish it would linger longer.

"I'm just an unreliable narrator." Then he looks at me in an odd, piercing way. "I don't know how to tell this story without darkening it with—" he stops and shakes his head. My heart falls into a delicate puddle at my feet. With her infidelity. He doesn't want to turn vindictive with his words. He sighs. "I'm too bitter now to write about love with any kind of reverence."

"Charlie," I whisper, willing it to not be, "that's not—that's not true." He doesn't respond. I clear my throat and hop up onto a curb. He looks at me, now nearly eye level, and shakes his head.

"Where are your chapters? How is *your real* novel?" he counters. My mind and its stupid romantic musings start to rage in unsolicited thoughts through my brain. *How's my novel? You mean my collection of sappy love poetry, my erotic reverence of love and praise of you and your hands?* I clear my throat, and continue to walk towards the park.

"I'm working on some short fiction instead." It is not a lie. Not entirely.

"The trouble with novels, Meg, is that they don't write themselves," he says.

"The trouble with *my* novel is that it's a shit fest and we both know it."

"What you wrote that day was not shit, it was the closest thing to truth you've probably ever written. You're avoiding, Meg," he argues. I nod, he's not wrong. The poetic musings aren't truth. They're fantasy. The pain is real. My life is real.

"Yeah, I am avoiding."

"Because?"

He forces the truth, that the real story was the one that hit me like a fucking freight train across his desk. He knows what I should be writing. I know what I should be writing. Things that come out like pyrotechnic vomit to the page are things that know they have a place in this world. They are a voice to be listened to. But it scares the shit out of me.

"It scares me," I say plainly and we stop at the precipice of the park. "It scares me to talk about her, to bring her back to life when I spent so long burying her." He looks down at me, his eyes watery from the cold, the tip of his nose red.

"I know it does, Meg." I want to rest my forehead on his chest, I waver forward.

"Why aren't you even trying to write Gina's play?"

"It scares me too," he says softly back.

I can't do this. I can't be so far away from him. I sigh, a big shuddering sigh and throw my arms around his waist. Snaking my hands between where his arms have pinned him together. He's knocked back, not expecting the audacity.

"Meg."

"Can we just have a minute?" I say, muffled in his chest. It's a lie, I'm speaking a lie right into his heart. I don't want a minute. I want all the minutes. He could shove me away. But he doesn't. Charlie lets me get away with far too much.

"You sap," he whispers and his arms go around me.

"Maybe we just need someone to help us feel brave," I say, because if I'm going to be a sap, I'm going all in.

"And who would that be?" he whispers and I feel Gina is waiting off stage to make an appearance. She made us brave. She was the buoy that kept us both afloat. Now she's the anchor. If I tell him my thoughts, he'll let go. If I say *each other*, he might let go too, and I don't want him to let go. I hold on a breath longer.

"I guess there's no one here but us," I pull away. "So? What are we going to do about it? And by 'we' I mean me and your eyebrows." He stops to scowl before continuing on down the path.

"You need a deadline," he says, as if I'm the only one in this park with accountability issues.

"*We* need a deadline," I agree, but then my mouth just

continues on and leaves my brain at the station. "Enforceable. And punishable by what? Spanking?" Oof, that thought came out loud to the world. His eyebrow quirks down at me. His eyes go far away even as they stare into mine. If that were the punishment, I wouldn't write a word.

"One month."

"One month?" My mouth goes dry, my head feels dizzy. He's not joking.

"You finish your first draft in one month. No excuses, no stopping. No matter what."

My stomach turns and pushes acid into my throat. "Then you'll finish your play about Gina. The first draft in one month, and pitch it on the first."

"Impossible," he grunts.

"Possible."

"I can't," he argues back.

"Can't isn't in your vocabulary, Horowitz!"

"Fine," he yells and I smile at him. This time he watches my lips and in doing so, he's given me permission to do the same. I feel strange and unsettled and worried that this is all going to blow up in my face. Writing this book, writing this play … finding a catharsis to our grief, will drop too many walls and everything will fall apart. And even though I'm used to life taking away the things I love, maybe if I convince myself that I don't love Charlie, then we can survive this somehow.

I don't love Charlie. I don't love Charlie. I don't love Charlie. The words are the mantra of my feet as we walk through the park, keeping the beat of lies while he talks about the latest NYT bestseller list and what a crock of narcissistic bullshit it is. I'm not sure if he's trying to give me hope that someday I'll see my name amongst them. I am full of narcissism and bullshit, so I'm practically halfway there.

CHARLIE

One night she comes in, drops her bag and her shoes at the door, sighs as silently as possible and heads up the stairs. Not even a hello, not even a trip to the fridge. Not even a little hint of complaint to draw my ire. I watch the way she slumps at her work. It's been weeks since my bed held her. Since I felt the weight of her in my arms. Weeks since I watched her sleep and wondered what would become of us if we stayed that way. Weeks since I lost myself in writing half-assed plays and stumbling starts. Weeks since I forced her into the same state of penance.

Weeks since we walked. I look outside. There's the mascot of late winter; the dull gray haze of clouds and not yet melted slush on the city streets below. The month is no kinder than the last and less hopeful. I'd hear the whoosh of traffic if I listen, but my ears are already attuned to the shuffle of papers up there. She's pulled me out of the screen. She's pulled me out of the lie. I stand up and stretch.

I miss my Meg. I miss our talks and the way she teases me. This doesn't feel like her. This doesn't feel like us. I look at Gina's closed door; untouched mausoleum that reminds me of what she asked me to do. I sigh and get my shoes and coat on. What did Gina know?

"I'm going for a walk," I say to the haunted sounds in the loft. I hear her chair scoot back.

Shit. Shit. Shit. I'm nervous and elated, and what is this feeling in my chest like I'm in the seventh grade and I just asked Judy Dorsley to hold hands? Meg is coming down the stairs and she's smiling and I don't want to scare it away so I meet her eyes as if I wasn't in love with her. We're okay. It wasn't life changing to see her in her underwear, I certainly don't think about that freckle on the daily, and neither of us is sure if I even really kissed her. We're okay.

"I'm going too," she says and puts on her coat and red boots for the slush. I want to tease her about them, but I learned from Gina to never make fun of a woman's shoes. Not under any circumstances. I put a hat on, and take one of my others from a hook. I shove it down over her hair. Perhaps the more ridiculous she looks the less I will love her. I look her over. It's not working. Talking or brooding. Either way, I'm probably fucked. So, it's the lady's choice.

"What's your poison today?" I ask.

"I dunno," she says and her next words stop my self-flagellation. "I'm feeling torn and unsure." *Join the club, Meg.* But my mentor side calmly says it will take this one, and responds more appropriately.

"Ah, finally a real writer, are you?" I raise my eyebrows at her. She smiles back at me and launches into self-deprecation, as is her style. I push her out the door before I can kiss her quiet. Not ten feet out she starts in on me.

"How's your play? Your *real* play?"

I put my hands quickly in my pockets to keep them from being thrown up in frustration. I avoid looking at her and instead scowl at the sidewalk. How do I even begin? I watch the cars slow to a halt at the light and rev back up on cue. The heart of the city, its veins in constant motion to transfer the people through. Constant contraction, and release. Aren't we in the right spot?

"Terrible." I say. She doesn't say anything back so I try to release. "I mean, not terrible. But it's a lot harder than I thought." That untruth was not too untrue, right? Sure, it's going but its turning into some sort of weird erotic rambling of poetry and life advice, and questioning my soul. I'm a fucking mess. I look out on the street, the cars, the overwhelming urge to run into traffic abates when she lands beside me and tells me she understands. That it's hard to play God in a story that already happened. She's right. How can we? We can't bring them back. My thoughts progress, even if I was a god, I'm not sure what I'd do now with that kind of power. Probably fuck up, on a truly epic scale. Kiss that freckle every day.

She goes to cross and I see the cyclist from the corner of my eye. I grab her and hold her back as the man speeds past and flips us the bird. I scowl after him, my hand still on the round apple of her shoulder, right where it dips into her chest, connects to her neck in the pale tent of her soft skin. *Fuck.* I take my hand away and vow that will be the last time we touch.

"I'm just an unreliable narrator." I try to keep my inner thoughts where they belong. "I don't know how to tell this story without darkening it with—" something creeps out of the locked gate. She's discovered, her gentle prying, something I haven't even realized. I'm afraid to deal with the truth of Gina and I's last moments. What if I turn vindictive? What if I ruin it all? "I'm too bitter now to write about love with any kind of reverence."

She argues, says *Charlie*, a soft plea for grace I don't deserve. How does a man *not* kiss a woman? He doesn't by digging a stick into old wounds instead of putting his lips where they don't belong.

"Where are your chapters? Where is *your book*?" I shove my hands harder into my coat pockets and pretend that I can't smell the sweet oranges that seem to come from her neck the soft tease of a cool spring around us. I feel her smile in her words. She does not bite.

"I'm working on some short fiction instead."

"The trouble with novels, Meg, is that they don't write themselves."

"The trouble with *my* novel is that it's a shit fest and we both know it."

"What you wrote in the lapse was not shit. it was the closest thing to truth you've probably ever written. You're avoiding, Meg," I say. I know she's too afraid of what's really lurking in her mind. Because *that* story is too raw. It's too close to the center of her wounds. That is the novel she *should* write. It's the play I should write.

These are the hearts of our festering wounds. The night after Meg's sleepover, my writing has been tumultuous and raging, like a white foam river over rocky bottom. So much want and denial that I feel disgusted with the lack of thought and the overabundance of heart and loin filling those pages. And the misguided anger at myself that comes from what the world tells me I'm allowed to feel, to have, and which wounds should never close.

Wounds we write about in frenzied states that cause us to forget to eat and drink and live. Wounds that make us tear apart our wives' rooms and spend desperate and naked hours alone with her ghost. I know what Meg should be writing. I know what I should be writing.

But I know why we don't.

"Yeah, I am avoiding."

"Because?" I ask, already knowing she knows.

"It scares me," she says, putting my thoughts into sounds that break ahead of us on the sidewalk like startled birds. "It scares me to talk about her, to bring her back to life when I spent so long burying her." We both stop on the edge. Of the park. Of our greatness, we're both stopped. I look down at her,

I want to cry. *I know kid*, I sniff back tears. I know exactly. I tell her so. She rocks on her toes towards me and I want to let her fall.

"Why aren't you even trying to write Gina's play?" she asks the cold tip of my nose.

"It scares me too," I whisper. She shakes her head, takes in a breath like we're going to fall off a cliff, and quickly threads her arms in between the tight huddle of my resolve. It is warmth and comfort, and heaven.

And I can't do this. I can't be so close to her. I step back, but she's too tightly wound, a creeping vine to old stone. The fucking beautiful audacity of her.

"Meg." I breathe in the smell of my hat on her head. The mixture of our lives thrown together and the river of sadness that runs beneath us. *Let go, Meg. Please let go of me, before I …*

"Can we just have a minute?" the words rise up from where she's nestled in, warm breath on my neck, warm arms holding the cage of my ribs closed, keeping my heart in, even as it fights to get closer to her. She's asking for a minute and I'm an asshole, because I want them all. And I don't want her to want me. Because then I have to tell us both no.

"You sap," I say and my arms betray my mind to wrap around her.

"Maybe we just need someone to help us feel brave," she says. What is she, a romance heroine? I pull away, but she's hanging on and my heart feels fear.

"And who would that be?" I say. The person I hung on to and who hung the moon, is gone. The one who's hanging on to me, doesn't understand that she doesn't need anyone to hang on to. That she's a free-standing monolith of thought and beauty.

But neither of us is brave enough to admit it to ourselves. That we'll be okay. That we'll survive. We're too scared to try. Because Gina was the brave one. She was the one that got us up onto life's stage and made us be seen. Now it feels like she's the curtain between us. Heavy. Meg lets me go, quickly like I burned her.

"I guess there's no one here but us," she says, mock serious as she levels on me in my own tone. "So? what are we going to do about it? And by 'we' I mean me and your eyebrows." I can't laugh. I scowl and continue on, all business.

"You need a deadline."

"*We* need a deadline," she corrects. "Enforceable. And punishable by what? Spanking?"

The power of the human mind to conjure up images withing split seconds and burn them into your gray matter is really a thing of beauty. I feel a brow raise as a vision of her across my lap, unfinished pages strewn around us, fills my head. Holy shit, Meg. I have to bring this back down. All business.

"One month."

"One month?" there's a question at the end, as though she thinks that's preposterous and unattainable.

"You finish your first draft in the next month. No excuses, no stopping. No matter what." We're a circle of attempted failures, always coming back to what we *will* do. When neither of us is so sad, or so alone, or so scared. That beautiful someday over a horizon we don't have to worry about because it forever stretches out, unreachable before us. Meg takes in a 'can-do' breath. Fuck, here it comes.

"Then you'll finish your play about Gina. The first draft in one month, and pitch it on the first."

"Impossible," I argue.

"Possible! It's mostly done. Just rough edges to work out."

"I can't," I argue, more feebly than the last time she pushed me.

"Can't isn't in your vocabulary, Horowitz!"

I look down at her and sigh. Not true. I *can't* love her. I'm not supposed to.

"Well?"

"Fine!" I yell, angry that she could be right about that. Angry that it scares me to do it. She smiles. Stupid wide smile, those green eyes sparkling like winter forgot to steal the last essence of color and fire from the world and the gods hid it in her eyes. Fuck and those lips.

I've written pages alone.

I can write a play. Writing plays is what I do and there was nothing more in life that I loved more than Gina, except writing plays. If the world took her away, I would bring her back to the world. Immortalize her. Maybe then, my heart can clear a shelf off. Maybe then I can …

I stop myself.

The only truth is that we've been wallowing too long. It's let our imaginations do stupid things. It's let us off the hook moving towards anything that's real. We aren't real. Meg in my bed, isn't real. And the sooner I can get her on her feet, I swallow hard, the sooner I can forget she was ever there. Let's get to the center of the wound. I watch her turn pale as she thinks through the month ahead. Yes, this is the spot we hit, where all the festering gunk is hiding.

I nod and we continue walking. I feel like she's bouncing beside me, a rhythm in her feet that may or may not be a march to our mutual deaths. But for today, I'm in the park, with Meg and we're talking like we used to, and the grayness of the sky feels two tons of clouds lighter somehow. The sun even breaks through to the tops of the highest buildings.

Maybe we can stay this way.

MEG

I do the unthinkable.

I do one of the absolute worst things one writer can do to another. But I can't help it. Charlie left it out, on the kitchen counter, unguarded. He took the trash to the curb and I set down my coffee cup to fill. And there it was. Just lying there. Next to the warm and full pot. When I see words on paper, I automatically read them. I can't help it.

And when they're good words, brilliant words, arranged in a way that carries one thought to the next as if you're watching it on a stage in front of you instead of actively reading it, it becomes hard to stop. Even ten pages in … eleven, twelve … Even when you hear the door slam and the snow being knocked off of shoes and his steps into the kitchen. I know that I need to stop and pretend like I didn't even notice it, but my eyes betray me and cling to the white paper and black ink even when my saber tooth tiger warning system tells me I'm being watched.

"Hey!" he yells. I gasp in air that his words caused me to forget to breathe. I jump away. But my eyes linger, I just want to read one more line. "Megan!" Full name and everything

"Charlie," I breathe in sharply and clutch my heart, not only from being startled but for feeling something that only Horowitz can evoke. The story that only he can write. The ache that only Charlie can put in the chest of his audience.

"That's not done yet."

"Then why'd you leave it out?" I say back. He purses his lips together, that's what they call it, right? When he clamps them down together in an air of annoyance.

Charlie purses his soft lips together when he stares at me.

"Because it's not ready yet and I need to you tell me what you think of the first act. And since I don't know when you'll actually be done, I thought this might inspire you to get some pages on my desk." *Ooo*, I want to hit him. I throw a dishtowel at him instead.

"You're showing me yours so I'll show you mine? Why didn't you just bring it to me? Why did you bait me?" I laugh. He laughs back and all is beautiful spring in the city. The entire world spins at just the right speed and I forgot life could be so bright.

"Because I know you're a master at it," he says, wiggling those damn eyebrows, and I feel my cheeks get hot.

"And I thought I was being quiet about that," I return and Charlie blushes this time.

I come back to the script and start to flip the pages again. He's got his arms crossed over his chest, one hand on his mouth, watching me read. My heart ticks up, my fingers flip pages faster. I'm on the stage. I'm in the audience. I'm in the story. I'm standing beside her. I've missed her so. Charlie has painted her, complex and bright, a star you can't gaze at too long. I am in her orbit again, and watching as she falls in love with Charlie, and the stage, and he falls in love with her.

Charlie in real life starts to pace. He puts his hands in his pockets, he leans against the counter next to me. Gina is fire and storm and I miss the way she tangled into my life with love and expectation, I feel my heart clench. He his building her into brightness and love, even when she caused him so much damage.

Charlie lowers his head while he watches me. It becomes distracting. I look up.

"What?"

"I'm waiting."

"For what?" I whisper and that's when I feel it. A tear slips down my cheek, then another, and another.

"For that," he whispers and reaches out to dry them with his thumb. I sniff and dry the rest. He's standing close now. His eyes fall to my lips and I bite them and shake my head.

"You'd better pitch this, now."

"It's not ready."

"Fuck you, it's not ready," I sniffle and shove his shoulder. "The world needs spring, Charlie. We've never needed it so badly."

He shakes his head at me. "It still needs reworking. It's not finished." He sighs and his hands hold my face while he plants a kiss on my forehead. "You're gonna be late for work," he says, then he's gone, back to his desk, back into his world.

"I'm supposed to work in this emotional state?" I grouch over my shoulder as I dump the coffee that has gone cold.

CHARLIE

I leave it out for her. I'm taking out the trash and I know she's going to look. Meg can't not read something that's out. I even put it beside the coffee pot, not to be missed. I take my time on the street corner. Huffing out clouds of air while I wonder what she's thinking of it.

Is she laughing? Is she crying? Is it the stupidest thing she's ever laid eyes on and she's already abandoned it. I come in, heart beat thrumming through my ears as if my blood can't be still. I knock the snow off of my shoes and hang up my coat, I trudge into the kitchen and stand at the doorway. She's biting her lip, she's hunched over it, greedily like she's trying to gobble it all up before I get back. My heart swells. How many more pages can she get in? Now comes the fun part …

"Hey!" I yell, hiding my smile as she takes in a deep breath and jumps away. She doesn't look at me because her eyes are addicted. Shit, is it that good? "Megan!"

"Charlie," she gasps and puts her hand over her heart. Such a Meg tell that she's been affected.

"That's not done yet." I'm trying to be serious, but the laughter is having a hard time staying contained and I have to press my lips together to imprison my growing joy. The game is too hard to play, and I can't keep a straight face when she throws a towel at me for scaring her. I tell her I did it to encourage her to get me her pages. So she knows that we're in this together. When she laughs the quiet Monday morning is a heaven I don't deserve but I'm going to steal the moments of anyway. Who knows how long it will last?

Meg goes back to the play. She flips the next page and the next and I can only stand in vigilance, refocusing my mind away from the way she bites her lip. I focus instead on the fear that at any moment she's going to push herself away from the pages and tell me it's all terrible. I pace. I feel the scratch of the stubble above my lip and put my hands in my pockets. I can't hold still, not while her eyes trace over and over and pages are flipping. I'm studying the way her face is changing, her eyes are filling, her teeth grab onto her lip and I long ... I ache. She looks up.

"What?"

"I'm waiting," I say, coming closer.

"For what?" she says, her lip shaking. My thumb picks up the first heavy tear but more follow down her cheeks.

"For that," I whisper. She sniffs and dries the rest on the cuffs of her sweatshirt. I don't want to step away, I don't want space between us. I need to be close to her thoughts. I want to be even closer to her lips, to feel the truth of them against mine. God, I'm lost.

"You'd better pitch this, now" she says.

"It's not ready."

She argues and shoves my shoulder. Angry and playful and shocking me back to myself. She tells me the world needs spring. That the winter has been cold and dark and the world needs the beauty of my words.

I shake my head. "It still needs reworking. It's not finished." I'm scared of the ending. I'm scared of what she'll say the ending should be. Or what it shouldn't. I want the moment in the park.

The moment she held on to me, so that we could both be brave. I hold her face between my hands and kiss her forehead instead of those lips. "You're gonna be late for work."

I can't kiss Meg; I can't finish the play. I can't do anything. I'm a man frozen in both want and fear. I take the unfinished play and all of my vulnerability and head back to my desk.

"I'm supposed to work in this emotional state?" she grouches over my shoulder and dumps her coffee in the sink.

Yeah, kid. If I have to, so do you.

MEG

I thought I'd reached the apex of stupidity. Perfected the art of crossing boundaries and shoving myself into his business, but the truth is, I have a panache for taking it one step too far. Especially concerning my faith in Charlie. This time I reached out to Jerry. Jerry's not a former actor-lover. He's definitely not a man-bun. Jerry is a mutual friend, and one who I know has been worried about Charlie. I sent him a teaser. I told him Charlie was working on something beautiful but that he was afraid to go too far with it. Afraid to finish it.

I wrote that it was really important that he finished this one. And could he take a look?

And I suppose it's a parallel train to the importance of finishing my own novel. So the world would know them. So that we don't have to carry all the grief in our gray matter, alone. We could spread it around, a shared load with the world. To let it be known that things we loved were taken. But we still remember. And now they can too.

My novel was a sputtering and jagged-edged trail that meandered from childhood, off the cliff, and back to adolescence and to the variety of Bradleys taking bits of my soul before they left, to my mother's job as a teacher, to how she lost it, getting drunk and falling asleep on recess duty. To the first time I bought a fitted dress, not from K-mart. To the loss of Gina. I'm trying to make sense of it but, much like my own life, it's a twisted footpath. Filled with brambles and mishaps, scraped knees and predators in bushes. I'm molding it together. Anytime I'm too quiet, he yells the days left us up the stairs.

It starts to make my stomach hurt.

CHARLIE

One day I get a call. I mean, I get a lot of calls, but this call is a bolt of lightning and unexpected. I wasn't even in the stages of wanting to send the play out. A week ago, Meg insisted that I talk to a few people in the business, feel out the concept. If, for no other reason, to dust off the dregs of grief and be able to finish it. I told her it still wasn't ready. So, I wasn't expecting this call and certainly not from a big director. A long-time friend of Gina's.

He has been through my catalogue. He knows my work. A funnier Tennessee Williams, says the guy. Fuck, please, no. Anything but that. But the concept of my newest play has struck a chord. It wouldn't have even been on the guy's radar, except he'd heard a rumor from a "reliable" source that I had something big coming. I scowl at Meg as she grabs a banana and scribbles on her first printed draft.

"Would you consider yourself a 'reliable' source?" I grumble. She looks up at me, mouth full of banana and talks around it like she's just won "Best Hog" at the Kansas State Fair.

"Huh?"

"Would you say my first draft is ready to pitch?" I change

tactics. She raises her brows and swallows. I watch her cheeks burn as she shrugs nonchalantly.

"Your first draft is another playwright's fifth, just do it."

"What about your novel? Have you pitched it to that agent I told you about?" I'd countered but she just shook her head.

"My first draft is just like everyone else's, a piece of shit."

She leaves the kitchen quickly, neither denying nor admitting her guilt. Jerry, big time director on the other end of the phone, wants to talk details over dinner. I have half a mind to kick her out for being so pushy. But if it turns out to be nothing, I would look like an idiot. Then again, if it turns out to be something, what does it mean?

I don't want her knowing where I'm going later that evening, so I yell at her that I'm going 'out' and she says 'fine'. And I wish it weren't fine. I wish she'd come down the stairs and worry for me, give me that hard-assed Midwest stare with her head slightly cocked, asking without words if my intentions are for the nearest bridge. But it's only 'fine'. Just fine and maybe she suspects I have enough to live for now.

Do I?

What if this meeting is something? I look back at Gina's closed door, and back up to the clicking sounds of Meg in bloom. Should I take it as a sign that this is the final act, and that maybe I should try to move on? Isn't that what humans always do? Even if I don't know how to human anymore? I grab Gina's scarf and head out the door, to the sound of typing and Meg sniffling, trailing from above me.

MEG

I think I'm busted. I hadn't expected Jerry to call so soon, but when Charlie asks if I think I'm a reliable resource after giving me that "what did you do?" look I think it's because I started pushing his play. It wasn't right of me. To leak the information, to force a conversation. But sometimes you stop building bridges out of your grief, even when they're leading to better places. I just put a couple of pylons down over that river in hopes he wouldn't stop building. He goes back to his work, and I stay upstairs like the kid who got caught stealing.

My phone has fifteen unanswered texts on it. I use the antsy energy, of what might be happening to Charlie right now to read through them. She asks if I can come home, or if she can come here. If we can see each other, at least once before the summer. Before the end. I haven't told Charlie she's found the back door into my life again. I haven't told him about my 'role' as her power of attorney, or of her resurgent cancer. And maybe that's because I haven't committed to any position in her life, and it still could end up being another one of Eileen's unfinished deals. But she's standing in my peripheral vision all the same. At least her imminent death is.

I haven't decided what to do. Maybe this is my bridge, half-built, that I'm afraid to cross. But nobody is carting in materials and building up pylons for me. It just me, standing at the edge of unfinished business, hesitating and making up excuses to never get over it. I've been keeping my heart and mind away from her. And my book.

I can't admit, even to myself, how badly I want to climb into Charlie's lap instead of being stuck in my own miserable words.

I hate to think of how badly I want him to press his loneliness into the hard lines of my avoidance. How I want to move past this awkward space between us that settled in the day I stumbled out of his bed. I know I shouldn't have ever been there, but even when I got up to write after that night, it was Charlie that brought me back to his bed. Charlie brought me to his bed. He could have woken me up and nudged me upstairs or dumped my ass on the couch. But he brought me back to his bed and let me sleep there. All night. I put my phone down, thinking.

I had been building up my self-blame for weeks now, but I never considered that maybe Charlie wanted me close, as much as I wanted to be close to him. But what do we do about it now? I look down at my shitty first draft.

I reach up and touch my forehead. He kissed me there too. After reading his draft. He moved me. The words blur in front of me and I sigh. If I can't make sense of my heart, how in the hell would he ever be able to? I pause, stare blankly into the page, a million miles from done, and all I want think about is Charlie. Not my mom, not all of the life that's spinning around me that I can't control or stop. Not this shadow of a novel that feels all at once too abstract and too precise when it cuts to appeal to any audience. And I wonder if this is my mechanism. When life gets too big, too hard, too heavy-weighted to the past, why do I always turn away from it to find the sunlight of distraction? Why not charge through the pit of it, and spare him the weight of me?

But Charlie is not so much sunlight, as a safe shore.

Something I feel compelled to reach; a home that knows. He is a story teller. He says I am too. I always have been. That I've hidden behind the screen of journalism, because it was easier for me to tell other people's stories than my own. I look down and my fingers tap the page. He carried the weight of me in the middle of that storm.

I think of my sister. Of the stories she never got to tell. Of the adventures she never spread her wings for. Of the love she never had and the Charlie she never found.

The thought punches me in the gut.

Life is so fucking fragile and unpromised that you could never have a Charlie in your life.

That the world may never know you.

Why aren't you writing?

I can hear him say, as if he's standing behind me. Not downstairs, pissed off that I meddled in his life. I feel my sister step up beside him, long flaxen hair, like wheat in sunlight, swaying past her shoulders, freckles sprayed across her nose.

Why aren't you writing?

I look at my screen blankly and shake my head. I close my eyes. I'm on the subway listening to Charlie echo back to me.

Why don't you write about her? And us answering each other.

"I did, Charlie," I whisper.

Not Cecily. Why don't you write about her?

"Who?"

Meg. My name on his lips is a whisper back, like the night he carried me to bed.

Meg. Megan, Meg ... My name like cold kisses behind my ear and I shiver.

"Why? Why me, Charlie? I'm a nobody." I say softly to the dark and empty. But Charlie is quiet in my mind. Because I know the next line. "So, the world will know her," I whisper softly, and my hands pause on the keys.

This story isn't Cecily's.

It's mine. I scoot my chair in and start to cut and paste the mismanaged notes into semblance. My whole being fires back to where I began. Steps from the past, and how they come back to my future. How not having a dad around, made me look up to any man that came along. How getting out of Kansas was as much an escape as a loss of myself. How on a dark Kansas highway, the intersection with a curve too tight, I was vaulted into an adulthood without a safe shore. It runs alongside a train where a man who would be my greatest inspiration and hardest battle was waiting at the end of the line, to ruin my first experience of New York by being perfectly Charlie.

Maybe that's what happens when you write the story that's been burning a hole in you. The doors open out and away from your grief.

"I'm going out," I hear him in my brain. I speak softly, like I do anytime I'm talking to myself.

"Fine."

I don't notice the time because I'm no longer in my loft, in the house, on the street. I am in the words and there is no other reality.

CHARLIE

I've been in the business for most of my life. Ever since I was a kid, wet behind the ears and full of stupid youthful optimism. So none of what Jerry says or talks to me about is a surprise. The themes and scenes he'd like to see made, the nuances that ought to be kept. The need for more pizzaz, the desecration of several of my ideas, that we can discuss later. None of it is surprising except when he says;

"I'm so glad to see you again, Charlie. You know, I thought you weren't going to write again. Then this ballsy reporter reached out to me to told me that she'd beta read this play and hoped I wouldn't be an idiot and pass it by." Jerry laughs in that kind twitterpated way that men do when they've been faced with the Kansas tornado that's currently occupying my loft in a fit of her own procrastination.

"Oh yeah? I'm not familiar with her," I lie. Jerry quirks an eye at me.

"No?"

"She's sounds like a meddling idiot."

"She was right. I'd be a moron to let this fall in someone else's lap. I'd like to take it. But Charlie, this has to be big. No side street Broadway. This is brilliant and I think it's gonna shine."

Jerry goes on and on, and this is a chance for a lifetime of something different, a new shooting star to pursue, a reason and purpose in my life again. A story about Gina, her life, her passion, a hit and maybe should we talk to a composer? He's really getting musical from this, and on his dynamic world building goes.

My brain is frozen on Meg. Fucking Meg Kent. Was right. And the world is tipping over. I'm not ready. I'm not ready to immortalize Gina. Because that means I have to let her go. Even in a small way. Jerry stops and I look up.

"That's a lot to take in," I whisper.

"It is. Let's meet next week on it. I'll talk to some people."

"Fine," I nod. "It'll be yours. If and when I get it done, I won't shop it around until we talk."

"Just what I wanted to hear," Jerry chuckles and checks his watch. "I gotta get to the *New Kids* after party." He pays for the meal, shakes my hand, but before he leaves, he turns back to me.

"If you don't know Meg Kent. You should get to know her. That woman has fire, I think she's going places." Then he leaves, on with life, a bee buzzing from one nectar pot to the next.

"Get to know Meg Kent," I grumble and feel her lips beneath mine, a memory on replay ever since the original. The world is moving too fast. And my grief is a parachute behind me. I get the waiter's attention and order a double on the rocks.

What will I do? Gina's words rumble around in the back of my mind like a loose watermelon in the trunk.

If you don't love that girl for the rest of your life, I'll never forgive you.

"If it were just that easy," I grumble and let the drink sink into my soul. If it were just that easy to love Meg Kent. If anything, it was too damn easy to love her. And I couldn't do it. Not in the way she needed love. I am an insufferable ass, and I can't love Meg Kent.

I'm a man unhinged. I don't know what to do with myself now that Meg has erupted inside of my chest. I guess I lied to myself, for a long time. Because I already had a love in my life. I already had Gina. Why would I ever ask for anything more than that? But Gina is gone now, and her memory has been soiled, by all the ways I failed her and all of the secrets she kept. All of the lies. It makes me forget the good we were. The beautiful life we really had on the surface of so many ugly things.

Meg, and all her horrible imperfections, was always just there, and so see-through and honest with her faults that I never saw her for the beautiful puzzle she was. That is until the night she fell asleep at her desk, toppling into my arms, trusting and warm, and asking me to take care of her.

Having her there all night next to me, the madness drained from her body and the creative genius spilt in ink across the page, was the best night I slept in over ten years. Waking up with her next to me, I couldn't stop writing. I couldn't stop creating. But the truth was, it really started the day she moved in, and I made her write at the table with me. To establish a boundary. This was to be a creative endeavor. But it built pathways, and I couldn't stop coming back to life. It shutters through me with guilt.

I can't love her. I'm not that kind of man to her and I never will be. I'm too old and I'm not available for a lifetime of love anymore. I've already spent that money. I am love broke. But Meg still has a chance. She should find someone, young and vivacious, someone who can still go places. I have already been. I stare down at the empty drink, and order another.

I knew I'd never sleep without it, because I don't think I'll ever sleep again. Now that I know I love her. That I know what it is to sleep with her in my arms. That I know it will never work out. And I'd rather not get on the train, than to get on just before the crash. The bartender sets the new glass down, and I begin the slow unraveling of my soul in an effort to forget that I ever loved Meg Kent.

.

MEG

Charlie isn't home. That's my first thought when I come out of the lapse sometime after midnight. It's not like him to be out even past ten. I inhale deep, sit up, stretch, save my work and stand. The house is quiet, the lights downstairs are still on. I go down to the base of the stairs and listen at the closed doors. Perhaps he's turned the corner and become the ghost. Or maybe the ghost is me, unaware of the living in the house, while I'm stuck in my own words.

My eyes fall on Gina's door. The room of ghosts. The mausoleum. The sacred ground that only one of the monks living in this brownstone can enter. I'm not worthy. But I am curious. And Charlie is still out. Perhaps he's fallen into the dark; the place I promised to keep him away from. Perhaps he's too much in the dark and I've failed her.

I've failed them both.

If she knew how much I loved him, would she hate me? Not even a year of her being gone, and I'm already too deep to back out. Even when I told him I should leave, tried to get away from my feelings, I couldn't. He wouldn't let me.

I look at her closed door again. I take in a deep breath, as though I'm going to plunge into cold, cold water, and maybe drown. A dozen chances to turn away and go back up the stairs line the path between me and that door. A dozen reasons, and excuses, and moments to change my mind, to make a different decision. But I keep stalking it all the same as if all the answers to the mystery of Charlie's quiet and closed heart, are just locked beyond the turning of knob. I stand, bare feet clenching on the precipice, and my hands grace the brass handle, the worn wood. What secrets are they keeping, together in her tomb?

"I'm sorry, Gina," I whisper and turn the handle. The click of the brass fitting scraping against its worn hole is loud in my ears and the door sticks, not on the old wooden jam, but on something against the floor. I push harder and the door gives way, trapping one of Gina's brightly colored scarves beneath it, and wedging the door open. A sharp shaft of light knifes against the far wall. Very Hitchcock. I should not be here.

I try to close the door but it's stuck on the scarf, so I have to bend down to undo it. My eyes fall to the paper shrapnel of letters and notes, cards and pages, some torn in half or in pieces, some clutched and blotched with dry stains. Tears. Charlie's tears. The bed is bare of covering, no sheets nor blankets. They're torn to the side too. Great heaps of destruction and remorse.

The air is thick and repentant, and I can feel him lying here. Night after night. A grave of a man, trapped in his own personal hell. A perfumed purgatory. Was it always this way? After the funeral, or did it only come after I planted the seeds of guilt in his bed? Because I crossed the line? Is this all my doing?

"Jesus, Charlie," I whisper and kneel down to read the scattered debris. I only make it through two of the love letters from Don. Then my stomach is sick and I want to throttle the man. I hate how angry I am with Gina. I hate that my head hurts in the center of my forehead, deep, like I've scowled myself into a migraine. How could she have accepted all of this?

When Charlie was here, right here in the same home with

her? When she had him in her pocket; all of his love, all his words and devotion, all of his mourning after her death. I tighten my hands into fists, crumpling the carefully poetic musings into the trash they feel like in my mind. He must feel discarded.

He must feel so stupid, so blind, so betrayed. Every night, all the nights. He must feel so unloved. The strange dropping in my stomach comes with questions.

Did being with me that night, the caring for me, the kisses to my forehead, the tender taste of his lips on mine, the way he'd carried me away from my grief and into a sanctuary of his arms ... Did it break something inside of him? Is he paying because I leaned on him? When the woman he loved so deeply, leaned on someone else? Does he think he was unfaithful? Does he think he is unloved?

I sniff and wipe my nose on my sleeve. Except he's not. I cough and drop the wadded-up love note next to her scarves and robes, and scattered jewelry and playbills and perfume bottles. I know I'm not the beautiful actress. I will forever be in the shadow of Gina, and the lifetime they had. I am a plain and poor substitute. Undeserving and common with my three pairs of shoes and nothing with designer labels in my closet. My unfinished novel and the destructive string of semi-talented actors behind me. My stupid tragic past with no character building to show for it.

I may not have a sparkling personality, or a voice that carries in a room, or a presence that commands admiration. But I have my heart. And my heart has been his since that first minute I stepped off the train all of those years ago, to stand in front of him and hear him call me *kid*. I've loved him at every turn of my life. I loved him when I told him about the latest boy leaving and probably secretly hoped he was jealous. I loved him when he held me close after the funeral and whispered *my girl* into my hair, even when I knew I wasn't the girl he meant.

I loved him when he saw me through the storm of my writing.

I loved him even more when he told me to get back into the torrent. I loved that he followed me into the streets and brought me back home. And I loved him for every wasted breath he spent in this room when a lesser man would have been with me.

I want to see him through this storm and bring him back home. Because I love Charlie and I don't want him to sit in this room anymore. Regretting a past he didn't choose and wasting away into the nothingness of loss. Not when he's my whole world. And everything I've ever loved about myself.

I leave the room; I wash my face. I brush my teeth and put on clean clothes. I take deep breath after deep breath and convince myself that there's no other way this can go. Not now. I've reached the tipping point and no play, or writing stint, or breakfast of bacon will be able to staunch the wound. It needs to bleed. The truth needs to bleed.

I pace. He's not home. I sit on the couch and wait, and my shoulders feel heavy and stuck. I stand up, I go to my room, flop on the bed, rub my eyes, stand up, go to my desk, and write. I write and write. I pull together my notes for the novel, anything to distract my mind from the atom bomb I'm about to drop.

The door downstairs bangs open and startles me. I pause and save my work.

"Charlie?" I yell.

There's shuffling, the door slamming closed, he coughs.

"Who do you think it would be?" There's a slur to his voice. Jesus, please don't tell me he's been drinking. I need him clear, to hear me out. I rush to the top of the stairs and he's there, staring up at me. Scarf around his neck, coat undone. Blue eyes sad. His fists are clenched.

"Charlie, are you ok?" I whisper and walk down, slow. Like I'm walking into the light at the end of my life. Or to a firing squad. I can't tell from his expression if its bullets or beginnings he's holding in wait for my heart.

"Why are you still up?"

"I've been writing," I whisper.

"Good," he says.

"How was … dinner?" I ask. He scowls down at me.

"Fine. Seems someone has a big mouth."

Heat erupts in my chest and I feel it spread to my cheeks. He must have been meeting with Jerry. I shrug. "Sometimes things need to be said." I take a deep breath as if trying to tell myself this was it. I have to fucking say something. But for all of the pep talking I'd done, I actually didn't rehearse what to say.

"Some things shouldn't," he turns away. I feel defeated already and angry.

"Damn it, Charlie! I can't stay quiet; you know this about me. Are you angry with me?" is what comes out of my mouth. Like my head and words decided to work against me. Charlie hangs up his coat and his hands pause on the fabric. His head falls.

"Yeah, Meg. I am"

"Please, Charlie I need you to tell me what I did wrong. Was it because I talked to Jerry? Or is it more? Because I slept in your bed? Was it because I went into a writing coma? Is it because I haven't finished yet? Is it because I hugged you in the park? Was it—"

"It's not any of that!" he yells and turns around, surprised that I'm closer than I was when he'd turned away. I'm surprised too. My body can't stand the separation, and I've moved closer with every desperate question.

"Meg," he whispers and rubs his face tiredly. I'm close enough to touch, to pull into his arms. I smell his skin, the undertones of scotch, the quiet softness of his exhaustion. The words tumble out of my mouth.

"I need you to know something important, okay? Because I can't … I can't stay quiet anymore."

"Meg—"

"I love you, Charlie."

CHARLIE

When I get home from the dinner, it's late. Later than I normally stay up. The bartender was generous and my wallet opened easy for a cab home. I know she's home. I know she'll come at me with questions and given what a romantic idiot I was the last night I drank (*I still can't believe I quoted Shakespeare into her breasts ... Jesus Christ*) I try to make a concentrated effort to get to bed undetected and unbothered. But just as I come in, the wind whips around me and slams the door into the wall.

"Fuck," I grumble at the ghost of Gina, no doubt calling Meg downstairs. To put in place a plan she'd long hatched ago. Maybe she's asleep or buried in her headphones. She doesn't stay up late. I'm taking off my shoes haphazardly, like a toddler kicking them off, just as hateful as he was putting them on.

"Charlie?" Her voice calls down and stops me. I trip over my shoe, bounce off the wall and nearly fall.

"Who do you think it would be?" I mumble. Just the stupid man who can't seem to get over any woman in his life. Who has all the ache to love but none of the heart to give. I look up, as she crests the stairs, the light from her lamp haloing her head. Christ, I want to fall to my knees and cry. Coming home, to Meg, anxious to see me. How did I ever let it get this far? My fists tighten at my sides. I've really fucked it up.

"Charlie, are you okay?" Her voice is soft, and she's coming down, slow, concerned. *No kid, I'm not.* Weeks of not saying anything of meaning, of pretending that I don't love her. Of having her retreat into her writing, yet every time she's near me the existential hope that springs in the dead cave of my chest feels like it might break me apart.

"Why are you still up?" My voice is a grating of gravel over iron.

"I've been writing."

"Good."

"How was dinner?" she stutters. Like she's nervous for the outcome. The play about Gina, me moving on.

"Fine. Seems someone has a big mouth." The accusation is meant to turn her away. In Meg fashion, it does not.

"Sometimes things need to be said." She's holding something back. Something big. She shuffles awkwardly, she puts her hands in her back pockets, she's rocking back and forth. What the hell is wrong with her?

"Sometimes they shouldn't," I warn her and turn around. I feel her rush towards me and the tense words hit my back, right up my spine.

"Damn it, Charlie! I can't stay quiet; you know this about me. Are you angry with me?"

I hang up my coat and my hands pause on the fabric. That's it, she's felt the way I've retreated. My head falls. Maybe this is the way I let her go.

"Yeah, Meg. I am," I lie.

"Please, Charlie I need you to tell me what I did wrong. Was it because I talked to Jerry? Or is it more? Because I slept in your bed? Was it because I went into a writing coma? Is it because I haven't finished yet? Is it because I hugged you in the park? Was it—" She goes on to list all of the beautiful, wonderful, stupid ways she's Meg and I can't listen to it. Because it's at once none of that, and also, all of that.

"It's not any of that!" I yell and turn back to where she's gotten considerably closer, right next to me. Her body's warmth permeates the cold air of the hall and beckons to my loneliness.

"Meg—" I am defeated and rub my face trying to sort through this mess on a brain half doused in Scotch. She's close enough to touch, to pull into my arms. I smell her skin, the cotton, the oranges, the light. The promise of something I have no right to even daydream of. Then I hear it come out of her mouth. Those words. Because she can't be quiet anymore. Because …

"I love you, Charlie."

She cringes, like I'm a bomb that might detonate because she cut the wrong wire. I cringe too, because she did.

Damn you, Meg Kent. Her words flood into my heart and suffocate me. It's too late, it's too late and I'm just going to fuck it up. I'll ruin her, just like all the other men in her life. Just like I ruined my marriage. I'll become disconnected and stuck in my work and she'll feel alone and abandoned and find another man, and I'll be angry and heartbroken. I know I'm right about this. I know I'm right. We can't do this. We're an Oppenheimer test, waiting to make nuclear wastelands of both of our lives.

"I love you, Charlie. And I haven't been talking to you because I'm confused and I don't want to say something I can't take back."

"You just did," I feel the blood drain from my head, away from my heart into my feet, ready to run or fight. My fingers tingle. The only way she'll listen is if I cut deep.

MEG

"Charlie, don't." My words falter in my mouth like too many things to chew at once and I stumble. *Don't, don't, don't.*

"You don't," his voice rises.

"What?"

"Don't do that. Don't say you love me."

"What? Why? Why not?" I say back, trying to decide if I should smile like I'm not a threat or let my face fall into darkness like his. Can't I just make light of this? Isn't love remarkable and stupid? The words were caged birds that are let loose and I'm horrified and elated at once.

"You know why not." He gets agitated, he stalks to the kitchen. But I don't understand, and I can't not press. Because, I don't *know* why not. My heart starts to bang against my ribs and I feel panic rising in my throat. He gets out ice, he pours another drink, not his first and probably not his last of the night.

"Charlie—"

"You know what? I should have just let you leave that night."

"What?" I pause in the stillness of this confession.

"When you said you should move out. I should have let you." He downs the scotch, without a pause and I feel my face get hot, tears bubble up and swell into the corners of my eyes. Hot tears, like the kind you make when you're stumbling through an emergency room hallway, towards a room with your sister's body, metal pole and all. Nothing good can come from the end of this hallway.

"Charlie—"

"You should leave," he growls.

"What? Come on!"

"Did I stutter? Get out, I don't want you here, go!"

"Stop that! Can't we just talk about—"

"No, Meg we can't!"

"But why?" I can hear them now. The tears have made it into my throat and they're burning down my cheeks and I can't breathe but to gasp. Charlie stares down his nose at me and shakes his head.

"There aren't any words after I love you."

"Charlie," I sound small, a girl, broken anew in my skin. He takes his next drink, stalks to his room and closes the door. I hear the click of the lock. A castle wall between us. A world. A whole fucking universe. A universe I'm no longer welcome in. In the only home that ever felt like home. The only place my heart beat normally in. Where I felt, but never was, loved. I sob into the back of my hand, a deep pitiful sound that echoes like a ghost mourning.

Who knew so much darkness could follow I love you?

CHARLIE

"Don't do that. Don't say you love me." I beg her, shaking my head furiously.

"What? Why? Why not?"

"You know why not," I growl and push past her to the kitchen. Cut deep, cut hard, show her I'm nothing but an abusive drunk. Cut deep. The things that Meg can't live with because they are the ghosts of her past. Cut hard. My heart starts to bang against my ribs in protest.

You idiot, don't do this. Don't do this to her.

It's the only way. It will hurt less this way. I get out ice, I pour a drink. I leave the bottle out. Cut deep.

"Charlie—" She's making this damn hard. Probably because she's spent years putting up with worse from people she loved. I can't break this character now. The audience must believe. I'm caught up in the madness of it. It's nothing but a play. The final act.

"You know what? I should have just let you leave that night."

"What?" That stops her, I watch her throat contract like she's trying to swallow the poison I'm forcing down.

I drink my poison, in one gulp. My eyes never leaving hers as

I force it down. *Let's both swallow it all, kid.* The hard truth of life that neither of us should have ever flown so close to the sun. Her eyes get teary and my gut whirls with disgust at the monster I've become. She deserves better. She doesn't deserve me. I will only fuck her up.

"You should leave," I force the lie through my lips.

"What? Come on!"

"Did I stutter? Get out, I don't want you here, go!" I lie, I lie. I hate the mouthfeel of these words.

"Stop that. Can't we just talk about—"

"No, Meg, we can't!"

"But why?" I hear her gasping for breaths between tears. I cannot falter now, I've almost freed her from the iron teeth of a trap around her heart. It's all just a stage. I die inside as I stare at her, cold calculation in my next words.

"There aren't any words after I love you."

Her voice when she says my name, her heart, both shrink in her chest. Shrunken but not broken, I'm sure. She is only newly in love. And newly in love is easily forgotten. I grip the glass, and turn my back on her, away to my room, and slam the door between us. I lock it. I sit against the wood and break down in a fit of hot, eruptive tears. Biting into the skin of my own arm to keep my cries quiet. When I hear her fly up the stairs and tumble back down again, I stop. I hold my breath. The front door opens …

An eon of time, enough to stop her, to rush her, to pull her into my arms and apologize and beg for her to understand, comes and goes. The door slams closed again.

I throw the drink at the wall and shatter everything in my life. I yell, a lonely howl, to the world that would play such a malicious game of chicken with two hearts. The truth is, I've only ever deserved what I've gotten out of life. Loss.

Who knew so much darkness could follow I love you?

MEG

Maybe he was right. I'm a fuck-up and when a fuck-up says they love you, there aren't words left to say. I fumble my way through the house, up the stairs, I pack up all my notes, my computer, I leave most of my clothes, my two pairs of remaining shoes, my hopes. My whole world. I stumble down the stairs as though my legs don't want to leave. As though my heart still wants to argue. But he's done arguing. He's done talking to me at all, it seems. I grab my coat. I don't put it on because I'm too warm with the fever of embarrassment and hurt. I close the door behind me, and it feels like an iron gate has closed on my life.

I don't know where I'll spend the night. There can be no substitutions. No Jonah or Bradley will ever suffice. I could find a hotel. But my heart begs me to not stay in this city. I don't know where I'll spend the rest of my life, but it can't be here. I stare up at the buildings as I rush down the dark morning street. I feel the loss of them in my bones. Wherever I go, without Charlie, it doesn't really matter.

He once told me that writing well was about killing your darlings, taking away the pieces of a story that you were in love with, because they often weren't interesting to the reader. I feel like I need to kill the darling that's sprung up in my chest. That main character, that girl. Who wanted more than she was worth, the thought that she could have things like love. And purpose. And a novel. And a chance at something supportive and stable. When all the rest of her life was nothing but a tragic roller coaster ride. I can't have things. Charlie isn't interested anymore. In life. In me.

And I can't help him now that he's disgusted by my heart. I think about apologizing to Gina, but it just makes me angrier. As though she set me up to fail. Because we both know that I do not deserve Charlie. I never did.

The truth is, I've only ever deserved what I've gotten out of life and that's loss.

I bite back tears as I get onto the subway. I ride it out of Manhattan, out of New York. I ride it to the last stop, sometime in the gritty, smog-laced morning. From there I take the bus, to the Pennibracken Depot, just outside of Pickering, Kansas.

Where things that were born, come back to die.

When I step off the bus, disoriented, scared, wondering what in the hell I thought I was doing with my life in coming here, it's shades of twenty-three-year-old me. Only there's no one to greet me. No Gina. No Man-bun.

Definitely no Charlie.

But even though he's not there, waiting at the bus terminal curb he's still 'there' in the back of my mind, standing at the closing door, telling me to get out. He'll always be there, the last picture burned into my mind. Twenty years I've spent, in both of these strange lands and I feel more homeless than ever. Unwanted. Unloved.

What did Bob Dylan say? You can always come back, but you can't come back all the way.

I can't go back. Not anywhere. All the way or part. I'm lost.

I turn to go to the counter. I'll buy another ticket and just keep riding, until I find a place that doesn't feel like it's ever known the taste of my bones on its streets or carried the ghost of my voice in its undercurrent. I walk up to the counter, pull out my wallet from three-day worn jeans. I barely have a change of clothes left me since I walked away and left it all behind.

They're all at Charlie's still and I wonder, distracted, if he'll toss them out the window like some bad ending in a movie affair. I pull out my thinning credit card. The man behind the counter looks up from his crossword, and I see Charlie across his coffee cup on a sunny morning.

Jesus. Nowhere will ever be far enough away, because Charlie has permanent, rent-controlled space in my heart and I don't have the strength to kick him out.

"Where you headed?" I shake the ghost from my mind and see the decidedly older man staring at me like I'm an idiot missing her village. He enunciates the question slower. "Where are you headed?"

"Megan?" The two voices speak at once and I'm confused how he knows my name. I stare at him for a whole moment before my name sounds again from behind me. I turn.

There she is, the shadowed bird of her former self. Shades of me in her shoulders and hips, hair sparsely graying. Brighter in her eyes. Sober.

"Thank God. I'm so glad you made it. I was so happy when I got your call." She looks worn thin, gray and specter-like under the harsh fluorescent bulbs. I'd forgotten I'd called, sobbing into the phone, somewhere between New York and here, with the last of my battery. A final cry of defeat. No one else to come to, nowhere else to be. *I'm coming home*. I said the word as if it had meaning. As if it were an actual place, and not the person I left in a dark Manhattan apartment. Tears burn in my mouth.

"Hey, Momma." I croak. My throat is dry. My body is a desert in the middle of this long-forgotten heartland. Why does she look like she's shrinking from the world? Why is she leaving now, when her eyes are so clear and she knows who I am, and she's wrapping me up in her arms like I'm just a little kid. I fall into her. I cry.

CHARLIE

Two months later and I'm a ghost, a dead soul, wandering the halls of my apartment, alone. I barely eat, I don't go to the loft. I have a few plays picked up at smaller theaters and a new edition of my screenwriting book in the works, but it's all mindless bullshit. Nothing I couldn't do just as well in my sleep. And that's where I am, in a constant state of sleep. Barely alive enough to know that I'm a suffering disaster. Not digging any deeper than I have to.

I've put a pause on *the* play. It needs rewrites, I tell Jerry, but he's still optioning song writers, so it can get into production as soon as possible. I sneer at every part of this fiasco, this raving over the love letter to my cheating wife. Knowing that someday, rehearsals will be in full swing with a grand composer being lassoed in to celebrate the bright and too short life of the Georgian Storm. Knowing someone will play my wife. And someone will play me. And neither have survived the knowledge that Meg won't be there to sit next to me. To tell me if I did her justice. If I told the story that was meant to be told.

Is she still writing?

I'm pacing my apartment in a weird trance, all of these

worries and regrets mingling like bad pills in my stomach, when a hunched over pile of woolen coats shows up on my doorstep with his discerning eyebrows and hawklike beak. Thank God I got my mom's nose.

"Charles Simon Horowitz," he begins and I want to close the fucking door in his melting face.

"Dad," I say.

"You're a grade-A moron."

This is where I get my charm from. "As has been noted before."

"Are we standing on the stoop to talk, like a couple of vagrants?" He looks up at me. Was a time when he was as tall as me, but the years wear the body down and I truly believe that bitterness has eaten away at his bones.

"Where is Meg?" Jesus, he starts it early with a wound right to the chest.

"She left. So what?" I move to close the door but the old guy has strength and speed that I don't expect and he's in my hallway before I can shut him and his rainstorm of judgements away.

"So," he leads as he hangs up his hat first, and then his coat. "Tell me what you did wrong."

"Of course you assume it was me that did something wrong." Of course he is absolutely right.

"I just want to know, why a woman who obviously loved you more than anything, would leave?"

"Why do you care?" I nearly yell, the pain of that truth gnashing at my heart. But I deny it because I'm still standing on a hill of righteousness that I somehow saved Meg from a fate worse than death. Loving me. My father is staring at me.

"She left." I whisper the words again. The words that have been on replay in my own head for weeks. No big deal. Not my whole fucking heart walking out the door and into oblivion. Not even a letter. Not a text. No call.

"Because?"

"Because I told her to."

"Why would you ask Meg to leave? I thought you were taking care of each other?" There is a strange penance in his voice. A sadness, as if he had hopes that someone was taking care of me.

"I'm a grown man. I don't need any one to take care of me."

"Shmegegge."

"Dad—"

"Look at you, you moron. Such a brilliant mind, so full of potential and blessed with the creativity to make worlds and bring people to tears and yet here you are, schlepping around like a hobo in your own home. Not a damn play written, not a damn article, or story to your name. Letting a woman like that, walk away from you."

"What do you even know about it?" My voice is rising. I'm a hurt animal, backed into a wall and he's poking at me with this sharp stick of all the ways I've failed, even through his compliments? My brain trips up.

Did my father just call me brilliant?

"Charlie," he says softly, "A man is lucky to hold the love of one woman in a lifetime. But to be gifted the love of two and deny his own heart? This is a sin against God."

"Don't put your god in my face," I choke back tears.

"Did you not love her? Or was I mistaken? I saw the way she mourned for you. I saw the way she stayed by your side, when the anger of your grief pushed everyone else away. I saw you—" he pauses, sighs, hangs his head with his hands clasped in front of him. "At the wake. You didn't hug anyone that day. But I saw you in the kitchen and when Meg came to you, you held her like a lifeline. She was the only place you could trust with your broken heart. I used to hold your mother this way."

I have never seen such softness in my father. He never talks about mom, except to say she was a 'good woman'. Which I always thought was code for she was obedient and didn't rock the boat. But maybe I don't know even an atom's worth about love, in a universe full of it.

"I just would have hurt her." I confess.

"Meg? My Meg? The woman has rhino skin and brass balls."

"Dad!"

He waves me off. "She's tough enough, Charlie. She's already loved you through the worst of this life."

My stomach sinks into the bowl of my guts and I feel like throwing up.

"It's too late. I ruined it. Like I fuck up everything else."

"It's not permanent. Fuck ups are steps to our lessons. Lessons learned are our lives in total. You fuck up a lot, you learn a lot. You become a better man." I can't help but smile when my father, well-respected and refined drops the f-word twice in one sentence. He drops my guard with them.

"I think it is permanent. I made it permanent. I couldn't do to her what I did to Gina." Dad looks at me and shakes his head with a sigh.

"Clear your head, Charles. Clear your space. You cannot reach for your future while hanging on to your past." He reaches up and pats my cheek with his cold hand. "Now sit down, you idiot, I'm making us lunch."

MEG

Mom has found a church, and God, and all the enlightenment that would have been more useful to me years ago. But who am I to judge? What in the hell have I ever found? Excuses, mostly. Excuses to not finish my Master's Degree. Excuses to not be "settled down" and "responsible". Excuses to not finish my novel. Excuses to not leave my shitty job. Excuses to stay with Charlie when I knew it would just break my heart. Excuses to leave town when he did break it.

I don't go to church with her after I get dumped back in Kansas. I gave up God long ago, somewhere on my way out of New York. I think I saw him waving at me from the bus station platform. I'm pretty sure I gave him the bird. I don't go in to church, because much like Charlie, 'fuck God'. But I told mom that I'd drive her there as long as she's well enough to go.

I wait outside in the dirt parking lot. I sometimes catch the hymns, floating through the clapboard walls and into the early spring air. It sounds like hope for a better world somewhere beyond this one. I'm cynical at first, but the longer I sit alone in that yellowing gray dirt, listening to other people high on faith, the more I learn to accept. Who can blame them? This world is pretty shitty. It only teases hope in front of you and taunts you with possibilities and dreams. Then it leads you off the edges of cliffs with those elusive dangling carrots.

Throwing the chances that you never took and the ones you shouldn't have taken back in your face.

She comes back to the car with a smile, and I wait until she buckles her seat belt before I go. Just like when I was a kid; the car won't move until you're safely in. Like she raised her daughters to do.

Like Cecily did the night of. I don't pray but I hope she doesn't ask me to drive up to the cemetery. She just hums quietly under breath as I drive her back down to the dusted white ranch, on a quiet side street, three blocks up from the school.

I find a part time job at the local newspaper, setting their ads and writing a column they call 'Current Events'. It's about three paragraphs, consisting of when the high school cross country meets will be and what the Senior Center is serving for lunch. Sometimes I work in a quote from a famous author. Usually, my boss takes it out for being 'progressive'. But it's something, every week, to write that at least someone is reading, even if it's just my mom.

I don't touch my notes. I don't open my laptop except for work. I had to buy a new charging cord from the old Radio Shack on 5th. I left my charger in the past. I feel like I'm being defiant by not writing my novel, because, fuck Charlie too.

I help my mom clean out the basement and garage. It is silent and dusty work that's nothing but morbid preparation. She waves so much of it off.

"You don't want this" or "that can be given away." As if I don't want any part of my past or of her. I help her take things to the thrift store or the dump. I squirrel away some stuff. Recipe books, as though I cook, and photo albums, and song lyrics

Cecily wrote, and my dad's military records. The Purple Heart nobody told me about, from a war that nobody talked about.

I've never wanted to think about where I came from, but living in the hospice of my mother's final chapter, sick to death of my own depression and loss, it gives me something oddly solid to cling to. There is purpose here, in Pickering, Kansas. Delving into my roots is the purpose I need.

I take her to her doctor's visits. I start to cook. I'm getting used to the grocery store, their odd hours and lack of choices. I'm learning to eat Kraft singles in my grilled cheeses again. Some things aren't so bad the second time around. Especially dipped in tomato soup with a side of pickles.

The days back home are quiet. Simple talks and small-town gossip of who's sleeping with who, who's kid got thrown in jail, who's left town, and who's come back. I never thought I'd be in the latter category. Mom's hair has grown back from the first round of chemo that she'd gone through on her own over two years ago. She didn't call me then. She thought she would beat it, and I would never know. Sometimes she asks me to brush it for her. It goes against every instinct to ask for and give help, but she and I are both learning how.

The curse of the midwestern woman is making sure no one worries over you, fusses over you, or is inconvenienced by you. The eternal 'I'm fine' complex. She tells me that I don't have to do the laundry, or clean up the mess, or grocery shop, or take her to her appointments, or sit in the parking lot every Sunday morning while she talks to God, preparing for her trip home.

You don't have to, Megan.

We can hire someone.

You should rest.

You should write.

Fluttering her birdlike hands and long-winged fingers like mine over the table in the morning. The drink left her with the shakes. And a liver that grew things it shouldn't have. It left her with years to atone for in the short span of months, and no more favors to ask.

"Don't worry about me. I'm fine," she says.

Me too, mom. Just fine. We're all fine.

CHARLIE

Not once in my life, have I ever thought my father was right. From the time I was a child, he has been the bull in the ring, and I am in constant fear of being gored or trampled. But now I see the truth. We are both bulls. Both stubborn, pushing with locked horns against each other. When my fading father, of eighty-seven years, puts on an apron and cooks me a meal from the meager pantry items I have left, and talks about my mother and the regrets he had in never loving her enough, I feel our horns fall to the ground. Two bulls, standing with our foreheads pressed together. Not out of will to win, but out of love to understand. I take him to the train station and come home to the quiet house, lying in wait for me to do something.

It's time I did something.

I get boxes from the recycling bin downstairs and I clear out Gina's room. I box up her photos, I fold her clothes neatly. I call on friends and her family and anyone who might want or need the lot of it. I put the furniture up for sale. Her room is now bare bones and before the hardware store on 35th closes, I buy a gallon of paint, and cover the walls into the late hours of the night, a calming blue gray. I send all of Don's letters back to him. Care of his wife. Because I'm an asshole, and I don't wish her the same fate of finding out on his deathbed that he'd parted his devotion. No one should have to suffer in that way.

I only keep a few things. Gina's blue scarf, I hang by the door, but it doesn't go around my neck anymore. That noose is too tight and I can't relive the night of the subway when her ghost followed me home and haunted me into a stifling grief.

I keep the pictures of us together. I take them from frames and put them in albums. But the ones with all of us; with me and Gina, and Meg … those go in a separate pile. Then into a shoe box on my nightstand. Just me and my girls; every night beside me, when I go to sleep. Grief and love in a convenient size-six box. Nestled into the dark, whispering of all my losses; those that were forced on me, and those I earned.

Sometimes I can't sleep. So I take the pictures out and I study our faces. Gina is always beaming into the camera, laser focused on capturing the world with her smile. In many, I'm looking at Gina. But Meg, if she's not shying from the lens, bundled up to her ears in her own shoulders, is smiling at me. In nearly every picture, she's not looking at the camera, she's looking at me.

What a couple of idiots.

I'm an idiot.

But so was she. I don't even know where she is. I can only assume she went to live with some former boyfriend. I'm sure her shitty apartment was long since rented out. Maybe she went back to live with her mom. What an uncanny idea; that she should be living with her mother, after all of these years.

I almost hope she's with a boy. It would be less destructive. But that's my doing, and the grief in my chest from it is my penance for being an idiot. Her mail stops coming. Wherever she is, she's had it forwarded.

I don't look her up. I'm not much of a social media guy. And last I knew, she avoided it because her job as a reporter had too many crazies keeping tabs on her slanderous side gig.

I hope she's writing. I hope she's writing. I hope …

From what I know of her first few chapters it was the story of her sister, her dad, her mother, and all the ways we pull ourselves up after every loss. It was fucking brilliant. Every page was a set of steps I still need to keep taking. I want more of that. Hers is a story in need of telling, because someone out in the world needs to know its survivable. I hope she is surviving. Those words that drove her to madness in their birth, are the exact ones other people need to read, to know they aren't alone in such grief.

I wasn't alone in my grief. I knew, I always knew, that Meg understood.

"Please, still be writing." The words are whispers on my lips as I trace my thumb over her face, grainy, taken on the night of my first opening on Broadway. I'm in the center of them. Gina's eyes on the camera, mine are closed in the joy and unexpected moment of triumph. Meg's looking up at me, brilliant smile below that freckled nose. Looking up at me like my joy is the root of hers. I close my eyes, I remember.

I remember my hand around her waist that night.

I remember it.

I remember thinking she's too thin, and is she eating, and can I just hold her a little longer? Will she let me hold her longer? I remember she was over the moon for my joy. For me.

Was she always in love with me? Have I always been in love with her?

I miss Meg. Deep. Like you miss your own soul when you stray too far away from who you are. I miss Gina too, heart of my heart, and the beautiful life we built, warts and all. But I *had* that life with Gina. We lived it and soaked in it until our fingers were pruney and the water turned cold. We wrung out all we could from that life. And she moved on.

Meg and I only dipped a toe in. The water was warm but we were … no, *I was*, afraid. I bring her upturned face to my lips and kiss her cheek.

"I wish I would have held you longer," I tell Meg, and set the photo down. I roll over on my side. I bury my nose in the pillow, breathe deep to catch anything left of her, and dream about the morning I woke with her curled, ass up, in my bed.

What an idiot.

MEG

I get an old, ratty letter in the mail. I don't even know how he found me. But Simon Horowitz, father of Charles Simon Horowitz has sent me a letter. I suppose he looked up my mother. Old people know ways to find people that don't include the internet. For all I know he talked to Charlie about me, but I highly doubt Charlie would have talked to his father about anything. Least of all me.

I let my fingers trace the edges of it. I hold it away from the unclean bills and funeral home arrangements, and upcoming sales at the latest businesses going under in Pickering.

"This one is for me," I whisper and tuck it next to my heart. Maybe the first thing of mine that wasn't a tragedy to carry since I left New York. Then again, like Schrodinger's cat, it could be tragic, or it could be wonderful. Both possibilities existed as long as I didn't open it.

I haven't had anything in the mail for me in a couple of weeks. Except the bills I had forwarded and they started to dry up when I wasn't in New York, eating out and taking subway fares. Going to plays. My tears stopped freezing on my cheeks two weeks ago too, so I guess winter is coming to a close after all. Even here, at the edge of such a desolate and cold world.

I forgot what it was to live in a place where you could still see a horizon of land against the sky. Without buildings being the architect of every sunset. I go home, with the mail and my letter.

I sort through the rest of it, pay the bills I can from a now joint checking account, and make my mother some lunch. I set up one of our old TV trays in front of her easy chair so she can watch Bob Barker make people decide the worth of the world. When I set down the soup and crackers with her applesauce, a memory flashes back to me.

A moment, when I was home from school and Cecily wasn't. I was sick. Mom picked me up. I remember the warmth of her arm around my body as she carried me in from the car. Set me up on the couch, let me watch The Price is Right and we had Jell-O cups. I pause, so stuck in the past my body has frozen too. She'd guessed every price right and I was sure she was a magician. I froze that moment inside of me, when I was young. I made that memory. It's thawed its way up to the surface.

"What is it? Aren't you gonna eat?" Mom snaps me back into the present and she's smiling up at me. I look into her eyes. My eyes. Clear and aware I'm in the room. I can't stop the dormant layer of tears that have been waiting for me to not have something to do.

I always have something to do.

"Megan? Honey?"

Our lives are defined by moments like this. I squeeze my eyes shut, tight. I take in the memory of the couch, and my mother's arms, I smell the chicken noodle, salty from a can, and applesauce too sweet and not enough tart. And I hold the sound of her voice into my cells and I make this memory, part of the first. And then, my knees buckle onto the floor and I cry into the sticks of her legs where she sits. Her hands go to my hair and I feel like every moment of comfort I've had, is still trying to catch up with every moment of pain.

"It's alright, Meg. It's okay now."

It's okay now.

~

WHEN MOM IS NAPPING, I SIT ON THE COUCH AND START A crossword. I look at my computer bag. I haven't written anything since last week's article on the FFA's good showing at State. Cal Walker was able to determine that the bum milk came from cows let loose in an onion patch, so all the world's problems seemed to be solved and zeroed out again. I snort. It still beats the life ruination that was BuzzFeed. Maybe I should write. Maybe the best revenge is to succeed despite Charlie Horowitz.

Charlie.

I remember Simon's letter. My eyes still sting from my breakdown over soup, and I wonder if I should open it now, or wait until a new day to cry. Might as well add to the mess I'm already in. I shuffle across the threadbare carpet and reach into my old coat for the letter. I cuddle back into the couch and run the pads of my fingers over the edges of it. There's not much in there, maybe one page. I tear it open, blow into the hole, and pull out a yellow legal pad page written in shaky black scrawl.

Meg, my girl,

The man is a mess. I do not know what idiocy he was up to, to make you leave but you must believe it is all his fault, and probably, partly mine. My son is stubborn, and headstrong, and believes he is always right. He also believes that he does not deserve happiness. That he suffers because he's not worthy of it. Sometimes, when he sees happiness, he pushes it away before it can leave him. I am at fault for not instilling in him the belief that he is worthy of love, no matter how big of an idiot he can be. He told me you fought. Or rather, that you had fallen in love with him and he sent you away. This is not the same thing as fighting. This is Charlie fighting his own heart. And it is not your fault.

God rejoices in love, Meg. Especially love pure of heart. But man fears it. Because women, their love, their tears, their deep understanding of life and connection to Yahweh make them hearts to the world, too big for us to carry. And we fear letting you down.

I do not have years left. Months at best. And I cannot leave this world with him unloved. I am all he has. You and I.

He is my son. The blood of my blood. And you are my friend. That you should love my son, is a blessing. That you should forgive him, would be divine.

Shalhom lakh Meg.
Simon

My heart hurts, my swollen eyes complain angrily that they've had their share of crying already. Forgive Charlie? For what? I fold the letter and tuck it carefully back into its envelope. I'm the one who fucked up. I said the words. The words that no other words can follow. I cross my arms over my chest and sigh raggedly. Tears, building up every ache I have to go back, rise into my throat.

He doesn't want me, Simon. He doesn't want me or I'd go back.

CHARLIE

The knock is brutish, and it's followed by the buzzing of my doorbell.

"What the fuck?" I grumble with gravel in my throat and a heavy regret in my lungs. I stumble from bed and Meg's picture falls to the floor. It's nine? How did I sleep in so late? The door buzzes again, another knock. I pull on my robe and stumble through the house. What if it's her? What if she's back? What if she needs me?

I look through the window on the door, and a scowl sets itself on my face like a vicious guard dog. It's a young man. A tall one. With a pile of beautiful, haphazardly curly hair, in a bun, above his lambskin coat and jeans, shifting nervously from foot to foot. Fucking Adonis in blue jeans. I glance down at my oversized slippers and my tattered robe, covering a body that has seen the battlefields of sedentary work and age. He knocks again. I know he can see my shadow through the glass. I growl and open the door.

"Godssakes what?"

"Hey—uh? Charlie, right?"

"Who the hell are you?" I grouch, but I know. I've always known who he was. From the cold morning conversation. The distraction. The body to warm hers when the apartment was cold and reality was too real. The one she didn't actually shack up with, because I made her live with me instead. Fuck, the man is pretty. Why'd she ever live with me, when she could have had him? Maybe she does have him now. Maybe he's here for her stuff. My heart breaks.

I love you, her words cry in the back of my mind and I want to hit the kid right in the jaw.

"What do you want?" I grouch, besides her things, because she can't bear to even look at me.

"I'm Jonah. I'm a friend of Meg's and I'm worried about her. I checked in at BuzzFeed but they said she just stopped showing up. They told me she was rooming with you, and I found your address on—" he's overcome with frustration. He scratches at his bun. "Look, I don't want to intrude, I just want to make sure that she is okay. That's all. It's okay if she doesn't want to see me, but is she here at least, safe?"

"No," I bite at him and my heart beats faster. "I don't know where she is. I thought she was with you." The young man's brow falls, like a taller Brad Pitt in scene. He shakes his head. There's a pit of worry opening up between us.

"She's not with me," Jonah says, "But it's not like her to not respond to my texts. Even to say she's busy. Or that she's working with you. Hell, I'd be happy if she even told me to fuck off at this point." He pauses to sigh and I feel every one of his words like they came out of my mouth. "Do you think she's okay?"

"I don't know. She left months ago."

"Did she say why, or where she was going?"

My tongue is dry and stuck to my mouth. It feels heavy with the lies I'm about to tell him and myself. I certainly can't admit to my part; *Well, Jonah, I was a grade-A moron who broke her heart and sent her out into the cold night after she confessed her love for me, and I didn't follow up, even though she's been my best friend for a quarter of a century.*

"She—she and I," I can't say the words. I can't admit to Jonah, and thereby myself, that Meg is not here, and that she could be in danger or dead, or in a drunken spiral in a gutter somewhere, and it's all my fault. "Haven't talked in a while."

Why didn't she go back to Jonah? He obviously likes her, cares about her. Might have even been the most decent one among the men who've claimed to love her. Jonah is studying me. He's not an actor, but I can tell he knows how to see through the bullshit of a poorly written line.

"You're a roadie?" I try to distract.

"Crew, yeah. You're the playwright?"

"I am. I was."

"Was? Don't you have that new one out that everyone's buzzing about?"

"Yeah, I guess." The wind is getting cold and I want to close the damn door on this conversation. I don't want to talk about the play. The one Meg made me write. Practically pitched for me. The hurt she made me face.

"Supposed to be good. I'm sorry about your wife, I'm sure that's been hard." He looks sincere. This kid's not from New York. I guess I could see why she was taken with him. Why she should *still* be with him. Why didn't she pick him? Why didn't she go back to him?

*I love **you**.* She says again, punching me in the arm. Somewhere in a park, in my mind.

"Thanks. I'm sorry I can't be of more help. I'm sure she's fine. She always lands on her feet." My throat closes and it sounds broken when I say it. I'm not sure she's landed on her feet. He sees it, in the crestfallen drop of my head. Jonah sighs. She's left us both and I suppose as odd-couple as we are, we share the same heart for a woman neither of us knew what to do with.

"If you hear anything, do you mind letting me know?" He

pulls a small scrap of paper from his pocket with his phone number on it, and hands it to me.

"Sure, kid."

"Jonah."

"Right, like with the whale."

"Right." He smiles at me, with fucking dimples no less. Jesus, she must have really loved me.

He nods and walks away, down the street, with his head hanging and worry settling heavy on his broad shoulders. I close the door, lock it, feel my heart rate climb and thrum in my veins. And then a small pain twinges in my arm.

Meg Kent's going to give me a heart attack.

I take the stairs to her loft two at a time. Most everything is still here. What in the hell did she leave with? And why didn't I come up sooner? Her clothes, her books, her pillow. I take it in my hands and put my nose up to it. It smells like her shampoo, the light orange scent of her face cream. Her notes are gone, her laptop. Her chucks. I sit on her bed, find a letter tucked in the unmade sheets. A letter from her mom with a copied form, from the Pickering Hospital Oncology Unit. Eileen Kent's last request of her daughter, along with her official results.

Inoperable.

3-5 months with palliative care given.

Come home.

Postmarked the week of the night she'd crawled into my bed.

"Jesus, Meg." I whisper.

The night she'd come to my bed was the night she found out her mother was dying. I never asked her what was wrong. She'd been so lost in her words. I was lost in my guilt and grief and both of us were ... lost. I feel the paper crumple between my fingers as I fall into the bed, my head on her pillow, curling up around the words she didn't tell me.

I didn't ask her. And she didn't want to burden me.

She only wanted to love me.
And I sent her out the goddamn door.
What a fucking idiot.

MEG

My mom shuffles into the kitchen one morning, a big brown folder in her hand. I rise, on the automatic response from my new care-giving anxiety, to help her. She waves me off and sits down.

"Can I get you tea?" I start to rise again and she lays a hand on my shoulder. The gentle shove back into my seat is the first motherly command she's given since I got home. She puts the folder on the table between us.

"I want to talk."

"Okay? Is this about Gladys Johnston? Don't listen to her bullshit, your cobbler tasted fine—"

"Why aren't you writing?"

"What?" My heart swings one-eighty in my chest and I stare at her. "What do you mean? I sent in my articles last night like always."

"No, Meg. I mean your book."

"How do you know I—what book?" My mouth is dry and I want to bolt out the door.

She ignores my fumbling denial. "What are you waiting for?

To not feel so much? Are you hoping if you wait long enough, the memories will just go away? They don't you know. You can't drink them away, you can't avoid them away either."

"Mom—"

"Cecily would have wanted you to write it." It's the first time, since I've been home that she's said my sister's name. And it puts the weight of grief, like a bowling ball, in my gut and I want to throw up my coffee. "*I* want you to write it."

"Listen—" I shake my head, angry heat swarming my cheeks. What does she know? About me, about what I can do about anything? She interrupts.

"But none of that matters if *you* don't want to write it. Don't you want to?"

"I—" all my excuses stop short in my throat. Yes, I want to write it. I was on my way. I was getting it done. I was on the right path and I felt like it was a living, breathing being, ready to spring out into the world the night Charlie kicked me out. Everything died that night. Everything left.

"You don't keep yourself alive in this world by taking a back seat, Megan."

"Mom—"

"Shush and listen! I don't have forever. You are the last link to the world this family has. You are the last one who knows the story. Her story. Mine. Yours. The only way you can keep us alive, Meg, is to write the story." Before I can stutter my way into an argument, she opens the folder. Packed inside, is a history, in situ, of all my writings, my newspaper clippings, my BuzzFeed articles printed out, my high school papers, poetry, the eulogy I wrote for Cecily's funeral, letters I wrote to my dad that I was sure I'd thrown away.

Every thought. The entire written history of the wounds and balms to my soul, in a simple brown folder. She kept them all. When I thought she was nothing more than a drunken ghost. I flip through them, the tears building up behind my eyes in burning waves.

"Why did you save all of these?"

"Because, I knew very few things for sure after your sister died. But I did know that you had a voice and you were going to use it in the world. I knew that you would keep us all alive by telling your stories. That you would go places, and do things, and show the world spring in the middle of winter. Meg," her hand alights on mine, a robin in the emerging grass, white circles around dark eyes, "life will take everything you have. It demands it. You are so much stronger than I ever was."

"I'm not."

"I see you. The way you came home broken. The hole where your heart used to be. I'm not sure what happened, but I do know that you can't run from it. You can't drown it, and you can't deny it. Grief requires your participation. Don't make my mistakes. Don't use me to run away."

"I'm not—"

"There will be life to live after me, Meg. You'd better live it. All of it. Give it all you have. You'd better not stay in Pickering once I go."

"Mom, please don't talk about that."

"Why not? It's happening. And you don't belong here. I'm happy to have you and I'm so grateful for your forgiveness. But this isn't your home."

I look up at her, the tears are well past trying to control now, and I wipe them away as quickly as I can.

Where is my home? I don't even know anymore. Maybe home is a place we build in our own hearts. Maybe for too long I've looked for it outside of myself. Maybe that's what she means. That I can't keep running from the nest of grief in my soul. I need to accept it as a part of who I am. And choose to keep living just the same.

"Now, what is this about Gladys not liking my cobbler? That hypocritical know-it-all." My mother smiles at me and the sun rises in Pickering, one degree higher than the last day. One more step towards spring.

CHARLIE

I've cleaned out the apartment, taken out the days of delivery containers and washed the laundry that had piled up in my closet. Gina's room is empty. Fresh paint. No soul to it left and I'm worried that I've somehow lost her. I sit in the middle of it sometimes, and close my eyes. Let my brain go down the littered roads of our past. The joy, the struggle. The lovemaking and quiet nights. The stage she came alive on and the silent hours she waited for me to come out of the alternate dimension of my writing. She was always waiting for me. Until she wasn't.

"I didn't know how good I had it," I say to the soothing walls. "I should have seen you, loved you, held you more." I feel her hand on my shoulder. Like the dream, when she asked me to look at the painful burn of a new day dawning. I close my eyes again and put my hand on hers.

We never do.

"So what am I gonna do about it now? Sit in your empty room and wait until I can go with you?"

And waste that brilliant heart of yours? You'd better not.

"My heart?" Gina smiles, squeezes my bones and I hear her laugh. "Is it even alive in there?"

I feel it beat, sudden and fierce.

It is alive. But it's not here.

I open my eyes, crawl to my knees and gain my feet. I walk out of the room, dream-stated and strange. My eyes fall directly to the plant on my desk. The plant Meg brought with her. The one I would not water. I approach it slowly, sure that the sticks and fallen leaves are a sign of its death. But when I get close, I see a new sprout forming on the tip of its scraggly branch. Like spring, or something akin, has drawn out the last hope of life from it, and it's taking hold.

I scramble through the papers for my phone. I dial the number without really thinking. When he answers, I don't bother with pleasantries.

"I need to borrow your car."

MEG

I'm called by the fading chime of the doorbell, from my kitchen duties. When I tear open the door, angry that my mom's resting and it's not the time of day for polite company to call, I expect neighbors or the pastor. The artist formerly known as Prince seems more likely. Anyone, dead or alive, seems more likely than Charlie-fucking-Horowitz on my doorstep.

"You're not even gonna call me?" The life-sized ghost on the other side of the screen door barks.

"What in the h-hell?" I croak.

It must be a dream. Or a stroke. Do I smell burning toast? I sniff. I touch the side of my face to check for drooping. The voice is too real, the outline of him behind the screen door too life-like. It must be a dream. I move to close the door and call an ambulance.

"Meg, come on!" His fist lands on the screen door with a thump. I don't talk. I don't believe in ghosts, so it seems silly to engage in a conversation with one. "Well?"

"What?" I say back, angry.

"Well, what the hell are you still doing in Butt Fuck, Kansas?"

"It's pronounced 'Pickering,'" I say and move to close the door.

"Meg, stop!" The voice of a man I once turned my world around for, sounds like god's breath after so long a silence. I interrupt it with the harshness of atheistic disbelief.

"What do you want?"

"I've been worried for months."

"And yet my phone says you couldn't have cared less what butt-fuck part of the world I ended up in."

His head falls, staring down at the jacket between his hands. He's in one of his old blue shirts, white T-shirt beneath and hair as wild as ever. "Can I come in?"

"No."

"Who is it?" Mom's weak voice drifts down the hallway like a dandelion wish on the wind. Before I can slam the door and deny that anyone is here, Charlie's voice calls back towards the darkness.

"It's Charlie Horowitz, Eileen!"

"You asshole." I glare through the grasshopper-eaten screen. He knows. He knows a small-town mom can't deny a guest who's traveled that far at least a cup of coffee. But Charlie doesn't belong in the house, he doesn't belong on the other side of the door. Charlie doesn't belong in Kansas anymore than a Manolo Blahnik heel belongs at a square dance. He's too New York. He's too smart and clever and savvy for my mom's shitty porch and her worn thin carpet.

Charlie doesn't seem to care or notice. In fact, all he's looking at is me. In my borrowed jeans and threadbare Van Halen shirt, dirty from cleaning and cooking and emptying puke buckets and giving sponge baths for weeks.

"Well? Are you comin' in?" my mom calls and I'm afraid she'll get up and fall the longer it takes me to swallow my pride and let him.

"Yes, ma'am," Charlie answers and takes away my choice to turn him out.

"Five minutes," I scowl and squeak the door open. I won't

stand near him. I won't get close enough to smell the familiarity of him. Irish spring and newspaper print. Soft cotton. They all hit me anyway and I want to cry for want of his comfort after so many months being the one being leaned on. Instead of falling into his arms, I push my willow tree of a body to the kitchen and pull out two mugs.

He didn't ask for coffee and I shouldn't offer, because coffee is a sit-and-stay-awhile gesture. And I can't have him staying. But the roots of Kansas have sprung up new branches in my short time here and when someone comes to the door, the pastor or neighbors, the good-hearted members of the tiny town, you invite them in and offer them coffee. It's as normal as flipping off cabbies in the middle of Broadway. All people have a gesture. My new one is Folgers in mismatched cups.

I pour it and hand it to him. He looks as though I've given him a ceremonial poison or truth serum. I hope it's both and neither.

"Thanks."

"Yeah. So? What are you doing here, Charlie?" I try to keep the tone of I-still-love-you-and-this-hurts out of my mouth when I say his name. Not like I've whispered it to myself over every blank page, or before I go to sleep at night, or in the depth of every crying fit that seizes me. I am grieving this too. I am grieving the loss of my one great love, just as he did. Only Gina never showed back up on Charlie's porch. How would he have taken it? He's looking at the coffee, he's sitting at the table. What he's not doing, is talking. And Charlie doesn't *not* talk.

"Well?"

"Well, it turns out that Jonah the Man-Bun came to look for you." Charlie's fingers toy with the handle of his cup. I feel disastrously horrified that a former lover showed up at Charlie's house. I feel the heat in my cheeks and my stomach threatens to heave up my breakfast of coffee. But Charlie doesn't seem horrified. He's just calmly drinking Folgers out of a World's

Greatest Kindergarten Teacher mug in my mom's dining room. He looks right at home.

"What? How in the hell did he know where I lived?"

The way I say 'lived' feels hurtful, probably more to my own soul than to Charlie's. I used to live with Charlie. We used to live together. I use to wake up to the smell of his soap and the sound of him running lines in the shower. I used to sit on the couch with him at night and argue over Jeopardy answers. I used to live …

"He tried looking for you at your work, and found out where I lived. Where we lived." Charlie interrupts and compounds on my thoughts. I turn away. I'd quit everything when I'd left. Except loving Charlie. I go back to washing the dishes that he'd interrupted. We are a case of constant interruptions, as though we've lost our rhythm.

"What did he want?"

Charlie scowls at me. "What do all men want with you?"

"A place to live and daily ego boosts?" I sniff, already knowing what's on his mind. Charlie grunts. "Wait! Did you give him a place to live? Do you have your own Man-Bun now?"

"He's quite lovely actually. He made me patchouli pancakes last weekend." I have the worst time keeping in the giggle that springs up, looking for Charlie. Long buried and repressed, it shocks me. I thought all my laughs had died away. Charlie sighs. "All men want to be with you. They just don't know how to deal with it when you start to outsmart them."

"Stop." *I couldn't outsmart you*, is all my mind thinks. *I couldn't outsmart my own heart.*

"He missed you. He was worried about you."

"Doubtful." I think of Jonah. Briefly, like the memory of an episode I once watched and quickly forgot.

"Seems like a sweet kid."

I grunt and lift the next pan from the counter into the small sink. Charlie doesn't say anything as I scrub it down and rinse it off. His silence is annoying. Mine is uncomfortable. I clear the hesitation and heartache from my throat.

"I'm sorry that he bothered you enough to drive out to the middle of nowhere." I put the pan in the drying rack, but Charlie continues to stare at me from the kitchen table. The oak kitchen table, where I once sat across from my mom and an officer and they told me my sister was dead. I close my eyes, rub a bubbly hand under my nose. I'm learning to accept. I'm learning to accept my losses, carry my grief, and move forward. Aren't I? Even when those losses show up unannounced and drink shitty coffee in my childhood kitchen?

"He was worried about you and it only bothered me because I —" Charlie pauses, leans forward with the cup between his long hands and sighs.

"What? Because you thought I was sleeping with him while we were living together? I was never unfaithful, after I figured out how I felt about you." I glare at him before setting to work on the spaghetti pan from last night.

The smell of it makes me nauseous. I cleaned up that puke too. But Mom had asked for it and enjoyed it on the way down at least. I want to throw up. I want to fall apart. I was doing so well, until he walked into Kansas and reminded me that I used to have friends. That I used to be something other than an agent of comfort. Charlie stands, puts the coffee down and glowers.

"It made me realize that if a man who only knew you a month would have the chutzpah to come and find you out of worry, why the hell wasn't I at least doing the same?"

"Because you didn't *want* me around anymore," I counter, my head dipped towards the pan and silence spreads between us like the miles that should still be there. I don't say more and I can feel him fuming.

"Will you just fucking look at me?" His voice is hurt, tense. So much Charlie and so much a man who never seemed desperate to me. What in the hell could he possibly want with me? There were no words after I love you, and yet here he sits, long legged and curly haired and giving me words.

"I—" I drop the pan in the sink and every nerve feels shocked and alive. "I don't know what to do here."

"Let's take a walk."

"I've got things to do."

"Nothing that can't wait an hour. When was the last time you left this place?"

I think he means Kansas, and I stare at him like he's an idiot, because he knows I left it over twenty years ago only to come back, a failure at life. Before I can speak, he walks towards me, taking his half-drank coffee to the sink and dumping it across my work. His voice is low and so near me that I can feel it, reverberating through my chest and tingling through my ribs.

"And don't say you went to the grocery store, or a doctor's appointment because that doesn't count. Your mind is a cancer ward and everything you do to fight it counts as being in the trenches." I shake my head but he goes on. "I know. Remember Meg? I know this place."

When I look up at him, he's not teary-eyed in the memory of how he'd also been the support structure for a building that was falling down. How is he so calm? Will I ever live through this to find that calm? I can't even wash a pan without feeling like I want to set myself and the whole world on fire.

"Fine," I whisper and dry my hands. It's cold outside. I grab a coat and a bag of stale bread that I was going to take with me and mom to the lake, so she could feed the ducks. But she hasn't been able to leave the bedroom the last few days and I don't want it to go moldy. I stop in to see her. Charlie waits by the front door.

"Hey, Momma," I whisper and she pulls herself from the dark sleep, adjusts her glasses and grasps at the book that's fallen to her side.

"Hey, honey. I was just reading a little."

"You were sleeping," I smile.

"Well, I was just trying to absorb the material." It's a small smile back, there's color in her cheeks. "You and Charlie should go to the lake, I'm sure he could use a walk after that trip. You could too." She might have fallen asleep, but the walls of the house were never thick enough to keep conversations or fights out.

"Will you be okay?"

"Oh, honey!" she waves her hand. "I'm just fine." I check that she has water, her tea, her phone, the emergency call bracelet, crackers and those nutrition bars she's supposed to eat but she says taste like waxy, chocolate cardboard.

"Are you sure you—"

"Go!" she says, and I feel my own soul in her. "Go take a walk with Charlie, it will do you both good." I sigh. So long without any confidante, my uncertainty presses through my lips.

"I don't even know why he's here."

"Because he loves you, Megan."

"Mom—"

"A guy doesn't travel thousands of miles on a Tuesday, from a huge, beautiful city to a dinky small town, on a lark." She shakes her head and I feel my stomach gurgle up into my chest.

"Maybe he's just lost." I say dryly.

"Maybe we're all lost," she says back. "Go on. Go get found. Don't keep him waiting."

Don't keep Charlie waiting? I don't know how that feels to my heart. But she's right, a man doesn't show up out of nowhere on a regular old day to not have something important burning a hole in his gut. Maybe after he says it, he can go back to being Charlie in his homeostasis. Maybe I can close the pages on the book that was never meant for me.

CHARLIE

When I see her, standing behind the faded noise of the old screen door I barely recognize her. That can't be my Meg. She's thin as a rail and there are half-moons of dark below each eye. She's staring at me and scowling like she can't understand what she's seeing. Before I can even speak, she starts to close the door on me.

"Meg, come on!" Desperation flies my fist into the door jam and she jumps. But she does not speak and I'm not sure if I'm face-to-face with her, or the ghost she's left behind. I whisper. "Well?"

"What?" she answers, as if I'm supposed to know what I'm doing here. I suddenly don't know what I'm doing here. Ripping both of our hearts back open, and to what end? The anger at seeing her so pale, so thin, and hands shaking takes over and I bellow.

"Well, what the hell are you still doing in Butt Fuck, Kansas?" *When you should be home with me,* my heart cries. She scowls and leans close to the metal barrier.

"It's pronounced 'Pickering'," she says, enunciating the *k* and goes to close the door again. I am desperate and I yell at her to stop. Stop closing me out. But my whole being wishes for more. For her to stop being sad, to stop disappearing before my eyes. Be Meg again. She asks what I want, and I'm suddenly at a loss. What I want and what I deserve are not the same thing.

I tell her I've been worried.

She doesn't believe me. Her voice is grainy, like her throat is dry. And I'm not sure if it's dry like a desert that's cried out all of its rain, or just cavernous from loss. I bow my head. I did this to her, and to myself. Only I can unfuck it.

"Can I come in?"

"No."

"Who is it?" I hear a weak voice drift over Meg's shoulder like the spirit in the house is investigating the visitor. I recognize it, the shadow of a woman that could have been Meg's mother in another life. I know her name from the letter tucked into my jacket pocket. Meg's hand twitches on the door.

"It's Charlie Horowitz, Eileen!" I yell out. *I am here, I am here. Don't let your daughter slam the door on my apology.*

"You asshole." Meg says and glares at me. She knows that I know that midwestern propriety will not let her turn away a visitor. I stare back at her, as soft as I can. I will take on all of the hate, the only sustenance in her belly. I will hold it all. I deserve nothing less.

"Can I come in?" I whisper. *Into your house, into your grief, into your arms ... Meg, please.* I can't tear my eyes from her. I want to hold her, and feed her, and beg her to rest. In my bed. In my arms. In my house.

"Well? Are you comin' in?" Eileen asks from somewhere in the dark, a co-conspirator to my ache. I can't deny a dying woman after all.

"Yes, ma'am," I yell back and nod at Meg. She purses her lips up in a scowl I've never seen before, and it devastates me to know that what New York couldn't do in all that time, I did in a few sentences. I've given Meg bitterness.

"Five minutes." She opens the door. I walk over the threshold, but she moves away, turns her back on me and floats towards the back of the house. The screen door slams behind me and I'm suddenly in the familiar pungent taste of bleach and Lysol and, faintly, vomit. Medicine bottles on tables and the quiet hiss of oxygen from where Eileen must be resting.

Meg is all alone. No nurses, or hospital staff. No loud and gregarious friends to take the load off, no throngs of admirers. No draperies of scarves and photos and bouquets to cheer the final curtain call. There's no one to bring her soup. Meg is carrying the end of her mother's life alone.

I regain myself and follow where my ghost-shaped Meg has settled. In the kitchen at the back of the house. Small, plain, oak cabinets and chicken wallpaper, cross-stitched sayings framed on one wall, and a picture of Jesus above fake flower arrangements on the sideboard opposite.

Jesus.

It takes me back to the way Meg was dressed when we first met her, and the wide-eyed way she studied New York for years. How I teased her for being so small town. This town, Pickering, this house, this kitchen, they were the only sets she had in a very sad first act.

She pours me a cup of coffee in an old red mug and puts it on the empty oval of a dining table where no family has sat for years.

"Thanks," I say, hoping this is the first step of our negotiation. She stands against the counter, her hands and arms crossed over her chest, a solid fortress against any incoming messages to the heart.

"Yeah. So? What are you doing here, Charlie?"

I don't know where to begin or how to tell her that I just want her. That I want to take away the weeks apart. That I want to start over, but not start over. I want to try and rewrite our lines. But the brain is stupid and I've been traveling for eighteen hours straight and I think back to what lit a fire in me to come here in the first place. Start at the beginning.

"Well, it turns out that Jonah the Man-Bun came to look for you," is what comes from my mouth. I look down at my coffee cup. You idiot.

"What? How in the hell did he know where I lived?"

I look up. It shouldn't surprise me that she hadn't told him we'd moved in together. She never talked about him when she lived with me. She slept in my bed, ate Chinese food out of my fridge, came home to me, left me waffles and wiped my toothpaste out of the sink. Meg loved me. My heart breaks and threatens to push itself out over my Folgers-laced tongue.

"He tried looking for you at your work, and found out where I lived. Where we lived." She turns her back to me. She's washing a sink-full of dishes. There aren't a million places to order out in Pickering, Kansas. The thought that Meg cooks seems like a disjointed entry in Wikipedia. I forgot she had a lifetime of taking care of herself before she came to New York. Her shoulders shake as she scrubs her anger away in the pan.

"What did he want?" her voice is broken.

I scowl. "What do all men want with you?"

"A place to live and daily ego boosts?" She's not wrong. We've done a grave injustice to Meg, as men. She stops scrubbing and looks at me. "Wait! Did *you* give him a place to live? Do you have your own Man-Bun now?" She is smiling, almost as if she forgot she was mad at me and it's the most beautiful thing I've seen in a lifetime. I smile back, a bridge of hope arcs between us.

"He's quite lovely, actually. He made me patchouli pancakes last weekend." I watch her throat contract, and her lips seal tight. The laughter that she wants to chew on is pushed back down into her chest, where it's gone to die.

I sigh. This is the dark night of our souls and maybe I'm too late.

"All men want to be with you. They just don't know how to deal with it when you start to outsmart them."

"Stop," she says. She outsmarted me. She knew me long before I knew myself.

"He missed you. He was worried about you."

"Doubtful."

"Seems like a sweet kid."

I swallow hard. *Meg, please don't. Don't keep punishing the world for my mistake.*

"I'm sorry that he bothered you enough to drive out into the middle of nowhere." She moves on to the next dish, the next mess to clean up, the next obligation. I can't stop looking at her, wondering if it's too late. Life cracked her, but I'm the one who split her in two. I've broken her. She sniffs, and wipes away emotion with her sudsy hand, like she's wiping away a stain.

"He was worried about you and it only bothered me because I —" I pause. I lean forward with the cup in my hands, my heart at the bottom of it. How do I fix what I broke?

"What? Because you thought I was sleeping with him while we were living together? I was never unfaithful, after I figured out how I felt about you."

I stand up and level my eyes on her. *Goddamn it, Meg, you hit me where it hurts and heals most.* I'm not walking out of this house, out of her life, until she knows.

"It made me realize that if a man who only knew you a month would have the chutzpah to come and find you out of worry, why the hell wasn't I at least doing the same?" The words rush out, a swarm of starlings at twilight over the field. The last hope of light.

"Because you didn't *want* me around anymore." She shoots them all down in one sentence, and doesn't even look at the carnage. She won't look at me, and I hope it's because she knows if she does, she might have to admit I'm still human. Still real. Still aching.

"Will you just, fucking look at me?" I'm begging now.

"I—" she drops the pan in the sink looks at it as though it was still hot. "I don't know what to do here."

I look around, the place is clean but it smells like a hospital and feels like death and I've planted myself and my love in the middle of it, without warning. A walk with Meg was the cure for nearly everything.

"Let's take a walk." I whisper.

"I've got things to do," she lies.

"Nothing that can't wait an hour. When was the last time you left this place?"

She stares at me like I'm an idiot. I take my coffee and come closer. I dump it in the sink across the half-cleaned spaghetti pan. I'm close enough that I can tell she hasn't gotten a shower recently. She smells like Meg and dish soap, and salt, and the faint trace of bleach. I can feel the warmth coming off of her. A dry desert, devoid of hope and love, and probably surviving on coffee and fingernails. She shrugs and looks like she's doing the math of how long she's been on call. I dive in, closer to her now, so my voice lowers.

"And don't say you went to the grocery store, or a doctor's appointment because that doesn't count. Your mind is a cancer ward and everything you do to fight it counts as being in the trenches." She shakes her head in denial. "I know. Remember, Meg? I know this place."

She looks up at me and I feel like I could take her into my arms now and smother her with kisses, but she's fragile and brittle and it just might break her. She needs a walk. Away from being the support structure of a monument in collapse.

"Fine," she says.

I step back as she takes her tattered gray coat from the hook by the kitchen door and a bag of bread from the counter. I'm not exactly sure what in the hell she's going to do with that. I hope eat. God, she looks like she needs to eat. I don't speak. I watch her move past me and down the hall. Towards her mother and the pet of cancer now growing bigger every day. I listen to their soft words, murmuring through the walls that raised her.

If she had invited me, I would have joined her. I would have talked to her mom. But she didn't. So, I stand, coat in my hand and look around the room. There's a couch and an easy chair. Books and crosswords on the coffee table. A bible near the chair. She certainly hasn't found God. She doesn't seem dumbly at peace. Everything feels sunken and brown. An old piano sits against the wall by the hallway. There are photos on top of it, and the keys are exposed. Does she play? I think she does. I recall ...

A late evening off of Broadway, going with her to pick up Gina, for dinner after the show. And while I discussed my next big plan with the director, and Gina was taking off her make-up and telling Don that she had plans with her boring, old husband, Meg had waited in the pit and started a stumbling rendition of the *Cheers* theme, across the keys. When I looked down from the stage, distracted from my schmoozing, and found Meg, in the same gray coat, knitted beanie and a smile, watching her hands dance across the keys, in stuttering imperfect melody, laughing at herself and the inability of her fingers to catch up to the rhythm, I remember thinking ...

What was I thinking?

"She was beautiful," I say out loud and startle to find Meg beside me.

"Yeah." It's a statement. I look at her and back to where I'd been staring.

Not into the past at a girl playing the piano, who I was unknowingly in love with for years. Not a girl who has always taken care of me and Gina, in her own stumbling way. Not at a woman who I hope will find forgiveness for my idiocy. I'd been staring at pictures of her. Young Meg, and a girl who could have only been her sister. My eyes take it in. The smiles, the shining blonde hair, the potential, cut down so brutally early. The loss.

Meg's hardest loss by far. Cecily was beautiful. In the bright-star way that Gina was. The kind of soul that life becomes so jealous of, that the cosmos call them to come back early.

The kind of beauty schmucks like us will never live up to. We just sit in awe, beneath the glow of them. I look at Meg.

"So were you."

"Yeah, well, emphasis on the 'were'."

I want to throttle her. "You still are."

She looks down at her ratty coat, her plain and very Kansas small town clothes. Probably what she would have worn her whole life, if Gina hadn't taken her under her wing. She touches her hair self-consciously.

"I'm a fucking mess. Don't bore me with empty compliments." I stare at her, every detail. Every worry line around her eyes, every crease of her forehead. The dusted strands of gray at the peak of her hairline and the ones beginning to show at her temples. She starts to fidget and bites her damn lip. God, her lips. To kiss Meg again, I'd die happy. Maybe I'm using too many words, maybe that's what I should do. She'd probably throw me out.

"I missed your face," I say.

"Come on," she whispers and passes me on her way out. I don't know where we're going but it becomes apparent that the bread isn't for us. She's tucked it into her pocket. I follow, slightly behind, as I would still manage to get lost in the ten-block town.

I did notice a newspaper building, next to the bank and one of the many bars. I wonder if she's writing. Is she drinking? She doesn't have that dull glow and red-eyed look. She looks, if anything, wired and awake, afraid to sleep and miss all of these last moments.

I watch her like my eyes can't fucking look away. I'm really the one afraid to miss any moments. I'm a starving man cleaning every grain of rice from his plate. Extracting every single frame from the walk down Pickering's quiet streets towards a lake in the distance. There's no rush of traffic. No horns, or voices, or electronic devices. Nothing to distract the mind from its millions of thoughts running their course from pleasant all the way to horrific.

How has she done it? I guess if this is the habitat you were raised in, it's not so difficult to fall back into the rut. I think of how she was always unbalanced in a subway car and how big and fast the world must have moved when she first arrived. How did she live in New York? She survived because grief makes you adaptable. I watch her shoulders drop and she sighs a few times as if she hadn't thought to breathe. Settling into walking next to Meg feels more like home than anything else. It's like Christmas, and New Year's, and the first day of spring. And I know I don't deserve any of it.

MEG

The lake isn't far and we start walking in silence. Until my stupid mouth speaks, because the farther away I get from the house, the lighter my shoulders feel, the more air I breathe, the more I settle back into myself. Walking next to Charlie feels decadent. And like I don't deserve any of it. But silence with Charlie, after months of it, seems sacrilegious.

"How's the play?" I ask, hands and bread tucked into my oversized pockets. He doesn't say anything and I look up at him, missing the sight of his profile in deep ways. His eyes are focused straight ahead.

"How's the novel?" he says back without looking at me.

I scowl at him. "You know how it's going, asshole. It's not."

"Neither is the play," he bites back. Then he looks down in frustration. He hasn't written since I left?

"Shit, Charlie, you need to—"

"What? Write? Write when the house is so quiet and there's no clicking of keys? Or your footsteps to the coffee pot, hoping you'd bring me a cup too? Or the way you would sigh and stretch and I was never sure if it was the chair creaking or you? When there's no you? I'm supposed to create without all of that?" My fucking heart shocks to life like someone hit it with AED paddles and my chest hurts.

"You did fine without me before, you'll be fine after."

"I'm not fine!" he yells back.

"Neither am I!" I return. We both huff, gray clouds of rural America between us. I break eye contact first and continue to the lake. The sooner the bread runs out the sooner the walk will be done. The sooner Charlie can get back on his plane, or train, or car, or whatever he used to get here. He can go back and feel better about himself and that he 'tried'.

"Why are you here really? I mean, just because you wanted to know where I landed?" I ask as we get to the end of the dock overlooking the lake. I take the bread out and he stands beside me.

"I needed to see you. I needed to talk to you."

"You could have called."

"Not for this."

"If you fucking tell me you have cancer, I swear I will push you into this lake." We freeze and he stares down at me with a smile. As if he's missed this exact moment. I hate the way I've missed it too. I've missed his face. His voice. All the ways he made me come alive, just by being.

If he has cancer …

"I don't have cancer," he says it with a soft smile. I turn away to look at the still gray glass beyond the edge. The fowl aren't dumb, they start heading towards the dock, leaving delicate V trails as they get closer to the ice shelf below us.

"I learned something about myself." It seems a heavy proclamation. One I don't have a whole heart to take in right now. My snark rears its head in defense of it.

"Is it that your eyebrows need trimmed?" I say over my shoulder and toss piece of dried bread into the ice floe where the ducks thrash over it and a rogue mallard steals it away from the group.

"My—what?" he says, stopped mid-thought, and scowls at me. I shrug and reach into the bag for another terrible idea. I bet I'm full of them, I wonder how many I can get out before he leaves. "My eyebrows are fine."

"I'm not saying you need to trim them; I'm just saying they've waved at me from across the country." I smile and turn back to the ducks. Man, I missed teasing him. It's like sustenance, to my heart. He comes to stand next to me and I can see that his scowl is turning up at one side.

"Jesus, Meg."

"It's okay to admit you're here because they missed me."

"They?"

I nod to his brows and wiggle my fingers at them.

"You're such an asshole."

I chuckle and hand him the bread bag. He grips it tight and looks like he might swing it into my face. It's quiet. I hate this quiet between us. Faster the bread goes, faster the torture ends.

"What did you learn?" I ask. His hand drops with the bread still attached. His eyebrows drop too. A furrow. I think that's what eyebrows do when they pull in like that. A furrow. Charlie's furious, furry furrow.

"It's not im—important," he stutters through it. He's losing his nerve. He turns away. I grab his coat's lapel and turn him back towards me.

"Don't lie. Nothing about you is unimportant," I whisper back. Charlie stares down at my hand and I hear him take in a deep breath. My fingers and my eyes drop to the open flap of his coat. I grip it, shaking around the woven gray. Oh god, to pull him in close, I'd die a happy woman. He puts his warm fingers over mine.

"Meg," he shakes his head "I need to say this." I drop my hand. I step back.

"What did you learn?" I hug myself, a poor substitute for hugging him, and bite my lip. I am Charlie's friend before anything else. No matter the stumbling questions in my heart, I will always be, his friend. Right now, he's asking me to listen, because nothing about him is unimportant to me. I'll just put aside the lifetime I've spent, slowly falling, irrevocably in love with him.

"I hide in my writing. I use it. To hide."

I stare at him. That wasn't what I was expecting and I'm shocked to find disappointment at the end of it. The ducks become restless and start to swarm around the dock. They know he still has what they want and we've only got a few minutes before they riot and leave the water to flap their orange webby feet all over our toes and nip at our ankles. I take the bread bag back and fish inside. I can relate to their feelings of frustration. He has what I want, but he's not giving it.

"Yeah. I know," I say softly and break apart the pieces in an effort to make it fair. Communion on the lake. A little piece to each of them. Of myself, of sustenance that failed me. Of all I have left. I divide it and toss it out. Better that it does some good in the world. Charlie's confession has done so little for me.

"I do," he argues as if I'd tried to deny it.

"I said, I know!" I yell back.

"That's why Gina had an affair. That's why you had to leave." The truth bolts out of his mouth like an arrow, misplaced and way the fuck off target.

I stare at him, the bread smooshing in my clenched fist. "What are you talking about? I didn't leave you. You kicked me out." The morning is cool, but I can feel my whole face explode with heat.

"I *made* you leave because I knew I couldn't pay enough attention to you. Gina left our marriage, our bed, years ago. That was my fault. You would have just done the same and we'd both be broken-hearted." I'm sputtering inside, a tea kettle over-heated and ready to explode.

"You don't get to tell me what I'd do! You don't *know* what I'd do. And you broke my heart anyway, the day you kicked me out!"

I argue with salty metal on the back of my tongue. The feeling I could jump into the lake and fall beneath the cold gray of it, never to return, washes over me. I try to breathe and I feel all the hurt piling up, waiting to give its lines on the edge of the stage. I feel the curtain draw back.

"You didn't even give me the chance to decide how to have my heart broken. I'm not her, Charlie. I could never live up to the life she made. I'm a weak substitute, I know that. But you don't get to shoulder all the blame for what happened between Don and her. Gina was Gina and she had a hunger for attention, but I don't. I don't want that. I just want to be—" What? What do I want to be? What is it?

"To be what?" Charlie's voice is sunken to a gravel pit.

"To be in your orbit. Whether you love me or not. All I ever wanted, from that stupid moment I saw you standing on the train platform waiting for me, was to be in your life. However you would let me." The tears are interrupting in harsh stops and starts, and they heave from my shoulders and chest until I want to die.

"However I would—" he stumbles, shakes his head as if confused.

"I would never leave you because you weren't paying attention to me. I know what it is to lose time, Charlie. I do it too. I go mad with it. I forget to eat and drink and I write until I'm numb and inconsolable. I hide too!" I throw all of the bread into the lake unceremoniously. The crowded fowl go insane and thrash below us in a hysterical argument.

"Then why didn't you come back?" he yells louder to compete with the coliseum of angry, feathered gladiators, pecking and dodging for the spoils. Their current of desperation carries up through the wooden dock and into my feet. Charlie's despair and self-blame land like a punch to my gut. I've lost all reserve, but it never did me any favors anyway.

"Because I knew it wasn't fair, loving you that much when you didn't love me back. I stayed away because you didn't want me, and I still love you too much."

"S—Still?"

I storm away from the statue of Charlie, leaving him staring in disbelief down the rickety wooden dock. His lips are sputtering useless noise that can't amount to words. I'm halfway down the plank of my own destruction when I feel the reverberation of his footsteps behind me, that same determined, hunched shouldered, heavy gaited walk. But faster.

CHARLIE

I am frozen. My brain processing the words, through the slow call center to my heart who's waiting anxiously on the other end of the line for the news. But Meg is walking away. She's leaving me again and I can't. The message digs in and the clouded gray of early spring in Kansas lifts to the warm blossoms of a Paris street.

Wait, I think. *Don't go*, I whisper. *You idiot, wait …*

I pound across the wooden planks like I'm Indiana Jones while the bridge gives away beneath him, until I've come close enough to catch my lifeline. Her wrist in my hand. Small bones, cold skin, barely enough to stay grounded and that's why she swings into my chest at the slightest tug. I don't let her pull away. I don't let our bodies part. I hold her close.

"You idiot," I whisper. She cries and flinches at the warmth; it's an affront to her efforts to be independent and unaffected. But I'm not unaffected. Since the moment I saw her in the doorway, I've itched to have her close. I need her in my arms, to need to hold her. I know too much now, of what I did wrong that night she walked out. We're both ridiculous. My eyes fill with tears and I hold her tighter. "You stupid, beautiful girl. I would have let you in. I'll always let you in, Meg," I cry.

"I'm not stupid."

"We're all stupid." I whisper into her hair.

God might exist when I hold Meg, because I feel celestial when she puts her arms around my waist and holds me like I'm the last breath she'll ever take. She starts to cry, hard like an angry rain and I am still waters for her to pour into.

I hold on, I hold on. I hold on.

I breathe in her sadness and her loss, and the stupid ways life has repeatedly torn the rug from beneath her, even when I was the magician who helped it.

Her cries become silent as if crying is her new breathing. She sniffs and rubs her face into my shirt. I'll never wash this shirt again. She tries to pull away, in the horror of sharing the desperation of her fluids but I don't let her.

I just hold on. And my fingers find her hair and my lips find the top of her head and I kiss into her gray matter, directly into the top of her beautiful brain, and I whisper things in the back of my throat straight into the neurons listening. *You are loved. You are loved. I love you*. She shudders in my arms. It feels like the last breath. Finally at peace.

I think of Gina. Of her last breath. Of how I begged her not to go. But still, even as the god of my world, she went. I look up at the cloud-clearing sky. Gods don't take requests, but then again, I hear Meg sigh and settle into my arms, maybe this time she did.

What now? I think to Gina. *What will I do now?* Is this really what she wanted all along? Us, crying and stupid on the edge of a lake, in Pickering, Kansas? Is this the future Gina imagined for me?

A hawk circles overhead. The ducks burst out from the safety of the dock and alight all at once. Their wings stir up the low and whistling notes of a hundred hearts beating. Meg stays still in my arms.

What's a world worth without all of this? Where have I been all my life, if not in her arms?

"Are you all done?" I say into her head. She sniffs. I wonder if she'll tell me to fuck off.

"Probably not," the words come out broken and staggered.

MEG

When Charlie's hand catches my wrist, I'm swung from my own momentum of escape into his chest.

"You idiot," he whispers into my hair, and his arms are so tight around me, his chest so engulfing, that I cry and want to pull away. But his arms are heavy, and warm, and his hand is threaded into my hair and he's holding me closer than his coat. Closer than the air between us, closer, tighter …

"You stupid, beautiful girl. I would have let you in. I'll always let you in, Meg." My heart stops beating to hear those words.

"I'm not stupid." I sniff. I'm definitely not beautiful. But I don't say that, because he says, 'We're all stupid.' And he's holding me and I can't think past those two lines.

We're all lost. We're all stupid. Those two truths run circles round my brain until I can't think straight. Because he's so close, and every cell of me has missed every cell of him. And I'm miserable and sad, though I'm not allowed to be, per the 'Caretakers Must Remain Stoic Act of 1972'. I throw my arms around his ribs, tight until they lock him down. His own personal Meg straight jacket. I try to breathe him in, my face to the hard knot of his sternum until I suffocate and cry. Big, heavy unanswered tears for all the life that's hit me and all the ways I've missed him.

I cry. Hard. Until it becomes silent, and draining. Snot and tears and probably even drool, unstoppable deluge of hurt and loss. And when I want to fall away I can't. Because he's just, holding me. He just holds me. And I think eons must have passed. Perhaps summer will be here when I emerge from my Charlie cocoon, and my mom will have passed on peacefully. And the world will make sense in bright green instead of the dead brown hospice of waiting.

If I can just stay here long enough. Maybe I won't have to go back to the world on the other end of the dock. The world where I'm not in his arms. Where I don't smell his soap or hear his heart beat or feel his fingers running through my hair. What's a world worth without all of this?

"Are you all done?" he whispers. I sniff and want to tell him to fuck off.

"Probably not," I say. Why would he want to leave this heaven? "You have a horse to catch or something?"

It's a line he used to tease me with when I was in a hurry to leave. Like people from Kansas still rode horses places. Like I was backwoods and simple. I am simple though. Too simple for the man whose old cashmere coat is soft against my cheek. I look up at his soft blue shirt beneath and realize what's missing.

He's not wearing her scarf.

"No horse. No plane, no train," he says.

"How did you get here?"

"I'm not on a schedule. I got here. Does it matter how?"

"Well, if I did stroke out back there and you are just a dream, I'd like to know sooner rather than later. So yeah, I need facts."

"All right, Megan Clark Kent, hard-hitting BuzzFeed reporter, you want facts?"

"Didn't I just ask you—"

Charlie's cold fingers tip my chin up and his lips press to

mine, soft at first, and then his hand tightens on my jaw and the warm pressing of his tongue against my bottom lip begs them to open. I dig my nails into his back and open my lips with a gasp. We are two souls finally catching a break and meeting one another, and my world of loss is filled again. He is passionate and giving. Charlie kisses like a man who loves kissing. Just the act of it, the warmth and wetness, the connection, with no accounting for where it will lead. He's curious and responsive and what I give, tentative or hungry, he returns in kind until I'm dizzy, and panting and clinging to his coat.

Fuck. How did I live before I kissed this man?

What have I been doing my whole life?

"Charlie—" *kiss me again. And again, until I die from it, just don't ever stop.*

"Fact; you're the most infuriating woman I've ever known." *Infuriating like your kisses, Charlie.*

"Fact; you're no picnic yourself," I say softly and look up at him where his eyes are moist and his lips are red, and I just want to silence the ridiculous banter with another kiss.

"Fact; Gina told me a week before she passed that if I didn't admit how much I loved you and promise to keep loving you for the rest of my life, she'd never forgive me."

My heart stops in my chest. "Charlie."

"Fact; When I tried to deny it, and kicked you out, I was the most miserable, ridiculous asshole on the face of the planet."

"Fact; *second* most miserable, ridiculous asshole on the face of the planet." I sound distant, like I'm sitting on Gina's hospital bed and she's begging me to take care of him.

"Fact;" he sighs. "I'm not leaving Kansas without you. Even if that means we need to stay here for the next year."

I get angry and I pull out of his arms. "Fact; you will die in Pickering Kansas from lack of things to do, sheer boredom, and putting up with my bullshit all day."

"Fact; I will not be bored! I am never bored with you. Jesus, I haven't even been in town an hour and I've already fed ducks! I've never fed wild ducks. I feel like I'm the Jewish Jack Hanna right now."

"Jesus," I can't tell if he's serious. I simply can't imagine Charlie in Pickering for even another day.

"What other amazing wonders are hidden in the streets of Pickering, Kansas? I won't know if you won't help me discover them." He smiles idiotically. This is the stupidest thing I've ever heard. I want to kiss him silent and tackle him on the cold and creaky boards and accept the absurdity of the last ten minutes.

"Shut up." I try not to return the infectious smile.

"Fact; you still owe me pages." He senses the escape plan brewing. Pulling up the long-forgotten contract that we both started, in order to save the other. Maybe he's desperate. Maybe he knows I need to write as much as I need him.

"Fact; you still owe me a play," I counter.

"Fact; I can't write without you. I can't live knowing that you're stuck, out of some warped sense of obligation. I can't bear the thought that this is all you might have, and that the book inside of your chest will die there, before its ever kissed a page."

The word *kissed* makes me want his lips on mine. It makes me want all the things I never deserved out of life, or even should have hoped for in the first place. I feel traitorous tears start back up.

"Charlie, I don't—"

"Fact, Meg Kent; your moments of being the side character in someone else's story aren't going to cut it anymore."

"Fact; you don't want me in your story."

"You are my story."

"Charlie—" What do you say when your heart feels cleaved in two? When your poor, battered heart didn't stand a chance from the start. When all of those therapists and counselors and years of trying to sort through all of my abandonment and grief, comes down to one man, on one lake, with one question.

God, it was easier thinking he left me, than to think I might actually get to have him in my life. I know so much about loss. I know so little of love. What would I do if I had to live up to the expectations of someone who's loved me for most of my life? Just as I am. What if I am unsalvageable? He scowls.

"Fact; if you don't get back into my arms right now, I'm going to march straight home to your mother and tell her I've asked you to marry me and I'll be helping to take care of her from now on." I glare at him and cross my arms over her chest.

"This is going to get fucked up. I always fuck things up Charlie, and I can't bear the thought that I will fuck us up too."

"You don't get to decide how my heart gets broken, Meg," he returns my words and turns away. "I'll see you at home!"

"What the fu—"

He starts walking away. No, he's running.

CHARLIE

When I look down, she's staring at my heart, tears still hanging on to the cliff of her eyelashes. I breathe in the relief. I got here. I'm here, with Meg, and she's in my arms, swollen eyes and nose. She shakes her head.

"I need facts."

I smile at this. She needs knowledge, she needs to know things. She never stops gnawing until she gets all the information from the marrow. And I love her all the more for it. She's going to make me confess it. And, frankly, the fingers of my heart are tired of trying to hold it all back.

"All right, Megan Clark Kent, hard-hitting BuzzFeed reporter, you want facts?"

"Didn't I just ask you—"

Writers don't tell. They show.

I kiss her. Both of us awake and perfectly daring. She is pliant and soft and the warmth of her is eager and seeking. The undercurrents of coffee and something sweet. The petals open, the flower exposed and tender and I can't stop kissing Meg. She matches my wit, her tongue warm and teeth delicately sharp against my lips. It sparks such heated need in me, I think I might have fallen into the inferno of hell for enjoying it so much.

I don't care what happens in the wide and horrific world around us, because kissing her is my only foreseeable *why*.

Why do you exist Charles Horowitz?

To kiss Meg.

Surely you can't be serious.

Surely I can. Yes. Again. I will never go back to trying to convince myself that I don't want to be the man who gets to kiss her.

I kiss her again and again. I want to do nothing else.

Can't feed yourself on kisses.

I can. I can if I'm kissing her. She is sustenance and light.

Can't build a life around kisses.

I have and will. I'll devote my life in piety at her lips.

She is breathless when I finally emerge from the heat and the need and she gasping against my cheek, her fingers tight on the lapel of my coat. Her fingers shake and she puts her forehead into my chest for a moment. I close my eyes. Catch my breath.

Fuck. How did I live before I kissed Meg? What have I been doing my whole life?

"Charlie—"

"Fact; you're the most infuriating woman I've ever known."

"Fact; you're no picnic yourself," she returns and looks up at me. Her eyes drop to my mouth. Yeah, me too kid. I could die of exposure out here, getting lost in your lips, but I have things to say. My eyes start watering, a burn in my nose follows.

I tell her about Gina, about the pact she wanted me to make, to love her, and how hard I fought it. I tell her all of the horrible vulnerable shit that I locked away, the months spent moping and pouring out my days over her pictures. Wishing I could have that one moment back again.

While I was stewing, she was at least doing something with her miserable existence. I've just been sitting in my underwear, staring out at a city that, even in the throes of spring, feels dead and in an eternal, loveless winter. I tell her I won't go back. That I'd rather stay here in this tiny, all-horizon town than live another minute away from her.

Heat swells between us. She pulls out of my arms, with her mouth puckered cutely up. Her eyebrows arrow down. Somewhere a dog barks outside of the courtroom where we've convened to debate the fate of two worlds, outside the ring of water that muffles our countering points, the trees hover around like a cocoon of confession. She tells me the boredom will kill me.

She doesn't understand. I'm never bored with her. There is always something new to notice, to discover, to talk about. To teach, to learn. She's rolling her eyes, and I can see the way she's attempting to sneak out from the fear that's threatening at the edges of her heart. A woman who has always been left, learns to let go first. I feel like it's desperate but, I test out the weakness of her armor with our original plan. With all the upheaval in our hearts and minds, the one thing that hasn't changed, is our need to write. She still owes me pages.

It backfires when she throws my unfinished play in between us. I'm done trying to lie, or sidestep the truth. I tell her I can't write without her, that I need her my life, that I can't stand the thought of her not doing what she loves. That she's my story.

She turns away, she hesitates. I've done this to her, me and about a dozen other people, have taught her the harder lessons of loss. But I'm learning too, that we don't love greatly from a place of safety. Love requires fear and hope in equal measure. It also requires a little bit of playing dirty. I tell her I'm going to tell her mom that I'm staying and we're getting married. She glares at me and crosses her arms over her chest, unconvinced.

Writers don't tell. They show. Words will not sway her. I start walking. I don't wait, I don't even give her the opportunity to decide. My gait gets faster as I start to reach the dirt road.

"What the fuck?" I hear her gasp before she starts after me, the fear of my dedication to fuck us up first, out-manning her stubborn insistence that she doesn't deserve me. She's getting closer and my body shocks in a strange excitement. I feel like a kid when she catches me around the waist and pulls me to a stop. The cool air rings with the deep-hearted laugh of a man who's found a why in the midst of loss. A woman who's found a why in a lifetime of grief. Life breathes spring into the edges of the lake and the dog stops barking. Ears perked up in the wistful dilemma of such joy. I turn and pull her into my arms.

My girl, I whisper, hands in her hair, loosening the threads of it from the binds of our weeks spent apart. "Fact, Meg. I love you."

"Fact, Charlie, I said it first."

"Then let me hold you longer as penance for not being the first to say it," I whisper. And she does.

MEG

Charlie strode back into my orbit and made his home on a dusty, old pull-out in the basement. I'd invited him into my dilapidated twin, but he shook his head.

"This isn't the time." And I can't tell if he's scared to sleep with me or if he's scared of the bed. Maybe it's because the genius knows me and worries that I'd be doing it to run away from the discomfort of grief. But it's slightly annoying that he won't put out and I tell him so with a smile that he returns, with an edge of nervousness. I wonder briefly, while we grocery shop in Pickering's one store, in its dwindling fresh section, if he's scared that he can't anymore, or doesn't remember how the steps to that dance go.

Sex is great, he'd once said.

I hold his hand and run a fingernail delicately down the inside of his palm. His hands have always fascinated me, and I trace across the length of his palm, to the pads of his fingers, meditatively while he's looking for one fucking cucumber that's not moldy. He looks back at me. A strange look, his eyes a deeper blue.

His fingers tighten around mine and he pulls me in for a

surprising and hard kiss, deep, hot, like he might take me against the wilting lettuce and really give Pickering something for the 'events' section. I gasp as he lets go of me and tells me to not do that in public again, before walking to the next item on the list. Maybe he does remember. I wonder what other, seemingly innocuous places I will find that spark his desire.

He's right, regardless. This isn't the time.

Mom's naps get longer and longer. She almost doesn't go to church on Sunday morning.

"Will you go with me?" she asks feebly over oatmeal she can't seem to stomach. I feel like she's the kid, asking me to come to her play. The one about the guy who dressed in robes and was fun at parties. Curing lepers and mixing drinks. Before I can get into an argument between my atheism and my boundaries, Charlie sets down a banana in front of her and pours her tea.

"Of course we will."

I scowl at him and he gives me his perfect old man shrug. *What could it hurt?* He's already eaten a pig's weight in bacon, he could probably survive a few Lutherans.

The last time I sat in a church was at Gina's funeral. The last time before that was at Cecily's. My palms are sweaty and I look down to the dress I've borrowed from my mom. It's, ironically, Easter and the lawn is turning green beneath patches of snow. Kids are in puffy dresses and hyped up on chocolate from early morning egg hunts.

"This isn't awkward at all for you, I'm sure," I mumble to Charlie as my mom visits with the woman in the pew behind us. Charlie shrugs.

"The world is full of death and rebirth. Faith is more about the need to believe in something," he pauses, as though he's got the space and the safety to really think about what it all means, if anything at all. I ache to know what's going on in that big, beautiful brain of his.

"What do you believe in, Charlie?" I whisper softly. I'm staring at the cross. I feel Cecily's hand in mine on the dozens of times we had to sit next to mom in this same pew, trying to stay awake, awash in boredom. Maybe I should have listened more carefully. Maybe then it would have given me some sign of comfort. Something to believe in and be bolstered by when loss crept slowly or barged in without warning. Charlie squeezes my hand in answer and turns his head down to look at our hands. Maybe comfort doesn't have to come from church.

"I believe in you."

I turn my head to look at him. He's crying. I put my hand on his cheek, fresh shaven, and shake my head. The asshole is going to make me cry in front of God and everyone. I feel the tears come out from behind my eyes, shy kids on a stage while everyone waits, as I study every line in his face, every laugh, every expression, every pit stop and place of interest.

"If you say you believe in my eyebrows right now, I'll tell everyone that you once called Lutherans, 'Catholic Light'," he says with a smile, cutting off any sappy response I might have been formulating.

"But they are and your eyebrows are godly," I whisper and do something I've wanted to do for over twenty years, I gently stroke one of them with the pad of my thumb and he laughs before closing his eyes. Who knew it would be so calming to the both of us?

The service speaks of rebirth and the everlasting life through God their light and Savior. Everlasting life isn't something I'm really interested in. I squeeze both Charlie's hand and my mom's. I just want to live as much as I can of this one, with the people I love.

Tuesday evening, I help my mom to bed and we talk and laugh about my Great Aunt Tilly who would sneak sips of communion wine from the nursing home and the smile on my mom's face glows before it settles.

"You're tired," I say softly and feel her forehead.

"It's been a long day," she says. Even though all she mostly did was sleep. Maybe she means the life has been long. She's right. We need some rest.

"Well, get tucked in, little chicken." I say to her, just as Charlie comes in with a cup of tea and a bowl of ice chips. She can't stomach too much water.

"Thank you, honey," she says and pats his hand.

"You're welcome, Eileen," he says back, leans down and kisses her forehead. He kisses mine too before heading back to the living room to read.

"Get some rest, Mom. Tomorrow, I'll see if you feel up to going to the lake. It's finally ice free," I say and lean down to kiss her cheek.

"That would be wonderful. I can't wait," she says, she pushes my hair away from my face. "I love you, Meg," she whispers.

"I love you too, Momma," I say it back, but I don't just say it back. I mean it back. I may have been a fuck-up most of my life. But I think we all are. We mess up, we keep learning. The bigger we fuck up the bigger the lesson. At this point in my life, I'm a learned woman. She smiles and cuddles into the pillow. I turn off her light.

When Mom is settled, I go back into the living room, to read with Charlie, maybe throw my tired body into his and hope he can catch me for a few hours. But Charlie isn't there. He's not in the kitchen. He's not outside. I go downstairs, but the sleeper sofa is empty, made neatly. I go back up to my room and peek my head inside.

There's Charlie, sitting up in my twin bed, looking ridiculous and large in the small frame, propped up on my pillow, reading, with his glasses at the end of his nose. Wild hair curly and falling into his forehead.

"What are you doing in my bed?"

"Sleeping," he lies and looks over his glasses at me.

"But where am I gonna sleep?" I say and walk closer, feeling the memory of our first night, accidental and disastrous, the catalyst that opened up more truths than either of us was ready for. A warm curl of heat spins in my belly when he smiles.

"Sleep here," he says and pulls back the covers. Him in his T-shirt and boxers, long legs crossed while holding a book makes my heart dances in my chest and I smile so wide my fucking face hurts.

"Yeah? What if I snore?"

"I'll smother you with a pillow," he says as I pull off my socks and shimmy out of my pants. He watches, slowly caressing my legs. I haven't shaved them or anything and I'm suddenly self-conscious. I move to cover the freckle, and he shakes his head with a gasp.

"Come here. Bring that fucking freckle with you. Be with me tonight," he says softly. There is a strange sadness in him. "I need you with me."

"Okay," I whisper, and crawl into the small tuck of a space. He shimmies down and turns out the light. My cheek is pressed to his chest, my hand splayed out over the beating of his heart. Our bare legs intertwined. He sighs, I moan. This is heaven. Right here in the middle of Pickering, Kansas, on a spinning ball in the middle of space. It's my heaven. My eyes close and his fingers comb through my hair until I can barely think straight for the calm river he's running in my veins.

"Love you, Charlie," I whisper in the night.

"Love you back, Meg." I feel him whisper into my forehead.

CHARLIE

Eileen doesn't dawdle long. In the days after arriving back in Meg's world I take the chivalrous stance and the old sleeper couch in their basement. It's awful and it kills my back, but if I were to crawl into bed with Meg, we'd probably do disastrous things to each other and I can't trust that she wouldn't be doing it to keep the grief at bay. I don't want to be an easy distraction to a time that should be hard. Though she invites me and it's the hardest fucking thing to say no. But I can see it in Eileen, the way I saw it in Gina. There aren't many hours left, and Meg can't be distracted for even one of them.

"This isn't the time." I tell her. But Meg is cagey and persistent. And with someone else to share some of the burden she begins to eat and seems more alive. Maybe it's the lack of desperation in missing me, (aren't I a narcissistic asshole?) Maybe she's finally relaxed enough to be free with her touch. But when she traces the delicate lines of my inner palm in the middle of the grocery store, while I'm distracted by the paltry choices, not yet knowing about my strange and charming erogenous zones, I nearly tackle her into the lettuce.

I pull her up, I kiss her hard and fast and hold her curves close to me. She gasps and falls away dizzy. I tell her not to touch me there. Thereby giving her exactly what she wanted. Knowledge that even I have buttons that like to be pressed, and that I want her pressing them. Just not right now.

This isn't the time.

Eileen is sleeping more. She's in bed most of the day, only coming out for meals and maybe a show. I haven't watched this much Bob Barker since high school. When she asks Meg if we'll take her to church, I know this will probably be her last chance to sit among her people and raise her hand, send a request, and ask if she can come to stay. It's morbid and it's hurtful, but Meg sighs when Eileen asks.

"Of course *we* will." I shrug at Meg as I set down a banana in front of Eileen and pour her tea. I know it will make her uncomfortable. But nothing about death is comfortable, so we might as well dive in together.

The last time I sat in a church was at Gina's funeral. My palms are sweaty and I watch Meg wipe her hands on her borrowed dress. I didn't account for it being Easter. Which is kind of ironic and I'm sort of enjoying the oddity of me sitting front and center to the crucifix.

"This isn't awkward at all for you, I'm sure," she mumbles at me.

"The world is full of death and rebirth. Faith, is more about the need to believe in something," I pause and stare up at the cross curiously, thinking through a lifetime of all those things, and how they just keep rolling along in cycles, across our paths, to our paths, to us …

"What do you believe in, Charlie?" she whispers, following my eyes and finding her own set of questions.

What do I believe? In this crazy, fucked up world? And all the different levels of hate and hurt? In all of the loss and beauty? I squeeze her hand and look down at it, lean and strong, intertwined in mine.

"I believe in you."

She looks at me, and I cry. Which is dumb, you should know when it's happening but I've been in thought, and the body just played out the subtleties. She puts her hand on my cheek and shakes her head.

Don't cry or I'll cry, she says with her frown.

I know my Meg, and I know what to do. I frown back. I make a crack about my eyebrows which causes a smile to seep onto her lips, and then the little shit starts petting them with the soft pads of her fingers. I want to pull away at her audacity. But it feels *really* good. So I just smile and let her. I feel like I'll be doing that for the rest of our lives. Smile and let her.

Tuesday evening, Meg helps her mom to bed and I hear them talk. I feel it. In the air and in the lower buzz of energy even through the halls of the house. I pause to look at the pictures over the piano. Cecily is smiling at me. I didn't know her. But I'm sure I would have loved Meg more all the same.

I walk softly down the hall to say goodnight to Eileen and bring her tea. *I can nurture Meg*, I'm saying to her. *I'll take care of her*, I think as I put the tea and ice chips down.

"Thank you, honey," she says and pats my hand. *I know you will*, she answers back.

"You're welcome, Eileen," I say and I lean down and kiss her forehead. I kiss Meg's too, taking one look at them smiling on the bed and nod before I leave. But I don't go to the living room or my bed. I wash my face, and hop into Meg's squeaky little bed. God, her poor back. Months of this. Ridiculous. I prop myself up and pretend to read while I listen to her make her way through the house, looking for me.

I feel like I'm eight years old, embroiled in the lamest game of hide and seek ever. I am giddy and nervous, waiting to be found. When she peeks her head in, she looks confused and then smiles.

"What are you doing in my bed?"

"Sleeping," I lie. When she starts to walk closer, shyer than I've ever seen Meg behave, I lift an eyebrow, beckoning to her. I pull back the covers and ask her to sleep with me. She smiles so big I forgot she had that many teeth. I chuckle at her joy.

When I watch her undress, I desperately remind myself, over and over ... *I'm not supposed to have sex with Meg* ... especially not tonight. But she's making it difficult to remember the why of that equation when her long pale legs remind me of the freckle. She pulls her shirt down self-consciously. Covering that beautiful, and kissable spot.

I tell her not to, that I want all of her here, next to me. She crawls into the bed and I turn out the light, nestle her into my chest, and smell her hair. Her bare legs curl around mine. The warmth of her body melting into mine makes me sigh. She sighs. This is my new heaven. I comb my fingers through her hair until I'm nearly asleep.

"Love you, Charlie," I hear her whisper.

"Love you back, Meg."

MEG

Mom is gone the next morning. I go into check on her and she is resting. Permanently out of pain. I'd forgotten her face could look so at peace. I sit on the bed with her, put her cold hand between mine and kiss it.

"We didn't have a perfect life. But we had something," I whisper and take a moment to let the wave of grief start from my bare feet and shiver up through my calves, my thighs, my gut. I want to throw up and scream. But I'm not sure if it's out of sadness or out of relief.

Should you be happy to see suffering end, even when it takes a life with it? The life of the woman who brought you into this strange and turbulent fuck-fest of a life? The world is so sudden and heavy, the idea of souls and rebirth and all the things I don't understand gets tapped on the shoulder and interrupted when Charlie steps into the room. When I look up at him, into his face, fallen in sadness, he's penitently waiting for me to acknowledge the weight of her absence in the room.

I realize, when he doesn't look at her, that he knew. He knew it would be last night. He knew that I shouldn't be alone. He stayed with me while she went on. He comes to where I sit and, kneels beside me.

"I'm an orphan," I say suddenly and the word opens the door to the hurt and loss that I've denied in the necessity of being her caretaker. But it's a loss denied for even longer than that. It's the breaking of the biggest lie of my life. Of being okay.

I was so okay, my whole life. I was okay when my dad left, I was okay when Cecily died. I was okay when my mom chose the bottle over me. Just dandy when I lost all of those useless men. Pulling through when Gina died. Trying to survive when I left Charlie. I've been so fucking okay my whole life up until this moment. When someone who loves me is kneeling at my feet and nodding in agreement that I shouldn't be okay, I realize that I don't have to be complacent to my grief anymore.

"It's okay, Meg. It's okay that this hurts. Let it hurt." His words are my thoughts, spoken out loud and turned into truth.

I collapse into Charlie's arms, hard and violently, and he holds on. He doesn't shush me or offer any stupid fucking platitudes. He just holds me. He whispers like the certainty of time marching.

I'm here, I'm here. I'm here. You aren't alone.

My mind sinks back to my desk the minute I hear that Gina has passed, after I'd thrown up, when I ask him what he needs. I don't know how to say what I need. I can't breathe, cannot speak for the ache of so many years holding on to the sharp blades of loss, on my own.

Just be here, he'd said.

"You're here," I echo, shaking and around breaths that keep catching on the pain. He nods and kisses my neck, my face, wipes my tears into his own hands and I wipe away his. He isn't crying for her.

He's crying for me.

"I want to go home," I gasp and churn in the ache for it. "I want to go home, Charlie." I beg now fingers curling into his chest and around his skin, "I want to go home," I sob, as I look at him, through the dusty veil of so many wasted years and all the saltwater still leaking out. I don't want to waste any more time or tears. He nods, pushes my hair out of the river of tears and nods on repeat.

"Okay, okay. We will. We'll go home, Meg. Of course." He kisses my swollen lips, hard, fervent with promise and a solid ground I've looked my whole life for.

CHARLIE

Eileen is gone the next morning. I don't know how I know, but I do. Maybe it's the irrevocable quiet. The machine isn't running and it's not beeping. I think she might have shut it off in the night. I give Meg a moment, I wait. If I hear two voices, I'll go make coffee. I wait. I don't hear any voices. I take a deep breath and go to her.

When I get to the back bedroom, I don't need to look into the peaceful mask on a soul no longer there. I only have eyes for Meg. Only a heart for her. Space and arms and whatever she asks of me. She's shuddering on the side of the bed. I can feel it moving through her. Even in the years of disconnect, you don't get out of this kind of loss unscathed. I kneel beside her.

"I'm an orphan," she says and the small shakes that rippled now become a tsunami that rips through her shoulders and her heart, her guts and her brain. I shake my head.

"It's okay, Meg. It's okay that this hurts. Let it hurt." She collapses into my arms, like she's hanging on to the only solid rock in the middle of a hurricane. I hold on just as strongly back, around the cage of her ribs, through the shaking sobs. I do not try to quiet her or try to manage the deluge of it. There aren't words strong enough anyway. I just hold on.

"I'm here. I'm here. I'm here. You aren't alone."

"You're here," she says. I nod and kiss her in any free space I find. I wipe tears and hold on. I rock and breathe slow for her, even as she gasps for air. She reaches up in great shaking hiccups and wipes away my tears.

"I want to go home," Meg sobs. "I want to go home, Charlie." She begs with her fingers digging into my skin and her teeth clenched. "I want to go home." Three times now through eyes drowning. I push her hair back. I nod softly and whisper.

"Okay, okay. We will. Of course, Meg. Of course." I kiss her. Hard. Without remorse. So she knows I'm here. In Kansas. In New York. Wherever in the world she goes. I'm at her lips, in her arms.

I'm here.

MEG

Eighteen hours in a car is a fucking tragedy, even with someone you like. Charlie and I have three fights over the music, one over the best version of Sherlock Holmes, and two over whether or not his dad loves me more than him. It's a draw. He tells me about the afternoon with his father. I tell him about the letter.

"I know you hate to do anything your dad tells you to." I narrow my eyes at him. He doesn't look away from the road.

"He might know a thing or two." I smile at him and he lets one corner of his mouth draw up. We stop often, because he gets antsy sitting and I have a small bladder. He says it's the soda and I should cut back as we get ready to check out, loaded up with the disgusting mixture of Doritos and Diet Coke. Charlie picks a goddamn apple of all things. At a gas station. The man finds an apple. It's a blasphemy to the god of road trips.

"An apple?" I scoff with my armload of poison and MSG.

"I'm watching my heart," he says, perturbed, and looks at me. "I need it now. For longer than I thought I would."

I drop all of the food in the aisle and replace it with Charlie in my arms. He lets out a 'oof' and curls into my hug. I don't know how affectionate Gina was. I'm sure I'm far too much. I have a lifetime of love waiting to be used. And Charlie always accepts it.

"I love your heart," I whisper right to it, so it knows. So he knows. There's no other heart in the world I want beating next to mine. He tips up my chin and kisses me slowly. The gas station melts away, the world melts away. His tongue is warm and I reach up on my tip toes to gasp against his lips, his hand tightens on my chin and he pulls away with a soft groan.

"Let's get home," he says and there's a deep, serious, darkness in his words, the kind that shivers through my skin. Charlie Horowitz just gave me the I'm-gonna-fuck-your-brains-out look, in the middle of the Gas n' Sip on an ordinary afternoon. I didn't know he had that look, but now that I think of it, it's the same one he gave the first time I was tumbling out of his bed. Has he wanted me that long?

When I fall asleep on the drive, I feel him touch my leg, caress my cheek. He's bringing me home. To the place we both belong.

CHARLIE

Eighteen hours in a car with Meg embodies a strange sense of freedom like when I first left for college. Or go the first trip to the grocery store I took on my own. I had to borrow my dad's car in all the cases. Meg teases me for the giant Cadillac but she's overjoyed it's not a bus. We have three discussions, that make me want to pull the car over and kiss her senseless, because I think that's the only way I can win, by pausing her brilliant mind.

We stop often, because I hate sitting for too long and she always needs the toilet. It's probably all the Diet Coke. We load up on snacks and I try to keep it to fruit and water. She shakes her head at me every time. Laugh it up kid, someday Doritos will seem like a horrible mistake of your past.

When I tell her that I'm trying to watch my heart, that it turns out I might actually still use it, she drops all of the food in the middle of the goddamn aisle and rushes into my arms. She knocks me back and I feel my heart racing, an overjoyed puppy to have her so close. To have her so close and knowing that I love her.

"I love your heart," she mumbles into my chest. I lift her lips to mine and kiss her, my bones shivering into warmth in the middle of a gas station, making the rest of the world outside of Meg's arms disappear. My hands hold her affection close and her heart closer. Goddamn it, I'd better live a long time. Twenty-three years wasn't enough and I need more.

"Let's get home," I say and look at her until her eyes dilate and her hand tightens on my ass. I narrow my eyes, in a promissory glare that I will, in fact, fuck her brains out one of these days. And it will take a while. Because the woman has a lot of brains.

Sometimes she nods off, and I steal glances over at her. Wondering what she's dreaming about. Wondering what she'll write next. Is she still throwing words across her grave, or is she climbing out to the sunlight. I put my hand on her knee. Brush hair across her face. I can't wait to be home.

No offense to Pickering, Kansas.

MEG

I'm almost as happy to see New York as I was to kiss Charlie for the first time. Almost, because nothing will ever make me that happy. Except the next time he kisses me. Except the acceptance email from an agent, that comes after querying nearly forty of them.

Except for the first time I come to his bed, not a stitch of clothes on, and his hands find doorways into my soul I thought were long ago walled up. Charlie makes love the way he kisses; for the pure joy, and heat of it. He's got unparalleled attention to detail and is a master of dialogue. Where every touch, every taste, every soft and darkly spoken word is on purpose and serves the story of us.

I'll never sleep with another man again, he's ruined me. His praising of the simplest freckle, the curve below my collarbone, his absolute lack of rush. His tempered and even joy that swings to serious study, and praising adoration that causes every cell to scream and cry and ache. The shuddering tightness of his body. The heartbeat of a man who has loved me more years than I have loved myself and the curl of his long fingers into every lonely muscle, that's held up every lonely bone, for all of my lonely life. I am fulfilled. I am, found.

WE SETTLE INTO LIFE IN A STRANGE BUT NOT SO DIFFERENT WAY. I hate the word *settled*. It sounds like *resigned*. Like *given-up*. We haven't given up anything. Except lying. Except worry. We are given in to something too long denied. There is peace, and space. We go to Raymond's. I order bacon but Charlie refuses. He says he's done being mad at God, if there is one.

"I didn't used to think there was one." I say, over my over buttered sourdough toast and relish the fact that nothing beats New York sourdough toast from Raymond's.

"And now?" Charlie's uninhibited brow arches over his coffee cup.

"Well, you're here."

"That proves nothing."

"It proves something. No way those eyebrows were made by nature alone."

"Jesus Christ," he scowls and points his finger at me, "you're getting spanked for that one later."

"More proof there is a God." I laugh and he blushes. "No, just, I think, there's divinity everywhere. There's something divine about all of us. We're like these perfectly contained universes, imploding and exploding and in constant states of flux, destruction and creation and—"

Charlie pulls me up from the chair and plants his lips on mine. "Let's go home."

"What? But I'm—" my breath won't let words out and my heart is in my throat because he kisses me again. "Trying to eat my toast and pontificating."

"Yeah, I know."

"Wait, is that what turns you on?" Charlie reaches into his

wallet, puts money on the table and pulls me out of the doors by my hand.

"That and about a dozen other things."

"Only a dozen?" I trip after him, waving to the confused waitress on our way out.

"Get in the cab, Meg, please."

CHARLIE

I haven't sweat this much since the first play I ever wrote went on stage in a Podunk little town in Kansas. The same play that Meg reviewed. She was there, on the night of my first play. My fingers stop fiddling with the tie when I consider it. Has Meg always been in my life? If I were to look back through the years, would I find her crossing my path during field trips and family vacations? It's an odd thought. I abandon the tie and stalk out of the bathroom, pacing. Sweating. Hurting. I hear the clicking and ticking from upstairs and I can't bring myself to yell. I know what it is to be in the storm. I sit on the stairs and listen. The sound fills my heart with a strange prideful joy.

This book. This next book. Over a year in the making for her.

It's good. It would even make a good play. I tell her so and she rolls her pretty green eyes at me. "There's no way we could work together. We'd kill each other."

I shrug. "Yeah, but think of the make-up sex."

Anytime I even say the word the woman pounces me and I'm lost in the sheets, and the love, and the decidedly ridiculous joy of Meg. My hands are propped on my knees and fingers woven together beneath my chin while I listen to her, telling the world her story. And how, even after so much brutality, the heart can love. Can breed kindness. Can hold a hand and forgive before saying goodbye.

Fucking Meg Kent.

"I'm coming, I'm sorry!" she yells down at me from her office. Just an office now. Her room is my room and I've never slept better. When she lets me sleep. I just can't say the *S-E-X* word. Or "make love", or "fuck me" even when I mean it in exasperation.

"Don't stop on account of me, you know and the biggest play I've ever put on, and the most nerve-wracking night of my life. Please, let's be late for that."

I hear her chuckle. "Jesus, Jewish mom."

"Can you use those two words so close together?" I roll my eyes upwards and she's at the top of the stairs. I stand and turn. Holy shit. Holy jumping Jewish Jesus. The gown is long, and hugs her, cuts low where it counts and I've never seen Meg in a dress like this, her hair piled up, long neck out for the world to see and I want to eat her.

I roll my eyes before I close them. Suddenly I'm not thinking about the play.

"What?" She looks worried. "Is it okay? I had to go through like ten dresses and the ladies at the store were starting to get really pissed. And I told them I don't wear anything but pajamas and besides that, you know I hate trying on—"

"Just shut up and get down here. You look fine," I grumble and try to not watch. But I can't not watch. What is life if you can't watch a beautiful woman coming down stairs just to meet you. She stops two stairs from the bottom and adjusts my tie that I'd forgotten about.

"You ready?" the softness in the question, isn't about the play. It isn't about the night or the people or the reviews that will come. It's not about the future. She means am I ready for the next small step. We don't think in large bounds. Just one word, one sentence, one scene at a time. I feel my eyes itch.

I miss Gina. I look down at the bright blue tie. Meg smiles at it, sadly, reverently. She straightens it, with grace, and tucks it neatly into my suit.

"She's so proud of you."

I just nod. I don't know what to say to that.

"She loved you so."

"She loved us both," I say back and cup her cheek in my hand.

"Let's go give the people spring," she says and kisses my forehead. I lean in.

Life doesn't ever happen in a straight line. It never happens in the way you plan and rarely even in the way you want. It takes, and it takes, and it takes, even when you're dry from the giving and not an ounce of blood left you. Still, it asks for more.

Life will ask for everything you have.

When I open my eyes, Meg is wiping away a tear. I know she misses Gina. I know she feels like she needs to take care of me. But the truth is that we take care of each other. I offer her my elbow when she slips on the heels. No red boots, but I know those will be back next muddy season. When we walk, hand in hand through the park. Tonight, the city is summer night cool, and I'm walking with my heart out into the world again.

MEG

I shift in the dress. Charlie is still in the bathroom and I can't stand pacing outside the door anymore. So I go upstairs and I start to write. A letter to Gina, a start of a new story. I'm on fire and alive and I have my own office to work in now. I hear him cursing lightly and the water running. I could ask him if he needs help, but I think he's just trying to work through the weight of this night.

He finally storms out and I try to finish up my thought, but the problem with being loved, and safe, and untethered is that when I start to write, the thoughts keep coming and it's always hard to find a good stopping spot. I check the time in the corner of my screen. I have time. Time for a few more sentences ... a few more words. I hear him sigh softly. He wouldn't ever say a word against my wording. He would never stop me. This book, this novel. It will be just as beautiful as the last, my agent seems to think so, I smile in the low light and take in a deep breath.

Charlie says I should turn it into a play, I say we'd kill each other if he took on my work and I had to let him mold it into something for the stage. He says the dialogue is good as is, but I need to simplify. Why? I say, when there are so many beautiful words to be had? He says that if we fight over it, then we could have make-up sex. He nearly sold me there. Even when we don't fight, we have great make-up sex.

Charlie is fucking insatiable. I just have to look at him from over my coffee cup some mornings and he's tugging me back to the bedroom or not wasting the time on that far of a walk and getting out our pent-up frustration and ache to be in such physical and loving bodies, right there in the kitchen. The countertops have never been so clean.

When I glance downstairs, there's that guy. Charlie, sitting on the third one up, propping up his head with his hands and trying not to worry over the outcome of tonight's performance.

Does the world even know how amazing it is to live in a time of Charlie? To share the stage and the air he breathes? This play, I touch my bare skin by my heart and try not to not let it swell into a size of a house with pride. It's so beautiful. She would have loved it. Even more than Downs. I wish he knew how amazing he is. And how much love he deserves.

Fucking Charlie Horowitz.

I turn and save all my work. Twice.

"I'm coming, I'm sorry!" I yell down at him and grab my wrap and a purse. I hope he likes the goddamn dress. It's way lower cut than I would have picked but the lady said I should 'rock it while I have it'? I don't even know what that means.

I hear him grumbling over his shoulder at me. "Don't stop writing on account of me, you know and the biggest play I've ever put on, and the most nerve-wracking night of my life. Please, let's be late for that."

I laugh, "Jesus, Jewish mom."

He rolls his eyes at me as I get to the top of the stairs. He stands and turns towards me. His mouth opens, his eyes are glassy. He watches me come downstairs the way a hero in a movie does to the heroine. I feel stupid and eighteen again.

He looks at me like he's never going to get tired of the sight.

I've told him, naked in bed, that he should have seen me in my twenties and he laughs, in the weekend sunlight, and says,

"I wouldn't want you any other way."

Broken and battered, leaning into the sagging body that has done so much for me so far. We love like two people who don't care what the level of disintegration, because our souls never grow old. I think they started off old, the two of ours.

I stop two stairs from the bottom and reach out. I don't know what he was doing in the bathroom besides arguing with his tie and getting into a fight with his hair. I adjust it softly, let my fingers feel the soft lines of silk and take a deep breath.

Shit, I'm nervous for him.

"You ready?" I ask him, hushed as if we're about to go into a wedding. I don't mean the play. I don't mean the night and the crowd, or finding a taxi, or schmoozing with a million people who have bought tickets. I don't mean taking the subway in these ridiculously refined outfits for two hack writers. It isn't about the play, because Charlie and I don't think in large bounds. Just one word, one sentence, one scene at a time. I feel my eyes filling up. My fucking mascara will run and then we will be late.

I roll my eyes skyward and ask Gina to help me get through this like a lady. With grace like her. Not fuck-uppery, like me. I miss her. I study the tie, the bright blue shade like the scarf that still hangs by the door. I smile at it and straighten it before tucking it into his suit.

"She'd be so proud of you."

Charlie nods. He's trying to find words, but sometimes there just aren't any.

"She loved you so," I say.

"She loved us both," he says and holds my cheek in his hand.

"Let's go give the people spring," I say and kiss his forehead. He leans into it; his fingers go around my waist and we hold each other for a moment. I can feel Gina, smiling back at us as she walks out the door.

Life doesn't ever happen in a straight line. It never happens in the way you plan and rarely even in the way you want. It takes, and it takes, and it takes, even when you're dry from the giving and not an ounce of blood is left to you. Still, it asks for more. It asks for everything you have.

Life demands everything you have.

I dry my eyes quickly with an annoyed sniff. He squeezes me before letting go.

"Come on Kent, get your shoes." I trail behind him, slip into the heels and pray to jumping Jewish Jesus to make sure I don't fall off them on this night.

I lean on Charlie, and he offers me his elbow. I know he misses Gina. I know he feels like he needs to take care of me. But the truth is that we take care of each other.

We open the door to the warm city, full in bloom and waiting for all the potential. All of the walks we'll take, the lines of the park we'll trace in any kind of weather. The shows we'll see. The dreams we'll bake up and get lost in. The coffee we'll bring each other, the eyebrows we'll laugh over and defend. Season after season, word after word, until we land on the right ones.

PLEASE REVIEW

We hope you've enjoyed *No Words After I Love you.* Please take a moment to rate and review the book, as every review helps our authors. Thank you.

Rate and Review: No Words After I Love You

MEET THE AUTHOR

Sarah Reichert (S.E. Reichert) is a novelist, poet and blogger. She is the author of The Sweet Valley Series (Raising Elle, Granting Katelyn, and Composing Laney) as well as two other sweet romances (Rewriting Christmas, Back to the 80s) from 5 Prince Publishing. Reichert is the Director of Writing Heights Writers Association, a local organization dedicated to the education and success of writers at any level. Her work has also been featured in several publications including "Rise: An Anthology of Change", Poetry Ireland Review, and "We Are the West: A Colorado Anthology". Reichert lives in Fort Collins with her family. In her non-writing hours, she is a mother to two teenage girls, loves being outdoors, and is a 2nd degree Black Belt in Kenpo Karate.

OTHER TITLES FROM

5 PRINCE PUBLISHING

www.5PrinceBooks.com

New to Newport *Emi Hilton*
Trusting the Alpha *Courtney Davis*
Sweet Summertide *Sarah Dressler*
No Words After I Love You *S.E. Reichert*
Demons and Tea Leaves *Courtney Davis*
Shadow of the Throne *Russell Archey*
Shadow Among the Stars *Courtney Davis*
The Pack *E.C. Saulness*
Keeping Kama *Emi Hilton*
A Winter's Wedding *Sarah Dressler*
Trimutant *April Marcom*
Soul Sacrifice *Courtney Davis*
Picking Pismo *Emi Hilton*
The Taste of Treachery *Emily Bybee*
Spring Showers *Sarah Dressler*
Secret Admirer Pact *Bernadette Marie*
The Publicity Stunt *Bernadette Marie*

www.ingramcontent.com/pod-product-compliance
Lightning Source LLC
Chambersburg PA
CBHW020528020726
47494CB00006B/1681